STRANGER IN THE HOUSE

An unputdownable psychological thriller
with a breathtaking twist

PATRICIA
MACDONALD

JOFFE
BOOKS

Revised edition 2023
Joffe Books, London
www.joffebooks.com

First published in the USA in 1983 by Pocket Books

This paperback edition was first published
in Great Britain in 2023

Cover art by Nick Castle

ISBN: 978-1-80405-787-2

As before, as always,
TO THE MEMORY OF MY PARENTS,
Olga and Donald MacDonald

Special thanks to Judith Curr,
for choosing to give this Stranger another chance

PROLOGUE

Propelled by a pudgy hand, the red sedan labored up the side of a pile of dirt and then zoomed down and tumbled into a trough on the other side.

"Mommy, look! The car crashed. It came over the hill, and it fell down."

Anna Lange halted the gentle rocking motion of the glider with her feet and smiled at her son. "You made it fall down, Paul."

The child beamed up at her, satisfied that she was paying attention. He wiped his dirty face with his equally dirty forearm and shook his head mischievously. "Unh-unh," he told her. "It just fell down."

Anna laughed in spite of herself at the picture he made, seated happily in the grass, his striped T-shirt and little blue shorts already smudged with dirt. Scooby-Doo winked and waved a paw from the bill of the baseball cap that her son was wearing. When Paul looked up at her, he had to tilt his head back to get a clear view out from under it. Anna noticed that his socks had ridden down and were already disappearing into the backs of his miniature Keds.

Making a revving noise with his lips, Paul extricated the auto from the ditch. "Have to hurry up and go to work now," he said. Waddling on bent legs, the child drove the car through the wooden gate of his play yard toward the sandbox, where a yellow steam shovel lay on its side. Paul abandoned the car outside the sandbox, clambered over the low wall of the box, and plopped himself down beside the large toy. He righted the steam shovel and carefully began to rotate the crank that lowered the scoop into the sand, all his attention now focused on his task.

Sunshine glinted off the stray amber locks which curled around Paul's cap as he bent his head to his mission. Anna gazed fondly at her son and wondered briefly what new vehicles were in store for him on his fourth birthday next month. So far her parents in Ohio had provided their grandson with every simulated make and model that Detroit had to offer.

A breeze rippled through the sultry afternoon, and Anna lifted her face gratefully to greet it. She placed a protective hand on her stomach. She was three months pregnant, and the heat seemed more oppressive, the humidity more stifling than it had been other summers. Sometimes she wondered if she should have given in and had central air installed in their historic old house. She'd never liked air-conditioning. She couldn't see why people tried to eliminate summer by staying inside in a frigid, artificial climate. But lately it seemed as if she always managed to be pregnant in the summer. "Well, Roscoe," she said, patting her stomach, "looks as if you'll be ringing in the New Year." She and Thomas had dubbed the newest addition Roscoe about a week after she learned she was pregnant, just as they had referred to Paul as Mortimer and called Tracy Clem in the months before their respective births.

Paul, who had been mumbling and humming to himself as he dug, added one scoop too many to the mountain of sand, and the pile collapsed into the hole as if struck by an earthquake. The child let out a yelp.

"Shhhh, Paul." Anna reproved him. "Tracy's asleep." She cocked an ear toward the house, where the back door and windows were open. Her daughter had contracted a summer cold the day before and had spent a feverish night. The pediatrician assured Anna that it was nothing serious, but the child had been whiny and disconsolate all night long. Finally, in the morning, she had fallen asleep, after a series of witch hazel baths and a lot of soothing from Anna.

Paul looked up at his mother with wide, innocent brown eyes. "Can Tracy come out now?"

"Not today, honey. She doesn't feel good today. You play."

Paul resumed his digging and Anna closed her eyes briefly. It had been a long night, trying to keep Tracy quiet so that Thomas could get some rest. He had an important meeting this morning and she knew he had to be alert. If Tracy's crying had bothered him, he did not mention it at breakfast. He had been his usual cheerful, preoccupied self. "It's amazing," she had told him once. "Sometimes I think you're at work before you even get out of bed."

Thomas had grimaced at her remark, but her smile reassured him. He worked harder than any man she knew, but it was all for her and the kids. She had planned to go back to work at her ad copywriting job after Paul was born, but two weeks after she got back to her office she found herself crying one day after talking to the babysitter, and she knew she wasn't going to be able to continue. Thomas was actually pleased by her decision to stay home. "I'll take care of us," he promised her, and of course, he had.

She opened her eyes and looked out across the rolling, shady backyard, bounded by woods that afforded a sense of privacy. The only sound that broke the peaceful silence was the singing of birds and the occasional, almost inaudible whoosh of the cars which passed by on the leafy Millgate Parkway, a dignified, tree-shrouded old highway which cut through back Stanwich, adjacent to some of the loveliest and wealthiest homes in all of affluent Fairmont County.

Theirs was far from the grandest house around. In fact, their lovely old home had once been the caretaker's house on an enormous estate. Their nearest neighbors, the Stewarts, lived in the manor house on the huge property, which had long ago been subdivided and sold separately. The Langes' home was small by comparison to the elegant Stewart mansion, but it was more than large enough for their young family and was magnificent in contrast with the other houses and little apartments they had lived in.

Anna smiled, thinking of the pride Thomas took in their home. She knew what it represented to him. His had been a chaotic childhood, with an absent father and an alcoholic mother who dragged him from boardinghouse to railroad flat and back. He had worked his way through college, and moved to New York City where they met and married. After a lot of effort, he attained the position of assistant treasurer in the Phelps Corporation, which was based in New York. It was not long after his promotion was announced that Thomas had taken her to see the beautiful old Victorian house in the suburb of Stanwich.

"It's too much," she had protested. "How can we afford it?" "We'll have to afford it," Tom had said, teasing her. "You have to have somewhere to spread all that junk of yours." She had laughed again at their old joke. It was true. She had a collection of antique bottles. She'd dried every flower he had ever given her, and she couldn't bear to throw away a magazine that had a sweater pattern or a recipe she might like to try. It had not taken long for them to fill up their new house. If Thomas worried about the cost, he never complained about it. But then, he was a master at keeping his worries to himself. After eight years of marriage she certainly knew that. Sometimes she worried that he would get an ulcer.

Tired of his job, Paul abandoned the sandbox and the play yard and went out exploring. She watched him as he tramped through the grass. He bent down to pick up a dandelion and blow on it.

Anna pushed herself out of the glider and walked toward her son. "Do you want a ride on the swing?" she asked him. Paul nodded eagerly and reached up to take the hand she extended to him. They walked along together toward the swing set at the back of the yard. When they were almost there, Paul disengaged his hand from hers and ran toward the swing, where he hoisted himself up on the seat and kicked his sneakered feet impatiently.

"Okay," said Anna. "Hold your horses." Just as she approached the swing set, Paul squealed and slipped off the swing. He began to tear across the yard as fast as his pudgy legs would move, shrieking and laughing.

"Look at the kitty," he cried. "Can we keep him?"

"That's all I need," said Anna, rolling her eyes skyward.

The fluffy black-and-white cat, which had appeared at the edge of the woods, stood frozen for a minute, whiskers on end, as the child barreled gleefully toward it, arms waving wildly. Then the cat turned and bolted into the safety of the trees. Paul started gamely after it, branches and leaves snapping against his short, bare legs.

"No, you don't, buster," said Anna, swooping down on her son and lifting him back into the civilized territory of the lawn.

Paul started to cry. "I want the kitty," he wailed.

"You're really getting heavy," Anna observed with a grunt. "I can't do this much longer. The kitty had to go home."

Paul continued to cry as Anna carried him back in the direction of the house. He stuck his thumb in his mouth and sucked noisily on it through his tears.

"What's this?" she chided him. "I thought you gave that up." He rubbed his eyes with small, dirty fists. Anna held him securely under his little rump.

As they approached the house, she heard the weak but unmistakable wailing of Tracy from inside. Anna placed Paul on the ground and offered him her hand. "Come on. We'll go and see how Tracy feels."

"No," Paul protested sullenly. "I don't wanna."

"Okay, then," she said, lifting him under the armpits and depositing him inside the large fenced play yard that Thomas had built. "You play quietly. I'm going to see how Tracy is. You be good." She wagged a finger at him and smiled as she lowered the latch on the gate. "You be a good boy, and I'll bring you a cookie when I come back."

Paul watched her forlornly, wiping his face again. Then he headed toward his sandbox. He threw one glance over his shoulder to the woods where the cat had disappeared. "Where's the kitty?"

"The kitty's gone, Paul. You play now." Anna ran up the back steps and threw open the door to the house. "I'm coming, baby," she called as she dodged the Wiffle ball and plastic bat in the foyer and mounted the stairs to her daughter's room.

Tracy was standing in her crib, whimpering, when Anna entered the sunny pink and yellow bedroom. One look at her mother, though, and the child burst into wails of misery. Anna lifted the fretting child in her arms and began to murmur to her. The child's summer pajamas were damp with perspiration. "Oh, poor thing. It's too hot to be sick, isn't it? Poor Tracy." Anna put Tracy back in her bed, and Tracy immediately began to howl again. Anna spoke soothingly to her daughter as she rifled the contents of the dresser drawer for a fresh pair of pajamas and then ducked into the bathroom and soaked a washcloth. Glancing at her watch, she realized that it was time for another teaspoon of ibuprofen.

After removing Tracy's damp pajamas and sponging her feverish daughter, she gave her the medicine and a cup of water.

"Hey, where's Fubby?" Anna hunted around under the crib for the stuffed rabbit that Tracy loved to chew on. She located the toy wedged between the leg of the crib and the wall and offered it to her whimpering child. Tracy clutched the rabbit and smiled wanly at her mother.

"You want a story?" Anna pointed to a stack of books piled on a table beside the rocker.

"No," Tracy said fretfully.

"How about a little song to sleep?" Anna asked her. Tracy nodded. "The Winky song," she cried. She settled down in her crib, and Anna began to sing softly. By the time Wynken, Blynken, and Nod were out on the silver sea Tracy's eyelids were drooping. Anna gently patted the little form and tiptoed out of the room.

Anna headed down the stairs to return to Paul. Just as she was passing through the foyer, the phone on the hall table began to ring. She rushed to grab it and caught it on the second ring.

"Hello."

"Hello, Anna. It's Iris. Did I catch you on the run? You sound breathless."

"Hi, Iris. I was upstairs with Tracy. She's got a little cold, and I just got her off to sleep."

Anna's neighbor was immediately remorseful. Oh, dear, I hope the phone didn't wake her up."

Anna listened up the stairs. "All's quiet," she assured her worried friend. "What's up?"

"Well, I've been meaning to call you about this. I have to go to a tea for the village green beautification committee, and I wondered if you wanted to go with me. Lorraine can watch the children. She can come over there if you don't want to wake Tracy."

Anna was bemused by the suggestion. Iris was a shy, ill-at-ease woman who trudged off reluctantly to countless social functions mostly, Anna suspected, at the behest of her appearance-conscious husband. Edward was an Ivy League-educated millionaire with a passion for high society, while his wife, who was born into a self-made immigrant family, seemed to dread rather than enjoy the social set. She often invited Anna to the endless teas and charity functions, freely offering the services of her maid, Lorraine Jackson, to mind Anna's children. Occasionally, Anna took her up on the offer, for unlike Iris, she enjoyed the company of the other women at these events, and it was a nice change from being home. However, a sick child had a compelling hold on its mother, which, Anna thought, Iris probably did not understand, having no children of her own. Anna passed on the tea party without a second thought.

"Not today, Iris. I couldn't leave Tracy. Thanks all the same."

"Oh," said Iris, and Anna could hear her disappointment.

"Well, maybe the next time." Anna felt a little sorry for her friend, realizing how awkward she felt at these gatherings. "I've got Paul outside," Anna said. "I'd better get back to him. Thanks for asking me, Iris."

Anna hung up the phone, listened once more up the stairs and then started toward the back of the house. On the way she remembered her promise of a cookie. Having detoured to the pantry, she rooted around until she located the butter cookies that Paul liked. Anna took two for him and then, after a moment's guilty debate, one for herself. It seemed, when she was pregnant, that she was always hungry. She returned to the back door, opened it, and stepped out onto the back porch.

"Paul," she called out, "I brought you a cookie." The child did not answer. She could not immediately see him in the play yard. He must be in the sandbox, she thought.

Frowning slightly, Anna descended the steps and hurried toward the play yard. "Paul," she called sharply. She rushed up to the fence and reached for the slats.

"Where are you?" she demanded. Gripping the top of the fence, Anna looked inside. She did not see her son.

Her throat constricted. Her gaze swept the play yard, searched the sandbox. The yellow steam shovel lay abandoned on its side. The red car leaned against the sandbox wall. The child was not there.

"Paul," Anna whispered through her tightened throat. Her frantic glance scanned the perimeter of the fence and then stopped short. She stared for a moment, disbelieving, at the gate, which stood ajar about two feet.

Anna held the fence for support, crushing the cookies between her hands and the slats. "Paul," she cried. "Paul."

At first she could not move. Her breath was short. Her limbs felt as if they had been set in cement. She looked out across the backyard, trying to breathe. Then her words came in a shrill rush. "Paul, do you hear me? Answer Mommy!"

The silent, empty yard shimmered in the heat of the July afternoon. Dragonflies whirred across the sun-dappled lawn. Beyond the swing set and the garden shed at the back of their property, the woods rustled, dark and cool. There was no sign of the child. He was nowhere to be seen.

Letting go of the fence, Anna forced herself to walk toward the back of the yard. Her eyes swiveled in every direction, starving for some brief glimpse of him. She searched the grass, the trees for anything. A swatch of his striped T-shirt, a splash of yellow from his Scooby-Doo cap, the glow of shell-pink skin. "Paul," she cried.

How could he get out? She stopped for a second and glanced back at the latch. One of the screws that held it to the fence was gone. It hung uselessly on the door. It mustn't have caught securely. I should have looked. Why didn't I pull on it to be sure? One tug was probably all it took, she thought.

Where was he? Immediately she remembered the cat. He had been fascinated by that kitty. He must have tried to follow it into the woods. He can't have gone far.

Running now, Anna plunged into the trees, crying out hoarsely for her child. She ran crazily in one direction, then another. A flash of waving brown-gold caught her eye. "Paul," she cried. A dried-out fern swam before her tear-filled eyes. She continued on, tripping through the mossy, leaf-strewn ground cover, her glance darting behind every tree. She could hear the sound of traffic beyond, on the highway, as she stumbled along. "Please, God," she whispered. "Please. Let him be all right. Paul, Paul, Mommy needs you." She could hear the choked bubbling of tears in her voice as she called out to him. The trees were silent in reply.

All at once she saw a sudden movement through the trees. Heart leaping with hope, she whirled to face it. There, beside a tree, sat the fluffy black-and-white cat, staring edgily at her.

Anna's lips and chin began to tremble violently. She could feel the shaking spread down her arms to her hands, in her knees, all the way to her feet. She was bathed in sweat.

She stared at the unblinking cat. Tears began to spill down her cheeks.

"Where is my baby? Paul!" she shrieked. Her anguished cry drowned out the intermittent drone from the highway, the rustle of the trees. It seemed to settle there on the dense, oppressive summer air.

* * *

"First thing in the morning," said Detective Mario "Buddy" Ferraro, neatly smoothing down his dark blue tie and buttoning his gray sports jacket over it. "We'll be here early, and we'll keep looking until we find your boy, Mr. Lange. I promise you. We'll do everything we can. Everything. But it's late now. We can't see anything, and these people need to get some sleep."

"I understand," Thomas said dully. He stared out the window at the motley group of men and women who were milling about in his backyard, waving flashlights and talking quietly together. They were policemen, neighbors, people in town who had heard about Paul's disappearance on the local television station. Even a bunch of teenagers, members of the high school key club, had volunteered to help in the search. Their numbers had swelled since three, when the search had started. Thomas gazed blankly at them, his face ashen above his white shirt. He was still wearing his suit, now rumpled and dirty from crawling in the woods and alongside the highway. His loosened tie hung like a slack noose around his neck.

"They need some rest, and so do you," advised the handsome olive-skinned detective. "Especially your wife. Did the doctor give her something to help her sleep?" he inquired.

"He was here a few hours ago," Thomas replied. "He gave her some pills to take. He would have given her a shot, but with the baby . . ." Thomas's voice trailed away.

"Try to get her to sleep," the detective urged. "We'll be back before she even wakes up. We'll find your boy, Mr.

Lange. We will." The detective gripped the stricken father's shoulder for a brief second and then released it. "Let me say good night to your wife, tell her we're going now."

The detective nodded in the direction of the dining room. In a fog Thomas led the way.

Anna sat at the dining room table, her head resting on her arms in front of her. Iris Stewart sat beside her friend, her hands clenched together in her lap. Her plain face was distorted by a worried frown as she stared sadly at Anna. Her husband, Edward, dressed in a perfectly tailored pin-striped suit, hovered behind them, a solemn expression on his face. Both the Stewarts looked up anxiously as Thomas and Detective Ferraro entered the dining room. Anna kept her head lowered on her arms.

Thomas answered the question on their faces with a curt shake of his head.

"Mrs. Lange," the detective said softly. Slowly Anna raised her head. Her face was puffed up; her eyes were red and swollen from crying. She flattened her trembling hands on the table.

Buddy Ferraro's stomach twisted at the sight of her face. "Mrs. Lange, I'm going to have to call off the search for tonight. Just for tonight. It's after two. We'll start again first thing in the morning."

"It's so late," she said. "We have to find him."

"We'll find him, Mrs. Lange. Tonight we need to get some rest."

Anna raised herself up shakily out of her seat. "I have to keep looking," she said. "You're giving up."

"Oh, no, Anna," Iris protested. "You mustn't think that."

The detective cleared his throat. "We are not giving up," he said. "We are just going to take a break, and we'll be back at it as soon as there is light."

An expression of exquisite pain suffused the mother's face. The tears began to stream silently down her cheeks again.

"Try to get some sleep," said the detective helplessly. "I'll let myself out."

"You two should go, too," Tom said to his neighbors.

"Let me spend the night here on the couch," Iris implored him.

Edward said, "Come along, Iris. We'll only be in the way here."

"It's okay," Thomas assured her. "You go on."

Iris hesitated and then clasped Anna's white hand in her own. "I'll be back first thing in the morning," she promised.

"Thanks for everything," said Tom. Edward shook his hand and then ushered Iris through the dining room doors.

The house was silent for a few moments. Anna moaned and hid her face in her hands. Then, without uncovering her face, she spoke softly. "I was gone for only a few minutes, Tom."

Thomas sat across the table from his wife, staring at the wall. "I know," he said in a choked voice. Then he looked over at her. "It's not your fault, darling. You can't blame yourself."

Anna did not reply. They sat in silence. After a few minutes he spoke again. "We'd better get to bed."

A feeble cry wafted down from upstairs. Anna started at the sound of the tiny wail. For a second she stiffened, and then she slumped over.

"Tracy's up," said Thomas. He watched his wife for a reaction, but she didn't move. "Do you want me to go?" he asked.

Anna avoided her husband's eyes. "If you don't mind," she said. "I want to clean up here." She waved a hand vaguely over the empty, stained coffee mugs that littered the table, left there by shifts of searchers.

"Don't bother with that, darling," Thomas said. "Come upstairs now."

"No, I want to." She got up from her chair and began to collect the cups and crumpled napkins with trembling hands.

Thomas opened his mouth to argue and then stopped. He lifted himself wearily from his seat and started to walk through the darkened living room toward the stairs. Suddenly there was a crash.

"Ahhhh . . ." Anna cried out. Thomas rushed back into the dining room. Anna was bent over double, clutching her stomach, pieces of broken china on the table and at her feet.

"Honey, what's the matter?" he cried, hurrying to support her in his arms. "What is it?"

All the color had drained from her face. She breathed shallowly, her arms crossed at her waist.

"What is it?" he demanded. "Is it the baby? Should I call the doctor?"

Slowly Anna shook her head. She breathed more deeply. She began to straighten up. "It's better now. It's passing."

"Please come and lie down," he pleaded.

"I will. As soon as I'm finished here." Glancing briefly at her husband's troubled eyes, Anna turned away from him. Tracy wailed out, more insistently now.

"Anna?" he asked.

"I will," she said. She gestured at the mess around her. "I'll be right up."

Reluctantly Thomas released her and started again for the stairs. From the darkness of the living room he looked back at her fearfully. Unaware of his gaze, she sank onto one of the dining room chairs and stared beyond her own lonely reflection in the window into the yawning blackness of the yard.

* * *

"What a night." Buddy Ferraro sighed, opening the door to his car and sliding in.

"What time tomorrow?" asked a patrolman, leaning against the open door of the detective's car.

"Say seven," the detective suggested. "I'll probably be here six or six thirty."

"I don't guess half an hour's gonna make much difference to this kid," said the patrolman, shaking his head.

The detective glared at him. "It could make a lot of difference," he snapped.

"Hey, no offense," said the young man. "I feel the same way you do. I'll be here early."

Buddy gave his young colleague a conciliatory wave as he started his car. "I'll see you in a few hours."

The young cop tapped on the detective's hood as the car rolled backward down the Langes' driveway.

Buddy Ferraro wondered if he would get any sleep at all that night. The sight of Anna Lange's face weighed down his heart. Her anguish had seeped into him, raging within him, giving the search an intensity that he had rarely felt in fourteen years on the force. To lose a child. It was a nightmare. The kid seemed to have just vanished into thin air. He thought of Sandy and of their own two boys, little Buddy and Mark. If anything ever happened to them . . .

He decided to take the Millgate Parkway home. It was faster than the back roads, even this late at night. He'd get off in two stops and nearly be at his door. He had called Sandy at around ten o'clock, ostensibly to tell her when he'd be home, but as the phone gave its third ring, he'd realized, by the tightening in his chest, that he just wanted to be sure they all were safe.

Following the signs for New York, Buddy crossed the overpass and drove down the curved entrance ramp to the full-stop sign. He braked automatically and sat for a moment, lost in thought. They hadn't found a trace of the boy, nothing. There had to be something, some lead they had missed. If it were there to be found, they would find it. He was determined not to lose this one. It mattered too much. He realized with a start that he was waiting for no reason. There was no other traffic on the parkway. He pressed his foot on the gas, and the car shot forward into the night.

Unnoticed by him not far from where he had stopped to yield, a child's baseball cap was wedged in a drainage ditch beneath the lip of the road. The low-hanging boughs of a hearty evergreen helped to hide the little hat from view. There were dark patches of dirt on the bent brim. And something else as well. A grimy Scooby-Doo winked and waved while across his smiling face and the balloon letters of his name, creases began to stiffen as the bloody fabric dried.

CHAPTER 1

Eleven Years Later

"How do you like your tea?" Iris asked.

"It's great," said Anna. "Fresh mint. Is it from your garden?"

The two women were sitting at one end of the plant-filled conservatory of the Stewarts' opulent home. The sun streamed in on them, and a breeze from the open doors riffled the leaves of the plants.

Iris nodded. "Henry brought it in this morning."

"I always mean to put some in my garden, and then I forget."

"I'll tell Henry to dig some up for you," Iris said eagerly.

"Would you? That would be great."

Iris and Anna relaxed in their chairs, enjoying the sun and the breeze. Anna leaned over the glass table and picked up a pile of envelopes that were lying beside the bowl, addressed in Iris's careful hand. "What are you up to here?" Anna asked.

A pained look crossed Iris's face. "Oh, we're giving a party. For the Hospital Guild. It's going to be rather a large affair, to raise money for the new cardiac wing."

Anna nodded. "I read about it in the paper. I didn't know the party was going to be here."

"Well, Edward is the chairman of the fund-raising committee, you know."

Anna nodded, noting that Iris was clenching her hands together in her lap. "You're good at organizing things," Anna reassured her. "It will be a great success."

Iris gave a small sigh. "I hope so," she said. "There's one for you in there." Iris pointed to the stack of envelopes.

Anna found the envelope addressed to the Langes and smiled. "Tracy, too?"

"Older children." Iris shrugged. "That was my idea, I thought they'd pep things up."

"Great," said Anna. "When's the party going to be?"

"A week from tomorrow. The thirtieth. I hope you're free. I'm a little late with the invitations."

"The thirtieth," said Anna softly, staring down into her glass of tea. "That's Paul's birthday." She looked up at Iris. "He'll be fifteen this year."

Iris's eyebrows rose slightly. For a moment she regarded her friend thoughtfully. "Is that so?" she murmured. "Well . . . that's good. Where's Tom today?"

"With Tracy. They're playing tennis. Is Edward home?"

"Oh, no. He had a business lunch today. He just bought another company. The Wilcox Company, I think it's called. They have something to do with helicopter parts."

Anna stirred the ice in her glass and looked up under her eyelashes at Iris. You would never know to look at her, Anna thought, that her husband was a millionaire. Edward, whose company manufactured private aircraft, was always a model of correctness and elegance in his appearance, while Iris dressed simply and seemed to give only the minimum attention to her hair and makeup.

Nonetheless, they seemed to get along together, and Anna had always ascribed it to opposites attracting.

"Well, I've got to be getting back." She placed her empty glass down on the end table and got up.

"Anna, I meant to ask you. How's Tracy's job at the vet's working out?"

Anna frowned, thinking of her daughter. "Oh, she loves being around the animals. She doesn't get paid for it, but she seems to enjoy it."

"There, you see! That's great," said Iris. "I had a feeling that all she needed was an interest."

"It's helped," said Anna absently, although she felt a twinge of annoyance at Iris's simplistic solution to the problems she had with Tracy. Her shy, introverted daughter was turning into a moody, difficult teenager who seemed to resent her mother more each day. But Iris always acted as if a little change in the routine would solve everything. And perhaps in Iris's pampered, childless life, that was all the solution she needed, Anna thought ruefully.

"Why don't I ask Henry to get you those mint plants right now?" Iris suggested, opening the glass door to hail the gardener in a straw hat, who was crouching in a flowerbed beyond the pool. Anna realized that she had been unconsciously staring at him.

"No, no," she protested hurriedly. "Don't bother him."

"It's no bother," Iris insisted.

Anna shook her head but smiled at her friend's kindness. She felt guilty for her uncharitable thoughts about Iris, remembering how often she had taken comfort in Iris's confidence in Anna's ability to make things right. Often, when she had been down, it was a visit from Iris that had forced her up. She gave her friend a brief impulsive hug. "Not today," she said. "I'd better be getting along."

"If you have to," said Iris. "Don't forget. Put that party on your calendar."

"I will," said Anna. She walked out the door and down the steps, then headed down the incline past the pool, greeting Henry, the gardener, as she went by. Her route home through the Stewart estate was long and meandering but it was a walk she always enjoyed. She followed the path through the gardens, skirted the frog pond, and wandered in the grape arbors until she came to the high hedges and the narrow stream that separated their properties.

Anna decided, before she went in the house, to get a few vegetables from her garden for dinner. She was proud of her garden this year. She had culled a few tips from Henry and had raised a bountiful crop of vegetables. Everything had grown vigorously, probably because much of the garden plot had lain fallow for so many years. After harvesting two lustrous inky eggplants, a few tomatoes and a bunch of beans, Anna headed back toward the house. Sometimes, especially when the fall came, and Tracy returned to school, Anna thought about going back to work. She always decided against it, although she never admitted her real reason to Thomas. She wanted to be home, just in case. Just on the unlikely chance that Paul found his way back to them, she wanted to be there. Anna walked past the spot where the children's play yard had been. She stopped and sank down on the rusty glider, staring dully at the patch of lawn. It was green now and planted over with flowers. I'd better not mention Paul's birthday, she thought. Tom will only get upset.

She knew how much he didn't like to talk about it. But each year she felt compelled to bring it up, as if it were somehow vital that his parents speak his name aloud, acknowledge his birth. Every year Thomas would turn away from her with a grim look on his face. She didn't do it to pain him. It just seemed that it was important. Then, last year, when she mentioned it, he had suddenly gotten angry.

"Anna, I can't stand it when you say that. Every year it's the same thing. 'Paul is eleven today. Paul is twelve today. It's Paul's thirteenth birthday.' Why do you always have to mention it?"

"Because it is his birthday," she insisted. "Because I want to remember it."

"It's like some grisly joke. Paul's birthday. As if he were still alive and about to walk in that door."

"But, Tom," she protested, "I do believe that he is alive. Don't you? I mean, we don't know any different. We need to have hope, darling."

But Thomas had turned away from her without another word, and the subject was closed between them once again, as it had been for most of the years since Paul was gone. She could not pinpoint the time when they had stopped discussing it. But the child's disappearance had been like an amputation on the body of their marriage. Tom wanted to cover it, to hide it and pretend it hadn't happened. Or so it seemed to Anna, as she restlessly sought help, advice, some reassurance that she would one day reattach what seemed irretrievably lost. As if by agreement, they avoided talking about it. It was the best they could do.

Anna examined the ground from her seat on the glider, to see if any trace remained of the play fence, any faint outline of where it had been. The grass had grown over it. There was not a sign. It was as if it had never existed.

Anna walked up to the back porch and entered the cool, quiet house. She placed the basket on the butcher block beside the sink and turned on the tap, placing a copper colander into the clean porcelain basin. The only sound in the house was the rush of the running water. Normally she liked nothing better than to be busy in her comfortable kitchen, but now a melancholy mood descended on her. She held her wrist under the water, like a mother testing a baby's formula, and gazed over the plants on her windowsill into the stillness of the sun-dappled backyard.

Suddenly she became aware of a sound like tapping. Turning off the water, she listened again. Someone was knocking at the front door. After wiping her hands off quickly on the soft terry towel next to the sink, she hurried through the house to the foyer and opened the door. At first she saw no one there. Stepping out onto the front porch, she observed the familiar back of a man descending the flagstone steps to the driveway where his car was parked.

"Buddy," she called out, "come back. I'm here."

Detective Mario Ferraro started and then turned slowly around to face the woman standing in the doorway. She was smiling in welcome. Over the years he had come to know her well. Long after Paul's case had been officially abandoned, she'd continued to call him with questions about psychics or other missing children or any case that bore any similarity to her own. He had responded with what he hoped was patience and care to each of her desperate hopes, tracking down any fillip of a lead that came his way. "It's that poor woman again," a rookie named Parker told him the last time she had called with news of a child who had turned up in Houston. That poor woman.

He knew that was how the others saw her, but secretly he admired her courage and her tenacity. After losing her son and then the baby, she had pulled herself together and committed herself to the search. Some people thought it was abnormal, but Buddy saw the logic in her efforts. But for the grace of God, he had reminded himself often, he would have had to make such a choice as hers. He had decided to help her. One night Thomas had taken him aside in the kitchen and apologized to him for Anna's relentless questions and leads. "There's no getting through to her," Thomas had said. In a way Thomas's reaction had bothered him more than Anna's. But he'd held his tongue. "I don't mind," he'd told Thomas. "I can imagine what she's going through."

"What's the matter with you?" Anna asked, squinting at him. "You look kind of sick."

Buddy Ferraro smiled with one corner of his mouth. "I'm glad you're here."

"I was out in the garden. I didn't hear your car come in. I hope you haven't been standing here for long."

The detective shook his head. Buddy climbed the steps haltingly. When he reached the porch where Anna stood, he looked at her and frowned, pressing his lips together. Anna linked her arm through his and led him into the house. "My garden," she said, "is really terrific this year. I've got something for you to take to Sandra. Eggplants and tomatoes. You get that wife of yours to make you eggplant Parmesan. No excuses. I'll give you a big bagful to take home."

"Anna . . ." he began.

Arm in arm they had passed through the foyer and into the bright L-shaped living room, which was filled with flowers, baskets of magazines, and needlepoint pillows on the furniture. Anna released the detective's arm and gestured toward a chair next to the fireplace at the end of the room. "Please sit down," she insisted. "I haven't seen you in such a long time now. I'm glad you came by. I was just in there starting to feel sorry for myself." She moved her knitting bag off the chair matching his and sat down opposite him.

Buddy perched on the edge of the seat and leaned forward.

"Can I get you something to drink? Club soda or a beer?"

The policeman shook his head. "It's good to see you," he said quietly. "But this isn't just a friendly visit. I have some news for you."

Anna gasped as if he had slapped her. Over the years she had been like a disappointed lover, waiting for a missive that never came. In time she had grown to expect the postman, not the letter. Now, suddenly, the detective was turning it all around. She stared into his eyes, trying to read what the message might be.

"Is Thomas home?" he asked quietly. "I think he should be here."

"He's not . . . he's out," she whispered, her eyes riveted to the detective's face.

Buddy Ferraro frowned. "Maybe we should . . ."

"It's Paul," she said. She clasped her hands together and pressed them to her lips. "Tell me," she whispered.

Buddy nodded and cleared his throat. "Anna," he said, "I don't know how to say this. It's going to be a shock."

Anna began to shake her head as she stared at him.

Buddy hesitated. "Paul's been found. He's alive."

Anna crushed her trembling fists to her mouth and squeezed her eyes shut for a moment. His words hung in the air before her, waiting for her to comprehend them. But a tingling fear suffused her, paralyzing her. She felt that if she tried to grasp what he said, take hold of it, it would somehow be snatched away from her. All hope, everything she had prayed for and clung to for all these years would vanish instantly and forever. "Don't lie to me, Buddy," she warned him in a shaking, nearly inaudible voice.

"I wouldn't, Anna. You know that. It's true. You can believe it. He's alive." Buddy was surprised by the tears that sprang to his own eyes. He pressed his lips into a crooked smile.

Anna sat frozen in her chair for a moment. Then, slowly, as if in a trance, she slid from the seat to her knees on the floor, clutching her arms around her chest. Her head was bowed; her eyes were shut.

Buddy sprang forward from his seat, prepared to grab her, thinking at first that she had fainted. Then, understanding, he exhaled and sat back in his chair. Bowing his head, he crossed himself quickly.

When Anna raised her head, her face was like a flower opening, turning out fragile petals one by one.

Buddy offered her his hand. Anna reached for it and kneaded it between her icy fingers. "Tell me everything," she whispered in a choked voice. "Where is he? Is he all right? Is he safe?"

"He's fine," Buddy assured her and reached into his pocket, removing his handkerchief and handing it to her. "Here."

While Anna wiped her eyes, the detective began to explain. "It happened this morning. We got a call from the sheriff of Hawley, West Virginia. He had been contacted by a minister in town who had evidence that Paul has been living all these years in that town as the son of a couple named Albert and Dorothy Lee Rambo. It seems that the woman was dying of cancer, and last week she contacted this minister, one Reverend Orestes Foster, and gave him a letter. Told him to open it at the time of her death, which occurred day before yesterday. The letter amounted to a confession that she and her husband had abducted Paul and raised him as their own son, and it also revealed Paul's identity, which apparently they were aware of all along."

"You're sure it's Paul."

Buddy nodded. "It's your boy all right. She still had the little clothes he was wearing when they took him. Pictures of him. The works. Evidently the woman believed that this terminal illness was some kind of punishment for her crime. She wanted to set accounts straight, make sure the boy would be returned to you."

"What about her husband?"

Buddy grimaced. "Well, that's a problem. It seems that she told him what she planned to do because he cut out of there before she even died. He's been on the run ever since. The man is a little disturbed, I'm afraid. From what I understand, he's had a history of hospitalization for mental illness."

"Oh, God, no."

"As far as we can determine, he never hurt the . . . Paul . . . in any way. He was just not quite right. The woman apparently was okay. She worked as a nurse and took care of them. Anyway, the police are looking for this guy, Rambo. And the FBI. They'll find him."

"Where is Paul now? When can I go there? I have to see him."

"He's still being questioned by the Hawley police. They're trying to find out what they can. Getting the story in bits and pieces. You've got to remember, this has come as a real jolt to all of them. They've known these Rambos for some years. You should have heard this sheriff on the phone. I could barely understand him for his drawl." Buddy chuckled.

"Buddy, I need to go to my son," Anna persisted.

Buddy squeezed her hand. "Anna, I want you to trust me on this. They're taking good care of Paul. You'll have him back here with you in a couple of days."

"I can't wait a couple of days!" she cried.

"We don't want a media circus. This is a shock for Paul, too. It would be best to keep it quiet."

Anna shook her head helplessly. "You're right. I know that what you say makes sense."

"There's a lot we don't know yet. The boy was too young to remember it. But we're getting what information we can. The important thing is that he's alive. And we've found him."

"I won't really believe it until I'm holding him."

"Believe it. Before you know it, you'll have your boy back."

Anna looked up at him with serious, tear-filled eyes. "I never gave up on him, Buddy. Sometimes I thought I was losing my mind over this. I always believed that he'd come home."

"You were right," the detective said.

Tears began to dribble down Anna's face again. For the first time in eleven years she pictured her son in her mind, and her heart did not twist in agony but was filled with joy. What did he look like now? How would he be? Would he know her, and she him? Suddenly she looked up at the detective. "I have to tell Thomas. And Tracy. I have to find them."

"Do you know where they are?" Buddy asked.

"They're over at the tennis courts in the park. I have to tell them." Anna scrambled to her feet and looked around the room confusedly. "I need the keys. Where did I put the keys?" She wiped her tears away, but they continued to flow.

"Never mind," said Buddy, standing up. "I'll drive you over there. You're in no state to be driving."

Anna raised her hands in a gesture of surrender. "You're right. Oh, let's go."

Anna and Buddy hardly spoke on the way to the park. Buddy glanced over at Anna briefly and felt a wave of apprehension at the sight of her delicate profile. The suffering she had endured was visible in the lines on her face, especially in her forehead. Her soft brown hair was streaked with strands of gray. But her eyes were shining now, and her skin had a high color that had been missing for a long time. These years had taken a high toll on her and her family, he thought. He offered a silent prayer that her ordeal would be over now. He wished he could dispel the uneasy feeling that had plagued him all day, whenever he thought of Paul's homecoming.

They passed through the stone columns which flanked the entrance to the park. Anna nervously directed him to the tennis courts, which were beyond the baseball diamond. As they pulled up to the courts, Anna could see through the climbing roses and the green chain links of the court walls the neon flash of Tracy's coltish legs sheathed in purple spandex bike shorts, and the back of Thomas's compact, muscular figure in white across the net.

"Okay," she said aloud, as if preparing herself.

"Do you want me to wait?"

Anna stirred and faced him in a daze. Then she shook her head. "Tom will drive home. Buddy, I can never thank you enough." She leaned over and embraced him fervently for a second. Then she began to slide out of the car. As she put her hand on the door handle, she turned back to him, a worried frown on her face.

"What is it?" he asked.

"Buddy, I keep thinking about this man, this kidnapper . . ."

"Rambo?"

"Yes. You say there's something wrong with him mentally. We don't know what he might do. . . ."

Buddy dismissed her fears with a wave of his hand. "I have a feeling that Mr. Rambo is trying to get as far away from you and your son as he can. I'll call you tomorrow with all the arrangements for bringing him home. We're going to do our best to keep it low profile. Now, go tell your family the good news. Go on."

Anna smiled and slammed the door behind her. "Good luck," Buddy blurted out, not quite knowing why. He watched her pensively as she hurried toward the court, bearing her precious piece of news. He had not told her all the Hawley sheriff had had to say about the severity of Albert Rambo's mental illness. Nor had he conveyed the sheriff's disturbing description of the sullen, uncooperative youth whose return Anna was anticipating with such joy. Why worry her? he thought. Things will all work out. But Buddy could not shake off the feeling of anxiety that had crept up on him again.

* * *

"Now you're in trouble," Tracy cried out as the racket connected with the ball at the sweet spot, with a hum and a thwack.

Thomas watched the ball and leapt for it. He slid into position and drew back his arm to swing, but his concentration was broken by the sight of Anna, who had thrown open the door to the court and was rushing toward him. He smiled and waved when he saw her, and then he frowned as he saw the expression on her face.

"Mo-ther!" Tracy cried in a voice shrill with exasperation. "Get off the court. You don't belong here."

Anna did not even seem to hear her daughter. She ran up to Thomas and then stopped short, a foot shy of him. She clasped her hands together and stared into her husband's baffled face.

"Tom, I have to tell you something."

"What is it, honey?" he asked worriedly. "What's the matter?" He took a step toward her.

"It's Paul."

Thomas's mouth tightened, and his eyes narrowed with wariness. "We're right in the middle of a game, Anna," he said.

"What's going on?" Tracy yelled across the court. The players on the adjacent court looked over at them through the mesh wall and then back at one another before resuming their game.

"Tom, Buddy Ferraro was just here. At our house. Thomas, Paul's been found. He's been found alive. The woman who kidnapped him died and left a confession. Tom, he's alive. He's coming home. Paul's coming home." Anna's face crumpled, and she buried it in her hands.

Thomas stared at his wife in disbelief. "What?" he whispered.

Anna nodded. "It's true. I'm telling you it's true. Paul is coming back to us."

It seemed to Thomas that the pulsing of blood in his ears was muffling the words she was saying. They were words he had never expected to hear. When he tried to picture the boy, there was only a blank spot in his mind, only the black hole with which he had willfully replaced his son's image through the years.

Anna was gazing at him now, gripping his hands. The warmth of her hands and the intensity in her eyes seemed to revive him. Feeling returned to him, in the form of an acute tenderness for her. She stood bravely before him, like a sapling that had withstood a pitiless gale.

He slipped his arms around her and drew her to his chest, his hands resting awkwardly on her back. "I knew it," she said, her cheek pressed to his sweaty tennis shirt. "I knew he was alive. I knew he'd come back."

Thomas stroked her hair, staring out over her head. "Paul's alive," he murmured. "You always said that. I never thought . . . I can't believe it."

Anna pulled back and looked into her husband's eyes. The tears were starting again in her own. "Oh, darling," she whispered.

Thomas squeezed her arms, wishing he could find his tears, but he felt as if they were trapped in a knot in the pit of his stomach. "It's wonderful," he said. "God, it's unbelievable."

"Forget it," Tracy screamed from across the court. She threw down her racket, which clattered to the ground, and started to stalk off the court. "I don't know what's going on here, but you can find yourself somebody else to play with."

"No, Tracy," Anna cried, disengaging herself from Thomas's arms and hurrying toward her daughter. She grabbed hold of the top of the net and leaned over it. "Tracy, wait. We have to tell you something. Wait for me." Anna did not want to yell the news out in front of the other players. But Tracy reached defiantly for the door of the court and yanked it open.

"Tracy, listen to me," Anna pleaded. "Your brother has been found. Paul. Paul is coming back."

Tracy turned around and faced her mother, who leaned toward her, clutching the top of the net between them. Behind her mother, her father stood immobile, his arms hanging limply at his sides.

Slowly the blood drained away from Tracy's tanned and freckled face. She seemed rooted there, staring at them, her eyes wide and blank. For a moment her hand remained frozen to the door of the cage. Then her hand dropped, leaden, to her side. The chain link gate swung back and clanged shut behind her.

CHAPTER 2

"All right, sleeping beauty, rise and shine."

Anna forced her eyes open like someone coming out of anesthesia and looked up groggily. Thomas was standing beside the bed in his bathrobe, holding a tray of food, decorated with one of the dahlias from her garden propped up in a juice glass.

She pulled the sheet up over her breasts and sat up with a sleepy smile. "Honey, what's this?"

Thomas looked down at the tray. "It's eggs, toast, coffee, and Bloody Marys!" Then he shot her a smile. "I forgot the milk. Here, hold this," he said, placing the tray on her knees atop the sheets. "I'll be right back."

"What time is it?" she called after his disappearing back.

"Almost eleven. I figured you needed the sleep."

Anna leaned back against the pillows and smiled at the tray on her lap. Then she gazed around the sunny bedroom. The wedding ring quilt was wadded up at the end of the bed, and their clothes were strewn on the bedpost and the floor, the telltale trail of lovers' impatience.

Yesterday, after they had gotten back from the tennis court, they had spent the balance of the day on the telephone and sharing with family and friends the incredible news. Thomas had gone out for Chinese food and brought it home at about nine o'clock. Tracy had pleaded an upset stomach and closeted herself in her room for the rest of the night. At about midnight Thomas had unplugged the phone and hustled Anna up to the bedroom, where, with an enthusiasm and a sense of urgency she had not seen from him in a while, he made love to her as if it were their last night together. At his moment of climax he had let out a cry so close to anguish that it startled her. She soothed him until he fell asleep, but she was awake most of the night, thinking about the miraculous news with a heart and mind so full that they would not admit sleep. It was nearly dawn when exhaustion finally claimed her.

The door to the bedroom opened again, and Thomas came in, carrying a small creamer of milk. He placed it on the tray and sat down carefully beside her on the bed. "Damn the crumbs, let's eat!"

Anna reached over and stroked the side of his face. "What a sweet thing to do," she said.

Thomas shrugged. "I thought we should celebrate. Besides, we hardly had a moment together yesterday. It was so crazy around here."

"Where's Trace?"

"She took off early on her bike. She left a note saying she was going to Mary Ellen's."

"I think she's upset by all of this," said Anna. Thomas stirred the Bloody Mary with a celery stalk and handed it to his wife. Anna obediently took a sip.

"It's a big change," said Tom. "It's a big change for all of us. But she'll be happy about it when she sees what a difference it's going to make in our lives."

Anna sighed and smiled at him. "I think so, too. Our son. Back home with us, and safe."

Thomas nodded and took a bite of the eggs. "We'll have a normal life again. Like other families."

Anna nodded, but she spoke a little defensively. "Well, we've had a pretty normal life, under the circumstances."

"I know," said Tom quickly. "I didn't mean that."

"It will just be that much better a life for having Paul back with us," she explained.

"I just meant," said Tom, "you know, that all that awful business will be over. You running off to every corner of the country every time we heard of a child somewhere. Those late nights on the phone and all that endless searching, contacting people. Nuts calling up every hour of the day or night with useless information. Reporters and police and psychics. If I never see another one of any of them, it will be too soon."

"They were all trying to help," Anna said.

"I'm sure they were, but they put you through a lot. You have to admit it. Now the . . . now our boy will be back, and we can stop thinking about it. We can get back to living our lives the way we should." He reached over and squeezed her arms. "You don't know how I've missed it."

Anna looked at him seriously. "I missed it, too," she said. "But what other choice did we have?"

Thomas picked up a napkin and wiped his lips. "Right. Right," he said. "Now you eat those eggs," he ordered, "before they get cold, and then I think I might just crawl back under those sheets with you."

Anna laughed and picked up a forkful of eggs. "These look good," she said. "I may let you have this job since you do it so well. Has Buddy called yet? He was going to arrange for us to talk to Paul today. I'm surprised we haven't heard from him."

"I don't know if he tried," Tom said. "I've still got the phone unplugged."

"Tom," Anna protested, "Paul may be trying to reach us."

"I wanted you to sleep," he said ruefully. "You were so tired."

Anna put the tray to one side and leaned over to the phone on the bedside table. "Plug it in for me, will you, darling? I'm going to call Buddy right now."

"Why don't you eat first?"

"Just let me find out."

Thomas removed the tray from the bed with a soft sigh and placed it on the floor. Then he bent down beside the night table and plugged the phone into the jack.

Anna leaned over the edge of the bed and kissed him on the cheek. "Thanks." She picked up the receiver and started to dial.

* * *

The arrangements, red tape, and waiting seemed interminable to Anna, but finally they passed. Now, by the light of the early-morning sun through her kitchen window, Anna sat planning the homecoming dinner. The butcher-block surface of her table was littered with open cookbooks. She could feel her cotton shirt already beginning to stick to her back. The August day had started to heat up early. There was usually a breeze that ran through the house, keeping it comfortable, and there were only a few days a year that she even thought of air-conditioning. She hoped to herself that this would not be one of them. She wanted everything to be perfect for Paul's first night home. She wanted him to like it here.

Anna returned her attention to the cookbooks. He was not coming until about nine tonight. She had to make something she could keep warm, or cook at the last minute. It was hard to know what to make, what he liked to eat. There was a recipe for lobster that looked good. Lobster was something special, and cool. But what if he had allergies to seafood? Lots of people did. She realized that she had no way of knowing about her own son.

She rested her chin on her hand and gazed out over the profusion of plants on the kitchen windowsill. She wondered what he was like now, how he looked. During the last eleven years she had seen him everywhere. On every playground, swinging on the swings, at street corners as she whizzed by in her car, coming toward her down the corridors at Tracy's school. Her heart would leap to her throat as she spied him, sure it was Paul. His name would be on her lips when, as she looked harder, the vision of his face would dissolve, and she would see before her some strange child with honey-colored hair whom she did not recognize at all. She would turn away quickly, before the little one could see the horror and woe in her eyes.

But tonight she would open the door and he would be there. Tonight.

Tracy, wearing zip-up black spandex and sneakers, entered the kitchen and slumped into a chair without a greeting. Anna pushed the cookbooks aside.

"Did you sleep well?" Anna asked.

"It's been so noisy around here it woke me up."

"Oh, I hope I didn't disturb you, darling. I got up early because I had so much to do," said Anna, ignoring Tracy's gloomy expression. "I dusted, waxed the furniture, and then I baked this." She got up, walked over to the counter, and lifted the lid on the cake dish. She held up the cake she had baked for her daughter's inspection. It read "Welcome home, Paul" in blue letters arching around the top half of the cake's chocolate icing. "I made chocolate. I figured all you kids like chocolate. Well, what do you think?"

Tracy stared at the blue writing and then looked up at her mother. "You made that?"

Anna nodded. "Does it look good?"

Tracy folded her arms across her chest and stared sullenly in front of her. "Yeah. Sure."

Anna returned the cake to the counter and replaced the lid after one last look. She wiped her hands on her apron and turned to Tracy. "What do you want for breakfast, sweetheart?"

"Nothing," said Tracy.

"Well, you should have something. You can't go out on an empty—"

"Juice."

"How about some cereal? I can get you some—"

"No! I said juice."

Just then Thomas walked into the kitchen, still buttoning a cuff on his shirt. He stopped short and looked at his daughter. "It's too hot to eat," Tracy insisted to him.

"There's no need to yell," said Thomas.

"She tries to force me to eat when I'm not even hungry," Tracy muttered.

Anna placed a glass of juice in front of her daughter and turned to Thomas. "You had such a restless night," she said. "I hope I didn't wake you getting dressed this morning."

"I woke up for a minute. It was pitch-black out. What time was it anyway?" he asked.

"It must have been about four thirty, quarter to five. I couldn't sleep," said Anna. "I was too excited."

Thomas put his arms around her and squeezed her, kissing her on the forehead.

"What do you want for breakfast?" Anna asked.

"I'm running late. I'll get something off the cart."

"Oh, Tom . . ."

"What's all this?" he asked, glancing at the pile of cookbooks.

"I'm looking for something to make tonight. I guess I should look through some of those magazines of mine, right?"

"I thought you were saving those for a special occasion," he said.

Anna smiled happily at the appropriateness of one of their standard jokes. "I'm so worked up I can't even think straight."

Tracy scraped back her chair and stood up.

Anna tried to get her daughter's attention. "What do you think we should have, Tracy?"

"I'm leaving," Tracy announced.

"Playing tennis this morning?" Anna asked.

"Mmmm . . ." Tracy mumbled.

"Before you go, dear, I want you to go upstairs and take your stuff out of the guest . . . out of Paul's room so I can clean up there."

"I'll do it later," said Tracy. "Bye, Dad."

Thomas smiled at her. "Good luck," he said.

Anna picked the glass up from the table. "I want you to do it now. I need to get into that room."

Tracy stiffened in the doorway. "I have a game this morning."

"It won't take you long," Anna insisted. "You've known you had to do this all week. There are things more important than your game. Your brother is coming home tonight."

Tracy turned on her mother, her small jaw hardening stubbornly. Her hazel eyes were icy with rage. "I don't care," she said. "I'm leaving."

Anna was momentarily speechless, stung by the cold defiance in her daughter's eyes.

"Tracy," Thomas ordered, "Do as you're told."

"Shit!" Tracy exclaimed, stamping out of the kitchen. "You both stink."

Anna shook her head and sat down. "God, she is really in a state about this thing. I don't understand it. Have you tried to talk to her? She just puts up a wall with me."

Thomas sighed, putting his newspaper in his briefcase. "No," he admitted. "It's the same with me."

"Maybe she's jealous of all the attention to Paul. You know, she feels usurped," Anna speculated.

"Well, it does seem to be the only thing anyone has talked about all week," he said.

"I know," said Anna, "but that's only natural. This is a miracle. Of course we're all excited about it."

"She might be feeling it's going to stay that way once he gets here," said Thomas.

Anna looked at her husband quizzically. "What do you mean?"

"I don't know," said Thomas, dismissing it.

He looked at his watch. "She'll come around," he said. "Listen, Anna, we'd better run."

Anna nodded, even though she wished they could continue the conversation. She got up and found her car keys in the little teacup she kept beside the sink. Their second car was in the garage for repairs; that meant she had to drive him to the station.

Thomas shrugged into his jacket and picked up his briefcase.

"I wish you didn't have to go in today," she said wistfully.

"It'll keep my mind occupied," he said. "Besides, I better not lose this job. I've got another kid to put through college now."

* * *

Leafy limbs of ancient maples canopied the quiet back roads of Stanwich. Stately houses overlooked manicured lawns, separated by orchards and stone fences. Few cars passed to disturb the tranquility.

Anna drove and Thomas rode in silence. He had his briefcase open on his lap and was leafing through the reports it contained.

"Tom . . ." she ventured. "Are you looking forward to tonight?"

Thomas rested his hands in the open briefcase and nodded slowly. "Yes, of course I am."

"I still can't believe it. It's incredible, really," she continued. "Our son finally coming back to us. We'll all be together again, the way it used to be. I'm just afraid . . . I hope that Paul will be . . . all right."

Thomas looked at her warily. "Why shouldn't he?"

Anna twisted her lip and did not reply immediately.

"Ever since we heard about Paul, I've been thinking," she began. "Worrying actually."

"About what?"

Anna hesitated. "Well, I was thinking it might be a good idea if we had some protection . . . for him."

She kept her eyes on the road, but she could feel his eyes scrutinizing her.

"What for? I don't follow you."

"Well, I just can't help worrying about him."

"Paul?"

"That man." She shuddered.

There was a silence. "Rambo," Thomas said.

"He's running around loose somewhere. We know the man is mentally unbalanced. We have no idea what he is capable of. He might decide to come after Paul. He might have some crazy idea that Paul is really his and come looking for him or something."

"I don't think we should borrow trouble, Anna. We have no reason to think he'll do anything of the kind."

Anna turned and stared at him. "How can you be so sure of that? He took our son once, didn't he?"

"Watch the road, Anna," Thomas cried.

The car swerved slightly as Anna came around a curve and then evened out.

"Look," said Thomas, "the police have told you . . . even your friend Buddy told you . . . the man is probably going to run as far and as fast as he can. He has a kidnapping charge to face if the police get him. The last thing he's going to do is come around here. Even Rambo is not that crazy. I think you should just forget about him."

"I understand all that about the kidnapping charge. But I also think that we're not dealing with a rational, predictable person. I mean, was it rational for him to take our son? How can you predict what a person like that will do? We know that he had a history of mental illness—"

"All right," Thomas interrupted her, "but if he knew enough to run away when he found out that his wife was planning to spill the beans, I think we can be reasonably certain that he is not going to walk directly into the arms of the police."

Anna gripped the wheel tightly. "Maybe you're right. But I have a bad feeling about it."

"For God's sake, Anna," Thomas said quietly as the railroad station came into view, "I thought now that you had the boy back, you would finally stop all this. I mean, do you get pleasure out of this constant worrying? Why can't you leave well enough alone?"

Anna pulled the car up beside the platform and shifted into neutral with the motor still running. "No, I do not enjoy the worrying, and you know it. But I won't just forget about this. Not after all we've been through. And your criticizing me about it doesn't help."

"All right, I'm sorry, I'm sorry," said Thomas. He opened the car door and got out. A rush of uniformly dressed commuters passed on each side of the Volvo. Thomas came around to the driver's side, glanced at his watch, and then bent down beside the open window. He kissed Anna's hair.

"Try to come home early," she said. "It's going to be a very happy night."

"I know." Thomas gave her a strained smile and turned away from the window. Anna watched her husband disappear into the ranks of commuters who milled around restlessly on the platform, their eyes searching the tracks for the train to the city.

* * *

The mingled smells of toasting bread, greasy bacon, and potatoes frying oozed through the grimy wall fan in back of the luncheonette and into the parking lot behind the little row of stores. The man who stood in the early-morning shadows was tantalized by the smells. He plucked at the skin on his face with rapidly moving fingers, leaving red blotches across the surface of his pasty skin. Inside the diner, the waitresses and the short-order cook ribbed each other above the clatter of dishes. Although he heard their words, the man could not understand their joking. He never understood what was funny about the things people said to one another or why they laughed.

None of the other stores on the street were open yet, but behind the grocery store sat a squat green metal garbage Dumpster — the reason he was here.

He moved deliberately across the backs of the stores to where the Dumpster stood. For two days he had had nothing to eat besides candy bars purchased in gas station machines. He had hardly any money and had been sleeping in his car in cul-de-sacs he found off the main highway. Finally he had had to stop. The voices had been so distracting that he had almost driven into a divider on the highway. He decided to put up for a few nights in that dumpy motel, but if he did that, he didn't have enough money for food, too.

Grocery stores threw out food, though. There was bound to be something in the Dumpster. Looking all around him, he lifted the heavy metal lid and held it up with one hand. The smell of rotting and decaying food wafted up from inside. He stuck his head under the lid and examined the loose garbage. Below a rumpled newspaper he saw an open egg box with three cracked eggs and two whole ones in it and, beside that, an open box of crackers with paper stuffed inside it. He reached in past a ripped and soggy milk container and fished for the egg box. He pulled out the newspaper first and threw it on the ground. As it fell, he saw the picture on the front page of his son, staring up at him.

Albert Rambo heaved a disgusted sigh and bent down to pick up the paper. He read the latest news article about Paul Lange's happy reunion with his family which was about to take place. His lip curled as he scanned the story. On the inside page was a picture of the Langes' house, a monstrous palace in the town of Stanwich, Connecticut.

A fit place for that scheming heathen to do the devil's own business, Rambo thought. Among the rich and godless up there in Connecticut. If the truth were known, he belonged in hell with the other devils, he thought. After all those years of giving up things for him, raising him as his own. He could still hear his wife's voice in his head. "The boy needs shoes. He needs a coat. Billy needs . . . Billy needs . . ."

Rambo gazed down at the house in the picture in the paper where the blaspheming little infidel, that acolyte to Beelzebub, would now be living.

Paul Lange. He snorted. Sounds like a young prince. Dorothy Lee's voice faded away as other voices began to grip him, whirling up through the hole in his stomach, haranguing him in insistent tones. The voices spoke of God's wrath against the wicked, His desire that they should be plundered, trodden upon like the mire of the streets. Urging him, urging him, arming him with conviction.

A squeal near his elbow made Rambo jump and the voices disappear. A bloated rat scuttled down the wall of the Dumpster and into the garbage. Rambo threw the newspaper back into the trash and with a furtive look around reached into the bin and pulled up the crackers and the eggs.

Stanwich was only about thirty miles from there, he thought, as he sucked the cracked egg greedily from its shell. He knew the exact spot. Billy's new home. He remembered it well. Stuffing the cracker box under his arm, he crossed over to his car.

CHAPTER 3

The gray towers of Manhattan were enveloped in a barley-colored haze of heat and soot. Thomas stared out his office window dreading the prospect of going into the streets again. The air had been thick and nauseating at lunch, and the asphalt in the streets threatened to turn viscous from the heat. He knew what it would be like tonight, walking to Grand Central Station. Pedestrians, like human bumper cars, dodging and colliding with one another, knees slamming into swinging briefcases.

Even from the twentieth floor, where he sat, Thomas could hear the whiny bray of the snarled traffic below on Madison Avenue. It was the start of the rush hour. With a sigh Thomas turned away from the window and looked again at the clock on his desk. His office, by contrast, was cool and air-conditioned, the temperate air shut in tight by large, clean, hermetically sealed windows. Even the decor was cool: beige carpet, beige walls, a muted blue print on the sofa and drapes. The only ornament which interrupted the sterility of the room was the framed picture of Anna and Tracy on his desk. Glancing at the laughing faces of his wife and daughter in the photograph, he realized that he would now have to put a picture of Paul there, too. At that thought Thomas felt an unpleasant tightening in his stomach.

He picked up the report on his desk without enthusiasm. He knew that he really should finish it before he went home. It concerned the new computer system that was being installed and how it could benefit his department. It was nearly five o'clock now. He counted the pages that he had left to read and calculated the time it would take him. Then he flipped the top page over and read the first paragraph.

There was a soft rap on his office door. He looked up, and his troubled expression dissolved into one of boyish pleasure at the sight of the smartly dressed young woman with wavy black hair who was leaning into his office.

"What did you think of my report?" she asked briskly.

Thomas indicated that the report was still in his hands. "I'm almost finished," Thomas said apologetically.

The young woman came into the room and eased herself onto the sofa across from Thomas's desk, then threw one arm across the back and crossed her legs. "So much for my brilliant analysis," she said, pouting.

"I think you're right about it," Thomas said earnestly. "I think we should have done it two years ago. You've done a very thorough job on this report, Gail."

"If you like, I'll give you a private summary over a martini. Save you all that boring reading," she said, running one hand lazily up and down her shin.

"Oh, I want to read it," he assured her.

"I'm only teasing you," she said.

"Oh," he said, embarrassed and flattered at once. He could feel her eyes on him and his scalp prickled at the sensation. He tried not to look at her legs. "Were you teasing about the drink?" he asked.

Gail Kelleher laughed aloud at the ingenuous sound of the question. "Nope. That was a solid offer."

For a minute Thomas could envision himself sitting in a cool dark bar with her, talking and laughing, a piano playing languidly in the background. Even as he thought of it, he remembered what awaited him at home, and he shook his head. "That sounds nice," he said absently. "I wish I could." He frowned and looked down at the report on his desk.

Gail caught the wistful note in his voice. Like everyone else in the office, she knew about Paul's imminent homecoming, even though Thomas hadn't referred to it voluntarily. Although their relationship was still only light and flirtatious, she had tried to let him know that she would welcome his confiding in her. A couple of times he had. Twice, when Anna had gone off on one of her missions in search of the boy, they had shared a drink after work, and dawdling over a second Scotch and water, he had vented a little of his frustration at Anna's relentless pursuit of the missing child. As soon as Gail expressed any sympathy for his point of view, Thomas had immediately withdrawn. But Gail had spotted an opening there. This man, whom she had found terribly attractive from the first time she met him, was not entirely happy with his lot. And today she saw the same glum, distracted look on his face that she recognized from those nights when he had gone so far as to linger for a drink. She found his reaction to the boy's homecoming interesting.

"You seem a little . . . down," she observed. "Are you worried about tonight?"

"What?" Thomas asked. "Oh, worried, no. Not really. Well, it's been a long day. Everyone's been either congratulating me or tiptoeing around me."

"It's hard to know what to say."

"I guess so." He sighed.

She bit her lip. "I'm just concerned about you," she said.

"I'm okay," he insisted, swiveling his chair and looking out the window. "I feel great. Happy."

Gail reached up and toyed with one of her earrings. "I guess Anna must be in quite a state over all this," she ventured.

Thomas grimaced. "Well, it's been hectic, kind of. Anna — she's just . . . it's so important to her."

"I imagine she's been awfully busy trying to get things ready for Paul."

"Yes," said Tom. "She doesn't think of anything else."

"Well, I guess she's never been quite normal since that happened."

"Anna!" Tom exclaimed, looking at her incredulously. "She's normal. She's perfectly normal. She's just . . ."

"Obsessed," Gail offered.

Thomas seemed to balk at the word, and Gail could sense that she had gone a little too far. He began to retreat from the conversation. She moved quickly to smooth it over.

"It's a great strain on everyone, of course. You just have to give yourself a little time to adjust."

Thomas ran his hand over his eyes and then nodded. "I'm a little bit tired, I guess."

With slow and deliberate movements, Gail uncrossed her legs and rose from the sofa. She walked over to where he was sitting and slid around behind his chair. "What you need," she said with mock sternness, "is a good relaxing massage." She placed her hands lightly on the back of his neck and then pressed down in a circular motion. She could feel his muscles tense up at her approach and then begin to relax at the pressure of her touch.

Thomas laughed nervously. "That feels good," he said, and then released a soft, involuntary groan.

Gail smiled to herself and kneaded his neck. "I took a course in massage one summer," she said.

"You must have gotten an A," he said. He wanted to speak in a carefree, flirtatious tone; but the pressure of Gail's hands on his back and neck seemed to be loosening something that was tight inside him, and he had to stifle a sob which rose unexpectedly to his throat. He closed his eyes in guilty enjoyment of the soothing manipulation, and as he did, he felt the sudden impulse to turn and embrace her, to bury his face in her stomach. His eyes shot open, and he pulled away.

"That helped a lot," he said as Gail released him. "Really." He made a point of looking at his watch.

"God, I'd better run if I'm going to make the five forty." He looked down at his desk. "I guess I'll take this home with me."

Gail shook out her fingers and headed for the doorway of his office. "Well," she said casually, "if you should want to talk about it over the weekend, just give me a call. Or drop by. I'm in the book. I hope everything goes okay with Paul."

"Thanks," said Thomas. "It will."

Thomas watched her walk out of his office, admiring the sensual way she moved in her very correct business clothes. He realized that he did not feel his customary eagerness to get home. Instead, he wished he were going to a dark bar with her and having a few drinks and forgetting everything. Everything but the feeling of her fingers on the back of his neck.

* * *

Anna unwrapped the silver foil and cocked her head to one side with a crooked smile. Then, holding the bottle by the neck, she reached over and embraced her friend. "Champagne. Iris, that's so thoughtful."

Iris looked at the label uncertainly. "Edward selected the vintage. He says it should be an excellent bottle. Are you all set?"

Anna glanced around the unnaturally tidy kitchen. "I guess so. I think I've done everything twice."

Iris nodded approvingly. "It should be just wonderful." The two women walked through the quiet house toward the front door and stood out on the porch steps. "It's going to be a lovely evening," Iris observed.

Anna nodded, scanning the sky for clouds.

"Don't worry, Anna."

"I'm getting nervous now," Anna admitted. "Maybe I should go in and wash the floor again."

At that moment a black Cadillac appeared around the corner, rolled down, and pulled into the Langes' driveway. The car's finish was lustrous, and above the grille, in place of the characteristic Cadillac trademark, the hood ornament was a gleaming golden eagle, its wings outstretched to full span. "Look who's here," said Iris. "They must have caught the same train."

Thomas emerged from the passenger side of the Cadillac and shut the door carefully. He came around the front of the car as Edward turned off the engine and slid out from behind the wheel. Both men were smiling, and that took Anna by surprise. As a rule they were polite but not friendly. Now, however, it made Anna feel good to see them walking, shoulder to shoulder, up the lawn.

She raised the bottle which she was cradling in her arm. "Look what Iris and Edward brought us," she called out to Thomas.

"Thanks, Iris, Edward," Thomas said. "We appreciate the thought."

"Well," said Iris, awkwardly grasping his hand and squeezing it, "we are very happy for you, and we will be thinking of you all tonight."

"Indeed," Edward agreed. Anna looked fondly at them both, remembering that they had been present and ready to help on another night, the night that Paul had disappeared.

"Would you like to come in for a drink?" Anna asked.

Edward waved his hand. "We have to be getting home. I have a lot to do tonight."

As Edward spoke, an aqua-colored van with a network logo printed on the side pulled up in front of the house.

"What's this now?" said Thomas as a man in a sport shirt slid out of the front seat and they heard the door slam. A blonde woman in a tailored suit came around the truck and skirted around the man in the sport shirt, who was opening the rear doors to the van. She hailed the Langes and started up the incline toward them.

Anna groaned softly, recognizing the reporter, Camille Mandeville, who had interviewed her many times in the years since Paul's disappearance. Anna hurried down the lawn to intercept her as another man emerged from the back of the truck and began to help the driver unload his videocam and sound equipment.

"Camille, you promised me," Anna said. "Not today. We want a private homecoming for our boy."

"Hello, Mrs. Lange," said the reporter, flashing her a dazzling, practiced smile. "Oh, we've been crazy all day. I was hoping to get here earlier."

"Everyone else has been very cooperative," said Anna. "I should tell you that the police have promised to intervene if we're harassed."

"Calm down, calm down," Camille said soothingly. "We're not staying." Thomas, Edward, and Iris had made their way down the lawn and were now surrounding Anna like reinforcements. "Hello, Mr. Lange. Are these relatives?" Camille asked pleasantly.

"These are our neighbors, Mr. and Mrs. Stewart," said Anna.

Camille gave Iris and Edward a brilliant, if distracted, smile as she shook their hands while sizing up the conditions for shooting on the lawn. "Pleasure to meet you."

"Camille, you must realize that we have so much on our minds right now," Anna protested.

Camille, who was signaling to her cameraman to join her on the lawn, turned to Anna and wagged a finger at her. "Mrs. Lange," she chided, "how many times have I, and this network, updated your story, given you airtime to try to locate your son? Now the people in this area have been very concerned about you and your family for a number of years. Don't you think that you owe it to them to share your feelings with them on this occasion? I mean, a lot of people have hoped and prayed for this day, just as you have."

Anna sighed. People had been kind to them. Sometimes their curiosity had upset her, but there were other times when their support was all she had had to cling to. Letters from other mothers, strangers, urging her to have faith, trying to offer a clue. She glanced at Thomas, who was wearing an impatient expression.

"All right," said Anna. "If you hurry."

"Why don't you all gather around Mrs. Lange?" Camille suggested, directing them with her melon-painted fingernails. "This won't take long. Come on."

"I'm sorry about this," said Tom to his unprepared neighbors.

"That's right," said Camille. "Gather 'round her. It looks good. People will like this. Friends, sharing your joy and so on. Everybody look cheerful."

"Can you keep it short, Camille?" Anna pleaded. "Our friends here—"

"Don't worry, Anna." Iris reassured her. "I think it's kind of fun!"

Camille raised both arms to indicate that speed was no problem and then accepted a microphone from a cameraman who was moving in on them. "Now," she said, "I'm going to introduce you all. I may ask each of you a question. Mr. Stewart, I may ask you how long you've known the Langes, if you remember Paul, that kind of stuff, okay?" Camille hesitated, peering at Edward, whose gray eyes widened with alarm.

Poor Edward, Anna thought as she glanced over at him. Television really isn't his medium. A discreet portrait photograph in *The New York Times* business section, perhaps, but not the ten o'clock news, sandwiched in with murders, fires, and city hall politics.

Edward licked his lips and nodded at the reporter.

"Now," Camille went on, "more of the same for you, Mrs. Stewart. And then we'll ask Mr. and Mrs. Lange to comment on their feelings tonight. All right, are we ready?" She smiled expectantly at them.

Anna nodded and tried to concentrate on all those people who had sent their prayers to her over the years.

"Folks, there's nothing to be nervous about. Just smile," advised Camille. "Mr. Lange, why don't you put your arm around your wife?" She turned to face the cameraman. "Once in a while a story has a happy ending," Camille began, "and here at the home of Mr. and Mrs. Thomas Lange one of those rare happy endings is about to come true."

* * *

Anna picked up one of the tasseled pillows from the comer of the sofa and squeezed it to her chest as she studied the arrangement of her living room. She crossed over, placed the pillow against the cushion of a wing chair, and stepped back to look at it. Then she picked it up again and circled around behind the matching chair across the room by the writing desk.

Thomas, wearing a clean sport shirt, stood in the doorway and watched her. "Is that a new outfit?" he asked.

Anna looked down at herself and then back at her husband. "Oh, yeah, I got it the other day," she said. "I forgot to show it to you." She picked the pillow up again and held it in front of her.

"It looks nice," he said. "Anna, what are you doing with that pillow?"

Anna sank down onto the edge of the sofa and placed the pillow beside her. She straightened the blooming begonia, the magazines and the large art books on the coffee table in front of her. "I was going to move it," she said.

"How long did Buddy say they'd be?"

Anna glanced at her watch. "He said he'd try to get him here by nine. Is the front light on?"

Thomas nodded and looked at his own watch. "Where's Tracy?"

Anna gestured toward the foyer. "She's still upstairs." Thomas sat down in one of the wing chairs. She folded her hands in her lap and tried to focus her attention on him. "How was your day?" she asked.

Instantly he thought of Gail's hands massaging his neck. He picked up a magazine and opened it. "Fine."

"How's that . . . um . . . computer business going that you mentioned?"

Thomas looked up at her warily. He had guilty thoughts of Gail, but at the same time he was pleased by Anna's interest. "The new system we're installing?"

"How long before you can start using it?"

"It won't be too long, I think."

"What remains to be done?" she asked, absently twisting her wedding ring on her finger.

"Well, I was just reading a report on it today. The software has been installed, but it's a matter of reorganizing information and also retraining some of our staff."

"People in your department?"

Thomas set down the magazine. "Well, I want the people in my department to know the quickest way to access information from it, but the main effort is going to be concentrated—"

A rapid series of thuds issued from the hallway stairs, and then Tracy shuffled into the living room, still dressed in her workout gear. Anna's eyes shot to the slim, disheveled figure and widened in dismay.

"Tracy," she blurted out, "why haven't you changed?"

Tracy looked from her mother to her father, who shook his head. "What's wrong with this?"

"You look like a mess," said Anna.

Thomas got up from his chair. "I'm having a drink. Do you want one, Anna?"

Anna tore her critical gaze from Tracy and looked at Thomas. "There's that champagne the Stewarts brought over."

"I'm not in a champagne mood," said Thomas sourly.

"There's regular wine," said Anna, taken aback by his tone.

"Well, I'm hungry now," Tracy said, flouncing past her father toward the kitchen.

"It's almost dinnertime," Anna cried. Thomas followed Tracy out to the kitchen and returned with a glass of wine. Then he looked at Anna. "Do you want one?"

Anna shook her head. "I'll wait until dinner. We're going to eat as soon as he gets here."

Thomas crossed over to his chair with his own drink and began to drain it.

"I'm having steak," said Anna.

"Oh," said Thomas, staring into his empty glass.

"I hope it will be all right," she said. "I don't know what he likes to eat. I figured all boys like steak."

"Oh, I'm sure he'll like it," said Thomas.

Suddenly Anna shot up from her seat. "Tom, do you hear?" Thomas placed his glass deliberately on the coaster and stood up. "It sounds like a car in the driveway." His voice was steady.

"Tracy," Anna cried out.

A crash from the direction of the kitchen was her answer. Anna ran through the dining room and threw open the kitchen door. "What happened?" she demanded.

Tracy faced her defiantly. Anna looked from her daughter's face to the ragged hunk of chocolate cake, upended and stuck to the linoleum by its icing. Jagged pieces of the cake plate were scattered about the floor. Another huge piece of cake tilted precariously on the edge of the sink. Icing was smeared on the countertop.

"I was moving the plate, and it fell when you screamed."

Anna clenched her fists. "You know you weren't supposed to touch that. I made that especially for Paul's homecoming."

"I didn't do it on purpose," Tracy said sullenly.

"Clean it up," Anna said. "This minute."

Thomas appeared in the doorway. "The police car is in the driveway. Hurry up."

"She has to clean this mess up," Anna insisted, backing out the kitchen door.

"Later," said Thomas. "Get in here. Both of you."

Tracy passed by Thomas, wearing the suggestion of a smirk. Anna gazed, as if mesmerized, at the lump of chocolate on the floor. Then she got down on her knees and began mechanically to scoop up the cake with her hands.

"Anna." Thomas bent over and lifted her up gently by the elbow. "Leave it."

Slowly Anna rose to her feet and wiped her hands on the towel that he handed to her. She looked helplessly at her husband.

"We'll close the kitchen door," he told her. "It will be all right."

The doorbell rang through the house from the direction of the foyer. Thomas and Anna's eyes met in a surge of apprehension.

"This is it, darling," he said softly. "Let's go."

Anna took his hand, and he led her out to the living room, where Tracy was sprawled on the sofa. Thomas reached for Tracy's hand, but she shook him off and jerked herself to her feet.

The doorbell rang again. Anna approached the front door and then stood still, as if paralyzed.

Passing by her, Thomas strode to the front door and opened it. Holding her trembling hands clutched together, Anna walked up behind her husband's back and looked out.

The night was dark, but the coach lamp beside the door threw its light over the front steps and the figure standing there. Drawn by the brightness of the light, a battery of dun-colored moths swarmed to the screen door and flattened themselves against it, beating their dusty wings in agitation against the grid. Through the whirring, jumpy mosaic formed by the congestion of wings, Anna saw the pale, narrow face of a teenaged boy. His brown hair was long and ragged, falling across his forehead like a dark scar. He wore faded jeans, black high-top sneakers, a T-shirt, and a faded camouflage vest with ragged armholes. His deep-set amber eyes, ringed by grayish circles, looked warily from the couple in the doorway to the squadron of nocturnal insects besieging the screen.

Thomas pushed the screen door out and motioned for the boy to hurry in. "Come in," he said.

Paul struggled through the narrow opening and stepped into the foyer. On one shoulder he supported an old duffel bag. In his other hand he held a cardboard carrying case. For a moment they all stared at one another.

Then Anna took a step toward him and reached out her arms.

The boy lifted the cardboard traveling box and held it between them. A cat's meow emanated from inside the box. "I forgot to ask you on the phone," the boy said, "about my cat."

Tears filled Anna's eyes, blurring his face out of focus. She nodded, unable to speak.

"Welcome, Paul," said Thomas, stepping back to let the boy pass by him.

"It's Billy," said the boy. For a minute Thomas stared at him.

The boy pointed to the name embroidered on the pocket flap of his vest. "I'm really . . . I'm used to Billy," the boy said as he edged into the house, clutching his few belongings.

CHAPTER 4

Although the weather-faded wooden sign on the La-Z Pines Motel billboard promised air-conditioned rooms, the unit in Albert Rambo's window was nearly impotent, and the sheen of sweat on his skin from the outside did not dissolve inside the room. Rambo wiped the film off his face and heaved a sigh. The hair on his head was thinning, and his white scalp glowed in the gloomy room. The smell of the chicken in the little striped cardboard box he'd found in the garbage can outside Kentucky Fried Chicken made him feel faint. He felt tired, too. Tired of running.

The thought of his predicament filled him with a sickish feeling. He had always kind of stayed put after he married Dorothy Lee. When he was younger, he had bummed around, but then they had settled down and got that trailer. They had moved only once or twice after that: once when they got Billy and then again when they bought the trailer. And of course, there had been the times in the hospital. But he didn't like to count those. He had long since lost his taste for moving around. Besides, Dorothy Lee had liked to stay put and make a home for the boy.

Remembering his wife caused a brief rage to stir in him; it then subsided into the familiar dead despair. How could she do this to him? Tell the minister everything and leave him to the wolves. After all, he had done it for her in the first place. It was his biggest mistake. He'd known it almost from the start. After the day they got Billy, she cared more for that son of Satan than she ever had for him. That little bastard with his evil eye. She denied it, but Albert knew it. And this was the proof. His eyes narrowed bitterly as they took in the parameters of the shabby room.

Having dragged himself off the chair, he walked over to the old Zenith TV set and flicked it on. He did not want to think about it anymore. He wanted to eat his chicken and just sit. Tomorrow he would make a plan of what to do.

The ten o'clock news came on as Rambo lifted a drumstick to his salivating mouth. The announcer promised that a visit to the Lange home was coming up. Disgusted, Rambo thought of changing the channel and then decided to leave it. The story fascinated him almost as much as it infuriated him. He only hoped that they did not show his picture on the TV again tonight. In a way, he was lucky that no one had ever cared much to take pictures of him. Once that kid came along, Dorothy Lee wasted all the film on Billy. The ones they usually flashed of Rambo were so grainy and distorted that you could hardly recognize him, the bill of his ever-present cap always throwing a shadow across his face. For a minute he wondered if he should get a different hat. Then he realized that he had no money to buy a new one. Maybe in the thrift shop. He might be able to pick one up for a quarter, although he hated the idea of wearing somebody else's dirty hat on his head. The germs could probably get into your body through the hair.

Sweat began to stream off him again at the thought of the spot he was in. His stomach felt knotted, and he suddenly felt unable to eat. He sat immobile on the bed, the drumstick dangling from his fingers, lost in a miasma of fears. Two voices inside his head began to chant something unintelligible about death. Rambo strained to make it out. Then his stomach growled, drowning out words, reminding him of his hunger. He lifted the drumstick to his mouth and bit into it.

The reporter on the tube was talking about a happy ending at the Langes' house, which was just visible behind the reporter. It looked like a mansion. Rambo thought of Billy, that evil little fiend, moving into all that luxury. Didn't that just tear it? Little old Billy bedding down in roses while he, who had taken care of that kid, had to spend his life running and hiding for his trouble.

Suddenly the drumstick fell from his hand as Rambo gaped at the picture on the set. The bitter cast of his face slackened, and his dull eyes flickered in amazement. Long after the report was over, Rambo still sat on the bed, his mind racing furiously. He was trying to take it all in before the voices could confuse him, trying to figure out what it meant. He was suddenly aware, though he could scarcely believe it, that what he had just seen on the screen could be God's way of sending him a message. Offering him salvation, right here on earth.

* * *

With the side of his fork Paul pushed the mushrooms away from the steak on his plate and tried to scrape off the sauce. Anna sat across the table, her hands in her lap, and watched him. Paul looked up and caught Anna staring at him. He quickly looked down again, to avoid her eyes.

"Well, P—" said Thomas. "What's, uh, what's your favorite subject in school?"

Paul picked up his knife and began to saw away at the steak with some concentration. "I don't know . . ." he said. "I don't like school."

"You don't have to eat that," Anna said. "I can make you something else."

The boy studied the piece of meat on his fork and then put it into his mouth.

"Really," said Anna, getting up from her seat, "it's no trouble. I have things in the refrigerator. I'll make you a hot dog or something."

"No. I'll eat this."

"Well, I didn't know what you liked, and I have plenty of other—"

"No," Paul protested.

"Anna," said Thomas, "he doesn't want anything."

Slowly Anna resumed her seat. There was a silence around the table. "I didn't mean to interrupt your conversation," Anna said. "What were you saying about school?"

"Nothing."

Tracy pushed her plate away and rested her chin in her hands, causing her eyes to narrow. "What did you use to do for fun?" she asked.

Paul shrugged and heaved a sigh.

"Don't you play sports or anything?" Tracy persisted.

The boy glanced at her. "I like hunting," he said. "I used to go hunting a lot."

"That's not a sport," Tracy announced. "That's disgusting. Killing animals for fun."

"Tracy works at the animal shelter," Anna explained. "Animals are her favorite people."

"Don't make excuses for me, Mother," Tracy said in a shrill voice, "I think it's disgusting. And it is."

"I like animals, too," Paul said. "I have my cat."

"Yeah," said Tracy. "Well, how would you like it if someone went hunting for your cat?"

"That's enough, Tracy," said Thomas.

Paul blanched as Tracy leaned back in her chair, crossing her arms over her chest. Her eyes blazed, and two spots of color appeared in her cheeks. Anna reached a hand to her, but Tracy jerked away.

"Well," said Thomas, "I'll bet you're going to like school here. They've got all the latest equipment. Lots of activities . . ." As his words faded away, Thomas cringed at the sound of his own voice. You can't think of a thing to say to your own son, he thought.

Paul kept his eyes down and carved off another piece of meat.

Anna smiled brightly at him. "We're right near New York here," she said. "There are all kinds of museums and shows to see. We'll take a trip into the city soon, if you'd like that."

"I heard there's a lot of robberies and criminals there," said the boy.

"Well," said Anna, taken aback, "you have to be careful, of course."

"I'd like to go sometime," said Paul. "My mom always said she'd take me someday—"

A silence fell over the table. Paul put the piece of meat in his mouth and started to chew noisily.

"Ugh. Can I be excused?" said Tracy, standing up.

"No. We're not finished yet," said Anna, glaring at her. She turned to Paul. "Let me get you something else to eat," said Anna. "Isn't there something you want?"

"Have you got any sweet milk gravy? Or even red eye?"

Tracy made a face, and Anna threw her a warning glance. "No . . . but," she said. "I've got ketchup."

"Okay," he said. "I guess."

Anna went into the kitchen and walked over to the refrigerator. She opened the door and reached in for a bottle of ketchup. Then she turned to the stove, put a kettle on, and quickly prepared the drip pot for coffee. From behind the door to the dining room she could hear an occasional muffled word. Mostly silence. The backyard was in total darkness now. Mercifully the worst of the heat had let up, and the night was merely warm. She gripped the edge of the sink for support as she stared over the flowerpots on the sill out to where the play yard used to be.

As a toddler her son had always been on the chubby side, with folds in his glossy baby skin. He used to laugh at nothing at all. It had been the most amazing thing. He could make people who saw him laugh, just in delight at him. She looked over at the closed door of the dining room. This boy, her son, was thin. His wrists were bony and looked as if they could snap like a twig under strain. His hair was dark and limp. She had yet to see him smile.

She realized now, with a sense of shock, that she had expected him to be the same. Gold in his curls and dimples of baby fat in his laughing cheeks. In these years of change she had lost the child. He was gone. She would never see her child again. She had lost her baby forever. Anna felt a sudden stabbing pain in her chest. Gone. Just as everyone had always said. Instead, this other boy, this stranger, sat at her table.

He is my son, she reminded herself. And he is here. It was all that mattered.

"My baby," she whispered. With a determined intake of breath Anna picked up the bottle of ketchup and pushed through the dining room door. The three of them sat at the table. Tracy leaned back in her chair with her eyes closed. Thomas was describing the town of Stanwich to the boy as if he were a member of the Chamber of Commerce. Paul kept his eyes on his plate, his face expressionless.

"We have a couple of tennis courts, and there is a nice beach here in town. Plenty to do. There's no reason for a boy your age to be bored here."

Anna slipped into her seat and handed the bottle of ketchup to Paul. "Here's the ketchup."

"Thanks," Paul said, and doused his sirloin with the gloppy condiment.

"I'm tired. I need to go up and take a shower," Tracy announced.

"We're almost finished. Then we can have some ice cream."

"I don't want any ice cream. It's so late already. Why can't I go?"

Anna looked to Thomas for a word, but he was staring down at the table in front of him. As her eyes swept past Paul, she noticed that he was holding his fork and knife rigidly upright in front of him, his eyes open wide. The veins on his neck were protruding, and he pitched forward in his chair.

"Paul," she said.

He made a gurgling noise in reply. Anna pushed her chair back and stood up. "Paul, what's the matter?"

They all swiveled their heads to stare at him. As Anna watched him, his pale skin turned dead white, and then the area around his lips began to turn blue. His eyes were bulging, the whites visible all around the pupils. He made another low, gurgling sound.

"Is he having a fit?" Thomas asked.

Anna stared at Paul, unable to move, and suddenly she saw his hand dip slightly toward the meat on his plate. In an instant she grasped what was wrong. "He's choking," she said.

Thomas jumped up and began to thump the boy on his back. Paul was rigid now and not exhaling any breath.

"No," Anna cried, pushing Thomas aside. She pulled the boy off the chair and wrapped her arms around him from behind, just below his waist, jerking in sharply with her forearms as she bent him over.

"Breathe," she whispered, jerking again at his diaphragm. She could feel his heart hammering above her arms. He stared at the floor, his body stiff, except for his fingers, which were slowly tightening into claws.

Anna pulled her forearms against him sharply. Tracy whimpered in the silence.

"Please," Anna prayed, "breathe."

In the hushed room Anna could hear only the strangled whistle from the boy's throat. "Oh, please," she pleaded softly.

All at once he gagged. With a terrible retching sound he expelled a hunk of gray meat from his windpipe, and it shot out to the floor. Gulping for air, the boy began to cough and retch. His body went limp.

"Are you all right?" she cried.

Paul nodded, his eyes closed, the sweat popping out across his waxen face. Anna guided his slumping form to the chair. He breathed in great gasps as the color slowly returned to his skin.

"I'm okay," he whispered.

"God," Tracy breathed.

Anna buried her face in her hands for a moment as Thomas held the boy awkwardly by the shoulders. "Are you sure you're all right?" he asked. "Maybe we should call a doctor."

Paul shook his head weakly. "No, I'm okay." He drew himself up in the chair and sat with his shoulders hunched, his arms crossed tightly over his lap. The dark circles under his eyes seemed to have deepened.

Anna wanted to reach out and embrace him, but she knew that he would flinch at her touch. He sat as if he were trying to shield himself from their eyes. He would not look up at her. "Thanks," he mumbled.

"I'm sorry," said Anna. "It was the steak."

Thomas filled a glass from the water pitcher and handed it to Paul. "Here," he said, "have a sip."

Paul drank the water.

"Are you sure you don't want a doctor?" Anna asked him.

Paul shook his head. "No. I don't need anything. I just want to go lie down somewhere."

"Of course," said Anna. "Of course you do. I'll take you upstairs."

Tracy looked fearfully at the boy, as if he might suddenly collapse again.

"You have your old room," Anna said. Paul looked at her blankly.

"I hope it will be cool enough up there for you," said Thomas. "Your mother refuses to get air-conditioning."

Anna saw the confusion in the boy's eyes. "He means me," she explained sadly. She reached out her hand and laid it on Paul's thin forearm. "You really scared me. I'm so glad you're all right."

"He looks fine now," said Thomas.

The plaintive wail of a cat could be heard in the room. Paul looked around the table and then stood up. "Where's Sam?" he asked. "I've got to put him out. He likes to hunt at night."

"Do you think it's safe? I hope he doesn't get lost," said Anna. "I've made him a bed in the kitchen."

Paul sighed. "I can't make him stay inside. Going out's the only thing he knows. It's bad enough he had to leave the woods."

Tracy got up from the table and started through the living room. "I'm going upstairs," she said.

"Good night sweetheart," said Thomas.

Paul disappeared into the kitchen, calling for Sam. Anna tore her gaze away from the kitchen door and looked at her husband across the littered table. "Tom," she said, "that was awful. I was so frightened."

"You acted very quickly," he said. "You probably saved his life."

"He could have choked to death."

"I know," he said. "It was lucky." They fell silent.

Thomas turned and looked blankly toward the kitchen. He ran his fingers absently through his hair.

Paul returned to the dining room. "Sam took off," the boy said glumly.

"Well, maybe he'll find some cat friends out there. I'm sure he'll be back. Cats are pretty good that way. Come on now," said Anna. "I'll show you your room."

"Good night," said Tom stiffly.

Paul picked up his duffel bag and followed Anna up the stairs to the room which she had readied for him. The garbled lyrics of a Backstreet Boys album emanated from behind the closed door of Tracy's room. When they reached the top of the stairs, Paul looked at Anna to direct him. She nodded toward a door down the hall, and Paul went over and pushed it open. He looked around and placed his bag on a chair beside the dresser. Anna felt for a moment as if she were showing a guest to a hotel room. "This was your room," she said.

He turned and saw her watching him. "It's big," he said.

"The bathroom is at the end of the hall. Are you sure you feel all right?"

Paul stood by the head of the bed, his hands jammed into his pockets. "Yeah," he said. "Fine."

There was so much she wanted to say. But it would have to wait. The look in his eyes was wary. "Well," she said briskly, "I hope you sleep well." She stepped over to him and placed an arm around his shoulders. He drew away from her, and the kiss she had intended for his forehead brushed his ear instead.

"Good night," she said, backing out of the room. He did not look at her.

* * *

For a few minutes after she had left the room, Paul did not move. He stood staring straight ahead of him. A silver cup was gleaming on the bureau in his line of sight. He walked over and picked it up to examine it. It was brightly polished, and on it was the name Paul, engraved in an elegant script.

He realized, with a queasy feeling, that the cup had been his. Someone had bought it for him, probably when he was born, years ago. When he had lived in this house. With these people. Paul looked around the strange room.

His mother had told him before she died that she had a terrible secret. So this was it.

Paul looked out into the darkness of the backyard, hoping for a glimpse of Sam, but the cat was invisible in the night. He took another look at the cup. What was the use in fighting it? he thought. They were going to call him Paul if they felt like it. He threw the cup away from him, and it rolled across the floor and landed against the wall under a chair.

Slowly he untied his sneakers and shook them off. He pulled back the bedspread and crawled under it, fully clothed. He was still wearing the camouflage vest he had found in the woods two years before. Dorothy Lee had washed it for him and patched it in a few places and sewn his name on it.

Despite the blankets and the clothes he was wearing and the heat of the night, Paul began to shiver. His teeth chattered, and he drew himself up, pressing his knees to his chest and wrapping his arms around him. No one had mentioned Dorothy Lee. Or his father. Not one word. Just as if everything were perfectly normal. Paul's lips drew back in a laugh. But his eyes were mirthless. He felt a pressure on his bladder, but he did not want to go out into the hallway. He didn't want to encounter any of them. His teeth were chattering more loudly now. He wondered if they could hear him.

* * *

Anna put the last dish in the dishwasher and wiped her hands. She turned the lock on the back door and jiggled the doorknob to be sure it had caught. Then she padded through the quiet house and put the lock and chain on the front door. From the den she could hear the drone of the television late news. Anna looked around at the windows. She wished she could lock them, too. But it was too hot for that. They all would suffocate from the heat. It worried her, though, to think they were open. She looked up the stairs. It was dark and quiet. Maybe he's asleep, she thought.

For a moment Anna pictured him again at the table, his face ashen, the taut cords in his neck, his hands helplessly clutching the air. Shaking her head, as if to dispel the image, she walked through the house and headed down to the cellar, where she locked the cellar door and windows from the inside. The light was on in the playroom adjoining the cellar, and she pushed the door open and went in. The room was still and empty. In one corner she spotted Thomas's golf clubs. She went over to the bag and, having disengaged one of the irons, pulled it out and turned it over in her hands. She just wasn't comfortable about the upstairs windows. At least she could lock the windows down here. No one would be down here. The heat wouldn't matter.

Anna leaned the golf club against the bag and made a circuit of the playroom, fastening the windows tightly shut. Then she returned to the golf club and picked it up again. The gleaming steel shaft and head of the club felt heavy in her hands. Anna hesitated, then gripped the club resolutely and started up the stairs.

As she turned on the landing, she saw a figure looming in the darkness above.

"Oh," she cried out.

"What are you doing?" Thomas asked.

"Locking up," she said, mounting the stairs to the top where he stood. He was holding the bottle of champagne from the Stewarts in his hands.

"I thought we might take this up to our room," said Tom shyly. "Kind of toast the fact that we got through it. Got our son home. Managed to avoid having to call the ambulance. You coming up?"

"In a minute."

Thomas noticed the golf club in her hand and frowned. "What's that?"

"It's one of your irons."

"I can see that. What are you doing with it?"

Anna edged past him and went through the hallway into the kitchen. Thomas followed behind her.

"I thought it would be a good idea to keep it up here," she said. "Just in case . . ."

"In case of what? Anna, give me that club. Let me take it back downstairs."

She drew the club back out of his reach. "No," she said. "We don't know . . . we might need it."

Thomas dropped his hand to his side. His jaw hardened. "Not this again."

"That man is out there somewhere, Thomas."

Thomas stared away from her, his eyes flinty. "I don't understand you, Anna. Don't you want to be happy? You have your son back."

"Our son," said Anna. Then she said quickly, "I'm sorry, darling."

Thomas glared at her and then turned his back.

"I think that's a nice idea, about having the champagne. And I will be along, Tom. Soon."

Thomas put the bottle of champagne down on the table and walked out.

"Tom," Anna pleaded, but she could hear him climbing the stairs. With a sigh she went into the living room. She pulled back the curtains and stared outside. The patterns of leaves on the driveway shifted as the trees rustled. Anna turned off all the lights in the living room and sat down in the chair beside the window. She held the club in front of her across the arms of the chair, her hands gripped tightly around the cold metal shaft. The light of the moon threw a sheen on the blunt head of the club.

One blow from this would do it, she thought calmly. You have to be careful with children. You can't take anything for granted.

Anna looked up at the clock in the comer. She could barely discern that it was nearly twelve. I won't sit here long, she thought. Just for a while. She decided that by one o'clock she would go up and get into bed with Thomas. He would probably still be up reading. She would bring the champagne and the glasses upstairs and surprise him. He wouldn't stay mad at her. He never did.

Soon. She would go up soon. Unless she heard something. If she heard something, she would sit here all night. Anna glanced out into the foyer at the murky gloom of the staircase. She would do anything that was necessary. Anything at all. She ran her hand over the cold dense head of the club. She wondered if she could sink that deadly weight into the side of someone's skull.

Her eyes traveled around the room to the fireplace mantel, where a photograph of a pudgy boy with brown-gold curls laughed into the darkened room.

Anna gripped the club tighter. You could, she thought. If you have to, you will.

It was not until the gray light of dawn had banished the shadows that her wary eyes finally closed in sleep. Her head drooped to her shoulder, but she slept lightly, her fingers curled around the shaft of the club.

CHAPTER 5

"Could you put out the cigarette, sir?"

Rambo looked up at the pig-tailed girl in greasy coveralls who was leaning into his car window.

"Sure, sure," he said, jamming the cigarette butt out in the ashtray.

"What'll it be?"

Rambo studied his narrow billfold and extracted a wrinkled five-dollar bill. "Five dollars' worth," he said.

The girl nodded and walked around to the back of the car. Rambo watched her in the sideview mirror, wondering why they let girls do jobs like this up North. It didn't make sense, what with good men out of work. He stuck his head out the window and called to her. "Pardon, ma'am. Do you have a phone?"

The girl pointed behind the station. Rambo adjusted his dark glasses, pulled down the bill of his cap, and got out of the car. Glancing around him in all directions, he walked self-consciously back to where the phone hung on the wall between the men's and ladies' room doors. He looked around; but it was early morning yet, and there was no one about. Reaching into his back pocket, he pulled out a slip of paper and deposited his money into the phone.

All night he had debated whether to call or not. He had waited for a word, a further sign, but none had come. He had read the Gideon Bible furiously, making notes in the margins and girding himself for his mission. At dawn he had decided to call. Now he dialed the number, which he had gotten from information, and put the phone to his ear, cradling it against his shoulder. Before it could even ring, the door to the men's room opened, and a young man wearing blue jeans and a khaki shirt with the station's name embroidered in red on the pocket emerged and greeted him with a wave.

"Morning," said the young man. Rambo quickly dropped the phone back into the cradle. His thirty-five cents came clinking down into the change cup as Rambo returned the greeting with a scowl.

The young man walked off toward the pumps, and Rambo watched him go, waiting until he disappeared to pick up the phone again.

Once again he dialed the number, trying to go over in his mind what he was going to say. There were moons of perspiration forming under the arms of his shirt, and the fabric was sticking to his back. He had to speak just right, to make the heathen understand that there was payment due. That the wicked had been found out and had to be punished. It was the Lord's will.

He held the receiver to his ear and waited, his eyes darting around the service station plaza to be sure no one came near him. For a moment there was a clicking sound. Rambo took a deep breath. Then a recorded message came on, advising him to leave his name and number at the beep.

"Damnation," he said aloud, and slammed the phone back down on the hook.

The girl in the coveralls walked out in front of his car and signaled to him that his car was ready to go.

Rambo thrust his hands in his pockets, and his angry eyes bored into the phone. Then, suddenly, he realized what happened. It had been the sign, the one he had waited for. He was meant to go strike without warning. No time to lose.

With a sigh of relief Rambo retrieved his change from the change cup and hurried back to his car.

It was a half hour's drive until he reached the Millgate Parkway, and Rambo kept his foot pressed lightly on the accelerator, his eyes shifting obsessively from the speedometer to the sides of the road the whole way. He was anxious to get there, but he did not want to attract the attention of any patrol cars that might be lying in wait.

The best thing to Rambo's mind about the Millgate Parkway was that hardly anybody used it since the Connecticut Turnpike had been constructed. The fewer cars and people he encountered the better. The bad thing was that no one seemed to bother to maintain it. Rambo's blue Chevy, which had newspaper plugging the body rot underneath and four nearly bald tires, struck each shallow crater with a shimmy. On the seat beside him the Bible, which he borrowed from his motel room, bounced over and struck his thigh. Rambo gripped the wheel and watched the road, muttering verses under his breath as he drove.

Although he had been on the lookout for it, he still felt a small jolt when he saw the sign indicating the upcoming exit for Stanwich. Surveying the area, he slowed down as his car took the last miles.

It looked the same. More than ten years ago, and still this anonymous exit was imprinted on his mind in precise detail. They had been coming the other way, of course, on that long-ago day, driving south after the funeral of one of Dorothy Lee's cousins up in New York State. That's what had made it all so simple. When they returned to West Virginia, no one had ever questioned the story they made up that Paul was the child of the dead relative, left alone in the world. Rambo's eyes darted across the highway. That was the spot all right. They were just planning to pull off the road so he could take a leak. That's when he had seen it. At first he had not understood what he saw. And then, before it was too late, he knew.

It was more than ten years ago since that day he had crouched there in the bushes, witness and then accomplice.

And he had suffered since, although never more than now. But he had endured. And now he would have his revenge. Rambo heard the voices like a knell in his ears. "Woe to those who turn aside the needy from justice and rob the poor of my people of their right."

The arrow for the Stanwich exit pointed right. His moment was at hand. Rambo turned the wheel and slowly exited onto the peaceful backcountry roads that cradled the homes of the privileged few.

* * *

"Buddy, I'm sorry to bother you. I know it's early. But I had to call you. I couldn't get any sleep last night, thinking about that man Rambo."

Paul stopped on the stairway. He could hear Anna's anxious voice on the phone cutting through the silent house. He waited on the stairs, listening.

"I would feel so much better if Paul had some police protection. Just until that man is captured. Please don't tell me I'm being paranoid. I can't stand to hear it again."

Paul's lip curled as he thought of his father. He was probably off on some street corner somewhere, raving about the Lord. The thought of Rambo's wild eyes, his accusations, and his rambling discourses on the devil released a sluice of bile into Paul's stomach. The hunger that had awakened him subsided. He could hear Anna in the kitchen, still pleading with the policeman.

"Buddy, we don't know that he's not dangerous. Just because he never hurt the boy before doesn't mean that he won't try something. I don't feel that my son is safe while he is still on the loose."

Paul crept down the last few stairs and quietly opened the front door to the house. He stepped out onto the front porch and closed the door behind him. The dewy yard sparkled in the morning sun, and the quiet backcountry road looked like something off a calendar. Paul's stomach churned as he looked over the peaceful scene. None of it looked familiar to him at all.

"Sam," he called out softly, hoping for the comforting sight of his pet. There were birds chirping in the canopy of trees, which meant Sam was probably not in the immediate vicinity. Paul walked down the steps and circled the house, going out to the back.

"Sam," he cried. He surveyed the rolling backyard, the glider, and the large vegetable garden. Out near where the woods started, was a small shed. He crossed the lawn to it and looked inside. Through the gloom he could make out a few rakes and some shovels. He closed the door and peered into the woods that spread out behind the lawn. Sunlight filtered down through the trees, and he could hear the distant hum of an occasional car passing on a highway that was not visible from the yard. He called out for Sam, but there was no movement in the trees.

After walking along the edge of the woods, he jumped across a small stream that meandered through the property on the other side. Beyond the stream was a long hedge of lilac bushes. Just beyond the edge of the lilac hedge, he saw the top of a huge house. It had a stucco facade and dark-framed windows, with a series of gables and turrets like a castle roof. He stood still for a moment, struck by the fact that it was the biggest house he had ever seen. Then he crouched down and began to scout the length of the hedge, searching for movement in the bottom branches and making his way in the direction of the house.

As he approached the mansion, his eye was distracted from the search for his cat by a blaze of aquamarine beyond the hedge. He peered through the branches and saw a large rectangular swimming pool shimmering in the sun. A model sailboat with a gleaming wooden hull and white sails billowing floated across the tranquil turquoise surface. The pool was surrounded by a patio furnished with black, wrought-iron chairs and a table.

Crouched on one knee beside the pool was a well-groomed man dressed in expensive sports clothes. He was controlling the sailboat's progress with a pocket-sized device in his hand and watching the boat's graceful movements with obvious relish. He caused the boat to crisscross the aqua surface of the pool; its white sails full and elegant in the light breeze.

Beside him, at the pool's edge, stood an elderly man with silver hair and thick horn-rimmed glasses, looking uncomfortable in a conservative business suit, with a white shirt and a somber tie. The older man watched the man with the boat anxiously for a few minutes, and then he cleared his throat.

"I realize," he said, "that it may be inconvenient for you to see me like this, at home on a Saturday, but this matter seems to me to be of the utmost urgency."

"It's no problem at all," said the man with the boat, although his rapt attention did not waver from the sailing craft.

The older man waited for the other man to get up and face him, but after a few moments it became clear that the man by the pool had no intention of doing so. Nervously adjusting his shirt cuffs, the old man began to speak to his host's back.

"Mr. Stewart, when I agreed to sell you the Wilcox Company, we made an agreement that you would keep on the president and all our officers. Now yesterday afternoon they all received their notices and were informed that you are bringing in an entirely new staff. I can only assume that there has been some kind of misunderstanding. That's why I wanted to discuss it with you immediately."

"No, there's been no mistake," murmured the man by the pool. He directed the boat over to the edge, where he knelt and lovingly adjusted the rigging on the sails. Then he gently pushed the boat off again without looking up.

The elderly man's face reddened, and his voice began to shake slightly as he continued. "Mr. Stewart, the Wilcox Company is a family business. My father started it, as you know, and we have always treated our employees as family members. In turn, many of these people have devoted twenty years or more of their lives to our company. They think of it as their home. I explained all that to you before the sale. The only reason I sold the company at all was that my health does not permit me to continue running it. But you assured me that my people's positions would be safe."

Edward Stewart turned finally and looked up at the indignant older man. "Mr. Wilcox, your company is not an especially profitable one. I am in business to make money. You and your officers have not done a very efficient job of making money. I intend to change that."

"But you gave me your word," the old man cried. "You promised me."

"Mr. Wilcox," said Edward Stewart patiently, "I thought it over, and I changed my mind. That is my prerogative. I am now the owner of the Wilcox Company."

The old man shook his head and clenched his hands into fists. "If I had known that was what you intended to do, I would never have sold the company to you. It is opposed to everything I have worked for and believed in. I took your word as a gentleman, and you lied to me."

Having risen to his feet, Edward Stewart walked around to the other side of the pool, his eyes, brimming with affection, glued to the sailboat. Under his command, the boat tacked back and forth across the gleaming surface of the water. After a moment Edward crouched down again beside the pool and shook his head in admiration. "Isn't she a beauty?" he said. "I believe this is one of the finest ships I've ever made."

Wilcox glared at the man by the pool, his eyes burning behind the thick lenses of his glasses. "I did not come here to admire your boats, sir."

Edward tore his gaze from the model and looked up at him coolly. "Wilcox," he said, "these boats are my hobby. I relax by working on them and then watching them sail. They provide me with great satisfaction. I can think of few things more rewarding than seeing one of my ships on the water, responding to my every touch of a button."

The old man stiffened, as if he were considering a physical assault. Then his shoulders slumped, and he turned away from Edward's impassive gaze. He controlled the trembling of his muscles with an effort.

"You should take up a hobby," Edward advised him, smiling vaguely. "You'll have plenty of time now. No more business worries. I heartily recommend models."

"I will take you to court, sir," said Wilcox, focusing a piercing gaze on Edward's face.

Edward shrugged. "You'll find you have great difficulty making a case. A hobby, Mr. Wilcox. A hobby will calm you down."

The old man's eyes were full of fury, but his every muscle seemed to sag. He turned and stalked off through the patio doors and into the house.

"The maid will see you out," Edward called after him, but the old man had already disappeared.

Edward shook his head and then knelt down again beside the pool. He brought the boat about, and when it approached the edge, he lifted it out of the water and began to examine the hull.

Paul felt himself trembling all over, unaccountably distressed by the scene he had witnessed. The old man's helpless anger filled him with pity, and he felt revulsion for the way the man with the boat had treated the old guy. Was this the kind of people, he thought, who lived in these big, fancy houses around here? He longed for his old life, the shabby trailer nestled in the hollow where he used to live. Well, he knew for certain, after what he had seen, that he was not going to ask that man if he had seen his cat. After a few minutes had passed and he felt steadier, Paul turned around and began to creep away. He had taken only a few steps when a familiar blur of fur slipped out from under the bushes.

"Sam!" he exclaimed.

Edward Stewart's head jerked up, and the boat slipped from his hands, landing in the pool with a splash. "Who's there?" he demanded.

Sam darted off in the direction of the stream at the sound of Edward's voice. Paul hesitated, thinking of trying to run away, and then, lifting his hands in a gesture of surrender, stepped out of the bushes. "I was just looking for my cat, and I saw him in this hedge."

The man blanched at the sight of the boy and stared at him without speaking.

"I was just coming along, looking for my cat," Paul repeated helplessly.

The man seemed to relax as Paul spoke, unclenching his fists and clearing his throat. "Do you know who I am?" he asked.

"Some big mucky-muck," said Paul.

"Indeed. Well, in future, when you come over here, Paul," said Edward, looking pleased, "why don't just announce yourself?"

For a second Paul was taken aback to hear his name. Then his face fell. "You know me," he said.

The man gave him a thin smile. "My wife and I have been neighbors of your family for some years." Edward looked at him closely. "Since you were a little boy, in fact. Perhaps you remember me."

Paul shifted his weight and looked at the ground. "Well, I was young then, when, you know, it happened."

"Yes," said Edward. "Of course."

The man began to stare at him again, and Paul had the uneasy feeling that the man was sizing him up, as if he were an escaped criminal. Paul cast about desperately for something to say. His eyes fell on the boat in the pool. "Is that your boat?" he asked.

"I have a workroom in that windmill over there," Edward said, gesturing vaguely in the distance. "I've made models of some of the world's greatest sailing vessels."

"Oh. Great," said Paul, nodding miserably.

The sound of a shrill, angry voice calling his name filled Paul with an unexpected relief. He and Edward both looked in the direction of the house and saw Tracy coming around the side toward the patio.

Tracy glared at her brother. "Mom's looking all over for you."

"I'm coming. I was just looking for my cat."

"I just passed him," she said.

"Hello, Tracy," said Edward.

"Hello, Mr. Stewart. You'd better get home." Without another word, she turned and headed back around the house. Paul sighed and started to follow her.

"I'll see you later," said Edward. Paul did not reply.

* * *

Tracy stomped up the porch steps past her mother, who stood clutching the railing.

"He was at the Stewarts'. He's coming," said Tracy as she slammed the screen door on her way into the house.

Anna closed her eyes briefly, and her tense frame relaxed. "Thanks, Trace," she said.

Thomas came through the porch door, dragging his bag of golf clubs. He set them against the railing and began to examine them without looking at Anna.

Anna watched him for a moment. "I replaced the iron," she said.

"So I see," said Tom coolly. "Did you find Paul?"

"He was next door. Tracy found him."

"Oh," said Tom. He unzipped the pocket on his golf bag, fished around inside it, and pulled out a couple of loose golf balls. "What was he doing over there?"

"I don't know," said Anna, leaning back against the railing and studying him. "When did Edward invite you to play golf?" she asked.

"Yesterday. On the way home from the station. I forgot to mention it to you."

"I doubt Paul knows the first thing about golf," she said.

Thomas looked at her. "I'll teach him," he said.

"I hope Edward doesn't get exasperated with Paul slowing down the game." Anna shrugged. "He's not the most patient person . . ."

Thomas smiled. "That's for sure. But he seems very interested in Paul. He said he wanted us to be his guests at the club. Maybe Iris put him up to it."

"Probably," Anna agreed, although she had trouble imagining Edward taking any of Iris's suggestions. "We're only going to play nine holes. I thought the boy might enjoy it."

Anna nodded. "I'm hoping we can all go to the beach later."

Thomas counted the tees in his hand and then put them back into the golf bag. "We can go this afternoon," he said, "after we get back."

Anna smiled at him. "I think it's great," she said. "You and Paul doing something together."

Tom sighed. "I hope so," he said.

"Honey," she said, "I'm sorry about last night. I meant to come up, but I guess I was so exhausted I fell asleep in the chair."

"It's all right," he said.

"Today is a fresh start," she said. She gave him a hug, and he returned it, holding on to her for a few moments after she had loosened her grip. She opened the door to the house and was about to go in when she saw Paul coming into the yard. She stopped and watched him as he walked slowly toward the house, murmuring to his pet.

Suddenly, as he reached the grassy spot where the play yard used to be, he stopped. Anna saw the expression on his face change from one of confusion to a grimace. All at once he dropped the cat, and it landed in a crouch on the ground beside him. Paul clapped his hand to his forehead and kneaded his eyebrow with one hand as the frown on his face tightened to a look of pain.

"Tom," Anna whispered, "there's something wrong with him." She let go of the porch door, and it shut with a bang. She hesitated for a moment and then rushed past her husband down the porch steps. She pressed her lips together for a moment, and then she called out to Paul.

"What is it? Are you all right?" The cat looked up at her, but Paul did not meet her eyes. "Yeah," he said, lowering his hand and walking toward her, his eyes on the ground. He brushed past her and entered the house. There was no trace of color in his complexion. She watched him go into the kitchen and greet Tracy, who was seated at the kitchen table. Tracy mumbled in reply.

Anna clenched her fists and looked back out to where the play yard had once been. The cat sniffed in the grass, carefully traversing the area. It picked its way across the unfamiliar territory, as if suspicious of every stone and weed.

CHAPTER 6

Dry branches snapped sharply against his bare forearms and flying bugs hovered around Rambo's face as he worked his way through the dense growth of trees and bushes known to golfers as the rough.

It had not been difficult to find Hidden Woods Lane when he got off the parkway this morning. He had parked his car in a little dirt road that forked off it and waited. He had seen the boy and his father being picked up by the man in the Cadillac and had trailed them to this golf course. He had climbed over a fence to conceal himself in the trees and overgrown bushes along the fairway. He had already gone six holes through the thickets, following the progress of play. It had made him laugh to himself to see the way the boy lagged behind the two men, clearly disinterested in the game, sweating under the sun in that camouflage vest that he always wore. He could see that the Lange man was trying to be patient with the little heathen, but the boy didn't pay attention to the instructions, trudging along without a smile, his shoulders slumping. He wondered bitterly if the man was satisfied now to have the stubborn little monster back again. The voices began to speak to Rambo once more, railing at the child's ingratitude and at his return to the land of silver and gold, where evil was called good. His own lips moved to form the words he heard, and he tried to control the muttering which rose from his throat, threatening to expose his hiding place.

Thomas picked up a club and whacked his ball far into the distance toward the seventh green.

Edward shaded his eyes with his hand and watched the ball drop. "You might birdie this hole," he admitted grudgingly. Thomas turned and handed Paul a club that he had lifted from his bag. They had been trading off shots for the first six holes, Thomas instructing the boy on how to set up a shot and how to swing. Thomas had tried to ignore the boy's sullen expression and had complimented him frequently on his playing. "Probably want to use this club for this shot. We could be on the green with this one."

Paul stared at the iron for a minute and then held it away from him. "I'm getting pretty tired," he said. "Is it okay if I go back?"

Thomas replaced the club in his bag, carefully arranging the heads. "Sure. I guess so." He looked up at their host. "Can he wait at the clubhouse, Edward?"

Edward Stewart nodded. "Of course," he replied. "You might want to remove that garment you're wearing though. Someone will mistake you for a grounds-keeper."

Paul ignored him, and kept his vest on. "Can I go now?"

"We're almost done," said Thomas. "We have only two more holes after this. Are you sure you don't want to hang in there?"

"No," said the boy.

"Okay, fine." Thomas watched Paul as he started slowly back toward the clubhouse.

Rambo thought that he didn't blame the kid. It seemed a dull game to him. He swatted a bug that was humming around his head and waited impatiently for Edward to shoot.

Edward addressed the ball in front of him, rocking a little on the sides of his feet, and then drew back his club. Rambo shifted lower to watch, and the bushes crackled. Edward swung a little wildly; the ball spun off in a curve down a hill and into a sand trap. Edward colored slightly and cleared his throat. "Did you hear those bushes rustling?" he asked. He looked around at the bushes as if to excoriate them. Then he walked over to the crest of the hill and looked disapprovingly down at the ball, as if it were a badly behaved child. "I guess I'll have to chip it out," he said. "You play on. Don't want to keep your son waiting."

Thomas rolled his eyes behind his dark glasses and then looked up the fairway where his ball was a tiny speck. "All right," he said. "I'll meet you up there."

Thomas began to stroll by himself up the fairway.

Seeing him pass by, Rambo tingled with anticipation. This was his chance. He licked his lips nervously and peered out between the leaves.

When Thomas was halfway up the fairway, Rambo edged his way over to the sand trap. Edward was treading gingerly into the middle of the sinking surface. Rambo parted the bushes and scurried to the lip of the trap. After looking in every direction, he cleared his throat.

"Hey, you."

Edward stiffened and stuck his chin out, humiliated at being observed in this predicament. He looked around coldly, prepared to wither with his glance whoever was summoning him. He frowned at the unexpected sight of the pale, nervous man in front of him. The man wore a cheap sport shirt, a baseball cap, and sunglasses. He might have been an aging caddie but for the shoddy black shoes on his feet. The man was clearly not someone of importance. Irritated by the interruption, Edward ignored him.

"You better come over here," said Rambo, his eyes darting around the sloping emerald hillocks of the course. "I want to talk to you."

Edward glared at the man and replied with an icy, imperious formality. "If you have any business being here, sir, you had better make it known to me immediately. If not, please leave these grounds. They are private, and you are interrupting my game."

Rambo stared at Edward. He raised one finger and shook it at him. "The word of the Lord is my business," Rambo chanted at him. "The Lord's justice is my aim!"

Edward heaved his shoulders in a sigh and shook his head. "If you know what's good for you, sir," said Edward, "you will go peddle your shibboleths elsewhere and get off this golf course this instant." He turned his back on Rambo and addressed the half-buried golf ball.

"The Lord has spoke to me. The Lord has given me a sign, not once, but twice, that I must render His justice unto you."

"I'm warning you," said Edward in a menacing voice.

"Your evil, your wicked ways. Easier for a camel to go through the eye of a needle than for a rich man—"

"That's it," said Edward, jamming his club in the sand and turning around to shake a finger at Rambo. "I'm having you bodily thrown out of here."

Rambo took a step back. "I saw you," Rambo hissed at him. "That day on the highway. Eleven years ago. I know what you did."

Edward stopped short. His face turned ashen under the brim of his golf cap. His knuckles went white as he gripped the shaft of the club for support.

"I don't know what you're talking about," Edward whispered.

"To the boy, your friend's son," said Rambo, flinging his arm wildly back behind him, the direction in which Paul had gone. "I was there in the bushes that day taking a leak. I saw it all."

Edward stared at the man, his body vibrating like a violin string. Suddenly he realized why the man looked vaguely familiar. Newspaper pictures of the wiry man, always wearing a hat. "Rambo," he breathed.

"That's right," cried Rambo triumphantly. "Albert Rambo. The voice of the Lord on this earth."

An incredible gnawing had started in Edward's stomach as he tried to absorb the shock of Rambo's words. It occurred to him, as his mind raced, that Rambo must be mad to have dared come here with Thomas and the boy so close by. He is mad, Edward thought.

But he knows.

Edward licked his lips several times and tried to think. But his brain seemed able to register nothing but glaring lights, offering only exposure, not refuge. "You are mistaken, sir," said Edward indignantly. "I have no idea what you are talking about."

"The Lord has a mission for me," Rambo cried. "I have work to do. I must complete His work. Yesterday the Lord spoke to me through the television . . ."

Edward felt as if an avenging angel had swooped down on him, threatening to destroy all he had gained. The day that he had always secretly dreaded had now come to pass. He forced himself to remain calm, reminding himself that this was a madman in front of him. "You heard God's voice through the television. Come now, Mr. Rambo," he said, with a condescending chuckle. "I doubt they would entertain that kind of testimony in court."

Rambo gazed down at the man in the sand trap. "I will have justice. The sword of righteousness will descend upon you. All the elders of the temple will see and know that the blood is on your hands and I am innocent as the lamb. . . ."

A shudder raced through Edward as the man raved on. His stomach was churning, but he knew that he needed to regain control of this situation. "Come now, Mr. Rambo. You're no innocent lamb and neither am I. If justice was all you wanted, you would have gone to the police. Why are you really here?" he said. "Is it possible that there is a certain price tag for your silence?"

"Filthy lucre?" Rambo thundered. "The truth has a price beyond rubies. . . ."

"Who else knows about this?" Edward demanded. "Get a hold of yourself and answer me."

Edward's bluntness seemed to jolt Albert back into reality for a moment. "Nobody. Just me. Dorothy Lee knew. She was with me when it happened. But she's gone now. And the boy knows, I guess you could say." Albert nodded to himself and rocked back and forth.

"You told him what happened?"

"He was there, wasn't he? Maybe he remembers. I don't know. Otherwise, nobody."

"You were following the boy and you recognized me," Edward said, half to himself.

"No," Rambo scoffed. "I told you. I saw you on the TV. You and your fancy car. On the news."

"The TV?" For a moment, Edward was confused. Then, he recalled the interview at the Langes', his Cadillac visible behind them in the driveway. He stifled a groan, remembering how he had been convinced to appear in the interview. There was a roaring in his head, but he spoke calmly.

"Mr. Rambo, you seem to have it in your head that I committed some sort of crime, when in fact, you are the man whom the police are looking for. I don't really understand," he said, picking up the golf ball and rolling it around in the palm of his hand, "how you figure you can go to the police with your so-called information. Given the fact that you face life in prison for kidnapping if you are caught."

"Well," Rambo dissembled, "I might not tell them directly."

Edward stared at his tormentor, and for the first time he began to feel his power, his control, returning. Rambo was a shabby, pathetic little man. A weak, sniveling creature. He reminded himself that he was infinitely superior to this nobody who threatened him. "How are you going to tell them?" Edward inquired. "Call in an anonymous tip?"

"I've got a way," Rambo insisted defiantly. He kneaded one bony hand with the other.

Edward trained his steely gaze on Rambo, who was shifting his weight nervously from foot to foot. He seemed disoriented and a little frightened, as if he were the one who had been cornered. "I don't think so," said Edward in a cold voice. "I don't think you do."

Rambo's face sagged as his voice rose. "Just give me some money," he cried, "or I'll show you." He fumbled in the pocket of his shirt and pulled out a cigarette and some matches. He thrust the cigarette in his mouth and lit it. He drew on the cigarette furiously, as if it were providing oxygen, rather than cutting it off.

"Let me tell you something, Mr. Rambo," said Edward in a cutting voice. "I belong to the finest social circles in this town. I have money and power, to be blunt. Who do you think would take your word over mine?"

A dose of spirit seemed to revive Rambo at Edward's words. "What will you do on the day of punishment?" he railed. "To whom will you flee for help, and where will you leave your wealth?"

Edward drew himself up and thundered over Rambo's chant, "You are a criminal on the run. A fugitive. A wanted man."

Rambo's shoulders slumped, as if his last outburst had exhausted him.

Edward felt the battle waning. "When you really think about it," said Edward slowly, "it's a preposterous idea."

Rambo stared helplessly at his intended quarry. "I need some money," he whined.

"I'm sure you do," Edward snarled. "But you won't get it from me. I'm not afraid of you. Now get out of here, before I call the police."

Rambo gaped at him for a moment as if trying to formulate a reply. "The day of punishment is at . . ." he mumbled.

"Now," Edward commanded. Rambo began to back away. When he reached the bushes, he turned and bolted into the trees. Edward could hear him crashing through the rough, like a rabbit fleeing from a pack of hounds.

Edward looked down at the golf ball in his hand. Drawing his arm back behind him, he threw the ball up and away, as far as he could toward the fairway. Then he scrambled out of the sand trap.

He saw Thomas standing up near the green, scanning the course. Plastering a smile on his face, Edward waved to Thomas, indicating that he was out of the trap and about to make his next shot. He selected a club from his bag.

As he was about to position himself over the ball, he noticed a little square of white on the edge of the grass bordering the sand trap. He walked over to it, squatted down carefully, and picked it up. Then he examined it. The object he held in his hand was a matchbook with *LA-Z PINES MOTEL, KINGSBURGH, NEW YORK* printed on it in letters formed by miniature logs. *GUS DEBLAKEY, PROP.* He stuffed the matchbook deliberately into his pocket.

Edward licked his lips and then gazed into the bushes where Rambo had disappeared. He saw it all, Edward thought again with a shudder. He saw me. He knows what I did.

* * *

"Do you like the beach, Paul?" Anna asked as Tracy and Paul got out of the car and Tracy started across the narrow road to the boardwalk that protected the dunes.

"I've never been," he replied, shouldering the aluminum-framed beach chair.

He looks like a waif, Anna thought. He was standing beside the car, wearing high sneakers without socks, a pair of black cutoffs, and his camouflage vest, despite the heat.

Anna lifted the plastic picnic basket out of the trunk. "I'll bet you'll be coming to the beach a lot from now on. We'll get you a beach pass and a bathing suit. Right, Tom?"

Thomas shut the door on the driver's side and adjusted his sunglasses over his eyes. "What?"

Anna handed the picnic basket to Thomas as Paul followed Tracy across the road. "You're awfully quiet," she said.

"Just thinking," he said as they followed the path of the teenagers.

"You didn't say much about your game this morning," she observed. "Did Paul enjoy it?"

Thomas peered at the boy, who was disappearing over the ramp down to the beach area. "I don't know. I guess he did."

As they came over the dunes, they could see the calm waters of Long Island Sound stretching out across the horizon. Anna walked up beside Paul.

"Well, what do you think?" she asked him.

The boy looked out over the pleasant summer landscape and nodded. "It's pretty cool," he said.

Anna felt a surge of happiness at his reaction. She turned to Thomas, who was setting up their chairs on the sand, to see if he had noticed, but Thomas did not look up.

"Well, spread your towel out," Anna instructed Paul matter-of-factly.

Tracy had found a group of friends who were oiled and giggling, sunning themselves at the foot of the lifeguard's chair. She avoided looking back at her family.

"You'd better put some lotion on," said Anna, eyeing Paul's white skin as he removed his vest.

"I'm going to look around," he said. Anna could see from the comer of her eye that Tracy's friends were whispering among themselves. One of them pointed to Paul's high tops and snickered. This started the whole group of them laughing. Paul did not acknowledge them, but Anna was filled with the sick feeling that he knew what they were up to.

Anna watched her son. He made a funny face at a child in terry-cloth trunks who was shoveling sand not far from the foot of his towel. The child laughed delightedly and pointed his shovel at Paul. The young mother, who was keeping a close eye on her toddler, smiled at Paul and then glanced over at Anna as Paul passed by.

"Is that your son?" the woman asked Anna. Anna watched the boy making his way down the beach toward the water. His skin was sickly pale in contrast with the browned bodies on the blankets. She tore her gaze from Paul and smiled at the young mother. "Yes," she replied.

"Nice young man," said the woman.

"He's fifteen," Anna said softly. "How old is your little fellow?"

The woman rolled her eyes and laughed. "Just two years, and he's into everything." As if to prove her point, the little boy waddled down and began to wrestle a pail away from a girl who was playing near a tide pool.

"Jeremy," the woman cried, and rushed over to separate them. "Give the little girl back her bucket."

The child settled in a heap near his new friend, and the woman returned to her towel. Anna smiled at her.

"You're so lucky," the woman said. "You don't have to watch him anymore. I can't wait until Jeremy's old enough that I don't have to keep my eye on him every minute."

"Oh, I don't know. They grow up so fast," said Anna, her eyes traveling back to the water's edge, seeking Paul. For a moment she could not find him. Her heart began to race. She scanned the shoreline anxiously. Then she spotted him. He was wading near the edge of the water, looking out at the ocean. She sighed and turned toward Thomas, who was sitting in a low beach chair, looking through the newspaper.

Anna sank onto the blanket next to his chair. She patted him on the knee, and he lowered his paper.

"Do you want me to put some lotion on your back?" he asked.

Anna nodded and handed him the bottle. He squirted some lotion into his palm, and he began to massage it in a circular motion on her bare back.

"Oh, that feels good," said Anna, leaning her head back, although she kept her half-closed eyes on the shoreline, where Paul was standing ankle-deep in the sea. "I think I'll sit and read a few pages of my book."

"You look tired," said Tom. "Why don't you catch a nap for a few minutes?"

"I don't know," said Anna. "I want to keep an eye on him."

"What for?" Thomas cried, tossing the bottle of lotion down on the towel. "He's not a baby, Anna."

"I forgot to ask him if he could swim."

Thomas studied Paul, wading at the water's edge. "It's not like he's going to be swept out to sea," he said.

Anna heard the impatience in his voice and tried to appease him. "I do need to relax," she said. "You're right." She opened her book, but she looked up surreptitiously every few sentences.

The sun was hot and soothing on her body, and it began to have a soporific effect. After laying the open book on the blanket, she stretched out and gazed across the sand. She had hardly slept all night, and weariness stole over her. The sounds of laughter and radios merged into a pleasant hum as her eyelids started to droop. She began to dream of a small boy in a pool of water and light.

Suddenly a horrible shrieking pierced her dream, frightening the dream child and then dissolving him, as Anna awakened with a jolt. The shrill squawking continued as she scrambled up from slumber, foggy and disoriented, searching for the source. The wail of a child filled her with dread. She looked around and saw a sea gull, perched on the edge of a wire mesh trash basket, a fragment of food in its beak.

"I'll get you another cookie." Jeremy's mother soothed him as the child decried the audacious bird's theft.

"Shoo," cried the mother, flapping her hands at the impassive bird, which eyeballed them from its perch.

With a sigh Anna sank down again to her towel. Then she remembered Paul. Immediately she turned over, and her eyes scanned the beach. For a moment she could not see him. Then she realized why.

Paul had not moved far from where he was before, but now a man wearing a loose-fitting shirt, dark glasses, and a baseball cap was standing directly behind him. Both Paul and the man in the hat had their backs to her. The man's hands were clamped on Paul's narrow shoulders. "Tom!" Anna exclaimed. "Look."

"What?" Thomas asked, lowering a corner of his paper.

"That man," said Anna, rising to her feet, her heart beginning to hammer.

"Where are you going?" Thomas asked as Anna started to run down the beach, her gaze fixed on her son and the man behind him.

She approached the man and the boy and spoke in a voice so loud it made them both jump. "What are you doing?" she demanded.

Paul and the man in the hat turned around and stared at Anna. Paul lowered the binoculars that the man had offered to him and backed away from her. The man, who had been guiding the boy's sights, frowned.

"I was showing him . . ." the man said.

Anna tried to grab her boy's arm, but Paul squirmed away from her.

"What's the matter?" the boy cried out. "He's letting me look."

Anna turned on the man. "What do you want with my son?" she demanded.

"Nothing . . ." the man protested.

"He was showing me those fish," Paul shouted.

The people nearby on the beach were staring at them now. All activity around them seemed to have stopped, as the bathers watched the scene.

"Come on, Paul," Anna insisted, trying to shepherd her son away.

"Leave me alone," Paul cried, pulling away from her. "Get away from me."

Anna's hands dropped, and she looked helplessly from the boy to the man.

The man in the hat drew himself up and took a deep breath. "Look," he said severely, "your boy asked to look through my binoculars. You're embarrassing me in front of all these people."

Anna felt herself shrink as her fright and anger oozed away. She passed her hand over her eyes. Her shoulders drooped. "I'm sorry," she whispered.

"Little overprotective, aren't you?" said the man, slinging his binoculars back around his own neck.

"I'm sorry," Anna repeated. "I'm not myself. I was afraid . . ." Her hands hung limply at her sides. She stared down at an airhole in the sand where some clam was burrowing, wishing she herself could disappear into the cool, dense muck.

"All right," said the man, pulling down the tails of his shirt. "You should be sorry."

Anna turned around, her eyes downcast, as Paul staggered up the beach, his pale cheeks flaming. Thomas stood in her path. He was watching her with grim, disbelieving eyes.

Anna shook her head, as if she could not begin to explain.

"Let's go," he said.

They walked in silence up the beach, past Tracy, who was hiding her face from the curious stares of her friends. "Do you want a ride home, Tracy?" Thomas asked.

Tracy kept her eyes averted. "No."

"Call me later, and I'll pick you up."

Anna walked up to their blanket. Paul had disappeared over the dunes. He was probably already in the car, hiding from the humiliation she had caused him. Her lips trembled as she bent over to pick up the picnic basket, still heavy with their uneaten lunch.

CHAPTER 7

Rambo slammed the door on his Chevy in the parking lot of the La-Z Pines Motel, unlocked the door to his cabin, and slammed that, too. He did not bother to turn on the light, although he did switch on the feeble air conditioner in the window. Then he flopped down on the sagging bed and sat there, staring at the drawn venetian blinds.

In his mind's eye he kept picturing Edward Stewart glaring at him. He shivered, remembering Edward's stony eyes. A gloomy sense of failure descended on him as he relived their conversation on the golf course. Rambo now realized that he had confronted Edward without any actual proof that the man had done anything. He had just been counting on his being so surprised and scared that he'd give in without a fuss. Besides, he'd had a sign from the Lord that he should do it. He had been sent.

Rambo reached across the bed, picked up his Bible, and began to pore over the marked chapter in the dim light of the motel room. But his eyes refused to focus on the words. After a few moments he snapped the Bible shut and put it aside. Slowly he pulled out his wallet and opened it. He stared at its meager contents a good long time without moving. The room was silent. No divine voices spoke to him, suggesting what he might do next. He faced the bald fact that his money would be gone in a day or two.

He folded the wallet over to insert it back into his pocket. A picture poked out from one of the loose flaps inside. He started to push it back in. Then, instead he drew it out and looked at it.

There was Dorothy Lee, wearing her nurse's uniform, smiling up at him. It was an old picture, from when she got her cap. She had been so proud of that.

He held the picture gently at its worn corner and thought about his wife. He had done it for her after all. Taken the boy. She wanted a baby so badly, and he couldn't give her one. The adoption people wouldn't even talk to them because of all the times he'd been in the hospital, locked up. So he had taken the kid. And look where it got me, he thought.

Dorothy Lee had always been after him to carry a picture of the boy, but he never wanted to. He wouldn't have a picture of that devil child anywhere on his person. It was bad enough when he'd had to look at his actual face. It set Rambo's teeth on edge just to think of the boy, who had ruined his life like this.

Once she had gotten that kid, it was almost as if she'd forgotten her husband, he thought. As if she hadn't cared for him anymore, just the kid. He could picture her, sitting there in the dark trailer on the daybed, watching TV, the kid cuddled up in her lap. She'd be crooning to him and playing with his hair and ignoring her husband. Rambo looked down again at his wife's picture and he could hear her dear voice inside his head. You'll never know what it's like to be a mother, Albert. A mother'll do anything for her child.

Even when he used to remind her that Billy wasn't really hers, Dorothy Lee had just ridden right over him. I am his mother, she would say, as if he was born from me. Albert sighed, and traced that sweet face with his fingertip. What would she think if she knew her Billy was living right next door to that man in the gold-eagle car? Oh, she'd be in a right fury over that. She'd be praying day and night for that boy.

And then a voice spoke aloud in the room. Not the Lord's voice, but his own. "The mother," Rambo said.

For a long time he sat in silence, turning his idea over and over in his brain. Then he crossed one leg over the other and rested the open Bible on his bony knee. Maybe there was a way he could honor Dorothy Lee's dying prayers, and still get out of this mess.

* * *

Edward closed the pages of the Princeton alumni magazine which he had been staring at and put it down beside his dinner plate with a sigh. He and Iris were seated at the table in their cavernous dining room.

Iris reached across the table to an untouched basket of rolls and picked one up. She tore off a piece and held it in her fingers. "How was Paul today," she asked. "What's he like?"

Edward peered disapprovingly at the roll in her hand and then picked up his fork and held it poised over the seafood salad in his plate. "I don't know," he said. "He seems like an ordinary boy."

Iris slipped the piece of roll into her mouth and chewed it with tiny bites. Then she leaned forward and looked earnestly at her husband. "Does he seem to be adjusting to the situation all right?"

Edward's eyes traveled from his wife's questioning face down to her sleeveless piqué sundress, where one of the seams revealed a small gap just above her thickening midriff. Edward gripped the fork he was holding and reached over toward her.

Iris looked at him in confusion and then flinched as she felt the cold tines of the fork press into her skin through the hole in her dress.

Edward's nose wrinkled in distaste. "Iris, you are splitting the seams of your clothing."

Iris drew back from the table, her face flushed, and folded her arms across her body in an effort to cover the gap in her dress. "I didn't notice it when I put it on."

"It would behoove you to be a little more observant when you dress," said Edward, wiping off the tines of the fork on his linen napkin.

"I know, I'm sorry," she muttered.

Edward finished off his seafood salad in silence as Iris picked at the food on her plate.

"Are the arrangements complete for the party?" Edward asked without looking up at her.

Iris bit her lip and nodded.

"Well?" Edward demanded, gazing at her impatiently.

"Yes!" Iris exclaimed.

Edward sighed. "You needn't shout, Iris."

"I . . . I talked to the florist and the caterer today, and everything is set."

"Oh, you may cross the Wilcoxes off your guest list," said Edward. "They won't be coming."

"That poor man seemed so upset when he left this morning. Is something wrong?" Iris asked.

"It is business, Iris," said Edward. "It does not concern you. Simply cross them off the list."

The maid came into the dining room to clear off the dinner plates. Iris lifted her plate and offered it up to her and then noticed Edward staring at the hole in her dress. She quickly lowered her arms to her sides.

Edward picked up his alumni magazine again and turned the pages. He found that he could not really concentrate on the articles, however, for his mind was distracted by the day's events. But it was easier to pretend to read than to look at his wife and the maddening hole in her dress. She had no shortage of clothes, although she had to squeeze herself into most of them these days.

He wondered for a moment what she planned to wear to the party. He didn't want to be ashamed of . . . her in front of his guests.

"Iris," he said, "I hope you have a decent dress for the party. One that fits."

"I do," she said.

The maid returned to the dining room and quietly put a bowl of ice cream down in front of each of them.

Iris smiled gratefully at the maid and picked up her spoon. "It's that blue dress," she said, "the one I wore to the ballet benefit. I received several compliments on it."

Edward watched with revulsion as she lifted a spoonful of ice cream to her open lips. He stood it as long as he could, then with a deft movement he rolled his magazine up into a tube and rose slightly from his chair. Thrusting his wrist forward, he plunged the tube of slick paper into Iris's bowl of ice cream. Iris let out a cry as the melting cream splattered up over the front of her dress and magazine page corners curled into the dessert bowl.

"Iris," he said evenly, "why, when you are already bursting out of your clothes, are you eating a bowl of ice cream? You don't need that," Edward informed her. "It will only add to your weight problem."

Iris stared down at the bowl as Edward lifted the rolled-up magazine and placed it gingerly on the serving tray on the sideboard.

"Now," he said, "please, go upstairs and change out of that dress."

Wiping her lips and the front of her dress hastily with her napkin, Iris stood up shakily from the table. Edward picked up his spoon and began to eat his ice cream as she left the table. In the dining room door Iris stopped and studied her husband for a moment with a resentful gaze. Then she left the room.

Edward glanced over at the magazine with its one soggy end on the tray. He rang the bell impatiently for the maid to come and remove it. It was a shame, really, that he had had to sacrifice the magazine to teach Iris a lesson. He always derived such satisfaction from reading it, for each issue confirmed his suspicion that few of his classmates had done as well as he had, although most of them had started out with advantages which he hadn't enjoyed.

It had not been easy for him. While the other boys frittered away their time on football games and the camaraderie of their posh eating clubs, he had held a job in a local diner to supplement his scholarship and had been forced to live off campus in the home of an old woman who was bringing up her orphaned grandson and needed the money.

At least it had been quiet there, and he had been able to study. He had paid no attention to the woman or her grandson, until that one bad time. He had left his term paper on the kitchen table for a few minutes, and when he came back the child had accidentally spilled a glass of chocolate milk on it. Edward had not thought to make a backup copy on the school's computer.

He pretended that it was not a problem. But, when the old woman and the boy were out shopping, he had gone into the garage and loosened the wheels on the boy's bike, so that the next time he went out for a ride, the wheels fell off and the child hit the pavement on his head. Edward had watched from behind the curtain in his room as the child lay still as death, the blood from his head pooling on the sidewalk. The boy needed a dozen stitches, and Edward felt satisfied. The old woman never accused him of anything, although she did ask him to leave the next day. It was an inconvenience, finding another room, but it had been worth it.

Edward shook his head and looked back at the alumni magazine, which the maid was now lifting, tray and all, from the sideboard. He had certainly come a long way since those days. He wanted to make a note to send the alumni magazine a notice of his purchase of the Wilcox Company.

He reached into his pocket for his leather note pad and pulled out, as well, the matchbook cover from the La-Z Pines Motel. Instantly his mind returned to his preoccupation of the whole day. At first he thought he had handled it so well. Intimidating Rambo like that. But as the day wore on, he was not as sure of himself.

The man might be a lunatic; but he was on the loose, and whether he had any proof or not, he knew a terrible secret about Edward. There was no guarantee that Rambo would keep silent if the police caught up with him. There was no way that Rambo could prove the story, of course. The police would have no case against him. But, there were other dangers besides the legal one. More than a few people would gloat to see him disgraced. So many people were envious of him. He thought, for a second, of the alumni magazine, shuddering at the thought of an item detailing the ugly accusations that could be made against him.

His concentration was so absolute that he did not hear Iris when she returned to the dining room. She inched into the room and stood behind her chair, wearing a different dress.

Edward gave her an annoyed glance.

"I was thinking," said Iris tentatively. "Perhaps I could go to a health spa for a few days next week. I've been thinking of doing it anyway, and I could trim down a little."

Edward picked up the coffee cup that the maid had brought in to him. "It's unfortunate that you didn't think of going before this party," he said.

Iris shrugged. "I think I'll go on Tuesday."

Edward opened his hand and looked down at the matchbook in his palm. There was only one way to be sure that Rambo's story would never reach the wrong ears. He had no choice, really. As long as Rambo was alive, nothing was safe.

"You're sure you don't mind, Edward?" Iris asked from the doorway.

"Iris," said Edward, "I'm sure I don't care."

* * *

Anna loosened her hair and removed the rest of her clothing. She lifted her summer nightgown off a hook in the closet and held it to her breast. She turned around and looked at her husband who was sitting up in bed, but he did not glance up at her. He seemed to be concentrating on the book he was holding. She pulled the nightgown over her head with a small sigh and walked over to her dresser to pick up her brush.

Thomas lowered his book and watched her as she pulled the brush back, her hair fanning out and then drifting softly to her shoulders. "I assume you're sleeping up here tonight," he said in a gruff voice.

Anna dragged the bristles across her scalp. "I've locked up," she said. "I guess it will be all right."

Thomas stared over the top of his book at the foot of the bed. Then he looked down blindly at the page.

"I can't tell how he feels about being back . . . with us," said Anna. "I mean, I don't expect him to feel at home right away. We have to be patient. Everything is strange to him. Sometimes I think he likes us a little bit. Of course Tracy's behaving terribly. But what else could you expect with a teenage girl?"

Anna came over to the end of the bed and placed a hand on his leg, which was covered by the sheet. "Tom, I'm sorry about what happened at the beach today. I'm sorry I embarrassed you. And the kids."

Thomas kept his eyes on his book and spoke in a tight voice. "You didn't embarrass me," he said.

"I think I was just overtired." She climbed into the bed beside him and pulled up the sheets. "I'm hoping we can have a quiet, relaxing day tomorrow, although we've got that party tomorrow night."

"I need to go to the garage and pick up the car tomorrow," he said. "And I want to get some stuff for the lawn."

"Maybe when you get back, we can all do something together," Anna ventured.

"I told Tracy that she should take Paul to the animal shelter with her tomorrow afternoon."

"Oh, no, Tom. Why?"

"Why not? They need to get acquainted. You just got finished saying that you want her to help . . ."

"But to go over there alone, just the two of them? Something could happen."

Thomas glared at her. "You let Tracy go over there alone all the time. You know it's perfectly safe around here."

"Well, yes, it's safe, but what about . . . you know . . . that man?" Anna shuddered at the thought of Rambo.

"Anna, when are you going to let up? That's what it was at the beach today, wasn't it?"

Anna bit the inside of her mouth and did not reply.

"You're not doing the boy any favors with this," he said. "You know you can't watch over him every minute of every day. Why don't you let him go about his business? Let him be."

"I'm concerned for his safety," she said. "I should think you would be, too."

Thomas's jaw hardened. He turned out the light and slid down beneath the sheets with his back to Anna.

She put one hand over her eyes, then reached out and touched him on the shoulder. "I'm sorry," she said. "I didn't mean that. I know you're concerned about him."

Thomas stared into the darkness. "It doesn't matter."

"I can't seem to help myself," she said. "With Tracy, you were always warning me, reminding me not to smother her because of what happened . . . to Paul. And you were right." She spoke softly to her husband's back, remembering their arguments over Tracy. How hard it had been for her to do what he said and let their daughter live normally. She caught her breath for a moment, remembering the constant fear. Reason had told her to listen to him, although everything inside had struggled against his advice. Once, when Tracy had gone on an overnight trip to Washington with her fourth-grade class, Anna had spent most of the night in the bathroom, throwing up from fear. "I tell myself that it's over, but somehow . . ."

She ran her fingers down his rigid spine. "It would help so much if I felt you understood. I need you now. I need to share this with you." She reached her arms around him tentatively and cupped his wrist, which was pulled tightly to his chest, in the palm of her hand. "We've always shared things before. If we could kind of . . . get together on this."

Thomas squeezed his eyes shut as she ran her fingers up his forearm. "I don't really know how, Anna. Maybe it's just that it's new. I have to get used to the idea of the boy's being back here and everything."

"It's not easy, darling," she crooned. "I know. But once they've caught up with Rambo, I promise you I won't be so anxious. I'm going to try not to worry. I only wish you seemed happier about all this. . . ."

He bridled reflexively at her suggestion. But at the same time he could feel her breasts pressing against his back, and that gentle pressure affected him like a clamp on his chest, squeezing out the air. The tumult of his feelings caused an ache in his throat. He wanted to roll over and press his stinging eyes to her soft breasts and clutch her to him with all his strength.

Suddenly she loosened her hold on him and sat up in the bed. There was a cold spot on his back where her body had been. "Do you hear something?" she said.

Thomas rolled over and looked at her, sitting up in the bed, the moonlight outlining her body in her thin nightgown. "What?" he said.

"Downstairs. I'm sure I hear something."

Thomas buried his face in the pillow.

"Don't you hear it?" she whispered. "There's someone moving around."

"I don't hear anything," he said, pulling the sheet up to his ears.

Getting out of bed, Anna pulled on her wrapper and tied it, straining to hear the faint sounds that came from the floor below. "It's probably one of the kids," she said uncertainly, but Thomas did not look up.

He lay, unmoving, shrouded in the bedclothes. "It's your imagination," he said dully.

Anna moved to the doorway and looked out into the hall. The doors to Paul and Tracy's rooms were shut, and the house was dark. She could sense her husband's irritation, but she could not help herself.

"I'm going to have a look," she said.

Thomas did not reply. Anna slipped out into the hall and turned the light on over the staircase. She went down quietly, one hand pressing against the wall, as if to ground herself.

The downstairs was silent and dark. She stood at the foot of the staircase, thinking that Thomas was right. She had imagined it. She moved out into the dark living room, making her way by instinct toward a lamp. Suddenly she heard a soft thud from the direction of the kitchen. "Who's there?" she said, switching on the lamp. There was no answer. She looked around the room as if to reassure herself that she was alone, and then she peered into the dining room. The heavy brass candlesticks on the dining room table caught her eye.

Her heart thumped as she rushed to the table and grabbed a candlestick. It felt heavy and reassuring in her hand. "Who is it?" she said again. "Tracy?"

Gripping the candlestick in a sweaty hand, Anna pushed open the door between the dining room and the kitchen and threw on the kitchen light. The room was empty.

Anna looked around and then walked over to the back door and tested it. The door was securely locked. She turned back into the room and noticed the pantry door was slightly ajar. She walked over to it.

Drawing back the candlestick, as if to strike, she gave the door a kick, and it swung back. Anna looked in and let out a gasp. "Paul," she cried, lowering her arm. "What are you doing?"

The kitchen light dimly illuminated the dark pantry. Halfway in, the boy crouched, looking up at her. The wide eyes of a cornered animal stared out from his pale face. His hands gripped the bottom shelf of the pantry, as if for support. He watched her warily, his eyes darting from her face to the candlestick in her hand.

"Why didn't you answer me?" Anna demanded, sharpness born of relief in her voice.

The boy shrugged, but his body was tense. Anna came toward him, worriedly examining his colorless face. She could see, as she approached him, that his body was trembling.

He scrambled to his feet before she reached him and sidled past her into the kitchen, keeping his back to the shelves.

Anna followed him and put the candlestick on the counter. She reached out a hand to him, but he pressed himself against the refrigerator. "I couldn't sleep," he said. "I was hungry."

"Paul, you don't need to hide from me," she said. "This is your home." The boy looked away from her. "Did you find something to eat?" she asked.

He nodded quickly.

She looked at him closely, not believing him, but decided not to press it. "What's wrong, Paul? Do you feel all right?"

He glanced at her and then took a deep breath. "I had a nightmare. It woke me up."

"Do you want to tell it?" she asked. "That helps sometimes."

The boy shook his head. "No. I'm going back up."

"Okay," she said.

"Night."

She waited until he had gone up the stairs, and then she turned off the lights and followed him. The thought of him, crouching there in the dark pantry, chilled her, and she tried to put it out of her mind. But she wondered what kind of dream it had been that had scared him so, made him cower from her like that.

Slowly she returned to her room. She opened the door. In the moonlight she could see Thomas's body, curled up with his back to her in the bed.

"It was Paul," she said. "He had a nightmare."

There was no answer from the bed. Thomas was making heavy breathing sounds. She knew that he was only pretending to sleep. Anna took off her robe and got into bed beside him. In the silent dark house, his breathing was like the sound of trees, rustling in a graveyard. She sat with her back against the headboard, willing herself to be calm. After a while Thomas's rigid body relaxed, and she could see that he had actually fallen asleep.

CHAPTER 8

The garage mechanic wiped his grimy hands on a ragged towel and rubbed his nose with his forearm. "Give me a few minutes, and then I'll add up the bill."

"No hurry," said Thomas, his hand resting on the hood of the car. "Was it bad?" he asked.

"Not too bad," said the mechanic. "About what I told you on the phone I expected."

Thomas shrugged. "I was surprised you were open on Sunday."

"Sunday, Monday, and always," said the man. "I'll be right back."

"Okay."

Thomas wandered away from the car and looked around the inside of the garage, which was filled with a dense, oily odor. On an aged bulletin board, there was a Dallas cheerleaders calendar and scores of notes about cars in an illegible handwriting. Piles of tires were stacked across the shelves in the back, and there were huge black stains on the cement floor of the garage. A plastic pocket holding a few maps and some pens with the garage name printed on them lay on a counter.

It had a kind of appealing atmosphere to Thomas's mind. It was a place where a man could have a beer and tell a dirty joke over a hero sandwich. It was a place where a man could bring his son, lift a hood, and show him how an engine worked. If he had a son. He tried to imagine himself bringing Paul here, and then he shook his head.

He had slept fitfully all night and had hardly spoken to Anna when she drove him to the garage. It made him feel guilty when he thought of the look in her eyes as she left him. She was ready to apologize again for getting up in the night to check the house, but he had turned away from her before she could.

When he really thought about it, he admitted to himself that she shouldn't have to apologize for it. After all, Albert Rambo was still loose, and he was a criminal who had kidnapped their son. Maybe it was only natural that she was worried about it. Maybe what was unnatural was that he didn't care about Albert Rambo. But he didn't. Not about Rambo and not about the boy.

Thomas closed his eyes, sickened by his own thoughts. It was wrong. It was wrong to feel that way. It wasn't the boy's fault that he had been found. It wasn't the boy's fault that his own father could not feel anything for him besides resentment. Thomas drew his foot back and gave the tire of his car a sharp kick.

"Tires are fine," said the mechanic, coming toward Thomas with the bill in his hand. "I checked 'em."

"Oh, good," Thomas said.

"Here's the damages."

Thomas looked the bill over and wrote a check on the hood of the car. "Thanks a lot," he said.

"No problem." The mechanic disappeared back into his officc as Thomas got into thc car.

He made a mental list of what he wanted to get in the discount store. He needed some weed killer and some new hedge clippers.

He remembered, as he began to drive out of the garage, that there was a men's clothing store next door to the discount house. He decided to go in there if it was open and see if he could get something for Paul. He had to try. There was no excuse for not trying.

That was wrong, too, he thought. To give a gift out of guilt. To give your child a present because you could not give him your affection. He wished he could feel something, some kindness toward the boy. But he could not deny the fact that he felt cheated. At least before the boy had come back, he'd had a wife. Now it seemed he had lost her, too.

* * *

"Keep your hands off the animals," Tracy snapped. "You can look, but don't touch." She donned a dirty apron and disappeared into a small room attached to the kennels.

Paul watched her go and then wandered among the cages, talking to the dogs and cats. The smell was powerful, and they all howled as if in misery at being caged. Paul looked around to see if Tracy had returned and stuck his hand into the cage of a little terrier that was slumped against the wall of his cell. Paul patted the dog's wiry coat. The animal whimpered and seemed to wince under his touch. Running his hand up over the dog's muzzle, he felt a warm nose. Paul frowned and touched it again. The animal sank lower in his cage.

"This one here's sick," he called out.

Slinging a bag of dog food, Tracy appeared in the corridor between the cages. "What is it?"

"This one's nose is warm."

Tracy dumped the bag at her feet. "I said not to touch them."

Paul stared back at her coldly.

"Which one?" she asked.

Paul pointed to the terrier. "Never mind him," Tracy said, but Paul noticed that she peered at the dog with concern. "Why don't you go outside? You'll just get in the way here."

Paul reached in and gave the terrier another pat. Then he left the kennel and emerged into the sunny yard behind it. A large, shady tree stood in one corner. Paul walked over and dropped beneath it. He was sweating in his camouflage vest, but he didn't feel like taking it off. He sat under the tree, and a small breeze fanned him. After a while Tracy appeared in the back doorway and came over to where he sat.

Paul closed his eyes and pretended to be enjoying the breeze, so he would not have to look at her. He heard her plop down onto the lawn near him. He opened his eyes and saw her sitting cross-legged a few feet away. On the ground in front of her was a little plastic bag filled with what looked like dried herbs. Tracy folded a white cigarette paper in half and sprinkled a little of the marijuana into it. She began to roll it up between her fingers. Paul watched her from the corner of his eye.

Tracy held the joint up to him. "Do you smoke?" she asked.

"Sure," he lied.

Tracy rolled the joint on her tongue and bit off the end. Then she took a pack of matches from her nylon knapsack and lit it. Paul watched as she inhaled a large quantity of smoke and held it in. He had done some experiments with cigarettes and whiskey, but he had never tried grass before.

Tracy held out the joint to him, and he took it from her fingers. He heard it was expensive, and he wondered how she could afford it.

"Do you get paid for this job?" he asked, gesturing toward the back of the kennel.

"What difference does it make?" she said, bristling. "I like doing it."

"No difference." He took the joint between his teeth and inhaled, looking around first to make sure that there was no one in the vicinity. His cat, Sam, had followed their bicycles over here and was sniffing around the kennels, but otherwise, there was nothing but the rustle of the trees. Paul handed the joint back to Tracy, and suddenly he began to cough.

Tracy eyed him disdainfully. "How do you like it?" she said.

Paul struggled to catch his breath. His eyes were watering. "Went down the wrong pipe," he explained.

"Take more," she said. He recovered his wind and took another toke. He could feel a fuzziness in his feet and his calves and an unpleasant dryness in his mouth. The radiant blue of the sky suddenly caught his attention. For a moment he stared up, feeling enchanted by the fleeciness of the clouds as they slowly passed. Then he looked over at Tracy, who had flopped down on her back on the lawn. She was lying there with a perplexed look in her eyes, studying him. She quickly turned away. Paul sighed and hugged his knees. He passed her the joint, and she took it without a word.

"What's this party tonight?" he asked offhandedly.

Tracy expelled some smoke in a snort of disgust. "Some boring thing for charity, at the Stewarts'. Mr. Stewart is some big honcho in all the charities in town."

Paul frowned and closed his eyes. He couldn't picture Mr. Stewart caring about good causes. He kept thinking about how mean he had been to that man at his house yesterday. It had been bothering him ever since it happened, and he felt he wanted to tell somebody. All the time they were at the golf course he kept looking at Mr. Stewart, thinking that he was just pretending to be nice. He thought now of telling Tracy about what he'd seen. He figured he could tell it in a way that would make her laugh and then see what she'd say about it. But suddenly he realized that just to spite him, she probably wouldn't laugh. She was like a porcupine. He tried to pretend that she wasn't there. Sam, who had been exploring the yard, came over and climbed up into his lap. Paul began to stroke his fur, which was warm from the sun. The cat lay, heavy, in his lap, and started to purr.

"I think someone just drove in," said Tracy.

Reluctantly Paul opened his eyes.

"I heard a car," she said. "I better hide this and go see what they want."

"I didn't hear anything," said Paul. His limbs felt heavy, and even his eyelids drooped as he looked at her. "What time is it?" he asked.

"How should I know?" said Tracy, standing up and brushing herself off. She picked up her knapsack and stuffed the bag of marijuana in a side pocket. "I'll be back in a while," she said.

"Okay," said Paul. He watched her as she disappeared inside the kennels. The cat, roused by Tracy's sudden movements, got up and leaped off Paul's lap to follow her. Paul missed the warmth on his legs where the cat had been.

He closed his eyes again and started to drift. Prisms of light sparkled and dissolved in the backs of his eyelids. The breeze was just enough to make him comfortable. His body felt weightless and at peace. He tried not to think of anything, but only to enjoy the sensations. A peculiar feeling stole over him as he let his mind wander in a cross between memory and dreams. The feeling had come and gone fleetingly several times since his return to the Langes. It was not memory, he thought, because he had absolutely no recollection of any of it. Not the faces, not the houses or anything. But once in a while some elusive sense of familiarity would overtake him. Paul wondered if under the influence of the marijuana, he could force himself actually to remember. With Tracy's face in his mind he tried to command his memory back, to picture her as a child.

He concentrated on her wary hazel eyes flecked with green and tried to picture them in a baby's face. In his mind's eye he roved over the house, trying to picture himself playing there with a baby sister. Suddenly the image of a wooden slatted gate burst in his mind like a flashbulb popping, leaving him with the uneasy certainty that he had remembered it, even though he had not seen such a thing at the house.

He tried to think about where he might have seen the gate, and as he focused on it, he was suddenly flooded by the memory of his nightmare from the night before.

Anxiety rolled over him in a wave as the nightmare replayed itself. He was lying on the ground, trying to move, but he couldn't. The ground was hard and cold beneath him. As he lay there, helpless, a huge black mass which he couldn't identify was moving toward him, as if to crush him. A large golden eagle appeared, flapping its wings and menacing him from where it hovered just above him. And then a man, familiar yet indistinct, was bending toward him, and he was awash in terror.

Paul's eyes shot open, and he scanned the silent yard behind the kennel. He had almost forgotten where he was. He rubbed his hands together, as if the terrifying dream had turned them to ice. There was a nagging pain over Paul's left eye. He had no idea how long he had been sitting there. He frowned as he looked toward the kennel. It seemed that Tracy should have been back by now. Suddenly he was sure of that.

Staggering to his feet, Paul ran across the yard to the back door of the kennel. "Tracy?" he called out. Inside their cages the animals began to howl and yelp with renewed vigor. Paul walked quickly through the kennel and up the stairs to the waiting room and the vet's offices.

The examining rooms were still, the tables lying empty. All the glass medicine cabinets were closed and locked. At the receptionist's desk the appointment book was open to Monday. The waiting room was undisturbed. Tracy was nowhere to be seen.

For a moment he wondered if something had happened to her. What if the person in the car had come to rob the place? His throat tightened at the thought, that someone might have been surprised to find her there and abducted her. He ran to the front door and threw it open, his heart beating fast.

There was no sign of a car in the driveway. Then he looked again. There was only one bicycle parked on the grassy side yard — his own. She had left him there.

Paul felt a surge of anger at her. He called out for Sam, but there was no sign of the cat either. She had just gone and left him. He realized just then that he did not know the way back. He had followed Tracy over, his eye trained on her red knapsack as she pedaled along.

He thought to call the house and then realized that he didn't know the number. He knew the street name — Hidden Woods Lane. He could call information. But he did not want to admit that he was lost. His anger at Tracy filled him with resolve. She probably thought it was funny. He did not want to let her know that he was scared. He would find the way.

Paul ran down the front steps of the shelter and got on his bike. He remembered that they had come up on the sign at the end of the driveway from the left. He would take it from there.

He could feel the sweat rolling down his sides as he started down the driveway, but he already felt a sense of relief, too. He glanced back at the shelter, feeling as if by leaving it, he had left that terrible nightmare in the backyard, where he had recalled it. All that remained of it was a headache that wouldn't go away. Slowly he guided the bike down the long driveway and turned to the right.

* * *

The cardboard bin held a chin-high display of plastic packages of paper napkins. *FAMILY SIZE*, read the poster written in Magic Marker. *ONLY 99 CENTS. STOCK UP FOR PICNICS*. Anna drew her cart up beside the display next to the checkout counter and stared at the pile of napkins. As she gazed at the brightly colored napkins, she pictured families, like hers in Ohio when she was a girl. Gatherings on long holiday weekends, with pies and barbecues. Everybody playing horseshoes and croquet on lazy summer days.

The first time she brought Tom to the annual July Fourth picnic he drank it in like a parched man at an oasis. "This is what I want for us," he told her then. "A family, like this."

Anna shivered in the nearly empty air-conditioned grocery store. Nobody shopped on a lovely, Sunday afternoon in the summer. But she figured she might as well. Tracy and Paul had gone off together to the animal shelter, unhappily yoked together by Thomas's command. Tom had informed her that he had a lot to do when she left him at the garage. Anna felt as if she just had to get out of the house and do something useful.

"That's a pretty good price," advised the overweight dark-haired woman in the uniform smock coat who was standing behind the cash register. She had been watching Anna staring at the napkin display and presumed that the shopper could not make up her mind. Anna smiled blindly at her and put a package in her cart, realizing as she did so, that she wanted the woman to think she had need of them for a large gathering.

Anna wheeled the cart around and began to unload her groceries so that the woman could check her out. One by one the woman rang up the items and began packing them in brown paper bags. Anna looked out the huge windows of the grocery store between the backs of the sale posters into the parking lot. Maybe, she thought, when she got back, the children would be home. Or Tom would be back. Tonight was the Stewarts' party. That will be fun, she told herself. But even as she did so, she realized that she held out little hope for it. With a sigh Anna lifted the paper bags into her shopping cart and, after thanking the woman at the checkout, headed through the electric eye doors and out of the store.

"Buy a chance?" cried a voice to her left as Anna left the store. She looked over and saw a man in a navy blue cap and shirt seated at a card table, waving an arm at the end of which was a hook, instead of a hand. Anna stared at the curved steel claw, which the sun glinted off as the man jabbed it at a pile of white tickets on the table. "VFW bazaar," he said. "You could win a station wagon."

The man beckoned to her with the gleaming hook, but Anna turned her head away. "No, thank you," she whispered, pushed her cart hurriedly onto the hot asphalt, and headed toward her car, which was parked near the island in the middle of the nearly empty lot.

She rested the cart against the rear bumper of the car and reached into her pocketbook for her keys. Her hands were trembling slightly, and she realized that she had been vaguely frightened by the man with the hook. She inserted the key in the lock for the trunk and turned it.

A few spaces down, a man in a blue car watched her movements. As she lifted the trunk hood, the man got out of his car and started toward her. He was wearing a gray baseball cap and dark glasses, and he looked nervously around him in all directions.

Anna lifted the first paper bag out of the cart and placed it in the open trunk. The man walked up to her.

"Miz Lange," he said.

Anna straightened up from inside the trunk and turned to face the wiry man standing beside her car. The instant she saw him, she knew who he was. Anna gasped and let go of the bag she was holding. Four oranges rolled out into the trunk, and a cereal box tipped over on top of them.

"Now take it easy," he said.

Anna stared at him. There he stood, the subject of all her worst imaginings: a thin, pale-skinned man with receding features, a dark-gray cap, and shiny shoes. She realized at once that she had no intention of screaming. It was as if she had always known that this meeting would come to be. Her eyes locked on the face of the man who had stolen her son.

Rambo lit a cigarette and spit out some tobacco from the end. He spoke rapidly in a nervous voice. "Now don't start hollering," he said. "I don't want the boy back or nothing like that. I just want to talk to you."

"I knew you'd come back," said Anna. She did not recognize the sound of her own voice. It was even and absolutely cold. "You can't have him this time. I'll kill you first."

Rambo put up both hands and pressed them into the air. "I don't want him back. Naw, I don't want him. That's not what I'm here to say. No, sir. I'm here on a mission for the Lord—"

Anna slammed down the lid of trunk. "I'm getting the police," she said.

"Don't do that," Rambo cried, lunging toward her and grabbing her arm as she tried to pass him.

"Let go of me, you filthy—" Anna struggled to free herself. His fingers clamped down on her flesh.

Rambo's eyes darted around the quiet parking lot. "Hey now, you listen. I'm taking a chance coming here like this. People'll come running. Be still."

A white-hot fury possessed her, and Anna turned and snarled at Rambo. For years he had been her absentee torturer. Now the fact that he seemed frail and ineffectual only angered her further. "You . . . you," she sputtered. "You won't get away this time."

With a swift motion she punched him in the sternum and jerked her arm free of his loosened grasp. Staggering away from him, she looked frantically around the lot for a policeman or a squad car. The parking lot was nearly deserted of cars, and there was not a cruiser in sight.

"Help," she cried out. "Police."

Rambo caught up to her and grabbed her arm again. "Listen to me," cried Rambo. "Don't."

"Let go of me," Anna snarled. "Help." Her eyes swept the shopping center, searching for aid.

They were stumbling along together now, joined by Rambo's grip. "I'm telling you something," he hissed desperately. "That boy's life is in danger. Don't you want to know?"

Anna wheeled on him with vengeance in her eyes. "You'll never get near him. You'll be in jail." She jerked free of him again and bellowed for help.

"Not from me," Rambo screamed at her. "But you better listen. It's a matter of life or death." It was his last try. He knew in a second he would have to run, the way she was hollering.

As she was about to cry out again, the man's words registered in her mind. In spite of herself, the words arrested her. She hesitated, hating herself for stopping, and turned to him. "What do you mean?" she said. The question made her feel low and helpless. "What do you know?"

"Listen here," he whispered urgently. "I'll tell you all you want to know. I know something about that boy that you better know. I swear to you on my wife's grave. But we can't talk here."

"Tell me what you know or so help me—"

"No threats, no threats," said Rambo. "This is the Lord's work I'm doing here."

Anna trembled and controlled the urge to spit at him, but she could not take her eyes off him. "You are a vicious liar," she said. "Why would I listen to you?"

"I'm not lying to you, ma'am," said Rambo. "Life or death."

"What's going on here?" A voice floated toward them, and both Anna and Rambo turned to look as the veteran with the hook was trundling toward them, his body puffed up with military importance.

Rambo saw that it was too late to run, although the panic rising in him made him wish he'd never come here. He glanced at Anna and saw the uncertainty on her face. The man was getting closer. Rambo clutched his car keys in his hand and hoped the old Chevy would turn over quickly if he had to bolt.

Anna watched the vet coming toward them, his face red and indignant, as if he were moving in slow motion. All she had to do was tell him and Rambo would be caught. Every reasonable sense told her to start screaming. But inside her, instinct warred with reason, telling her something alarming and awful. Rambo was not lying. He was telling her the truth. And he was the only one, the only person alive, who knew about Paul's lost years and could tell her.

Images of Paul filled her head: his pale complexion; the headaches that made him wince; the way he crouched in the pantry, trembling and disoriented, plagued by sleeplessness. He could be sick. He could be in danger. The last, lost eleven years could hold secrets she could never hope to learn any other way.

The vet was in front of her now, puffed up and angry. "Is this man bothering you, ma'am?"

Anna stared at her would-be rescuer for a second. Then, with a sickening feeling in her stomach, she shook her head. "It's nothing," she said. "Just an argument. I'm sorry I yelled out like that."

The vet glowered at Rambo, who was staring down at the asphalt, the bill of his cap covering his face. "If she hollers again," he threatened, brandishing his hook, "I'll have the police here. I know just about every cop on the force. So mind your manners."

"Thank you," said Anna. "Thank you so much for coming over."

The vet grunted and gave a casual salute before he turned and started back toward his ticket table.

Anna watched him go and then turned to face Rambo. The bargain was struck between them. Rambo was shaking. "Tell me now," she said. "You have to tell me."

Rambo shook his head. "Not here. Every minute I'm here I'm in danger." He handed her a piece of paper. "This here's the address," he said. "Come tomorrow morning. No police. No one but you. The door will be open. When I'm sure you're alone, I'll show up and tell you it all."

"I'd have to be a fool," said Anna weakly, half to herself.

"Up to you," he said. "That boy's life could depend on it."

Anna looked into Albert Rambo's shifty eyes. "What's in this for you?" she said. "If the police catch up with you . . ."

"Well, a modest donation would help me, I admit," he said. "Just enough so's I can get away from here and continue doing the Lord's will in greener pastures."

"Why should I help you get away?" she cried furiously. "You stole my son."

"Ma'am," he said, "as God is my witness, I saved your son." Before Anna could reply, he backed away and hurried to his car.

CHAPTER 9

Anna wiped her hands on a dish towel and glanced up at the clock. It was nearly five, and Thomas was still not home. In a way it made her angry, and in another way she was relieved. She wondered how she was going to conceal the turmoil she was feeling when he did come in. The less time they had before the Stewarts' party, the better.

Using the towel in her hand, Anna began to wipe the counter, which she had just finished cleaning. Usually she loved to be in her kitchen, which was her haven and the center of the house. But now, as she looked around the room, she felt a rising panic. Everything was neat and in its place, yet her life seemed to be in a state of chaos.

No feeling sorry for yourself, she scolded herself. You have to do it. What's the point of debating it with yourself a million times? Thomas had once railed at her that there was nothing she wouldn't do to get Paul back. Now she had him back, and she intended to protect him. I don't care what Thomas says when he finds out, she thought, although she was already apprehensive about his response. She could not tell him, though. She could not take the chance.

Anna heard the sound of the front door opening. She walked into the dining room and saw her husband coming in the front hallway. He was carrying a large white box under his arm.

"Sorry I'm late," he said sheepishly. "Where's Paul?"

"Upstairs in his room," she replied. "He's kind of upset. He thought his cat was with Tracy, but apparently she hadn't seen it. The cat still hasn't come back. You know, he seems so attached to that animal." Anna picked some dead leaves off a plant. "How's the car running?"

"Oh, fine," said Tom. "I went shopping after I picked it up," he said. "I bought him a birthday present."

"You did? For Paul?"

"It is his birthday. After all . . ."

"Well . . ."

Thomas looked at her in surprise. "What do you mean, 'Well'?"

Anna spread her hands helplessly. "I wished him a happy birthday this morning, and he said his birthday was in October."

"What?"

Anna winced. "They made up a birthday for him."

Thomas's face puckered in disgust.

"It's not his fault."

"I know."

"What did you buy? Let me see." She came toward him.

"It's a jacket. I figured he needed something for the Stewarts' party tonight."

Anna smiled nervously at him. "Take it up to him. I'm sure he'll like it."

"I suppose," said Thomas. He peered at her for a moment. "Are you okay? I'm really sorry I took so long."

"Fine," she insisted. "I was afraid you'd forgotten the party."

As Thomas started up the stairs, Anna turned away so that he wouldn't see the tears that rose to her eyes. He had remembered Paul's birthday and brought him a present. Maybe things would work out after all. He seemed less angry than he had been all weekend. Maybe once this whole thing was over . . .

Anna glanced up the stairs. She knew she should tell Thomas about Rambo, about what she planned to do. Then she shook her head. He would insist on the police. She couldn't take the chance. She would tell him everything once it was all over. Just then, Anna heard the sound of raised voices over the wail and thud of rock 'n' roll from Tracy's speakers upstairs. Then a door slammed, and Thomas came pounding down the steps, glowering.

"He doesn't want it," said Thomas. "He wants to wear that filthy camouflage rag that he goes around in."

"Oh, Tom, I'm sorry."

"I told him he'll wear this jacket and like it. I'm not taking him anywhere looking like some bum."

"You didn't say that to him," she said.

Thomas glared at her. "Yes. That's exactly what I said. And I meant it."

"He's just so attached to that old vest of his. It must have sentimental value to him."

"I'm going to take a shower," Thomas said.

"How about a glass of wine? We could sit outside," she said hopefully.

"No," he said, and stalked off down the hall.

Anna sighed and looked at the clock. It was almost time for the party. She needed to get ready, too. But first . . . she wiped her hands nervously on her shorts and started toward the staircase. First she would go and appeal to the strange boy upstairs.

* * *

The crescent moon hung like a sugar cookie in the violet sky, and garlands of pastel paper lanterns cordoned off a large area of lawn and patio behind the Stewart manor. A three-man combo in dinner jackets played mellifluous jazz on the patio near the French windows, although none of the guests were dancing. Clusters of sleekly dressed people talked and laughed in the twilight. A few teenagers, who had come with their parents, were huddled by the pool, the boys shoving one another into the girls, who shrieked as sodas splashed on summer dresses.

Anna fiddled with the bracelet on her arm and glanced at Paul, who stood stiff-shouldered in his new jacket in the doorway leading out to the patio. Tracy had already rushed past them, greeting the Stewarts on her way, and joined the tight little group by the pool.

"Doesn't it look pretty?" Anna asked the boy.

Paul studied the glowing yard. "They must be loaded."

Anna nodded and then looked gently at him. "You look nice in that jacket."

"I feel like a prize sow," he said.

Anna watched his eyes shift nervously over the scene, the tables covered in white linen, waitresses hovering as the band played. She could tell that he wanted to back away quietly and just avoid it. Anna was all too aware of the knot in her stomach. She could not relax enough to make it easier for him. She watched him helplessly as he squared his thin shoulders and stuffed his hands in his pockets. She did not want to push him out into the throng. She just wanted to keep him there, standing still and safe on the edge of the party.

Anna looked away from the boy and saw Thomas watching them with indignant eyes.

"Shall we go say hello?" asked Anna.

Paul jumped and shrank back. At the same moment Iris spotted them. She was talking to a woman with strong features and short, wavy brown hair who was wearing an Indian caftan and long, dangling earrings. Iris motioned toward Anna, and the woman in the caftan accompanied Iris to where Anna and Paul were standing. Anna could see by Iris's high color and her nervous, fluttery gestures that she was in a state of total agitation about the party. She felt a sense of real empathy for her, but for once Anna felt as nervous as Iris herself.

"You must be Paul!" Iris exclaimed. "I'm so happy to have you here. I'm Mrs. Stewart."

"Hello," said Paul.

"And I want you both to meet Angelica Harris. She's my ceramics teacher and one of the hospital's most prized volunteers."

Anna smiled at the woman and shared a firm handshake with her. "You're quite a teacher. Iris has shown me some of the beautiful things she's made."

The ceramics teacher smiled broadly, revealing a gap between her front teeth. "Well, she's my most talented student." Iris blushed and smiled.

Edward joined them, casting a critical glance over the ceramics teacher's flowing dress, and then turned to his wife. "Iris," he said with a thin smile, "I hope you won't forget all our other guests."

Iris blanched and looked down at her clenched hands. "If you'll excuse me," said Angelica, obviously aware of Edward's disapproval, "I'm going to mingle."

All but Edward smiled at her as she left. "Thank you for inviting us," said Anna to Edward, "and for taking Tom and Paul to play golf yesterday."

Edward nodded. "My pleasure," he said. "Paul, why don't you go over there and join the other young people by that table? They seem to be enjoying themselves," Edward suggested, clasping his hands together behind his back.

"That's okay," Paul demurred, his eyes straying anxiously over the knot of laughing teenagers by the pool. Anna placed a hand on his shoulder and then removed it instantly as he twitched his shoulder blade. She wanted to intercede for him, but she knew she couldn't say what she was thinking. *I need to keep him here with me. I need to watch him every minute. He may be in danger.* For the hundredth time that day she asked herself what Rambo had meant. Was the boy ill? She thought again of his headache the other day and his sleeplessness. She could just take him to the doctor and be done with it. But what if Rambo knew something specific about his condition? Or perhaps it was not illness at all. Perhaps it was a vendetta. Some enemy of Rambo's or his wife's. She looked at the back of Paul's head in front of her. She wanted to run a hand gently over his hair. She could not imagine anyone wanting to hurt him.

Paul shoved his hands farther into his pockets. There was panic in his eyes, which he strove to conceal.

Iris, no stranger to social uneasiness, seemed to notice. "You know, I don't think Paul has even been inside our house yet," she said. "Would you like a tour, Paul?"

Paul weighed this prospect against that of joining Tracy's friends. "I guess so," he said.

"Iris," said Edward, "you have scarcely exchanged a word with any of our guests. Don't you think it's about time you attended to that, rather than retreat back into the house?"

"Oh, well, I didn't think I'd be missed. I mean, I offered to show Paul . . ."

Edward studied the nervous boy with a critical gaze. "Go ahead," he insisted. "I will show Paul around the house."

Paul winced, realizing too late who his guide would be, but there was no way out of it. With a glance back at Anna, Paul followed Edward, who had started to march in the direction of the house.

A passing guest collared Iris, who turned and forced a smile. Thomas walked over to Anna, who was watching her son disappear into the house with Edward. He touched Anna on the arm, and she started.

"What did you do? Bribe him to wear the jacket?" he said.

"He was willing. He's a good boy, Tom. He just needs some understanding," Anna said irritably,

Thomas shrugged. "I see Edward is giving him the grand tour. Rather an undignified chore for the lord of the manor, don't you think?"

"Maybe he likes the boy," Anna replied defensively. "He's just trying to be nice."

Thomas raised his hands, "Sorry I said anything."

Anna sighed. "You're right. I didn't mean to jump on you."

"Mmmmm . . ." said Tom.

"Do you think Edward minds taking Paul around?" Anna asked.

Thomas shook his head. "He probably loves it. He can show off all his possessions. It's just a shame that the kid won't appreciate how much everything costs. On second thought, Edward will probably tell him."

"Thomas Lange, that's unkind," Anna said with a smile. "It's true, though."

Just then Iris returned to them, carrying a martini glass, which she handed to Anna. "I thought you might want this," she explained.

Anna thanked her for the drink.

"Anna," said Iris, "he's such a lovely boy."

"Tom bought him the jacket he's wearing," said Anna, glancing at her husband.

"He looks very handsome. I'll bet he was pleased."

"Mmmm . . ." said Anna.

"Will you excuse me?" said Tom abruptly. "I need another drink."

Iris frowned at her friend. "How are you doing? All this must be a strain. You seem a little edgy."

"I'm tired, that's all," said Anna quickly. "And you're right. It is a strain."

"Have you heard anything more about that man Rambo?"

Anna started, and the drink she was holding spilled over the rim of the glass. "No, No. Not yet."

"They will catch him, Anna," said Iris earnestly. "You should try not to worry."

"I know," said Anna, staring at the glass, which shook in her hand.

"Poor Paul," said Iris, glancing back at the house. "I hope he won't be too bored hearing all about the house."

* * *

"This is my room," said Edward, gesturing toward the closed door of the upstairs hallway. He opened the door, and Paul looked past him into the dark, heavily curtained bedroom with gleaming dark furniture and a leather chair in one corner.

Edward held on to the doorknob and closed the door again after Paul had glanced in. "And this is Mrs. Stewart's room," he said as they passed a room with eggshell-colored walls and rich floral chintz-covered furniture. The bed had a canopy over it.

Paul had never heard of married people having different rooms, but he decided that it must be something peculiar to the rich. "That bed's got a roof," he observed. "Is that for when the roof leaks?"

"Amusing," said Edward, unsmiling. Paul hadn't actually meant it as a joke. Music and laughter drifted up from the party through the open windows, and the strange party suddenly seemed preferable to this tour of the Stewarts' house. Edward, however, was oblivious to Paul's discomfort.

"Those are guest rooms and baths down the hall," said Edward. "Here, come in this room, and you can see my pride and joy."

Paul obediently followed Edward into the bathroom and looked out the window. He looked toward where Edward was pointing, but he saw nothing but the darkness and the shapes of trees.

"My windmill," said Edward proudly. He noted the perplexed look on Paul's face. "I suppose you can't see it in the dark. You can scarcely see it in the daytime. It's quite a distance, and the trees cover it. Well, I'll take you out to it and show you."

Paul looked back up from the landing as they started down the stairs. "Oh, that's all right. You don't have to," Paul said.

"But I want to, Paul," said Edward, descending the stairs behind him, twisting his wedding ring on his finger. "You used to come here as a small child. Do you remember that?"

Paul shook his head. "I don't ever remember being in a house as big as this. I don't remember anything from back then, really."

"Well," said Edward reassuringly, leading Paul through the winding hallways of the first floor, "it was a long time ago. Now," he said, "watch your step here. And follow me." The two stepped out into the night and skirted the edge of the party in the darkness.

Paul followed Edward up some terraced steps beside the house and up the graded lawn. He wished he had a flashlight to pick out the path, but Edward seemed to know the way and did not stumble or make any missteps as he negotiated the path. Paul glanced back at the island of sound and light in the dark where the party was rolling and hesitated.

Edward turned and looked back at him. "Come along," he said.

Paul continued up the path, watching his feet as best he could until Edward put up a hand to forestall him.

"There," said Edward. Through the trees Paul saw the stout, obelisk-shaped structure looming above him, the wide blades of the windmill outlined by the dim light of the crescent moon. The outer walls of the building were shingled in dark, rough slabs. The tiny windows were black holes gouged in its sides.

Edward walked over to the door and pushed it open, flipping on a switch inside. A weak yellow light warmed the doorway and lighted the panes of the windows. "Welcome to my workshop," said Edward, motioning for Paul to follow him in.

Paul slipped past Edward through the door. It was silent inside, and he blinked his eyes to adjust to the light. He rubbed his eyelids with his fingers and then looked around the six-sided room that formed the base of the windmill. It was colder inside the windmill than it had been outside. Edward stepped over to the workbench, which took up one of the six walls, and flipped on a light over the counter area. The workbench was a catacomb of drawers and compartments, each filled with a precise assortment of bolts, screws, and nails. Books, tools, sandpaper, and tiny boat parts were carefully organized into separate areas on the counter tops which lined the walls.

Paul looked up and saw that the wooden floor of a loft formed a ceiling above them. A ladder going up to it rested against the side, surrounded at the top by sailing magazines and tin cans of paint. Edward gazed fondly at the orderly workroom. "This is where I am creating my fleet," he said.

Paul felt suddenly uneasy about the faraway look in Edward's eyes. He moved away from him toward the door. "Well, thanks for showing it to me," he said.

Edward looked at him strangely for a moment. Then he stepped into the center of the room. "Have a look around," he said. "Take your time."

After a moment's hesitation Paul began to pick his way through the assortment of ships. Edward stepped around him and closed the windmill door. He watched the boy as Paul stooped over to examine the boats.

"You sure have a lot of boats," Paul said.

"Sit down," said Edward, indicating a chair. Paul sat down and glanced around the room. It looked too neat to work in, but he could see that Mr. Stewart really liked it that way. He shivered involuntarily.

"Are you cold?" Edward asked, leaning up against the workbench.

"It's kind of chilly in here," said Paul.

"Stone floors," said Edward. "I really should cover them."

Paul felt a little hemmed in, seated on the chair with Edward taking up most of the rest of the free space in the room. He wondered how Edward could stand to be so cramped up in the windmill.

Edward reached over the working surface of the tool bench and picked up a piece of bright, multicolored silk which was lying there in a heap. He unfurled it for Paul to examine.

"This," said Edward, "is a spinnaker for that sailboat over there." Edward indicated a large, delicate model with a deck of golden wood and a gleaming white hull. "I sewed the edges on that machine."

Paul looked at the old Singer sewing machine which was nearly hidden in one corner. "You can sew?" he asked, giggling nervously at the thought of Edward seated at the spindly machine.

"Indeed, I can," said Edward.

"My momma used to have a sewing machine. She wanted to teach me how to use it but my daddy said no way was any boy of his . . ." Paul's voice trailed away.

Edward ignored the interruption. "Here, take a look at this. Seven different colors in this one sail."

Paul reached for the sail in Edward's fingertips. The slippery material eluded him, and the sail floated from his fingertips to the floor. Edward started to bend over to retrieve it.

"I'll get it," Paul offered, sliding from the chair and crouching down to get the sail, which had fallen at Edward's feet. He put his hand on the sail, leaning over the toes of Edward's wing-tipped shoes. Edward loomed over him, blocking the light from the workbench.

Paul started to stand, but he felt a sudden dizziness come over him. He folded his body back into a crouch. There was a flash in his head and the fragment of an image on his eyelids. A golden eagle swooped toward him from a black cloud, talons extended, its eyes cold and enraged. Paul covered his right eye with a trembling hand. His complexion turned a chalky white.

Edward's cold eyes were riveted to the boy's bent head. "What's the matter? Are you ill?"

Paul shook his head. "I don't know."

Edward bent down toward him and reached out a hand to support him.

"No," Paul screamed, and scuttled away from him. In his haste he bumped into the table holding the white sailboat. The model teetered and then fell over. The delicate rigging crunched as the ship hit the stone floor.

Paul staggered to his feet, his breath coming in gasps. He stared down at the model, but for a few seconds he did not seem to see it or to realize what he had done.

Edward froze where he stood, his left eyelid twitching as he fixed the boy with a gaze that dissected him. "That's too bad," he whispered after a moment.

Paul seemed to awaken at the words, and he looked, aghast, at the broken ship on the floor. "I'm sorry," he said. "I'm sorry."

Edward licked his lips and stared down at the broken vessel at his feet. "That model was the only one of its kind," he said in a low voice. "It was custom-made for me."

"I'm sorry," the boy cried, looking up at Edward with alarm in his eyes. "I don't know how it happened."

Edward's gray eyes were as blank as rivets in his head. "That was careless," he said, staring at the boy. "There's no excuse for carelessness."

"I know, I'm sorry," Paul repeated miserably. "Can I go now?"

Edward stepped over to the windmill door and held it open, looking out into the night.

"Maybe I could pay for it," the boy offered hopelessly.

Edward turned and watched him for a moment. Paul began to feel again as if he couldn't breathe. Then Edward spoke. "You may consider it forgotten," he said, in a voice that did not sound forgiving.

"Thank you," the boy mumbled, and bolted out of the door and down the path in the direction of the glowing lights of the back of the patio.

"I'll be right along," said Edward. He watched the boy go, and then he looked back at the wreck of his ship on the floor. Carefully he crouched down and began collecting the broken pieces.

* * *

A dull throbbing in his head had replaced the feelings of panic and disorientation. Each time he put his foot down, Paul felt as if he were jarring the pain into a greater fierceness. His stomach had begun to churn in concert with the headache, and he kept on breathing deeply to hold the nausea down. Paul reached the periphery of the party and then hesitated, unwilling to enter the crowd of strangers. The light from the lanterns seemed to hurt his eyes.

From the edge of the patio Iris peered into the darkness and spotted the boy standing there. "Paul," she called out. "There you are." She came toward him, smiling. "Did Edward show you around?"

Paul nodded. His eyes searched for Anna in the group, wishing that he could see her and tell her he wanted to go home. He thought of asking Iris where she was, but he did not know how to refer to her. He could not bring himself to say "my mother."

Iris gestured toward the rest of the party. "Why don't you come along now and sit down with the young people and have something to eat?"

Reluctantly he let himself be led to a table occupied by teenagers. Paul sniffed the aroma of marijuana as they approached the table, but Iris seemed oblivious to this. She indicated a chair, which Paul lowered himself onto. "I'll send a waitress with some food," she said.

Paul smiled mechanically at Iris. Out of the corners of his eyes he could see Tracy watching him across the table.

"You have fun," Iris urged, patting his shoulder as she left. Paul nodded, but his head was throbbing.

Tracy leaned across the table and looked at him with narrowed eyes. "Where were you?"

"Inside. With Mr. Stewart," Paul mumbled.

Tracy said something quietly to her friends, and their mocking laughter rang out. Paul tried to ignore them. A waitress walked over to the table and placed a plate of food down in front of Paul.

Paul looked down at the slab of pink fish on his plate. "What is this stuff?"

"Salmon," said Tracy. "Didn't you ever have it?"

Paul shook his head. "I'm not hungry." He tried not to look at the fish on the plate, but he imagined that the odor was overwhelming him, making him feel even queasier.

"Have some of this," said Tracy, producing a glowing joint from under the tabletop. "You'll be hungry."

A pretty brown-haired girl in a clingy, hot-pink dress sitting next to Tracy burst out laughing at this and covered her mouth with her hands.

"I don't want any," Paul said, and pushed the plate of salmon aside, as if to remove it from sight.

"Mary Ellen wants to ask you something," said Tracy slyly.

Paul stiffened and quickly eyed the two girls. The girl in the pink dress started to laugh, and Tracy punched her in the elbow. "Go ahead," Tracy ordered. "Ask him."

Waves of pain seemed to be surging through him now, and he felt as if his eyes were aching from it. He could hardly focus on the girl's face.

"Did you *ever* . . ." Mary Ellen dissolved into laughter, and tears began to spurt from her eyes.

"Mary Ellen, you ass," said Tracy, elbowing her friend. Paul squirmed, but he tried to make his face impassive to whatever assault might come.

"Did you . . ." she cried, and collapsed into giggles again.

"Oh, shut up," said Tracy, "and let Paul eat his salmon in peace." She gave the plate a shove, and it bumped Paul in the arm. The slab of fish slid off the plate onto his jacket. The two girls started to laugh uncontrollably, although the sound of their laughter seemed far away because of the thudding pain in his head. Paul picked up the fish, and it felt cold and slippery in his hand. He thought he could smell the vilest odor off it. He tossed it away from him and stood up abruptly. All of a sudden he felt a lightness in his limbs, and black spots appeared before his eyes. He could see Tracy and her friend staring at him, but they seemed to be receding as the darkness descended in a cloud that came, then lifted, and then, in a rush, blacked out his sight altogether. He fell with a thud to the ground, pulling down a chair with him as he collapsed.

Tracy screamed, and there were gasps from the people all around him. The hum of conversation gave way to anxious murmurs as people began to crowd around the fallen boy. Paul came to in the midst of the worried onlookers, his body feeling weak and drained. He tried to drag himself up on the edge of the chair seat without looking at the faces of any of the people surrounding him. He felt as if their warm bodies were imprisoning him, suffocating him. He was trapped there, still trying to remember what had happened to him.

Suddenly Anna was beside him, her hands firmly gripping his shoulders. "Paul," she said.

He looked up at her briefly. "I fainted," he said.

Galvanized by the helplessness in his eyes, Anna asked no further questions. "Okay now," she said in a firm voice to the people who surrounded him. "It's all right. We're going now." Resolutely she helped him to his feet. "Leave us alone." Paul stumbled to his feet beside her. Thomas took a step toward them and then stopped. Anna was miles away from him, completely in control.

"We're going," she said. Anna turned to Iris, who was shaking her head with concern. "I'm sorry. I'll call you, Iris."

She forced a path through the guests, and Paul followed her blindly, his young face haggard and deathly white.

CHAPTER 10

Edward strode out across the sloping lawn of his estate. All the Japanese lanterns had been extinguished, and the extra people they had hired were cleaning up the remains of the party by the illumination of the terrace floodlights and the pool.

Edward spotted Iris just out of the floodlights' range. She was dressed in a flowered kimono and slippers, and she was eating a cream-filled pastry horn, which she had lifted from a tray that was still on one of the buffet tables.

She started as she saw Edward approaching her and quickly tried to put the pastry back down on the table. Edward glared at her and then turned on one of the women who were cleaning up at the other end of the table.

"Remove this food at once," he ordered. "Why is this cleanup taking so long?"

The woman looked up, surprised, and then quickly came over and collected the tray.

Edward turned back to Iris. "Well," he said, "I hope you're satisfied."

"With what?" Iris asked, baffled.

"The evening was a total disaster."

"Oh, I didn't think so, Edward. I thought everyone had a nice time."

"That boy's display threw a pall over the entire party. As soon as that happened, everyone started to leave."

Iris shook her head. "The poor thing. I felt sorry for him. He was so embarrassed."

Edward snorted. "I was the one who was embarrassed. I was humiliated in front of my guests."

"I'm sure everyone understood," Iris suggested meekly.

"The question is, why did you invite those people in the first place?"

"What people?"

"The Langes, Iris. The Langes. They don't belong in our set. They are completely out of place here. And now they managed to ruin my party."

"Edward, that's not so. They're our friends."

Edward turned away from her in exasperation. Iris stood uncertainly, wadding up the belt of her kimono. "I guess I'll be going to bed," she said.

"And who," Edward demanded, "was that woman in that muumuu? Whatever was she doing here?"

Iris squirmed and looked down. "I invited some of the volunteers from the hospital. She's my ceramics teacher. She works at the hospital, helping the children."

"That outfit she had on looked like something out of the circus."

Iris sighed. "I'm awfully tired, Edward. I think I'll say good night."

"They won't be invited again," said Edward. "Any of them."

"Good night, Edward."

"I'm going to do some things in the windmill. I have to relax somehow," Edward announced.

"Oh," said Iris, surprised to be informed, "fine."

Edward watched her as she walked back toward the house, her dressing gown billowing out behind her like laundry hanging on a line. She was a graceless creature, he thought. She had always been that way, even when they met.

The first time he had ever seen her was at a party, much like this one tonight. The party had been given by a rich lawyer from one of New England's finest families to reward all the people who had worked on his victorious primary campaign for the Senate. Edward had joined the campaign in hopes of meeting some of the right people who could further his young career. The race had proved unsuccessful for him, however. He had done a thousand errands and kissed as many rear ends. But he had ended up at the party without the offer of a position or even a promising lead.

He was irritable that evening and frustrated by the fact that, just as they had at Princeton, these wealthy people had closed their circle to him. The only reason he had noticed Iris at all was that she was behind the punch bowl, ladling punch in a drab dark outfit. He mistook her for a servant and was becoming increasingly angered, as he waited in the line, at the slow and awkward way that she was serving. When he reached the punch bowl, she offered him a glass which, unbeknownst to her, had a crack in it. Edward stared at the cracked cup, and the rage began to boil in him. He felt as if this low-class serving girl had somehow singled him out to receive the damaged glass. He drew the cup back and was about to toss the red punch at the front of her dress and slam the cup down on the table when the campaign's largest contributor, a paper mill magnate, came up, kissed her on the cheek, and introduced her to the victorious candidate as his daughter. Overhearing that remark saved Edward from an embarrassing faux pas and turned Iris from a frog into an heiress in his penetrating eyes.

All in all, marrying her had been a shrewd thing to do, he thought. It was true that she was an embarrassment to him, of sorts, but her father's money had gotten him started in his business. The rest he had done himself. Now he had it all, all the things he had dreamed of and missed as a boy. He was important, rich, and powerful. And he had made it happen.

One of the cleaning women came by and gathered up the tablecloth off the buffet table. "It's about time," Edward muttered. "And take all that food out of this house." At least, he thought, there would be nothing left for Iris to gorge on before she went off to her spa.

He shook his head in disgust. It was a waste of energy to think about Iris when he had much more important things on his mind. The night still held a difficult task for him, and he anticipated it with a twinge of anxiety. The cleaning people were beginning to leave the yard. It was almost time, he realized, to get over to the windmill and gather up the equipment that he needed for the night ahead.

* * *

Thomas peered out the back window at the shape of the boy sitting hunched on the glider.

"He's still sitting out there."

Anna sighed and looked out the window again. "I don't know what to do."

"Maybe we should just let him be," said Thomas.

Tracy came into the kitchen and took a pear from the refrigerator. She rubbed it on her bathrobe and took a bite out of it.

Anna shook her head. "He's terribly upset. Maybe if we talk to him . . ."

"He might not feel like talking right now. He might want to be alone," said Tom.

Anna turned to Tracy, who was seated at the kitchen table, eating her pear, and staring vacantly into the center of the room. "Tracy," she said, "what happened at the Stewarts'?"

"Nothing. Why? We were just fooling around, and then he just stood up and fainted."

"What do you mean, 'fooling around'? Did anyone say something to upset him?"

"No," Tracy cried. "We were just having some fun."

"Fun? At Paul's expense? Maybe this is the problem. Maybe you owe him an apology," Anna said.

"Me? Why me?"

"Do as your mother says," Thomas barked. "Go out there and apologize to your brother."

Tracy scowled, but she knew better than to argue with her father when he looked angry. She did as she was told. She opened the back door and stepped out into the darkness. She waited for a few moments while her eyes got used to the dark. Then she walked over to where Paul was seated on the glider. She stood several yards away from him, waiting for Paul to acknowledge her. He did not look up.

She did not know how to get him to look at her. In movies people always coughed to get someone's attention. She decided to try it. She coughed. He continued to ignore her.

"Don't you think you better go in?" she asked in a soft voice. "It's pretty late."

"No," he said stonily, staring across the nocturnal landscape.

"My parents are worrying about you. Why don't you come in?"

Paul did not reply.

"Look, we were just kidding around over at the Stewarts'. I didn't know you were sick. You should have said something." Tracy glanced back at the house. She could see Anna's silhouette in the kitchen window, watching them. Tracy sighed and tried again.

"I guess, you know, with your cat running away and everything, you probably feel bad. But why don't you come in now? If you want, I'll help you look for him tomorrow."

Slowly Paul stood up and turned to face Tracy. For a moment she felt relieved that she had accomplished her task. Then she saw the fury in his eyes.

"What did you do with him?" he said.

Tracy frowned and took a step away from him, drawing the tie on her bathrobe tight around her. "What?"

"What did you do with Sam? Where is he?" Tracy shook her head.

"You did something to him. I know it."

"That's a shitty lie," she said through clenched teeth.

Paul took a menacing step toward her. "You and your friends probably had a good laugh about it."

Tracy stuck out her chin. "You asshole. I wouldn't laugh about that."

"I'm an asshole, right?" He turned his back on her, returning to the chair. "Get away from me."

Tracy hesitated, stunned for a moment by his accusations. Then she approached the chair, fighting back the tears that were forcing their way out. "You're just acting like a baby. Blaming it on me. It's not my fault your cat ran away. It's not my fault you came back here. I didn't want you back."

He kept his eyes averted from hers, staring coldly ahead of him. "Thanks," he said. "I know."

Tracy's face turned scarlet. "I didn't mean it like that," she said.

"Yes, you did," he said. "You're a spoiled little brat. You get all the attention. That's the way you like it, don't you? Well, I've got news for you. I don't want to be here either. I hate your ugly face."

Tracy charged the glider where he was sitting, and landed a glancing whack with her fist on his shoulder that set the seat in motion. "I hate everything about you," she cried.

Paul jumped up from the glider, whirled around to face her and grabbed her wrist. "Don't touch me," he growled at her. He gave her a shake and then released her. Suddenly he let out a groan. He gripped his head with his hands and slowly sank to his knees. Tracy watched in astonishment as he collapsed on the ground. The back door of the house slammed, and Anna sprinted across the yard.

"What's going on?" she cried out. "What are you two fighting about?"

Tracy looked up at her mother in bewilderment as Paul rocked back and forth on the ground, holding his head. "He said I was ugly," she cried.

"I ask for your help and this is what you do," Anna said grimly, bending down beside Paul.

"He said I did something to his cat," cried Tracy, staring at the boy on the ground as he writhed.

"What is it?" Anna pleaded with her son. "Tell me what's wrong."

"My head," he groaned.

"I didn't even touch his head," Tracy insisted.

"Go inside, Tracy," Anna ordered. "Haven't you done enough damage for God's sake?" Tracy backed away from her mother and the boy on the ground, her eyes wide. "Let me help you," Anna pleaded with Paul. She put an arm under his and clambered to her feet, pulling Paul up beside her.

"Come on," she said, "we're going to the hospital."

"No," the boy cried. "No hospital." He tried to wriggle free of her. "Just leave me alone."

"All right," she said soothingly "All right, no hospital. But please, come inside."

They approached the back of the house through the soft grass. The air was filled with the hum of crickets and other peaceful summer-night sounds. Anna could feel her son shivering. "I'll help you," she said.

"I feel better now," he said as they slowly climbed the steps to the house.

* * *

He was asleep as soon as he lowered his head to the pillow. She sat at one end of the bed and watched him fall away, his thin face white from the strain of the headache. His mouth fell open, as if he were gulping to breathe, and in the moon light his face was all shadows and hollows. His hands fell open outside the sheet, weak and helpless. There was a sheen of perspiration on his forehead and upper lip.

He is sick, she thought. There is something terribly wrong with him. That's what Rambo meant. Try as she might, she could not stop thinking the worst. A brain tumor. Some kind of cancer. That had to be it.

She thought that maybe she should get up tomorrow and just take the boy directly to the doctor and never meet Rambo at all. It was utterly clear to her now that Rambo knew about this illness, and that was what he was going to tell her. A doctor would probably be able to diagnose it in no time. But the thought nagged at her that perhaps Rambo knew something about it that was vital. After all, the boy had grown up in his household. Perhaps he had sustained some injury, taken some kind of drugs, or something. She had to find out what Rambo knew. He might disappear, and she would never find out what he really meant. Anna felt her thoughts racing around her head like a dog chasing its tail. She did not want to waste precious time with Rambo if the boy was ill and needed to be hospitalized. But it was her only chance to find out. She tried to steady herself. Do as you planned, she told herself. Courage. Tomorrow you will know.

She wished for a minute that she could talk to Thomas. But she knew he would not let her go. She shook her head. She would do it alone. Anna stood up quietly from the end of Paul's bed. He was breathing normally at last. She opened the door and let herself out. She closed the door behind her and started down the hallway.

As she passed the door to Tracy's room, she noticed a faint light emanating from the crack beneath the door. Still up, she thought. Then, from behind the door, she heard the sounds of gasping, as if someone were trying to catch her breath. For a moment Anna hesitated. Then she put her hand on the doorknob and tapped. There was no answer. She pushed open the door to the room and peeked in.

A tiny reading lamp threw a pool of light on the floor of the darkened bedroom. Tracy sat at the edge of the circle of light. Her head was bowed, and in her arms she held Fubby, the stuffed rabbit she had loved from when she was a baby. Tracy's shoulders shook as she cradled the rabbit to her chest.

"Tracy," Anna whispered. Tracy jumped and whirled around, hiding the rabbit behind her and staring defiantly at her mother. Anna could see that her daughter's eyes were pink, and there were tears still dribbling down her freckled face.

"Go away," Tracy cried.

Anna stepped into the room. "Tracy, what's the matter? Tell me what's wrong?"

"Just get out of here," the teenager wailed.

"Please, Trace," Anna pleaded, "talk to me."

"No," Tracy spit out.

Anna bit her lip and put a hand out to touch her daughter's flushed, contorted face. "I'm sorry I yelled at you, Trace," she whispered. "It's all so stressful. But, I shouldn't have snapped at you like that."

Tracy jerked away from her touch and turned her back to her mother, hiding the rabbit in her folded arms. Anna sighed and put her hand on the doorknob.

A small resentful voice came from Tracy's huddled frame. "I'm just sick and tired of being blamed."

"Oh, Tracy, I don't blame you," Anna assured her, relieved to have an opening. "I know I got mad at you, but I was just worried about Paul. These headaches of his. I'm afraid it might be something serious—"

"You always blamed me," she said bitterly.

Anna shook her head. "It probably seems that way to you. I just have so much on my mind right now, but believe me, it's not you. I mean, brothers and sisters fight. I'm sure that's just the first of many . . ."

"Not only for that," Tracy interrupted her furiously. "For back then, when they took him."

"When they took him?" Anna looked at her daughter in confusion. "What—"

"You always blamed me," Tracy said accusingly. "You always thought it was my fault."

Anna's face slackened in amazement. Tracy was holding the stuffed rabbit tightly under one arm. Tears welled in her angry eyes, but she seemed oblivious to them.

"Of course, it wasn't your fault, Tracy. No one in the world ever thought it was your fault," Anna protested, wrenched by the sight of her daughter's misery.

"Yes, you did." Tracy corrected her bitterly.

Anna shook her head helplessly. "I never did."

"You always did," Tracy insisted.

"Tracy," Anna cried, "you were just a baby. It was something done by grown-ups. It had nothing to do with you." She reached out her hand to her daughter.

Tracy spurned her touch and shook her head.

"Why would you ever think that?" said Anna.

"You said so."

"I didn't."

"I *was sick*," Tracy cried. Anna stared at her. "I was sick."

Anna shook her head, uncomprehending.

"Every time you told it that's what you said. I was sick. And you came in the house to take care of me. And then he was gone. You always say that. You had to come in because I was crying. Because I was sick." Tracy looked down at the rabbit under her arm as if she had just remembered it was there. "I was sick," she mumbled. "And so they came and took my brother."

Anna felt tears stinging her own eyes. "No, no," she whispered.

"I didn't want them to take him," Tracy said. "He was my brother."

Guilt sizzled through Anna as she stared at her daughter's unrelenting eyes. "I never thought . . ." she said.

For a moment Anna wanted to beg for forgiveness. But she was struck by the sense that she needed time first, to consider her crime, repeated time after time, for years, without thinking. She felt stunned by it, like someone who had learned that the cigarette she thought she had stubbed out had set a house on fire.

"Is that what you thought, all this time?" she whispered in a stricken voice.

"Leave me alone," said Tracy. Ignoring Anna, she climbed into bed, tucking the stuffed animal in beside her. She turned her back on Anna. Anna walked over to the bed and put a hand on Tracy's shoulder. "Sweetheart, I'm so sorry you ever thought that. It's not true. I didn't mean it that way . . ."

Ignoring her mother, Tracy switched off the reading light beside the bed.

Anna stood there in the darkness, wondering how she could make it right. She gazed at her daughter's form, curled up and still in the bed. I'll make it up to you, she vowed silently. But she wondered, even as she promised, how she ever would.

* * *

Albert Rambo gave his head a shake over the empty basin, and a shower of coffee-tinted droplets hit and clung to the sides of the sink. Rambo stood up and smoothed his wet hair down on his head, spreading the thin hair evenly over his white liver-spotted skull. Then he stepped back and examined himself in a three-quarter profile on each side of the bathroom mirror. His normally graying hair was now a deep, robust auburn. It looked pretty good, he thought. He decided he would grow a mustache and dye that, too, the same shade. There was still plenty of dye left in the bottle. He hadn't liked the way the Lange woman recognized him so easily. Tomorrow, when he got the money, he would buy a new hat also, before he took off.

Picking up a bathroom towel, he gingerly patted his balding head dry. Then he wadded up the flimsy plastic gloves and put them, along with the glass bottle of dye and the squeeze bottle of stabilizer, back in its box. After looking in the mirror approvingly one last time, he shrugged on his shirt and buttoned it. Then he took the hair coloring kit with him from the bathroom to the bedroom and shoved it into a corner of his valise. He fingered his upper lip absently, wondering how long it would take him to raise a mustache. He had never been the hairiest guy. It might take a couple of weeks of looking untidy. By the time he grew it, he mused, he'd be far away from here.

Just then there was a flurry of raps on the motel room door. Rambo froze, staring at the back of the door, his heart accelerating with fear. Police, he thought instantly. They'd found him. Maybe the Lange woman . . . but why would they knock? It must be a mistake. Maybe if he was quiet, whoever it was would realize that he was at the wrong door and go away.

At the second set of knocks Rambo clenched his fists. But then a low voice followed the knocking.

"Sorry to bother you. This is the manager, Mr. deBlakey."

The manager. He exhaled with relief and then became immediately irritated. "What do you want?" Rambo barked.

"It's your car, sir. I'm afraid it's parked in front of the wrong cabin, and the other guest is making a fuss. I know it's late and all, but could you just move it over here in front of your place?"

Rambo shook his head in annoyance. "Okay, hold on a minute," he answered gruffly.

"Thanks a lot, Mr. Rambo."

"Wrong space," Rambo muttered under his breath as he slipped on his shoes and unlocked the door. "I parked it right outside here. Where the heck were you supposed to park?" Just as he was pulling the door open, he remembered. He had signed the register Smith. Mr. Willard Smith.

A force from outside shoved the door open, ramming him back into the room. For a second Rambo was paralyzed by the shock, his throat closing on him. He could not even cry out. The man in the doorway reached for him, and Rambo began to struggle, flailing the other man with ineffectual punches.

The man grabbed Rambo's head and pushed his face into the rag he was holding in a gloved hand. Rambo gasped and tried to jerk his face away from the suffocating smell which filled his throat and nostrils. He began to hear the voices crying faintly in his ears, and then, as the eyes disappeared, there was silence.

CHAPTER 11

Anna watched the side of the road anxiously as she drove, looking for the sign for the La-Z Pines Motel. She was afraid to miss it and lose any more time. It was past noon already. She had gone to three different banks to withdraw a few hundred dollars, and had stopped twice in the town of Kingsburgh before she found someone who could direct her to the La-Z Pines.

The sign came up suddenly on her right, and Anna made a sharp turn into the driveway and slowly crossed the gravel courtyard. Driving at a crawl, she deciphered the cabin numbers, looking for Number 17. A tall gray-haired man in work clothes, carrying a pail and a mop, stopped and watched for a moment as she drove in. Then he turned and went down to the cabin at the front marked office.

Anna waited until he had disappeared inside the screen door, and then she pulled her car up and parked it. The motel courtyard was quiet and almost pleasant, shaded by dense pines. The walls of the little cabins were graying from their original white, but the trim on each window and doorway was freshly painted forest green to match the surrounding trees. Anna sat in her car, feeling the seat of her skirt and the back of her shirt sticking to the car seat. On the seat beside her, in a brown paper grocery bag, was the money. She hadn't known how much to bring. It was ironic, she thought. There was a time when she would have welcomed a ransom note, some sign that the person who had stolen her son had done it for gain, that there was some possibility of an exchange.

Now here she was, ready to pay for help from the man who had stolen Paul from her. To pay for information that was probably useless, and in so doing, she would be helping her son's kidnapper to escape. She would take the risk. Anna felt certain he knew something important about the boy. And after Paul's attacks of the night before, she was more convinced than ever that she would pay any price for that information.

Anna glanced in her rearview mirror to see if she could spot Rambo skulking anywhere. He had said he would leave the door open and wait until she was inside. She saw nothing but a few scattered cars, closed blinds, and the unmoving foliage of the trees.

Okay, she thought. Here goes. As she got out of the car, she pulled her skirt away from the seat and picked up the paper bag, which she put under her arm. Quietly shutting the car door, Anna looked all around and then hurriedly traversed the patchy grass to the doorway of Number 17. There was a single step outside the doorway. Anna mounted it and rapped twice on the door. She glanced all around, but there was no sign of anyone watching her.

With one swift movement she reached down, turned the doorknob, and leaned forward to push the door open. It did not budge. The handle turned back and forth only a fraction of what it should. Anna stared at the doorknob and then rattled it as hard as she could. The door did not move.

Blood rushed to her face as she tried to force the locked door. Then she stopped and spun around, to search the surrounding cabins and trees with her eyes, in case he was watching her, enjoying her distress. Nothing stirred in the quiet courtyard. She put her face up to the door and softly called out his name. "Rambo. Rambo, open up." There was no answer from inside.

For a moment she stood staring into the courtyard, not knowing what to do. Over on her left she heard a door opening. She looked in the direction of the noise and saw a chubby man and a redheaded woman in bowling shirts emerge from a cabin two doors down and look her over. They got into a long Chrysler and drove away.

Clutching the paper bag tightly, Anna retreated to her car. She slid into the front seat and slammed the door. Her eyes blistered the locked door of Cabin 17 as she thought about Rambo, that weasel of a man, controlling her life once again.

For a moment she was tempted to treat it like a hoax and drive away. Just forget the whole thing. But even as she thought of it, she knew she could not let it rest like that. If she could only get into Rambo's room. Even if he had lost his nerve and was on the run, he might have left something behind, something for her to go on. She had to keep on trying.

Resolutely she got out of the car again. She hesitated about taking the bag of money with her. Then she decided that she'd better not leave it lying there. She walked down to the cabin marked office.

The La-Z Pines office consisted of two plastic-seated chairs, a high Formica-topped counter, and a wooden rack on the wall holding a few scattered brochures about the Kingsburgh area. The floor of the office was covered in a cracked brown and black linoleum.

Behind the counter sat Gus deBlakey, absorbed in his favorite soap opera, *The Young and the Restless.* He'd been watching it on and off since it started. He felt a twinge of annoyance when he saw the woman with the Volvo coming into the office. He had a feeling that she had more than just a yes or no question on her mind. He had figured she was in the wrong place when he saw her come in. She didn't look much like one of his customers. Probably lost, he thought.

He tore his eyes away from the screen and looked up at her as she leaned over the counter. "Help you?" he asked, one eye on the man in a tuxedo who was declaring his love to a girl in a hospital bed.

"I'm looking for someone," said Anna. "A . . . friend of mine. He's in Cabin 17."

Gus furrowed his brow and looked at her again. She didn't seem like the type to be friendly with the guy in 17. He was that sleazy guy who drove the blue Chevy.

"Didja knock?" he asked, his eyes drawn back to the small screen.

"There's no answer."

"Must be out. His car there? It's a blue Chevy," said Gus. "Look outside."

Anna stepped outside the office and looked down the row of cars. Parked not far from 17's door was a dirty blue car with a large dent in the front fender.

She called in to the man behind the counter. "Is that dirty blue car out there a Chevy?"

"What?" Gus called back, leaning forward as the couple embraced on the hospital bed.

Anna came in and approached the desk. "Could you come and look? This is important."

Gus glanced up at her irritably and then, with a sigh, reached over and switched off the set. He got up, came around the counter and followed Anna to the door. She pointed at the battered fender just visible from where they stood.

"That's it," said Gus.

"But he doesn't answer the door," Anna protested.

Gus shrugged. "It's a free country. Maybe he changed his mind." Then, seeing the distress on Anna's face, he said more gently, "Maybe he went for a walk."

"He was expecting me," she said. "He's got to be there. His car is there."

"I don't know," said Gus.

"Please, sir, could you just open the door for me? I'm afraid he's ill or something. If he's not there, I'll just leave him a note with you."

Gus began to shake his head.

"Oh, please," Anna entreated. "If I could just look in."

Gus frowned. He knew better, but there was something about this woman that got to him. Whatever she wanted with this guy, it obviously meant a lot to her. And the guy really was paid up only until noon.

"Okay," he said.

"Oh, thank you," said Anna. "Thank you so much." She followed the man down the courtyard. He fiddled with the keys on the chain on his belt as he walked, finally locating the one he wanted.

"This is it," he said, stopping in front of Cabin 17. He knocked on the door and called out, "Mr. Smith, you in there?" Then he turned to Anna. "I hope he isn't just passed out drunk or something."

That's probably it, Anna thought. The explanation suddenly made perfect sense to her. And if she walked in with the manager, Rambo would never talk. She'd ruin everything. She watched the manager insert the key into the lock, wondering frantically if she should tell him to stop. "All right," said Gus. "I hope you two are real good friends."

He pushed the door open and walked into the gloomy room. Anna followed behind him, peering around his arm. All the blinds were drawn, and the lights were off in the room. The double bed was rumpled, but not unmade. Rambo's few belongings were heaped in an open valise lying on the floor beside the bureau. On top of the bureau were car keys and a tiny pile of change. Well, thought Anna, at least he didn't leave town.

"Where's the light?" she asked.

"There's a lamp beside the bed," said Gus, pointing to it. Anna leaned over and turned it on. Its dim bulb illuminated only a small corner of the room.

"He probably went out for cigarettes," said Gus, pointing to the crushed packs and the pile of butts in the ashtray on the bedside table. "There's a little Seven-Eleven store about half a mile down the road. He probably walked over there." Gus walked to the window and tried to raise it. "Phew," he said. "It stinks in here."

Anna tried to take in as much of the room as possible, knowing that the manager would soon be insisting that they leave. She noticed that the bathroom door was ajar about six inches, but there was no light coming from the bathroom.

"Which direction is the Seven-Eleven?" she asked. "I should think I would have passed him as I was coming in," she said, walking over to the bathroom door and pushing it. She switched on the overhead light as she did so.

"We'd better clear out of here," said Gus impatiently. "You'll just have to come back and meet him another time. There must have been a mix-up." He waited, but there was no reply from the bathroom.

"Come on, now, Miss. You'll have to come back later," he said, but there was still no answer. Gus walked over to the door and stepped up behind Anna, who still stood in the doorway. "Holy Jesus," he cried.

A pair of shiny black shoes swayed only inches in front of Anna's face. The legs hung limp, pants stained wet in the crotch. The hands were open and stiff, the fingernails blue. A rope which hung from the light fixture cut deeply into the broken neck, and Rambo's tongue protruded, swollen and gray. His sightless eyes bulged from the bluish, mottled skin of his face. A few auburn-colored clumps of hair stood up messily from the white scalp.

Anna's face was as pale as tissue paper. She stared at the gruesome sight before her.

Gus pushed past her and nearly tripped over the straight-backed chair from the bedroom which was lying on its side. "Christ Almighty," he breathed, standing the chair up with trembling hands.

"Oh, God," he heard the woman behind him whisper. "Oh, my God."

* * *

Buddy Ferraro looked from the piece of paper in his hands to Anna's tired face. "So that's all he said to you? That's everything?"

They were seated at Anna's kitchen table. A glass of iced tea, untouched, formed a wet ring by Buddy's elbow. Thomas stood with his back to the sink, his arms folded across his chest. The summer night had softly descended, and crickets hummed outside the screen door of the kitchen.

Anna nodded. She noticed as she looked at Buddy that the hair at his temples was turning gray. For a moment she wondered when that had happened. Buddy folded up the paper and put it in his jacket pocket.

"What do you think?" she asked.

"I think he was a desperate man," said Buddy.

"I don't understand why he killed himself before I even got there," she protested.

Buddy gave her a baleful look. "I still can't believe you did that, Anna. You know better than that. How many cranks came to us over the years, offering information for money?"

"But this was Rambo. And he really did know something." Anna ran a hand over her eyes. "And now he's dead. There's so much he could have told us."

"Well, I grant you there are a lot of questions that I would have liked to ask Albert Rambo."

"Buddy, why would he do that? Say those things about Paul if they weren't true?"

"Anna, the man was up against the wall. Listen. Number one, the man was not right in the head. We know that. He was a kidnapper on the run. He was down, literally, to his last few cents. It all was closing in on him. And then you got there a little late. I guess he decided he was out of options."

"I understand about the suicide, I guess," said Anna. "But I'm convinced he really did have something to tell me. He wasn't lying to me. I'll tell you what I think," said Anna. "I think there's something physically wrong with Paul. And I think it had to do with that. I'm afraid he's ill."

Thomas quietly pushed himself away from the sink and walked out of the room without a word to either of them. Buddy watched him go. Then he turned back to Anna, who was frowning, deep in thought.

"Well," said Buddy, "I suggest that you get him to a doctor then. And while you're at it, you look like you could use some rest yourself."

"Oh, I'm taking him," she assured him. "First thing tomorrow."

Buddy stood up to go. "How's the kid handling all this?" he asked.

Anna sighed. "It's hard to say. I heard Tracy asking him about it, and he said he didn't feel anything about it. He's been up in his room for hours."

Buddy shook his head. "That kid has had it rough. Well, I'll be going. Got a busy day tomorrow. Sandy and I are driving Mark up to college."

"Tomorrow?" said Anna. "How great. How long a trip is it?"

"Coupla hours," he said. "We're going to go up and spend a few days there. They have a little inn. We have to go to all kinds of teas and cocktail parties and whatnot," he said casually.

"It sounds lovely." Anna beamed at him.

"It oughta be lovely, for what this year is going to cost me," Buddy observed, feigning exasperation.

Anna started to rise, but he gestured for her to stay in her seat. "I know my way out," he said.

Anna sighed. "Well, at least I can forget about Rambo lurking around every corner."

Buddy looked at her thoughtfully. "You take care of yourself while I'm gone."

"I will," she said, smiling at him. Buddy frowned as he turned away from her. He had his doubts about this suicide, but he had decided not to burden her with them. He knew she would seize on them, and she did not need any more worries. He raised his hand in a relaxed salute as he left.

"Thanks," she called after him. Anna could hear him going through the house and the sound of the front door closing behind him. She sat in her chair, her hands resting limply in her lap. She was afraid to close her eyes, even though she was exhausted. She was afraid to see it again in her mind's eye: Rambo, dangling there; the hideous color of death; the bulging tongue and eyes.

"Ugh . . ." She made a retching sound and forced herself to her feet. She did not want to sit alone there, thinking. She felt a sudden, urgent need to talk things over with Thomas. They had not really had a chance to talk yet. There had been the police, the reporters, the hospital, and Paul, all afternoon. Thomas had been quieter than usual, and it was hard to tell what he was thinking. As tired as she was, Anna felt that she had to explain it all to him now and make him understand.

Anna walked through the house to the staircase and trudged slowly up the steps. The door to their room was open, and the soft light of the bedside lamp spilled out into the hall. The house was quiet. Tracy wasn't even blasting her boombox, stunned into silence by the strange events of the day. Anna walked quietly into their room.

Thomas stood by the bureau, his shoulders sunken, running his fingers over the back of the silver brush. The sight of him caused an aching in her throat, and Anna started toward him, ready to slip her arms around him from behind and rest her cheek on his broad back. But as she walked across the room, she saw the packed suitcase, standing at the foot of the bed. She stopped short. "Tom," she said.

He turned to face her, putting the brush down on the bureau top.

"What's this?" she asked incredulously. "Tom, what are you doing?"

He walked stiffly to the nightstand and picked up the book that was lying there. Then he unzipped the front pocket on his suitcase and shoved it in. "Packing," he said.

Anna sank down on the bed and sat on the edge, struck speechless for a moment. Then her words came in an urgent rush. "Tom, I don't blame you for being angry. But we have to talk. I probably should have told you what I was going to do. Believe me, I agonized over it. I wanted to tell you; but he threatened me and said I would never find out if I brought you, or the police, or anyone else into it, and I couldn't take the chance."

"I've heard the story," said Thomas in a dull voice. "All day."

"It's not a story, Tom. It's the truth," said Anna.

"Okay. It's the truth."

Anna leaned toward him. "But, darling, I'm still sorry. Can't you forgive me for not telling you?"

"You don't need to explain," said Thomas. "I understand why you did it."

Anna spread her hands. "Then what's this all about? Why are you packing?"

Thomas was silent for a few moments, and then he turned to face her, his eyes like ice-covered pools of pain. "Because it's endless, Anna. I can't take it."

"What's endless? What do you mean?"

"You. Your preoccupation with Paul. All those years he was gone, all the searching, and the phone calls, and the newspaper stories. All the times I felt you were only half with me, I didn't complain. But when I heard that the boy was coming back, I thought it might end. I thought you might finally let go of this . . . obsession. Only it's worse than ever."

Anna felt indignation flare at his accusation. "How can you say that? An obsession. I had to search for my son. I couldn't just say, 'He's gone,' and forget about him. I couldn't have lived with myself. Is that what you expected me to do?" Thomas did not answer or meet her gaze.

"And when Rambo approached me and said he knew something of life-and-death importance about Paul, yes, I had to find out what it was."

"For Paul's sake," Thomas interjected in a flat voicc.

"Yes," said Anna. "That's right. I had to try to protect him."

"And what about Tracy and me? What if something had happened to you?"

"Well, I intended to be careful. It seemed that there was never any real danger to me."

"A criminal on the run. A lunatic . . ."

"I was desperate. I had to know what it was that Rambo was hiding. He said our son was in danger. . . ."

"Listen to yourself, Anna," he cried. "Don't you see? No sacrifice is ever too great for Paul. First it was the searching. Then it was Rambo. Now you've taken it into your head that the boy is sick, and it will be a round of doctors. And then what will it be after that? Where does it end, Anna?"

Anna stared at him for a moment, about to protest, and then she shook her head. "It doesn't end," she said quietly. "My concern for my own son — that will never end, any more than my concern for you and Tracy would end. . . ."

Thomas snorted. "Concern. Is that what you call it?" He stalked over to the closet, pulled open the door, and quickly inspected its contents.

Anna rose from the bed and shook her head in disbelief. "You know, have you ever stopped to think that maybe it's you who's being unreasonable? Ever since we heard that Paul was coming home, you've been withdrawn. You won't talk about it. You never once showed any real happiness about it. This should have been the best moment of our lives. Our own child coming back to us. Why don't I feel that from you?"

Thomas looked at her with tired, bleak eyes. "He's a stranger, Anna. He's someone we don't even know."

Anna stared at him. "How can you say that?" she whispered. "That boy is your son."

Thomas shook his head and slammed the closet door. "To me, he is a stranger. I can't pretend to love him. I don't feel anything for him."

Shocked by his words, Anna could not speak for a moment. Slowly she recovered her voice. "Then maybe you should go."

Thomas walked over to his suitcase and zipped up the front pocket. Then he picked up the handles. "I can't help it," he said. "That's the way I feel."

"Well, go then. Go," she said. She grabbed the bedroom door and pulled it open. "You don't belong here."

Thomas hesitated and then, carrying his suitcase, he walked out. Anna heard his footfalls, descending the staircase. "How could you?" she said softly as she stared at the empty doorway.

* * *

The sound of harsh voices filtered down the hallway through his bedroom door, but Paul could not hear what they were saying. He sat huddled up in the chair beside his bureau, his arms wrapped around his knees, which were pulled up to his thin chest. The only illumination in the room was the moonlight coming through the window, throwing the objects in the room into monstrous shadows.

Once, when he was younger, he and another boy had stumbled onto a body in the woods. The man was a hobo. They found him not far from the remains of a dead campfire. It was wintertime, and the hobo's rags had not been enough protection from the cold of the mountains. Paul had never been able to forget the sight of that stiff body, curling up into itself, the tattered clothes fluttering slightly over the man's blue limbs, the eyes and mouth open and frozen into an expression of resigned terror. Every time he tried to imagine his father hanging in a motel room, he kept picturing that dead man in the woods. He could see his father's mouth open, like that, the stream of invective and religious ramblings silenced forever. Those agitated, angry eyes staring, fixed into eternity. Paul wondered uneasily if despite all his preaching, Albert Rambo would end up in heaven. If there was such a place, Paul suspected his father could get there only through the intervention of his mother.

But no, they both were kidnappers, doomed to be punished. And now they both were dead. He tried to decide if it was his fault that they were dead. The thought made him feel weak and woozy. They were gone, though. Both those people who had been his parents. And Sam was gone, too.

Every trace of the life he had known seemed to have been swallowed up by the earth.

Although he felt that he should, he could not feel sad about the death of his father. Not the way he had felt when his mother died. But he did feel afraid. For as long as Albert Rambo had been alive, there had been someone who knew who he was. Now, with his father gone, he was truly alone. Alone with these people. The Langes. He was Paul. Their son. It was as if his life were a huge lie, and now he was forced, for the rest of his life, to live in that lie.

But even as he emitted a sob at that terrifying idea, he thought again about how Anna, the mother, had gone to meet Rambo with money, just to try to find out about him. It seemed like a kind of stupid thing to do, in a way. But Paul felt a tiny spot of warmth in the pit of his stomach when he thought of it. For a second the yawning loneliness lifted, and then it descended again.

CHAPTER 12

Thomas drummed his fingertips on the surface of Gail Kelleher's cocktail table. "Thanks for inviting me over," he said. "I guess I needed to see a friendly face."

Gail tucked her legs under her and leaned back into the cushions of her plush sectional sofa. She took a sip of wine and gazed at him over the rim of her glass. "That's all right," she said. "I'm glad you called me."

"I wasn't sure you'd be home. I just took a chance. I figured a girl like you would be . . . I don't know . . . busy."

Gail smiled ruefully. "Out dancing till dawn and drinking champagne out of a slipper," she said.

Thomas shrugged. "Something like that," he said.

"Let's see," she said, throwing her head back as if she were reading something off the ceiling. "This past weekend I met a guy for a drink whom I knew from college. He had three stingers in a row and tried to maul me in the cab on the way home. I ended up in bed with a good mystery. One day I did my laundry and met my girl friend for a hamburger down the street. Yesterday I watched a baseball game on TV. Pretty glamorous, no?" She smiled at him, raising one eyebrow.

"I'm surprised," he said. "I pictured it differently. You're so attractive. And you're single."

"Oh, I meet a lot of men," she said. "Not many that I really like. They all seem to be preoccupied with their investments and their sound systems. It's rare to meet someone who is really warm. That you feel you can talk to . . ."

Thomas looked up at her and felt a tingling sensation at the intensity of her glance. He quickly looked away and gazed around the modem, elegantly appointed apartment. "I like your place," he said, although he felt a little out of his element in the sleek decor. He glanced again at Gail, who was barefoot and dressed in a V-neck summer dress that seemed to have only one button holding it closed at the waist.

"It's about time you got over here," she said lightly. "Want a glass of wine?"

"Yeah, okay," he said nervously.

He watched her as she walked over to the ice bucket on the bar, picked up a wineglass, and filled it, "You still haven't told me why you're here," she said. "You just said on the phone that you were spending the night in the city."

Gail walked back to the sofa and handed him the glass. Then she settled down beside him, somewhat closer than she had been before.

Thomas stared into the pale liquid in the glass. "I . . . I left home," he said, feeling, as he said it, like a small boy who had run away and was trying to appear to be brave.

"What happened?" she asked, watching him closely.

"Well, you probably heard about Anna's finding the kidnapper at the motel and all. . . ."

"It was on the news," said Gail.

Thomas sighed. "I don't know. I just couldn't take any more,"

"Why did she do that?" Gail asked. "It was such a crazy thing to do."

Thomas felt himself shrink from the harshness of her judgment. He felt an instinctive urge to defend his wife. "She's been under a lot of pressure lately. She can't seem to stop thinking about the boy."

"It sounds kind of sick to me. I don't know how you've put up with it for as long as you have."

Thomas sighed and stared at his hands, which were clasped together. He did want to talk about it, and he knew that Gail was only trying to take his side in it; but he could not bring himself to say all the things that he felt about it. He felt guilty, talking about Anna that way. He felt only a kind of inchoate need for comfort. He had the urge to reach over and touch the smooth, tanned skin on Gail's arms.

As if she had read his mind, Gail put a hand on his forearm, and Thomas gazed down at it. He started to speak several times and then stopped. "When Paul showed up on Friday . . ." he said. Then he shook his head and frowned. "He doesn't look anything like he used to." Thomas could feel a sob welling up inside him that he wanted to stifle at all cost. "I don't know what I was expecting. I feel so far away from him. . . ."

Gail tilted her head to one side. "It's been rough, hasn't it?"

Thomas was silent for a few minutes. Then he shook his head. "I'm terrible company tonight," he said. He finished his wine and put the glass down on the table. "I'd better be getting over to the hotel."

Gail put her glass down beside his and moved over to him. As she came near him, he could see her bare breasts inside the plunging neckline of her dress.

"You don't have to stay at a hotel," she said.

Thomas looked up into her eyes, which were dark and deep and full of sympathy for him.

"I'm glad you came to me," she said softly.

Thomas closed his eyes and swallowed. Despite the air-conditioning in the room, he was suffused with heat. He could feel her fingers burning into his arm. With a groan he reached out for her.

* * *

Sprawled on the bed in her rumpled clothes, Anna groped across the quilt for the familiar mound of Thomas's body and came awake, grasping a wad of the cotton mosaic in her fingers. Turning her head, Anna gazed at the undisturbed bedclothes beside her. The shafts of sunlight which fell on her made her wince, her eyes grainy from the angry tears of the night before. At least, she thought, the awful night was over.

Anna rolled over onto her back and stared up at the ceiling. The memory of Thomas's words, the vehemence with which he had disavowed their son still stung her. But with the morning and after a few hours of sleep, she felt more incredulity than anger. She had known for a long time that he had held out no hope for Paul's return. Well, she thought, not to hope was one thing. But he seemed to be saying that he hadn't even wanted him back. Not at all. It made her feel that there was a whole side of him which she had never known about. She tried to think back, to the point where she had lost track of what he really felt.

In the year or so after Paul had been taken, and she had lost the baby, she would often come awake in the night, jerked from her fitful sleep by a sense of dread that was suffocating, that made the sweat stream from her body. Inevitably he would awaken moments later and turn to her, to encircle her tense, sleepless body in his arms, as if even in his sleep her needs were known to him. His embrace was meant to comfort her, but she could always sense that he was fearful of her dry-eyed grief, and his arms felt like a weight on her. One morning she complained of it to him. After that he still woke, but he would only take her hand, and gradually he learned not to touch her, but would lie there beside her, staring into the night, unable to help, unable to sleep. After a while he got a prescription and took sleeping pills. From then on she awoke alone. She was relieved, actually, to be alone with her thoughts, not to have to answer his unspoken anxieties about her. She would look at him dispassionately, lying there beside her, sleeping like an exhausted soldier, eyes encircled with shadows, mouth open. When had he stopped waiting for Paul? she wondered. Was it then, when he started to sleep?

For her part she had remained a sentry, without consolation, for a long time afterward. When she finally was able to sleep through the night, make love again, resume her life with him, they never mentioned those other times.

There were so many things that they had never talked about, subjects too tender to touch. Now she wondered if they ever would. She felt a stabbing pain in her throat, as if she were being strangled by the painful thought.

First things first, she reminded herself. She had to get ready and get Paul over to the doctor's office. She was convinced now of his illness, and as much as she feared the verdict, she could not bear to wait. In a sense she was grateful to have a mission of such urgency. It enabled her to get out of bed.

She dragged herself up and slowly shed the wrinkled clothes she was wearing. She grabbed a wrapper, went into the bathroom, and ran a hot shower. The water spilling over her felt good, and she marveled for a second at how such small pleasures were enough to keep a person going. She recalled those days after Paul had gone and she had lost the baby. She would focus on small, pleasurable sensations to lift herself up — the curve of a shell she found at the beach; the feeling of clean sheets on her legs; the blaze of an icicle struck by sun, hanging from the porch roof. These sensations would jolt her, sometimes forcing tears to her eyes, always reminding her that she was alive. The heartache had numbed her but not killed her. As she slowly dressed, she realized she thought that those days were over, that they had ended on the day she learned Paul was coming home. She shook her head, feeling pity for her own hopefulness.

Leaving her room, she noticed that the doors to Paul and Tracy's rooms were still closed. She went quietly down the stairs, hoping not to disturb them yet. She had a feeling that Paul was dreading this doctor's appointment, although he had not actually said so. As for Tracy, Anna did not relish the prospect of telling her that Thomas had left. He had always been closer to Tracy than she had. She wished that they would sleep a little longer and give her some time to collect herself.

Anna went into the kitchen and put a few things for breakfast out on the kitchen table. She stopped short, thinking again of Thomas and wondering if he had eaten. He had never been able to take care of himself. He was probably having a doughnut at his desk and drinking black coffee till his hands shook. One thing was true of him: He had never taken for granted the way she took care of him, unlike most husbands she heard about. Anna sighed and poured some milk into a pitcher for the table.

"Mom?"

Anna turned around and saw Tracy, dressed in a T-shirt and running shorts, standing in the doorway to the kitchen. They had not spoken to each other very much since Sunday night, when Anna had gone into her room, but Tracy's storm of accusations seemed to have eased her anger, as if an infection in her had burst and was draining away. Anna felt a sickening certainty that the news of Thomas's departure would create a whole new climate of resentment. She placed the pitcher of milk on the table and began to fuss with the gauge on the toaster.

"Hi, darling. When did you get up? I didn't hear you."

"Just now," said Tracy. "Where's Daddy?"

That was quick, Anna thought. She sighed. "He's not here."

Tracy picked up an orange from the basket on the table and started to peel it. "Did he go early?" she asked casually. She pulled out a section and slipped it into her mouth. She watched her mother warily.

Anna could sense the tension in Tracy's stance. For a second she realized that Tracy knew instinctively that something was wrong. She wondered how the child could be so perceptive, but at the same instant she understood, with a heavy heart, that Tracy had been bred on calamity. She must have a presentiment for it, based on experience. There was no point in trying to conceal the truth from her. Anna sat down carefully in one of the kitchen chairs and laid her hands, palms down, on the tabletop. She was not sure how to begin.

Tracy saved her the trouble. "What happened?" she asked in a matter-of-fact tone, but Anna could hear a tremor in her voice.

"Tracy, your father and I had an argument last night, and he decided to go away for a little while."

"What do you mean?" Tracy asked incredulously. "You mean, he moved out?"

Anna was poised to deny it. Then her shoulders slumped, and she nodded. "For a little while." She mitigated the admission.

"What's a little while?" Tracy cried. "When's he coming home?"

Anna was silent for a moment. Then she replied, "I don't know."

Tracy spit an orange pit into her hand. "You mean, never," she said.

"I mean, I don't know."

"He just left, like that? He didn't even say good-bye to me."

"You were sleeping. He didn't want to wake you. You'll see him, Tracy. It's not you he's mad at."

"What did you do?" Tracy asked accusingly. Then she blurted out, "I can't believe this." Tears spurted to her eyes, and she angrily wiped them away.

Anna stared sadly at her daughter, who was trying to be defiant about this, her latest loss. What have I done to you? Anna thought. "Tracy, I'm sorry. I know you're going to feel as if I'm to blame, and I know how much you care for him; but I did what I had to do, and I'd do it again if I had the chance. I'm going to try to make your father see that, but if I can't . . . well, I don't know."

"Did what? What did you do to make him leave?"

Anna considered claiming that it was private. She felt too tired to face her daughter's reaction and the cementing of her conviction that her mother was to blame for all her misery. But perhaps there had already been too many things kept inside. Anna drew a deep breath.

"Your father was very angry at me for what I did yesterday."

"What do you mean? For finding that guy?"

"Not for finding him. For going to see him. I went to see him without telling Daddy what I was going to do. You heard the whole thing yesterday."

"Yeah, I heard it," she said. "He was going to tell you something about Paul."

"Yes," said Anna carefully. "I knew he was wanted by the police but that didn't stop me. I knew that he wanted money for the information about Paul, and I planned to give it to him. Without telling your father."

"Is Daddy mad about the money?"

"No, darling. He is mad because he thinks I acted recklessly. He feels that I didn't give any thought to his feelings, or to yours for that matter. That I just went ahead and did it without caring about the two of you. That's not true, but he didn't believe me."

Tracy inserted another orange section into her mouth and then sucked on it thoughtfully. "I don't get it."

Anna looked up at her.

"Did he think we should have come with you? How could we do that?"

"No, he meant that if something had happened to me, I mean, if Rambo had been lying and done something to me . . . that I just took a dangerous chance . . . for Paul's sake."

Tracy nodded and picked another pit off her tongue. She deposited the pits in her hand into the trash. Then she wiped her hand on her T-shirt. "Yeah, but you had to try to find out what he knew about Paul," she said simply.

Anna felt momentarily stunned by the unexpected endorsement. She looked up at her daughter with her mouth open. Then she bit her lip. "Yes," she said. "That's what I thought." She started to say more but stopped, afraid to break the fragile understanding with a load of explanations.

Tracy sank down into a chair beside Anna and rested her head in her hands. "This sucks," she groaned.

Gingerly Anna placed a hand on Tracy's back and rubbed it in a circular motion. Tracy let her do it.

"It'll be all right," Anna assured her softly. "We'll make him understand. Don't worry," she promised, gathering determination as she spoke. "You'll see."

* * *

Boarding the morning commuter train was like stepping through the open door of an inferno. Edward gasped and stepped back as the blast of heat hit him. Behind him, a pileup of briefcase-toting commuters began, and he could hear their murmured complaints. A trainman in a blue uniform came trudging up the center aisle of the car, bawling, "Step inside, plenty of seats, watch the closing doors."

Edward stood still, glaring at the conductor, as some of the other men slid by him, grumbling and flattening themselves against the seats. The conductor glanced at him and then shook his head, anticipating his complaint. "I know all about it," the conductor said in a bored voice. "Nothing I can do. The whole train's like this — a steam bath."

Edward bristled at the man's casual attitude about the breakdown in the air-conditioning, but it was clear that the conductor just didn't care. Complaining under his breath, Edward marched down the aisle, settled himself in the window seat, and began removing his jacket. He hated driving into Manhattan, but this was insufferable. He should have called a town car to take him into town today. Too late now, he thought.

Edward instinctively smoothed out the fabric of his suit to prevent it from being wrinkled by the man who sat down heavily in the seat next to him. He arranged his jacket carefully before glancing over at the man in the adjoining seat and stifled a groan when he recognized Harold Stern, a member of his country club. Harold had made his money in the department store business, and Edward did not consider him suitable for membership in his club. Edward looked quickly away and pretended not to see him.

"Hello, Edward," said Harold, disregarding the snub. "It's hot in here today, isn't it?"

Edward gave him a mirthless smile of assent, and the two sat in silence for a moment.

"Hey," Harold said as Edward began to open his copy of *The Wall Street Journal*, "this whole thing with Tom Lange's family is really incredible, isn't it. You're pretty friendly with them, aren't you?"

Edward gave Harold a rather patronizing nod. "We have been neighbors for some time, of course. The boy's coming home, you mean."

"Well, and then his wife's finding the kidnapper yesterday. They say he killed himself. My God."

"Anna found . . . that man?"

"My wife heard about it on the radio last night."

Sweat broke out at Edward's hairline. "I don't understand. How could Anna . . . ?"

"I don't know the details. There might be something in this morning's paper, though. They love anything sensational, especially in the suburbs." Harold snapped open his briefcase and pulled out a copy of the *Daily News*. "My wife told me I'd better bring it home tonight so she can read about it. I just got it at the station."

Edward watched in horrified fascination as his seatmate pored through the scandal-ridden stories in the front of the paper.

"Here it is," Harold cried. "Page three."

"Let me see," said Edward urgently.

"Just a second," Harold said, frowning as he read.

"Let me see it," Edward demanded in a shrill voice. Harold looked up at him in surprise.

"They're our friends. It upsets me terribly," Edward explained, tugging the paper from Harold's hands.

Harold released the tabloid, and Edward stared down at the account in the newspaper, the details just sketchy enough to leave his own fate hanging in the balance. Edward's face paled as he read, and the words seemed to throb in front of him. For an instant he imagined a phalanx of policemen waiting to meet him as he stepped off the train at Grand Central Station. His heart was pounding, and the gnawing in his stomach was almost audible.

Harold Stern watched Edward as he stared at the paper. "God," he said. "You look awful. Are you all right?"

Edward gripped the paper, the ink staining his dampened fingers black. "I'm all right. Shocking news," he mumbled.

"Well, it could be worse. At least nobody got hurt. Except that nut."

"It's this heat," said Edward, handing him back the paper and turning toward the window. How *could* Anna have found Rambo? She must have spoken to him at some point. And how much had Rambo told her? He had to get back to Connecticut and find out. He would not even leave Grand Central Station. He would just turn around and take the next train out. If the police were not already waiting for him, he reminded himself.

CHAPTER 13

A phone rang, and Anna looked up sharply as the nurse behind the desk answered it and spoke in a low tone. Anna's restless gaze strayed around the doctor's waiting room. Over in one corner a pair of neatly dressed girls with strawberry-blonde hair were squabbling desultorily over a jigsaw puzzle. In a chair beside them a man with red hair, dressed in khakis and a Lacoste shirt, alternated between glancing at the door and consulting his watch. In a chair by the window a heavyset woman in a flowered dress was leafing through a *People* magazine, raising her eyes occasionally between pages.

Anna sighed and looked up at the clock. It had been nearly forty minutes since Paul went into the examining room of their family doctor. She wondered what Dr. Derwent could be doing with him all that time.

"Mrs. Lange," the nurse called out pleasantly as she returned the phone to the cradle, "Dr. Derwent would like to talk to you in his office." The nurse gestured toward the closed office door. Anna smiled wanly at her and got up from the sofa; her legs felt numb beneath her. One of the children by the jigsaw puzzle began to cry.

Anna passed through the office door and into the diploma-and-book-lined room that the doctor used for conferences. She sat down nervously in a black leather chair beside the desk and waited. In a moment the door opened, and the plain, bespectacled face of the doctor appeared in the doorway. He gave Anna's shoulder a squeeze before he sat down in his chair. "Paul will be out in a few minutes, Anna," he said. "He's getting dressed."

Anna tried in vain to read the familiar but expressionless face. "How is he, Doctor?" she asked, steeling herself for any response.

Dr. Derwent leaned back in his chair. "Well, I did a number of tests on him today, and we won't have all the results of those tests for several days, of course."

Anna knotted her fingers together and stared at them. "I understand."

"But from what I have seen of him this morning, I would say that you have nothing to worry about."

Anna's head jerked up and her eyes widened in disbelief. "He's all right?" she whispered.

The doctor raised a cautionary hand. "I'm not a specialist in this area, as you know. But the presence of a tumor on the brain is something that can often be detected by examining the patient's eyes, testing his reflexes. Paul seems perfectly fine. I'm sending his blood work to the lab, and I want him to have an EEG. But what I've seen so far looks quite normal. Perhaps I shouldn't be telling you this without all the results; but I want to put your mind at rest about all this."

"But I don't understand," said Anna, "The headaches and fainting spells. The nausea . . ."

"Well, there are a lot of reasons for a person to have headaches which are not organic, Anna. The boy has been under a lot of stress. It's clear that he is exhausted. He needs to get some rest."

"He has nightmares," she said.

"I can give him something to help him sleep. And I do think you should bring him over to the hospital tomorrow afternoon to have these other tests done on him."

Anna gave him a puzzled look. "I just don't know what to think."

"Anna, you should feel free to take him to a specialist if that will make you feel any better. I'll give you a referral and I won't be insulted. But I feel pretty confident about this."

Anna shook her head and gave him a crooked smile. "I can't tell you how grateful I am, Doctor. This is wonderful news."

Dr. Derwent smiled. "Glad to be the bearer of good tidings."

Anna rose shakily from her chair. "I'll have those tests done on him right away."

"Anna," said the doctor, getting up from behind his desk, "you might want to have the boy talk to a psychologist or a counselor or something. This whole thing may have an emotional origin. And I think the situation certainly calls for it."

"I suggested it to Tom before he even came home," she said. "He didn't really go for the idea. He thought we should just let things get back to normal without a lot of interference from outsiders."

"Suggest it to him again," the doctor advised. "Tell him I said so."

Anna nodded, not wanting to get into the fact that Tom had left home. She walked out of his conference room and back to the waiting room in a kind of daze.

All right. He's all right. Anna waited for the unexpected verdict to penetrate, but she felt numb all over. She had created a wall of readiness around her heart, so that she could tolerate whatever the doctor had to say without collapsing. She had endured for all these years, and she was not about to collapse now.

He is fine, she repeated to herself. No brain tumor. You were so well prepared for the worst that now you can't even grasp the good news. Anna looked up and saw that the others in the waiting room were eyeing her curiously.

She tried to force a smile, as if to let them know that she was happy with the news. I *am* happy, she reminded herself.

He's all right. It's over. There's nothing more to fear. For a moment she wondered if everything Thomas accused her of was true. Maybe she needed the anxiety, just to survive. Maybe worrying was an end in itself, a way of life that she throve on. She should be hugging herself for joy. At that thought a tiny stab of happiness and relief suddenly pierced through her.

It's just a delayed reaction, she told herself. You'll feel it when you get home. I'll take him to a movie, she thought, or anything he wants.

But if the boy was not ill, she thought, why had Rambo said his life was in danger?

"Hi," said a quiet voice.

Anna started and looked into the drawn face of her son. "Paul!" she exclaimed. "How do you feel?"

"All right," he said. "Can we go now?"

* * *

Thomas studied the array of muted silk ties that stood on the men's accessories counter. He held one between his thumb and forefinger and stared blankly at it. Then he let it drop and turned away.

He stood in the aisle between the two glass counters as women with their shopping bags brushed by him. His eyes traveled to the gilt clock above the elevators, and he tried to calculate how much of his lunch hour was left before he had to get back. But the numbers on the clock did not seem to make sense to him, and he felt as if he were in a stupor. A determined-looking young woman in an olive green jump-suit squeezed by him, muttering, "Excuse me," in an irritated tone. Her perfume remained in her wake, and Thomas recognized the scent with a start. It was the perfume he had chosen for Anna on their anniversary some years ago, and she had worn it ever since on special occasions.

"I think this one will go," said Gail, coming around beside him and examining a silk tie with a maroon stripe in it. She looked up at Thomas's bewildered expression and smiled. "What's the matter? You look shell-shocked."

"It's so crowded."

"It's always like this at lunchtime," she said matter-of-factly.

"Let's get out of here," he said.

"What about the tie? You know you need something to go with that gray suit. You said so yourself."

Thomas shrugged. "I guess my mind was elsewhere when I was packing."

Gail felt a cold little knot form in her stomach at the faraway look in his eyes. She trained her eyes on the tie in her hand and spoke briskly. "Well, what about this one? This would go."

Thomas looked down at the tie in her hand without enthusiasm. "Yeah. That's fine. Let's buy it and get out of here," he said. He reached in his jacket for his wallet, but Gail brushed it off.

"I'll put it on my charge," she said brightly. "A present."

Thomas smiled briefly at her.

"You wait outside," she said, shooing him.

"Thanks," he said. "I'll be over at Saint Pat's." He watched her line up at the counter where a primly dressed saleslady with glasses on a chain around her neck was talking calmly into the store telephone. He threaded his way through the throngs of shoppers and pushed through the revolving door out onto Fifth Avenue.

The crush on the sidewalk was nearly as bad as it had been in the store, but he heaved a sigh of relief to be outside. He inhaled the humid summer air, heavy with the smell of burned hot pretzels and automobile exhaust.

Thomas crossed the street over to St. Patrick's Cathedral and sat down on the steps outside, heedless of his well-pressed suit. On the opposite corner, a black man in a red knit cap was running a game of three-card monte for a crowd of gullible passersby. Behind him, a Latino family posed proudly at the portals of the great cathedral to have their pictures snapped.

Thomas turned away from the family and stared vacantly across the street. They are probably back from the doctor's by now, he thought. All morning he had found himself wondering, with an intensity that surprised him, what might be discovered wrong with Paul. He did not like to think of Anna's dealing with bad news, if bad news it was, by herself. He realized, with a sickening sense of guilt that his leaving last night had probably robbed her of her sleep. She would be exhausted today. He could picture the weariness in her eyes. You wanted to punish her, he reminded himself. And it was true that last night he felt she deserved it. But with the morning had come the old impulse to hover near her.

He opened his briefcase, and pulled out his cell phone, weighing it in his hand. He could just give Anna a quick call, to ask about Paul, he thought. Then from the corner of his eye he saw Gail mounting the steps to where he stood, watching him. There was a flat package under her arm and she was tearing a piece off a giant pretzel. Thomas slid the phone back into his briefcase. If Gail had noticed him holding the phone, she didn't mention it. She held out the pretzel to him, but Thomas shook his head.

"That saleswoman was infuriating," said Gail. "I thought she'd never get off the phone."

Thomas nodded. "Persistence won the day, I see."

Gail handed him the box and he tapped it against his thigh. "I guess we should be getting back," he said.

Gail nodded and they started off together down the steps. He could sense that she was studying him, hoping that he had enjoyed their outing. He did not want to hurt her, but he could not seem to shake the melancholy mood that had descended on him. I'm hardly the picture, he thought, of a man on the town with his new mistress. He wondered if he was not so distracted whether he could concentrate on her.

"There's a nice little Italian place in my neighborhood," said Gail brightly. "Does that sound like fun for dinner?"

"Sounds nice," he said with a forced enthusiasm.

Gail's high heels clacked on the stone as they descended the steps. A little farther down the sidewalk, she spotted a wire trash basket about five feet away from them. With a flick of her wrist she tossed the remains of her uneaten pretzel dead center into the trash.

Thomas squeezed her arm and smiled.

"College basketball," she admitted with a rueful smile.

Thomas shook his head. "You're a marvel," he said. "Is there anything you can't do?"

Gail did not answer but flashed a cheery, uncomplicated smile as she slipped her arm through his and held his forearm in a firm grip.

* * *

"Cutchee, cutchee, coo," crooned the proud grandfather, and his breath formed a cloud on the plate glass window in front of him. Gus deBlakey waved energetically and beamed at the newborn, swathed in a soft blanket, which the nurse in a face mask held up for his inspection. The wails of the other babies were muffled by the window pane as they flailed their miniature red fists and feet drunkenly against the sides of their little beds. Gus's infant grandson blinked and yawned but did not cry as the nurse showed him off.

"What a good little fella. Yes, you are," Gus exulted, his face distorted by a besotted grin, his eyes disappearing into crinkles. "You're a little angel, just a perfect little angel."

"Excuse me, Mr. deBlakey?"

Gus turned away reluctantly from the window and faced the handsome, neatly dressed man beside him. "That's me," he said. "Hey, does one of these belong to you?"

Buddy Ferraro shook his head, and Gus turned back for a last look as the nurse replaced the baby in the little bed. The child started to wail with his nursery mates as he was released onto the sheet.

"Have a stogie," said Gus, reaching into the pocket of his work shirt and fishing out a cigar. "His father's out on the road in his rig, so Grandpa gets to do the honors for him." He pressed the cigar on Buddy, who took it and slipped it into his jacket pocket.

"I'm sorry to bother you, Mr. deBlakey, but I need to talk to you."

Gus peered at Buddy with pursed lips. "Another cop," he said with resignation.

"I stopped by the motel a while ago, and the chambermaid said I could find you here."

"Don't tell me," said Gus, biting off the tip of a cigar ferociously and spitting it into the palm of his hand. "That Rambo character again. What a mess this turned out to be."

"I'm afraid so," Buddy agreed. Gus shot one longing look back at the babies, who twisted and yawned in their newborn slumber. It took him a moment to locate his pride and joy. "Isn't he cute?" he asked.

"Fine boy," Buddy assented.

"All right," Gus muttered. "Come on outside. Can't smoke in here." Waving his cigar, Gus led the way out to the hall and down the corridor to the waiting room. "I thought I told you guys everything there was to tell," Gus grumbled, but Buddy detected the familiar note of authority which being a witness to a crime often conferred.

"I'm not from Kingsburgh," Buddy explained. "I'm from Stanwich, where the Langes live."

"Oh," said Gus, shaking his head. "That was something. Well, what do you want to know?"

Now that Buddy had the man's attention, he was not precisely sure what he wanted from him. He could not fully accept the idea that Rambo's death was a suicide for two reasons. One was his gut reaction, which simply made him uneasy. The other, more specific reason was his own observation that Albert Rambo had dyed his hair on the day of his suicide. Despite all the other evidence of suicide, Buddy was plagued by that fact. He could not understand why any man, even a crazy man like Rambo, would dye his hair just before taking his own life, and then carefully save the remaining dye in his suitcase. It didn't make sense and it was making Buddy lose sleep. He was supposed to be on his way, right now, up to Mark's college, but he had kept his family waiting while he decided to make another stab at the motel owner's memory.

"I'm trying to find out if by chance Rambo had any other visitors, if anything suspicious happened while he was staying at your place."

"Nope," said Gus. "The only one was the Lange woman. That I know of."

"Did you see any automobiles you didn't recognize in the area or anything like that?"

"Hey, mister," said Gus, "it's a motel. There's always cars there I don't know."

"What about when you went through the room?" Buddy persisted.

"Nothing," said Gus. "Anyhow, the police made a list of everything he left in that room. They kept all his stuff. They'll probably let you look at it."

"I've looked at it," said Buddy with a sigh.

"Well." Gus shrugged. "I wish I could help you."

"I know," said Buddy, "I know. Look, I've got to go away for a few days, take my son up to college, but I'll give you this card. It has my name and my number at the police station in Stanwich." Buddy had reached into his wallet and extracted a card, which Gus took and studied. Then Gus slipped it into his pocket.

"If you think of anything, even if it seems stupid or unimportant, would you just give me a call?"

"Sure, I'll call you," said Gus, "although I don't know why you'd care about this guy after what he done to that kid. I say good riddance."

"I guess I've just been following him for so long I can't quite give up on it so easily." Buddy grimaced and then walked away.

CHAPTER 14

A half-eaten tuna fish sandwich lay on the plate with a couple of potato chips beside it. Anna picked up the plate and put it on the counter beside the sink. At first, when they got home from the doctor's, Paul had said he wasn't hungry, but when she put the sandwich in front of him, he had managed to eat some of it. Then he had gone upstairs to rest.

I'm going to fatten you up, Anna thought. That's my next project now that I know you're all right. All right. She felt a thrill of happiness at the doctor's verdict, which had finally begun to register. He was going to be fine. Her strong, healthy son. And now that Rambo was dead, there was nothing more to fear from that quarter. For a moment Anna rested against the sink, counting her blessings. Her son was safe. She could stop worrying, despite what Thomas had said. Stop worrying and concentrate on putting her life back together.

A faint sound from the front of the house drew her attention. Tiptoeing through the dining and living room, she walked to the foot of the stairs and put her hand on the banister. She strained her ears to listen for him, but all was silent from the rooms above. He's all right, she repeated to herself. He's going to be fine. For a moment she wondered how Thomas would feel if he knew. She felt a sudden weakness, a need to share the news with him.

She stopped by the phone in the foyer, her hand hovering above the receiver. It would be a way to open up communication with him and to let him know that she still wanted to share her life with him. Then she remembered what he had said about Paul: that he was a stranger.

Shaking her head, Anna turned away from the phone and walked resolutely to the kitchen. She went over to the sink and with a fork began to scrape the sandwich and prod it through the garbage disposal, followed by the chips. She didn't really like using the garbage disposal. She hated the idea of those teeth inside her sink, so powerful that they could twist a piece of silverware like a coil of clay. But Tom had insisted on it when they had the kitchen redone a few years back, to make life easier for her. She sighed and shoved the last of the food through the rubber sleeve into the disposal. Then she turned on the water and flipped the switch.

The disposal went to work, its harsh din making Anna flinch, as it always did. She had seen forks tied into knots by that thing. She hated to think what it could do to human fingers. She noticed that a corner of bread was still in the sink. Gingerly she pushed it toward the opening of the disposal, ready to jerk her hand back as soon as it disappeared. Suddenly she felt a hand clap down on her shoulder, pushing her forward. She cried out, bracing herself against the sink.

Edward Stewart drew back his hand apologetically and tried to shout her name above the racket. Regaining her balance, Anna leaned over and turned off the switch with a trembling hand.

"Edward!" Anna exclaimed, placing a hand on her chest as if to calm her heartbeat. "I didn't hear you come in."

"The front door was open."

"Oh," she said, exhaling a deep breath. "I was daydreaming. Here, sit down, sit down." She cleared a pile of clean, folded dishtowels off one of her kitchen chairs and glanced at her guest, who was wearing a business suit. Seeing him sitting there in her kitchen unnerved her somewhat. It was the first time in their years as neighbors that Edward had come calling on his own.

"Aren't you working today?" she asked.

"There was very little that needed my attention, so I came home."

Anna nodded, although she knew very well that Edward was a driven man, who spent as much time as possible at the office. She and Tom sometimes wondered when he and Iris ever saw each other.

"Anna," he said, "I came by to make sure that everything here was all right. I read the ghastly news in the paper this morning about that man's hanging himself and you finding his body."

So that was it, Anna thought, both surprised and touched by his concern. Even the unflappable Edward had been shocked by this latest turn of events. Perhaps he was human after all. "It has been harrowing," she admitted. "It was so nice of you to come by."

"I . . . we had no idea you had been contacted by that monster," Edward said. "Whatever did he want?"

Anna rubbed her eyes with her hands. "Oh . . . this whole thing. He came up to me in the parking lot at the shopping center. Sunday, I guess it was."

"Sunday," Edward murmured, mentally calculating, "the day of our party."

"He said that he had something to tell me about Paul, that Paul was in some kind of danger. And he wanted money for the information."

"Good Lord," Edward said.

"I know," said Anna. "Are you sure I can't get you anything? A beer or a soda or something?"

"No, nothing," said Edward quickly. "Was that all he told you?"

"I begged him to tell me more, but he wouldn't."

Edward felt like laughing with relief, but he kept his expression grave. "But why did you go? Why didn't you just call the police?"

"Well, to be honest, I had had my own suspicions that there was something wrong."

Edward jerked forward in his chair. "I don't understand," he said.

"About Paul. He hasn't been . . . well, he's been ill, as you know. That incident at your house was not the only time. He's had these blinding headaches, nightmares. Ever since he got . . . home."

"How terrible. But then the man was dead when you got there. He wasn't able to tell you any more."

"No," Anna admitted. "It was quite a shock. But I took Paul to the doctor this morning, and Dr. Derwent did a number of tests on him. He hasn't got all the results yet, but the doctor seemed to feel Paul is all right, that there is nothing serious to worry about."

"You must be relieved."

"I am," said Anna. "I am. It's a great relief."

"Well," said Edward, "it's probably best to just get life back to normal." He stood up from his chair. Please tell the boy that I stopped by to see about him."

"I will," Anna assured him. She found his interest in Paul peculiar, but rather endearing, as if she were seeing a side of him that she had never known existed. She had always assumed that the Stewarts were childless by choice. Edward's choice. Now, for a moment, she wondered about it.

"And remember," he said, "if you ever need anything, you can call on us. Iris and I are always—"

A wretched cry cut through their conversation. Anna lunged for the staircase. "It's Paul," she cried.

"What's wrong?" Edward asked.

Anna was already taking the stairs two at a time. Edward followed her up the steps, his breathing heavy.

Anna ran down the hall and threw open the door to her son's room. Paul lay, fully clothed, on top of the bedspread, whimpering and letting out intermittent moans. Anna sat down on the bed beside him and took one of his clammy hands in hers. With her free hand she pushed the damp hair back off his forehead. The boy's eyes were open but glassy and unseeing. Anna began to murmur to him.

Edward tiptoed up behind her. "Is he awake?" he asked in a whisper. Paul's whole head swiveled toward the sound of Edward's voice as if he were blind.

"What was it?" Anna murmured. "Was it a dream?"

Paul's vacant eyes rested on Edward's face for a moment. Then, all at once, he began to howl like an animal in a trap. He struggled to free himself from Anna's hands, crawling away from her over the bed. "Help me," he cried. "Help." The word was barely recognizable, croaked out in a frantic voice.

"It's all right," Anna said soothingly. "It's all right."

The boy scrambled back and grabbed the bedpost, his dazed eyes locked to Edward's face as he cried out, "Help me, don't leave me."

"Paul," Anna cried, grabbing his wrists and shaking him, "wake up now. Stop it." Intent on her son, Anna did not notice her visitor standing behind her. Like a man facing a rattler, Edward began to inch backward, his eyes trained on the dangerous beast in front of him.

"Please, Paul," Anna pleaded.

The boy's head rolled back, and he went limp in her grip. He seemed to awaken. He blinked at Anna and then relaxed against the headboard. "What's going on?" he said. She released her hold on his wrists.

"You had a dream . . . again."

"Oh," groaned Paul. He crawled slowly off the bed. "Oh. Oh, yeah," he said. "I remember."

"What do you dream of that scares you so?" Anna asked.

Paul walked over to the bureau and looked in the mirror. He began to flatten his unruly hair down with his hands, and then he pressed his palms to his forehead, his face screwed into a grimace. "It's always the same."

"Can you remember it?"

"I remember a part of it. I know I'm lying on the ground. And there's this big black mass coming toward me, and there's a big golden bird flying over me, swooping down on me. It's got its claws out like it's hunting."

"Is that it?" asked Anna.

"No. There's something else. A man coming toward me. Leaning over me. Sometimes I think this really happened!" he exclaimed, surprised at his own words.

"What's the man doing?"

"I don't know. But he's going to hurt me. I know that. And I can almost see his face, but not quite."

Paul shivered and then shook his head. "Every time I get to sleep . . ."

"It must be something troubling," Anna observed, "if it keeps waking you up like that. You really gave us a scare," said Anna.

The boy looked at her. "Who's us?"

"Mr. Stewart and I . . ." said Anna, turning around. She stopped, seeing that Edward was no longer in the room. "I guess he left. He probably saw how upset you were and didn't want to intrude. He seems very concerned about you, Paul."

"Yeah." The boy nodded. In the hallway Edward could hear their voices perfectly, but he could not move. His arms felt stuck to his sides with sweat, and his heart was hammering within his chest, so hard that he was having trouble breathing. He felt the need to urinate and a twisting in his stomach that made him feel faint.

He wondered, as he listened to Anna soothe the boy, why he had not realized it before. He had been so preoccupied with Rambo that he had not really considered the boy. But just because the child had not remembered him yet did not mean that he never would. And if the memory surfaced and he blurted it out . . . Edward felt a tightening in his chest at the thought. Anna was a fanatic on the subject of that child. Everyone in town knew it. If he were to be accused by that urchin, she would never let it rest. She would pursue it to the bitter end and see him ruined before she was satisfied.

It was the kind of story that the newspapers would delight in. An important man like him, brought low by a child's accusation. There would be no end to it. All those who were jealous of him would laugh and gloat to see him cut down. It all was so clear now. Getting rid of Rambo was not protection enough.

Edward was almost swooning from the need to get some air, to sit down, to get out of there. He could not let anyone see him in this condition. Forcing one foot ahead of the other, he started quietly down the stairs. It was lucky, he thought, that he had been here and heard what he had. It had finally brought him to his senses, and none too soon.

As he descended the staircase with the lightest possible tread, he admitted that he had always known it, deep down inside. Ever since he had learned that the boy was coming back, he knew that he would have to silence him. At least that was now clear to him. He had no other choice.

* * *

A steady stream of people flowed by Thomas, who leaned against the wall in the skyscraper's lobby. Girls from word processing with magenta lips and high heels clacking laughed and chattered on their way to the subway. Sober, colorless men and a few women in business suits with briefcases, as well as the forest-green-liveried building staff, passed by without looking at him.

Thomas held his cell phone in his hand, tapping it against his thigh. He knew he would have to make up his mind soon. Gail would come along, and once he was with her, he probably wouldn't call. By the time he got back to her apartment it would be too late.

He wished that he had not agreed to stay there again. It was obvious to him when he woke up that morning that his accepting her invitation implied something he didn't really feel. After tonight he was going to have to get a hotel room.

He didn't feel that Gail was trying to pressure him, one of her most appealing qualities to him. Still, he knew that she would not be pleased about his calling Anna.

He just wanted to talk to her. That was all. He wanted to find out how Paul had made out at the doctor's. And how Tracy was doing. He had left without even saying good-bye to her. Just those things, Thomas told himself, and I'll hang up. He set down his briefcase and punched in the number.

He turned and gazed out the lobby doors to the busy street while he waited for the number to connect. Maybe Anna wouldn't even speak to him. It was possible. Thomas felt his stomach do a sickening flip-flop at the thought. He had never been able to stand it when Anna was angry at him. Part of the reason he had fallen in love with her was that she had such an even temper, and it was easy to make her laugh. On those rare occasions when she got angry, it turned him into a child again, helpless in the face of his mother's constant rages. If she tried to stonewall him, he would just insist that she let him speak to Tracy. You have a right to know about the children, he reminded himself. They're your children.

The phone rang a few times, and he felt a queer, sick feeling all through him. He found himself half hoping that she wouldn't answer and then, as it rang again, panicked at the thought that he wouldn't be able to reach her.

"Hello."

Thomas started and thought of hanging up. He cleared his throat.

"Anna?"

"Oh," she said faintly. "Hi."

Her voice sounded guarded but not angry. Thomas took a deep breath and continued. "Am I taking you away from something?"

"Not really," she said. "I'm cleaning some vegetables."

He could imagine her there in the kitchen, looking over the windowsill into the backyard.

"What do you want?" she asked in a flat voice.

"Well, I . . . I've been wondering all day. Did you take Paul to the doctor's this morning?"

"Paul?" Thomas could hear the mistrust in her voice. "Yes, I took him."

"I was just curious. What did he say?"

"He said . . . I took him to Dr. Derwent, and he seemed to think that Paul is okay. He's going for some tests tomorrow, but he said there's not a tumor or anything."

"That was good news." He was surprised at the genuine relief he felt at her words.

Anna hesitated. "Yes, it is good news, but then this afternoon he had another bad dream. Woke up screaming and in a sweat. Well," she said coolly, "I'm sure that's not what you wanted to know."

He wanted to protest that he was interested, but the coldness in her voice daunted him. There was silence on the line for a few moments.

"How's Tracy?" he asked finally.

"She's all right. I explained to her that you and I had a disagreement, and she seemed to understand."

"Can I talk to her?"

"She's not here now. She went over to Mary Ellen's for dinner, and then she's going straight to the animal shelter."

"Oh, that's right," Thomas murmured. "She works tonight." He waited for her to ask how he was, and realized how unlike her it was not to question him. He could feel that the conversation was coming to an end.

"Anna," he blurted out, "I think we should talk."

She hesitated, and he winced at the silence. Then she answered carefully. "I think so, too."

Relief flooded him, and he felt like kissing the receiver. "Good," he said. "When?"

"I don't feel like discussing things on the phone," Anna said.

"No, not on the phone," he agreed hastily. "We should meet."

"All right," she said. He thought he heard relief in her voice also. "How about tonight? Could you catch a train into the city? I'll make reservations at that French place we like on the West Side."

"Tonight?"

"Yeah. We can have dinner there and talk. I think it's on Seventy-Fourth Street. Le Chevalier Blanc."

"I don't know about tonight," she said.

"Why not?" He withdrew, feeling wounded by her reluctance.

At her end Anna thought of Paul, who was listless after his day of tests and bad dreams. She did not like to leave him alone in the house. For a moment she was torn, but she realized that she could not use Paul as an excuse not to meet Tom. That would only drive them further apart than ever. She had to make the effort.

"All right," she said. "I'll meet you at that place. I can be there by seven thirty."

"Good," he said.

There was an awkward pause. "Good-bye," she said.

"Bye." He hung up and slipped the phone back into his briefcase. His underarms were wet, and he felt weak, but the nauseated feeling had been replaced by one of anxious excitement. As he stood gazing absently across the lobby he realized that Gail was at the newsstand inside the front door, handing over money for the newspaper. She turned and looked at him, and their eyes met. He tried to smile at her, but she gazed at him gravely for a moment. Her mouth was downturned, and there was an unfamiliar flush in her face.

His relief at the phone conversation was tinged by guilt. There was no easy way to tell her, he thought, that he was meeting his wife for dinner, the night after their affair had begun.

CHAPTER 15

"Hello, you two," said Anna, walking across the terrace to the edge of the pool where Iris and Edward were sitting. Iris's face lit up at the sight of her friend.

"Please sit down," Edward said, getting up.

"I can't stay," said Anna. "I've come to ask a favor."

"Of course," said Iris. "What is it?"

Edward urged the chair on her, and Anna sat down on the edge of the seat. "Tom called," she said, "and he wants me to meet him in the city for dinner."

"That sounds romantic," said Iris, picking up a towel and patting herself dry.

"Not really," said Anna with a grimace. "We had a pretty big fight last night."

"Did you make it up?" Iris asked.

Anna shifted in her chair. She was used to confiding in Iris, but she felt uncomfortable telling her marital problems in front of Edward, even though she assumed that Iris shared their confidences with her husband. "Well," she said, "he stayed in the city last night."

"Anna, no!" Iris exclaimed.

"So it's important," Anna went on hurriedly, "that I go. We have really got to work a few things out."

"Of course you do," Iris agreed. "How can I help, though?"

"It's Paul," said Anna. "I had him to the doctor today."

"Oh no," said Iris. "Is he all right?"

"He seems to be," said Anna. "But he's still edgy and suffering from the headaches. I'm worried about leaving him alone there."

Iris bit her lip and grimaced. "I'm supposed to leave for my health spa tonight. I guess I could put it off until tomorrow."

"No, don't do that," said Anna. "I just wondered if Lorraine or anyone was going to be here, in case he needed to call someone."

"Well, Edward will be home, I think," Iris ventured, looking uncertainly at her husband.

Edward sat up very straight in his chair. "What about your daughter?" he asked.

"She's at the animal shelter until around ten," Anna explained.

"Well, I should be home," said Edward. "Tell him to call me if he needs anything."

"Thanks so much," said Anna. "I'd hate to have to tell Tom I couldn't come on account of Paul. That would not go over too well."

Iris's eyes were sad and worried. "Anna, I hope things work out with you and Tom."

"Me too," said Anna sincerely. "When will you be back from the spa?"

"Sunday," said Iris, stretching out the bathing cap in her hand.

"Yogurt and massages, eh?" Anna said, teasing her.

Iris looked slightly pained. "It's not really like that."

"I'm only kidding you," Anna assured her. "I know they work you pretty hard at those places. I hope you'll enjoy it, though. Of course, we're all going to miss you," she said, turning to Edward for confirmation.

Edward gave her a tight smile of agreement.

"Well, I feel better," said Anna. "I'm going to go get ready." She bent over and gave Iris a pat on the shoulder. "Call me as soon as you get back," she said. She straightened up and smiled at Edward. "Thanks for everything. I'm sorry about this afternoon," she said. "He's been so jumpy and upset."

Iris looked questioningly at her husband. Edward avoided her gaze. "Think nothing of it," he said.

Anna smiled at both of them and then started off around the side of the house.

"Wait up," said Iris. "I'll walk around with you and go in through the solarium."

Edward's eyes flickered as he watched the two women go off together around the side of the house. The boy would be alone in the house tonight. It was more than he had hoped for, and it had fallen right into his lap. He had to act quickly and without any hesitation. Edward's eyelid began to twitch, but he ignored it as he began to formulate a plan for the night ahead.

* * *

Points of light danced across the cut surface of the topaz earrings as Anna twisted her head from side to side, studying her reflection in the mirror. The earrings were her favorites — a gift from Thomas. She had hesitated about wearing them tonight. In a way they seemed a poignant reminder of a happier time. But now that she had them on, they looked right. Be optimistic, she thought. Maybe there are better times ahead. She was about to turn away from the mirror when she remembered her perfume. He had chosen it for her. With all the deliberateness of a courtesan, she applied the scent to her pulse points. Then she straightened her navy silk pants suit and started toward the stairs.

She could hear the television in the den when she came down to the foyer. Following the sound, she went down the hall and into the den. Paul was curled up on the sofa, staring at the TV set.

"I'm going to go now, Paul," she said. "Are you sure you'll be all right?"

The boy nodded, his eyes trained on the television.

"Tracy should be back around ten," said Anna. "If you need anything, Mr. Stewart will be home tonight. Just give him a call. His number is by the phone."

The boy continued to stare at the flickering images in front of him. "Okay," he said absently. Then he turned to look at her. "You look nice," he said.

Anna's anxious face broke into a beaming smile at the unexpected compliment. "Thanks."

"It was because of me, wasn't it?" the boy said.

"What?" Anna asked, surprised.

"He left."

"No," said Anna quickly. "It was something between us."

Paul looked back at the TV set. "He hates me," he said simply.

Anna felt shocked for a moment. Then she picked up the remote and muted the sound on the set. She stood in front of the set, blocking the picture. "That's not true," she said. "He doesn't hate you."

Paul shook his head. "He wishes I never came back," he said offhandedly. "That's why he left." He stuck out his chin at her, defying her to disagree with him.

Anna looked at him blankly for a moment, remembering Thomas's angry words about Paul and not wanting to reveal her thoughts by her expression.

The boy nodded, as if satisfied.

"Wait a minute, Paul. Your father . . . you don't know what it was like for him. For all of us. All those years of worrying and wondering . . . after you disappeared. It was terrible," she said. "Agony. We never knew from one day to the next."

"Maybe he started thinking he was rid of me," said Paul casually.

"Rid of you?" Anna flared. "How could you think that of your father?"

Paul did not look at her. Anna shook her head. "I'm sorry. You don't really know him. He doesn't always say what he feels. But you . . . you meant the world to him. Why, when you were born . . . oh, he was in heaven," she said, seizing upon a memory that she was sure of. "You never saw anyone so happy."

"He's not happy now," said Paul.

"It's not that . . ." Anna protested. "I don't think he . . ." She stared unseeingly at the shelves of books above the sofa, trying to find the accurate description of her husband's feelings. The boy was silent, but there was a tension in his body as he waited for her to speak.

"You see, I always believed that you would come back to us. And he . . ." She groped for the right word. The fair word. "He couldn't."

Paul looked at her curiously.

"I remember," she said. "I don't recall when it was exactly. He began to think . . . he would say to me that I should try to prepare myself for the worst. But I always said that I thought you would come back. He couldn't understand how I was so sure of that." Anna shook her head, her eyes far away. "One day we argued about your room. He wanted me to clean out your room, and I wouldn't. He said it was unnatural to leave it the way it was and we could use the space." Anna bit the inside of her mouth and was silent, for a moment, her eyes darkening at the recollection.

"God, I was so furious at him. We hadn't really talked about you for a long time before that. But I guess I knew how he felt, although we never discussed it. Until this one day — it was just after one of your birthdays — and he started in on how we should clean up the room. I wouldn't have any part of it. I hated him for it. I remember that very well. He went upstairs, and I could hear him rummaging around, throwing things in boxes, and I just sat there in the living room, as if I were made out of stone. He began bringing boxes down to the basement, and I could hear him taking things out to the garbage cans in the garage. And I was just sitting there, watching all this and thinking that I would never forgive him for it." She gazed over at Paul, who was watching her intently.

"He was working, not saying anything, and then he came down the stairs, carrying a box under one arm, and under the other he was holding this elephant. It was a fuzzy blue elephant, stuffed, that he had bought for you when you were born. He brought it right to the hospital for you. He couldn't even wait until you got home. So he came downstairs, carrying this thing. And he was crying," she said quietly. "Tears were just streaming down his face." Anna's eyes filled suddenly at the memory. "He didn't say anything to me, and I was too angry to care. I remember thinking, Serves you right. You don't deserve to have your son back."

Paul studied her face as she remembered that moment. There was an expression in her eyes like that of someone trying to make out a sign from far away. She shook her head sadly.

"So why did he leave now?" the boy asked softly.

Anna hesitated for a minute. Then she said, "I think he's afraid."

"Of what?"

Anna looked quizzically at the boy. "I'm not sure," she said. "I don't think he ever expected things to turn out right. He's afraid of having all this . . . hope."

Paul and Anna looked soberly at each other. Then Paul nodded.

"Well," she said, "I guess I'll go." She handed Paul the remote.

"Good luck," said Paul.

Anna wanted to lean over and clasp the boy in her arms, but his wary glance forestalled her. She settled for kissing him lightly on the hair. Then, with a wave and a crooked smile, she headed for the door.

* * *

"It's getting dark earlier and earlier," Iris said wistfully as she gazed out the library windows. "I hate to see the summer end."

Edward looked at his watch. "Isn't it about time you were going?" He picked up a letter opener and began to tap it impatiently on the surface of his desk.

"I just . . ." She faltered and then continued hastily. "I hope you'll be all right here while I'm gone."

Edward stifled the urge to laugh in her face. "I'll be fine," he said. "All you need to worry about is getting rid of some of that." He pointed the letter opener at Iris's stomach.

Iris sighed. "All right," she said. "What are you going to do tonight?"

"I'll probably work on my boats," he said.

"Okay, well, I guess I'll be going. I'll see you on Sunday."

Edward nodded indifferently. "Take your time."

"Don't forget about Paul," said Iris, turning back to him.

"What?" he said sharply.

"I told Anna he could call if he needed anything. Remember?"

"Oh, yes," he said. "I won't forget. Don't look so worried."

Iris hesitated as if she had more to say, but then she turned and left the library. Edward waited until he heard the slam of her car door and the sound of the car leaving the driveway. Then he looked out the library window toward the windmill. He could not see it from that window, but in his mind he visualized it. Tapping the letter opener on his palm, he went over all his tools in his mind, trying to decide which one to use. The idea was to use a tool that a burglar might have. He would break into the house, take care of the boy, and then mess the place up. Ransack it and take a few valuables, to make it look as if the boy had been killed in the course of a robbery. It was simple, and it made sense. These houses were isolated and clearly affluent. There was always the danger of burglary. A crowbar might be a good weapon, he thought, but it was large to carry. He didn't own a gun. He had thought of a chisel, but it did not seem part of a burglar's equipment. The best bet was probably a knife. In the windmill he had a set of large hunting knives he sometimes used. That would do, he decided. He could put it in a sheath under his jacket. It would be messy, but that was all right. He kept a change of clothes in the windmill anyway. He would just wait for a little while and then . . .

Lost in thought, he did not hear Lorraine enter the room and did not notice her until she appeared beside him like a dark ghost. He jumped a little as she said his name.

"What is it?" he demanded.

"You said you wouldn't be needing me . . . my brother is here to pick me up," the maid said.

"Fine," said Edward. "We'll see you next week then." He walked with her to the door after she had picked up her suitcase in the foyer. He waited in the gloom until the taillights of Lorraine's brother's car had disappeared. Sweat gathered under his arms as he stood there in the silent house. He was keenly aware of each passing minute. His blood was singing in his ears, but the rest of the house was tomblike. Without bothering to turn on a light, he walked back through the house, headed out the patio doors and into the night.

CHAPTER 16

Paul studied the *TV Guide* as the sounds of Anna's car faded away. Using the remote, he flipped the channels for a few minutes and then he turned the set off. There was nothing on that he wanted to watch. He wandered through the house to the living room, where he sank into a chair and picked up a magazine from the brass rack beside it. He thumbed the pages restlessly and then dropped it back in the rack and got up again.

Anna had made him some dinner before she left, but he still felt hungry. He went into the kitchen and opened the refrigerator. Help yourself, she always told him. And there certainly was plenty to eat. His mother's refrigerator had never looked like that, except for the freezer, which had stacks of frozen dinners in trays in turquoise boxes with pictures of the food on the front. Dorothy Lee always worked the three to eleven shift at the hospital; he'd heat one up and eat it quick so he could be done before his father came around. Paul looked down at the shelf and saw a piece of cream pie left in a pie pan. He could have eaten the whole thing standing there, but he felt uncomfortable about it. After getting out a knife and plate, he cut off about a third of the piece, only an inch across the back, and ate that. It was gone in an instant, and he thought about taking more; but he closed the door instead.

After taking his plate and utensils to the sink, he washed and dried them and put them back in their places. He surveyed the kitchen and then hung up the towel, satisfied that no one would be able to tell that he had taken anything.

The house was quiet, still seemed strange to him, and for a moment he wished, more than anything, that he had someone to talk to. He thought of Sam and then sighed, and tried to dismiss the thought of his lost pet.

He walked idly from room to room, looking at the furniture, the plants, and the pictures. It was like something from a magazine, he thought, or that you saw on TV. Probably if anyone from Hawley had seen him in this house, they would have thought he was the luckiest person on earth, living in a place like that.

Paul wandered to the living room window and pulled back the drapes. He looked out into the darkness. Every day he thought about running away. Every single day. He could just pack his few things in his bag and go. Maybe if he got away from here, the headaches would stop. And no one would miss him. Well, the mother maybe.

He sighed, realizing that he wouldn't know where to run. And he had no money, so he couldn't get far. There was probably money in this house, but he didn't want to steal from them. As much as he hated to admit it to himself, he was afraid to run. Yet he cringed at the thought of staying. I don't belong here, he thought.

There was no answer in the darkening yard. He dropped the curtain and turned back into the room, to look for something to do.

* * *

Pressed against the window, the boy's pale face appeared to be melting against the pane. Edward's cold eyes focused on the mournful visage as he crouched below the porch, looking up at him. He had been making a circuit of the house, scouting the best point of entry when he saw the boy's face appear at the window. For a moment he thought the boy had heard him in the yard, but as he watched, trying to quiet his racing heartbeat, he could see that the boy was not searching the yard but simply staring, his thoughts far away.

Edward's knees ached as he crouched there, his pants cutting into his legs. The indignity of the position made him feel angry and impatient. He wished the kid would hurry up and get away from the window. He did not feel like hiding in the damp grass much longer. He wished to be done with it and safely back in his studio.

The curtain dropped, and Edward breathed more freely as he rose to his feet. He knew how he was going to get in. At knee level there was a set of windows that opened into the basement. He had seen them from the inside and knew that they were latched with only a simple sliding fastener. It would be easy enough to open one of them and slide inside the house. With the aid of his penlight he had seen a sturdy chair below one of them. That was the window he would choose. As he stole around the house to the window, he repeated his plan to himself. The basement adjoined a playroom. He would go through the door into the playroom and up the stairs into the house. Edward reached the window that he wanted and bent down beside it. He slipped his knife blade through the side of the frame and began to worry it around until he caught the hook. Carefully he jimmied it with the knife point. After a moment the fastening began to move.

* * *

Paul passed by the door to the playroom stairs and stopped, remembering that there was a CD player down there. The silence of the empty house oppressed him, and he thought that perhaps some music would help. He opened the door and started down the stairs. An unfamiliar noise reached him, and he stopped on the steps, listening. It was quiet. Hearing things, he thought. Baby.

He wondered, as he shuffled down the stairs, how the big reunion was going. That story she had told about the father's carrying down the elephant had made him feel prickly at the back of his neck. He thought that the elephant seemed familiar. Maybe the father wasn't so bad. The mother was nice, and she liked him.

There was no telling why people liked each other. He had never been able to figure out his parents . . . the Rambos. His father had always been weird and crazy, although Dorothy Lee never said anything bad about him. Still, it had been so humiliating in school and all. Paul had actually been relieved to find out that Albert wasn't his real father. For a minute Paul felt a wave of pity, followed quickly by revulsion, at the thought of his father's hanging himself all alone in that hotel room. What a way to end up.

Paul cocked his head to one side and read the titles on the edges of the CDs arranged in a plastic tower. Most of the good ones were Tracy's and they were up in her room. He didn't want to go up there. But there were a few good things in the playroom CD tower. Paul picked out a Beatles anthology and examined it. At home, or in her truck, his mother played country music. No one he knew in Hawley ever listened to much rock 'n' roll, but he had always secretly liked it. He'd heard of the Beatles and he knew they were an old group from the sixties that people still listened to. He'd heard a lot of their songs. Curious, he put the CD into the player and plugged in a headset, planning to lie back on the rug to listen. Just then he noticed, on the bookshelf above the CD tower, a pair of fat brown leather books with photos sticking out under the covers. He reached up curiously and pulled the top one down, still holding the headset in his hand as the lyrics of "Norwegian Wood" squawked. He opened the unwieldy book, and an envelope of snapshots fell out. The album was full of photographs neatly mounted and captioned. Crossing his legs Indian style, Paul opened the album on his knees and then settled the headset over his ears. Absorbed in the pictures, he did not see the door of the playroom across the room opening behind him a millimeter at a time.

The bright faces of the people in the pictures smiled, heedless of their images, which were fading with time. They were like people waving from the deck of a ship that was disappearing out to sea. Paul turned the pages carefully, tapping his foot and gazing at the photographs. There were pictures of Thomas and Anna toasting at their wedding and shy, smiling pictures of them, tanned shoulders touching, on a honeymoon in Bermuda. She was always smiling out at the camera, while Thomas kept his gaze on her face.

On the next page a baby appeared, and Paul realized, with a start, that it was himself. He traced the outline of the strange baby's head, which the infant struggled to lift from a blanket. There were pictures of him in every imaginable pose, one or the other of his parents holding him, in and around a house which was not this one. He laughed out loud at a picture captioned *PAUL'S 2ND BIRTHDAY*, in which he, a toddler now, was perched behind a lit cake, sporting, at an angle, a shiny, pointed foil hat. An older, dark-haired boy behind him was blowing a noisemaker right into his eager, squinting face. The music drummed in his ears as the Beatles sang about seeing a face they couldn't forget.

A shadow fell like a scythe's blow over the page, darkening the cheery faces in one swipe. Paul's head jerked up as he felt the presence behind him. He yanked off the headset and twisted around to stare at the figure that loomed above him. For a moment he looked up, bewildered. Then he spoke.

"What are you doing here?" he said.

Tracy cocked her head and glanced at the book he was holding. "I brought you something," she said.

Paul looked at her in confusion as she shrugged her backpack off her shoulders and carefully opened it. She reached in and pulled out the struggling, crying gray-and-black-striped cat.

"Sam!" Paul exclaimed. "Where'd you get him?" He lifted the animal from her grasp and crushed it to his chest. The cat protested angrily and leaped away from him.

"He turned up tonight at the animal shelter," Tracy announced with a satisfied smile. "They let me come home early, to bring him."

Paul's gaze lingered on the cat, which had jumped up on the sofa. "Thanks," he said softly.

"That's okay." Tracy flopped down on the daybed. "You looking at those old pictures?"

Paul nodded.

Behind them the door to the playroom began to close, imperceptibly slowly.

* * *

"Would you like to walk a little?" asked Thomas, as they left the restaurant.

"Yes, why don't we?" Anna agreed.

"I could use a walk," said Tom. "The food there is so rich. The sauces and all."

Anna murmured agreement, although she had noticed during dinner that he hardly touched his meal.

They set off walking down Columbus Avenue, joining the meandering stream of pedestrians taking the night air on the West Side's most fashionable avenue. Although it was warm, it was not humid, and a few stars were visible in the city sky. The dinner conversation had been halting and Anna felt, as she faced him over the table, that she really understood the meaning of the word "estranged." Now, however, as they made their way side by side down the avenue, she felt more normal, their steps meshing neatly, turning automatically at the same corners, even though they had no stated destination. They both heeded the flashing don't walk signs, while the New Yorkers around them spilled contemptuously into the intersections.

Anna stole a glance at her husband's profile as they waited on one corner. He had ordinary, rather blunt features except for his eyes, which were clear and expressive. The expression in them now was one of anxiety and a trace of sadness. She felt an impulse to slip her arm through his, but she restrained herself.

"Shall we go over to Lincoln Center?" he asked. "It's only a few blocks down."

Anna nodded. "I'd like to see the fountain."

They walked along in awkward silence. "Is that a new tie?" Anna asked him.

Thomas reached up and fingered the knot at his throat. "Yes." He cupped her elbow. "Our light," he said.

Anna noticed a slightly guilty expression on his face as he propelled her across the street.

"I didn't pack too well," he said when they reached the opposite curb. "I've got to go to Boston tomorrow on the ten o'clock shuttle, and I don't have the clothes I needed for the trip."

"Are you going for long?" she asked coolly.

"Just overnight."

She stifled the impulse to say that he should have asked her to bring what he needed. He left you, she reminded herself. Walked out, remember? But she could not muster her anger against him. He seemed vulnerable to her. His hand burned on her arm. "Where are you staying?" she asked.

"In Boston, you mean?"

"No, here."

Thomas squirmed visibly at the question. "On the East Side. Not far from work."

They crossed the street and climbed the steps to the plaza in front of Lincoln Center. Anna caught her breath as she always did at the sight. The murals in the opera house were a giddy burst of color, the chandeliers sparkling through the huge panels of glass. In the center of the plaza ringed by theaters, a round fountain gave off sprays of water and light. Thomas and Anna walked slowly toward the gushing fountain.

Thomas gave Anna a tight, pained smile and offered her a seat on the fountain's edge.

"Thanks," she said.

Another silence fell between them, and Anna had the sense that their time was running out without their having made any progress. She cast about in her mind for some way of reaching him without starting a fight.

Suddenly Tom spoke. "I was really relieved to hear about Paul today," he said.

Anna looked at him in surprise. It was the first mention of the boy between them that evening. She thought of just agreeing with him but decided to plunge in instead. "We talked about you before I came down tonight."

"You and Paul?" he asked.

"Yes. He thinks you hate him."

Thomas closed his eyes, and Anna could see the pain in the grim lines around his mouth. He swallowed hard, as if trying to ingest some bitter tonic.

"I told him that wasn't true," she said.

Thomas looked at her in surprise. "You did?"

Anna nodded. "I was trying to explain to him. I was telling him about you. About when he was born and how you adored him. Things like that."

Thomas stared out across the plaza, as music lovers hurried toward the theaters. His gaze was pained. "How could I hate him?" he said. "Poor kid." He was quiet for a long time. Anna watched him helplessly, wishing he would look at her. Finally he spoke. "I think I hate myself," he said.

"Tom," she protested, "don't say that."

He shook his head. "You don't know how I feel," he said. "It's different for you."

"What's different?"

"Oh, you. You were always so sure he'd come back. Always believing he was still alive. Hopeful. Even the tiniest thing would make you hopeful." He turned and looked at her for the first time.

"I never was hopeful, Anna. I never expected to see that boy again."

"But you had no way of knowing. Nobody did."

"I gave up on him, Anna. My own son." Thomas sighed and bent forward at the waist. He looked away from his wife and held himself around the middle, as if he were going to be sick. "When I see him, I feel so . . . I don't know. I feel so guilty—"

"Guilty! Tom!" Anna exclaimed. "You have no reason to feel guilty."

"I did love him," he said. "It's not as if I didn't."

"I know that," she said. "He knows it, too. I'm sure he does. Or he will. It will just take a little time."

"I hated the way you were always looking for some good sign, finding reasons to hope," he said.

"I just had to," she said.

"Sometimes," he said, "I wanted to scream at you because of it. But how could I? You were the noble one, the one who refused to give up."

She groped for the words to try to explain it to him. "I didn't do it to be noble," she said. "I often thought it was a delusion. But I had to cling to it. I couldn't have gone on living without hope."

Thomas reached over and put his hand on hers. They sat quietly at the fountain's edge. The meshing of their fingers was like a circuit completed. The consolation, the connection in their touch made Anna feel a sudden, fierce desire for him — her husband, her man. She closed her eyes and felt the heat throughout her body. She imagined turning to him, burying her face in the curve of his neck, feeling his hands on her again. She was trying to think of a way to say, "Come home." And then she realized that "Come home" was all she needed to say. She did not think she could speak aloud. She decided she could manage to say it in a whisper.

Suddenly Thomas released her hand. "That's not all I have to feel guilty about," he said quietly.

The portentous note in his voice was an icy bath over her. She sat up straight and stared at him. "What does that mean?"

A pair of lovers who were sitting at the other side of the fountain got up and, arms around each other, began to stroll across the plaza. Thomas watched them walking away.

"Tom?"

"I don't know how to tell you this. But I have to. I don't want this secret between us. I'd always be afraid you might accidentally find out." He licked his lips nervously. "I've been . . . with another woman," he said.

Anna rocked back on the granite ledge as if he had struck her a blow in the face. In all her concerns for him and for the children, the possibility that he had someone else had never even crossed her mind.

"I don't know why I did it," he was saying. "I was feeling lonely and angry at you. I couldn't talk to you. These are some pretty . . . miserable excuses, I know."

"Who is it?" said Anna.

"It doesn't matter," said Thomas. "You don't know her."

"I see," said Anna. The young couple had traversed about half the plaza when suddenly the man stepped back and slid his arm around the girl's waist as he lifted her hand in the air. The girl looked momentarily startled, and then she laughed. The two began to waltz across the plaza, to music of their own devising.

"So that's why you left us?" said Anna, placing her pocketbook under her arm and sliding off the edge of the fountain to her feet.

Thomas, who had been rubbing his eyes with his hand, looked at her in surprise. Anna was staring at him coldly, a pulse beating visibly in her neck. "No," he said. "Of course not."

"Fine," she said. "I understand now."

"Wait a minute," Tom protested. "What are you doing?"

"I'm going home," she spat out at him. "To my children."

Tom stepped in front of her and blocked her way, trying to get into her line of sight. "Anna," he said, "you don't understand. It happened. Yes. But I don't intend to continue it. I just felt I had to be honest with you. I'm telling you it was a one-night thing. A mistake. I never meant . . . I want to come home, to you and the kids."

Anna brushed by him angrily. "I don't want to talk about it," she muttered. She dodged his open arms and started walking quickly across the plaza, passing the dancing lovers, who did not look at her. Anna descended the steps and held up her arm for a taxi. Through the blur of tears she saw the lighted sign of an empty cab getting closer to her.

Thomas approached her side. "I don't blame you for being angry. But don't I get another chance?" he asked softly. "After all these years? I was feeling sorry for myself and I acted like a fool. My feelings for you may have wavered for a night, but they didn't change. Can't you forgive me?"

Anna glared at him but he stuck out his chin stubbornly.

"I wanted to be honest with you," he said. "I thought you would be able to forgive me," he said.

Anna closed her eyes briefly, and then she looked at him. "I can't take any more right now," she said.

"We have to talk, Anna. I have to go to Boston tomorrow. I'm not going to be able to think straight for worrying about this."

"I can't help that," she said. "I have to do some thinking myself." She got into the cab and slammed the door behind her. As the taxi pulled away from the curb, he reached out forlornly, as if to hold on to it, and then the cab disappeared from sight in the tangle of traffic and people.

CHAPTER 17

With anxious, stealthy movements Edward pulled the cellar window closed and crept across the lawn toward his own property, silently cursing the starlight. The sudden blaring of music from inside the house startled him. He stopped for a moment, perspiring profusely, and waited. Then he continued on, his hand wound around the handle of the knife under his shirt.

It had crossed his mind, as he hid behind the doorway, prepared to strike, that he could try to kill them both. He considered it and then decided against it. It was too messy, too dangerous. Still, the rage he had felt when he saw the girl come in with the cat had almost been enough to propel him through the door and into a frenzied attack on the two of them. Everything had been perfectly calculated, and then the stupid girl had ruined it.

Despite his show of restraint, Edward still felt the anger churning inside him at the way his plans had been thwarted. He had been ready. Ready to finish this business. Now he was left with his anger, his frustration. Edward made a wide circle around the back of his house as he headed for the windmill. He could see the blades jutting up black against the night sky, beckoning him. There was still time. He would find a way to do it tomorrow. He tried to keep his mind on that as he skulked along.

Edward reached the door of the windmill and pulled it open. He had imagined himself all day, coming back here, hiding his weapon, and changing his clothes, his business done. If only, he thought, it had been done. If only he had gotten it over with.

Stepping into the cool confines of the windmill, Edward pulled the knife from under his shirt and threw it onto a workbench, where it landed with a clatter. Then he turned back to close the door behind him.

"Edward."

Edward whirled around, slamming the windmill door shut, his face drained of color. Standing in the shadows beneath the loft, kneading her hands together and smiling tremulously at him, was Iris.

"Iris, what are you doing here?" he demanded in a shout. His whole body was shaking, his eyes bulging at the sight of her.

"I'm . . . I'm sorry," said Iris, recoiling at his outburst. "I didn't mean to startle you."

Edward stared at her, his mind racing. The thought that he might have walked into the windmill covered with blood and been surprised by her filled him with a terror that left him speechless. It didn't happen, he reminded himself. She didn't see anything. He tried to calm his pounding heart with that thought, but he was still unable to speak, his eyes glued to her puzzled face.

"I thought you'd be here when I got back. Then, when you weren't, I just waited."

Edward shook his head as if he didn't understand, not trusting his voice.

"Where were you?" she asked. "Why did you have that knife?"

His natural impulse was to scream at her, to drive her from the windmill with a shaking fist. But he knew instinctively that she would only wonder more about what he had been doing.

"Whatever were you doing out there with a knife?" Iris asked. "Did you hear something outside?"

Edward looked at her with a sudden sense of relief. That was it. She had provided his excuse. "Yes," he said. "I thought I did. I thought I heard a prowler. So I picked up this knife and went out to look. That's . . . that's why it startled me so to find you here. For a second I thought that whoever it was had sneaked in here." Sweat was dripping from his forehead now, but he knew that he was safe. She was looking at him with anxious, sympathetic eyes.

"Did you see anyone out there?" Iris asked.

"No, no," said Edward finally, collapsing against the counter. "Nothing. It must just have been the wind. Or my imagination."

"I don't know, Edward. Maybe we should call the police."

"That's hardly necessary," he said. "I'm sure it was nothing."

Iris had another thought. "Paul!" she exclaimed. "He's all alone over there."

"I told you. There was no one outside."

"Perhaps we should call and check."

"Iris," Edward demanded, "What are you doing here? I thought you went to the spa."

It was Iris's turn to look first surprised and then uneasy. "Well, I was on my way," she said. "And then I came back. I'd been wanting to talk to you, and I thought I'd come back."

"Why didn't you just phone me?" he asked, as if it were the obvious solution that only the simpleminded would overlook.

Iris bit her lip nervously. "I thought we should talk in person. Edward, I've been thinking a lot lately about us . . . about our marriage."

Edward tried to stifle the disgust that rose in him at her words. She wants to talk about our marriage now. It was almost laughable. He knew right away what had caused this crisis. Anna was having problems with her marriage, so naturally Iris had to jump on the bandwagon. Monkey see, monkey do. He assumed a long-suffering expression and stared at her. "Iris, what are you talking about?"

"This is so hard to say," Iris continued, looking pained and almost fearful as she spoke. "I don't think I am really making you happy anymore. If I ever did. You deserve a wife who can be the way you want her to be."

Edward could scarcely believe his ears. The incongruity of her earnest confession made him feel almost amused, but he kept his expression grave. The trembling in his body had subsided by now, and he could barely concentrate on her words for the relief he felt for his narrow escape. All he wanted to do was to get rid of her, propel her back onto the road toward her spa, and sit down to plan his next move.

"Iris," he said, "is this really the time and the place to discuss this? Can't it wait until you get back?"

"I suppose it could," said Iris miserably. "I'm just . . ."

"I'm tired," said Edward. "I was looking forward to a peaceful evening, working in the windmill."

"But I feel sometimes that you would be better off without me," Iris blurted out.

Edward looked at her with an expression of amazement, as one would at a display of exceptionally bad manners. "I haven't complained about our marriage," he said coolly. "Why must you bring this up now? Must I spend my life reassuring you that your position as my wife is secure? I think that shows a rather pitiable lack of self-confidence, Iris. I am satisfied with our marriage. I see no reason for you to doubt that."

Iris sighed, and her shoulders slumped. "I suppose you're right," she said.

"Why don't you get along now, so that you can arrive at the spa before it is too late? It's not a good idea to be driving late at night. Go ahead, and don't worry anymore about this. As far as I am concerned, everything between us is as it always has been."

Iris sighed again, and nodded, and walked toward the door of the windmill.

"Shall I accompany you to your car?" he asked.

"That's not necessary," said Iris.

"I think I had better," said Edward smoothly. "I'm still a little apprehensive, even though the noises turned out to be nothing. Watch your step in the dark," he called to her as he followed her out the door.

* * *

The soulful singing of Alicia Keys greeted Anna as she opened the door to the house and walked in. She saw Tracy's jacket draped on one of the dining room chairs. Home early, Anna thought. She had not seen any lights on upstairs as she came up to the house. She walked over to the door that led down to the playroom.

"I'm home," she called out.

"Hi . . ." The voices of both of her children floated back up the stairs. Anna raised her eyebrows in surprise and then smiled. She walked over to the refrigerator and opened the door. There was an open bottle of club soda on the shelf. She pulled out the bottle and poured herself a glass.

As she sipped it, she thought about her meeting with Tom. All the way home on the train she had gone over it again and again. He had slept with another woman. She wondered if there were signs she might have noticed, if she hadn't been so preoccupied with Paul. If she had been paying attention to him.

The worst part was the thought of him in bed, in someone else's arms. Probably someone who had no lines around her eyes or gray hairs. Someone whose body was trim and taut and very willing. It made Anna's face flame to think about it.

A warm swish, like a feather duster across her calves, made Anna jump and let out a little shriek. She looked down and saw Paul's cat, rubbing against her legs. Anna quickly bent over and picked him up.

"Sam!" she exclaimed. "Where'd you come from?" Anna went to the top of the stairs and thought of calling down. But the volume of the music discouraged her. She started down the stairs, carefully cradling the cat in her arms.

At the foot of the stairs she stopped, surprised by what she saw. Tracy and Paul were sprawled on the round braided rug, each studying a hand of cards.

"Ten," said the boy, laying down a jack.

"Twenty, for two," Tracy announced, savoring the move as she matched his jack with her own.

"Hey," said Anna, "look who I found." She held up the cat for their inspection.

Paul looked up and smiled with such unexpected sweetness that Anna drew in her breath. It was as if, for a moment, she had glimpsed her lost toddler again.

"Tracy brought him," said Paul. "He came back to the animal shelter."

Anna smiled into the cat's furry coat. "Welcome home, Sam."

"What did Daddy say?" Tracy asked, her gaze glued to her cards.

"Well." Anna hesitated. "He sends his love. To both of you," she added pointedly.

Paul lifted his arms for the cat, and Anna placed the animal into them. The boy began to stroke the fur.

"Come on," said Tracy. "Play."

Still holding the cat under his arm, Paul reached into his hand and put down another card. "Twenty-six," he said.

Tracy glanced from the card to her hand, her fingers hovering above the fan of cards.

Anna wrapped her arms around herself and watched their game. She wished that Thomas could see them at this moment. She dropped down on the daybed, to be closer to them. "All quiet around here?" she asked.

"Yeah," said Paul.

"So, what else did Daddy say?" Tracy asked, playing another card. "Is he coming home?"

"I don't know," said Anna. She laid her head back against the sofa and gazed out across the room. I wish I could say yes, she thought. "I hope so," she added, surprised to realize that it was true. She turned her head from side to side, trying to release the tension that had built up in the back of her neck. As she rolled her head around, she noticed that the door to the basement was not completely shut. With a sigh she got up and went over to close it.

"Who left this open?" she asked.

"I don't know," said Tracy. "That's six," she corrected Paul, pointing to his cards.

"Did you, Paul?"

The boy looked up. "Not me."

For a moment she hesitated, and then she pushed the door open farther and walked slowly into the dark cellar. Skirting the boxes and old pieces of furniture, she walked over and pulled the light chain in the center of the space. Despite the bulb's illumination, the corners remained gloomy, while the rest of the basement's jumble of contents was illuminated. Maybe I didn't shut that door tightly, Anna thought. She glanced around at the once useful junk that was stored in the damp cellar. I've got to clean this out one day, she thought wearily. She reached up to pull the light bulb chain again, and as she did so, her gaze rested on the window.

One of the cafe-length curtains which she had made to cover the low windows was caught, partially trapped between the closed window and the frame. The twisted material ballooned out awkwardly. Anna walked over and touched the curtain. Then her fingers traveled to the latch, which was unfastened.

Anna felt her heart thud as she stared from the open latch to the snagged curtain. In a sharp voice she called out, "Who opened this basement window?"

"Can't hear you," Tracy called back over the sound of the music on the CD player.

Anna backed away from the window, her eyes focused on the captive curtain. Halfway across the basement she turned and hurried toward the light of the playroom.

Paul looked up, holding a card poised to drop between his fingers. "What's the matter?" he asked. Tracy, who was hunched over one bent, upright knee, turned and looked at her mother.

Anna stood stiffly in the doorway, staring at her children. "Did either of you open the cellar window?"

The two shook their heads in unison. "Why?" Tracy asked.

"Did you hear anyone outside there?" Anna asked. "Either of you?"

"No," said Tracy impatiently.

Paul frowned for a moment and then shrugged his shoulders.

"Paul?" Anna asked.

Anna stared at him, trying to remember when she had last checked that window, knowing that she had locked it when Paul came home and not opened it since.

"Maybe Daddy opened it," Tracy offered.

Anna looked at her daughter and considered the suggestion. "Maybe," she said. Anna nodded, wanting to reassure them, to convince them they were safe and had nothing to fear. As she watched them resume their card game, she knew that they really weren't fearful. They were young, and never thought in terms of what could happen.

She shivered, worrying over the open window. It was probably Tom. It probably was. But she felt vulnerable all the same. You could not be too careful. Not where your children were concerned. That is one thing, she thought, I know for sure.

* * *

Iris tapped tentatively on the door with the closed sign visible behind the panes. In a few minutes she heard movement, and then the door was thrown open by a woman with short brown hair, wearing blue jeans covered with gray dust. Long silver earrings with turquoise stones dangled below her curly hair. The woman's dark eyes softened when she saw Iris, and she smiled to reveal a gap between her front teeth.

"Are you working?" Iris asked timidly.

"Just firing a few pots. Come in." The woman stepped back, and Iris entered the studio. Coils of clay and chalky looking pots occupied the countertops. A potter's wheel sat in the center of the room, while two black kilns took up most of the back wall. The room seemed to have been dusted with a soft gray powder.

"Where are your suitcases?" the woman asked.

"I put them in the bedroom in the house," said Iris, turning to face her. "I'm sorry I'm late, Angelica."

The woman put her strong, clay-caked hands on Iris's shoulders. "I wasn't worried about you. Yet." She drew Iris close to her, and the two women kissed each other gently on the mouth. Iris sighed and pulled herself away from the lingering embrace. Angelica released her and walked over to a little stove and sink on the side of the studio. She poured a cupful of boiling water into a ceramic mug and handed the mug to Iris, who sat down on a stool and rested the mug on the counter.

"Herb tea," said Angelica. "Looks as if you need it." Iris sighed again, and Angelica cocked her head to one side and smiled at her. "What's the matter?"

Iris shrugged her shoulders like a dejected child.

"You didn't tell him, did you?" said Angelica.

Iris looked at the other woman beseechingly. "I tried to tell him. All day I wanted to tell him. But I couldn't find an opportunity. And then tonight I went back, after I had started out for here, and I told myself that that was it. That I was entitled to my happiness and that it was time to speak up and tell him. And I started to . . . but then I couldn't."

Angelica lit a cigarette and held it between her teeth as she shook the match out. Then she took a drag and removed it and had herself a sip of tea. "Maybe you don't want to tell him," she said. "Maybe you don't really want out of the marriage."

Iris looked up at the other woman with woeful eyes and shook her head slowly. "Oh, no," she said. "I am going to get out of it. I promise you that."

"Don't promise me," said Angelica archly. "I mean, don't do it for my sake. If you can't take the pressure and the scandal, well, I understand. I'll be your backstreet girl."

Iris reached out for Angelica's hand, and squeezed the dusty fingers between her own. "No," she said. "This is the first time in my whole life that I have ever really been happy. I feel as if I were asleep before I met you. Now I know what I was missing in life, and I want to live with you. I don't care what people say."

The other woman squinted at her and took another drag on her cigarette. "It's not going to be pleasant. He will make it miserable for you."

"He told me tonight he was satisfied with our marriage."

"Satisfied." Angelica snorted. "Honestly, Iris, I don't know how you have put up with him as long as you have. The way he treats you is inexcusable. I don't see why you should care how he feels about it."

"I can't help it," said Iris apologetically. "I feel guilty. I'm afraid I never really cared for him. I married him to please my father, and I haven't been much of a wife to him, you know. And the scandal of this is going to be awfully hard on him."

"You don't have to make a public declaration and do time in the stocks, you know," Angelica said. "Lots of people get divorced these days. The whole world doesn't have to know why."

Iris looked up at her friend with shining eyes. "I want the whole world to know," she said. "For the first time in my life I'm in love, and I feel like shouting it."

"You're so sweet, Iris," said Angelica kindly. "You're a bit naive, but that's something I love about you."

Iris blushed, and tears sprang to her eyes. She wiped them away quickly. "I will tell him," she said. "In a couple of days. Maybe I'll just call him and tell him I'm not coming home when Sunday comes around. I just don't want to spoil these next few days we have together," she said earnestly.

"All right," said Angelica. "Whatever you think will be easiest on you." She put out her cigarette and smiled. "I'd better check the kilns. Don't go away."

Iris shook her head and followed her raptly with her eyes. "I won't," she said.

* * *

As Gus deBlakey was rolling down the front blind of the La-Z Pines Motel, he saw a sight that made him grimace. A pair of the Methodists, husband and wife who were in town for the big Methodist convention, were striding up toward the office with that look on their faces that said, "The toilet's stopped up, and we're paying good money for this room." Gus looked at them reflectively. He recognized them all right. They were in Cabin 17. Well, it surely was the cleanest one in the place. It had been scrubbed down pretty well after that guy was found swinging in there.

Gus had an inkling now of what the problem was. Someone probably had told them about the guy's hanging himself in their cabin, and now they didn't want to stay there. He hoped, briefly, that the word didn't get around on Cabin 17, or he'd be stuck with one useless piece of real estate.

The door to the office opened with a jingle, and the middle-aged husband and wife came in.

"Evening, folks," said Gus, pasting on a smile. "What can I do you for?"

The husband, who had steel-rimmed glasses and hair the same color, cleared his throat. The wife just stood next to him, looking indignant.

"Well, sir," said the husband, "my wife and I are staying down there in one of your cabins."

"Seventeen," said the wife.

"That's right," said the husband. "We're members of the Methodist Church. Here for a convention." The man held up the Gideon Bible as if by way of explanation.

"It's a pleasure to have you folks," said Gus. "How do you like your room?"

"The room's just fine," said the man, "but we aren't too happy about this." The man wrapped both hands around the Bible and gave it a little shake.

Gus looked at it with a frown, wondering if the Methodists used another version of the Good Book in their religion. He didn't know too much about Methodists, although if they were anything like the Baptist conventioneers he'd had last year, they'd be complaining because they didn't have a minibar.

"Disgraceful," the woman stated, sniffing at the Bible.

"We put those in all the rooms," Gus started to explain. "It's an old custom. For the weary traveler."

"I know that, sir, and a fine custom it is. But this Bible in our room has been defaced."

"Defaced?" said Gus.

"My wife wanted to read a few passages this evening, and when she opened it up, this is what she found." The man opened the book and held it up for Gus to see. Gus swiveled around to have a look. The margins of the page he indicated were covered with scrawled handwriting lapping over onto the text. Gus could see at a glance that some of the words were of the obscene variety. He quickly lifted the Bible from the man's hands and put it behind the counter.

"I am so sorry about that, sir," he said, going into a drawer and bringing out another copy, which he offered the offended conventioneer. "You do get the occasional guest who has no respect for the Lord's Word. I'm terribly sorry."

The woman opened the new Bible and looked through it. "That's better," she announced.

"Will that be all?" Gus asked, worried that there might be more.

"That's fine," said the man, putting his hand on his wife's elbow. He turned to Gus as he reached the door. "I wouldn't keep that lying around here, you know. Some child could get his hands on it and have a terrible shock."

"I'll take care of it," Gus assured him. After the couple had gone, Gus took the Bible out from under the counter and began to examine it curiously. He leafed through the pages until he found the offending section and turned the book upside down and sideways to read what was written there.

It was that nut, he thought, deciphering the passages in Jeremiah that had been amended by Rambo's jerky handwriting. The writing did not make much sense; that figured, to Gus's way of thinking, and he soon gave up trying to figure out the gist of it. Gus was just about to stash the defaced book away under the desk when he noticed that in one corner of the page was written, quite clearly, the name Edward Stewart and, beneath it, a phone number.

Gus pondered it for a while, wondering if that name, or any of this crazy business, would be of any use to that detective who had come over to the hospital. The detective had wanted to know if Rambo had been in contact with anyone during his stay here. Could this Edward Stewart be some friend of Rambo's who might know something? Gus thought for a moment that it wasn't a good idea to get involved, but he didn't see himself as one of those kind of people you heard about in New York City who never bothered to call the police, even when they heard their neighbors screaming bloody murder. He fished in the pocket of his shirt and pulled out the card with the detective's name and number on it. It wouldn't hurt to give him a call, he thought.

Picking up the phone, he dialed the number of the Stanwich police station and waited. He looked up at the clock while it rang. A gruff male voice answered, identifying himself as Sergeant McDonough and announcing the Stanwich police station. Gus squinted down at the card in his hand and asked to speak to Detective Mario Ferraro.

"He's not here now," said the cop at the other end. "Can I help you?"

"Off duty, is he?" Gus asked, trying to sound knowledgeable. "When do you expect him?"

"Actually," said the policeman, "he went away for a couple of days. Who's calling, please?"

Then Gus remembered. The detective had said something about taking his son off to college. "When'll he be back then?" said Gus, unwilling to go into a whole long explanation with somebody else.

"A couple of days. He's due back in on Friday."

"I see," said Gus, looking down at the writing in the Bible. He would be curious to see what, if anything, the detective would make of it.

"Can anyone else help you?"

Gus shook his head. "No, I don't think so. I'll give him a call when he gets back. Friday, you say?"

"Want to leave a message?"

Gus hesitated. "No," he said at last. "It'll keep. I'll call when he gets back." He hung up the phone and put the Bible back under the counter. Then he picked up all his keys and switched off the light in the office, leaving the emergency number facing out on the door. He decided not to tell his wife about it. She'd tell him he should have minded his own business. But as he locked the door and went out toward his car, Gus felt a lot better for having done his duty as a citizen.

CHAPTER 18

The morning sun fell across Anna's shoulders as she crouched down in front of the clothes dryer, pulling out the warm laundry and folding it into a plastic basket. She heard Tracy's sneakered steps in the kitchen and called out to let her know where she was. Tracy appeared in the doorway and then came over to where Anna was working. She bent down and kissed her mother briefly on the cheek.

Anna felt a flutter of surprise and pleasure at the kiss, the first sign of affection from her daughter in what seemed weeks. She tied two socks together and affected a jaunty tone. "You're up early."

"Mary Ellen invited me to go sailing on their boat with her older brother and his girlfriend."

"That sounds like fun."

"Are you wearing perfume?" Tracy asked.

Anna stood up and put the laundry basket on top of the machine.

"Lipstick and everything," Tracy said. "Where are you going?"

Anna took a deep breath. "To the airport," she said.

"The airport?" Tracy cried.

"Your father is going to Boston on the shuttle this morning. I've decided to see his plane off."

"Oh," said Tracy, trying not to betray her happiness at this news.

"We have some things to talk about," said Anna. "Will you take these up to your room, darling?"

Tracy accepted the pile of folded clothes from her mother.

"I was thinking of asking Paul to go sailing with us," the girl announced offhandedly.

"That was a nice thought," Anna said "But I've got him scheduled at the hospital this afternoon. More tests. I'm going to take him with me to the airport and then we'll go to the hospital. We should be back from the airport before noon." She didn't want to tell Tracy about her renewed fears over the basement window.

"He gets to go see Daddy off, too?" the girl asked, a note of petulance in her voice.

"You can come, if you want," said Anna. "Although I don't know how your father and I are going to get a chance to talk with both of you there." Mother and daughter were silent for a moment.

"No," said the girl reluctantly, "I'm going sailing. Can you drop me at Mary Ellen's?"

"Sure," said Anna. "Wake Paul up for me, will you? We're going to have to leave before long."

"Okay," said Tracy. She glanced at the little stack of sweat socks and dungaree shorts on the washer. "Is that his stuff? I'll take it up."

Anna rubbed her daughter's back between her shoulder blades for a moment. Tracy pretended not to notice. Clutching the two piles of laundry, she headed off through the house.

Anna walked into the kitchen and sat down at the table by the phone. She had been up most of the night, but she did not feel tired. On the contrary, her entire system was racing, and she was anxious to get going.

After her discovery of the opened window she had carefully checked the house and then called the police. The officer she spoke to could barely conceal his impatience. He explained to her that they did not generally come out to investigate windows that had been opened. He advised her not to worry, and said that they would send someone only if she insisted. Anna had debated it and then decided to insist. An officer had dutifully arrived, checked the house in a perfunctory manner, and assured her she had nothing to be concerned about. Anna had ignored the officer's indulgent manner and, after he had left, tried to put the open window out of her mind and concentrate on her other problem.

The long night, alone in her bed, had given her plenty of time to think about what Thomas had said. He had been to bed with another woman, and now he wanted to be forgiven and to make it up to her. All night she had wrestled with her feelings, unable to decide what to do. She had fallen asleep at around 4:30 a.m., and when she awoke, she knew.

Now that her mind was made up, she could hardly wait to get going. She had one phone call to make now, before they left. It was still early. In all likelihood Edward had not yet left for work. Anna dialed the Stewarts' number and waited for several rings.

* * *

The glass doors of the apartment house lobby were opened by a small-boned, balding man in aquamarine livery. "Good morning, sir," said the doorman politely. "Lovely day, isn't it?"

"Yes, isn't it?" Thomas mumbled, slipping into the elegant lobby.

"Whom did you wish to see, sir?" the doorman asked. Thomas recognized the doorman as the same one who had been on duty when he had left with Gail the previous morning. He wondered if the man remembered him and was just being discreet. He felt as if the gold of his wedding band was flashing on his hand. "Miss Kelleher, please. On the twentieth floor."

"Who's calling, please?"

"Mr. Lange."

The doorman nodded and walked over to the house phone on the desk in the lobby. Thomas sat down in one of the lobby sofas and placed his bags on the floor. He had to be at the airport in an hour and a half, but he felt that he couldn't leave without talking to Gail, as much as he dreaded it. After having left Anna the night before, he had gone to a hotel, where he had been up most of the night with his thoughts and a bottle of bourbon. This morning he was weary, and his head ached; but at least he did not feel guilty.

"You can go up, sir," said the doorman.

"Thank you," said Thomas. He stood up, picked up his bags, and went to the elevator. He figured that Gail would not be too surprised by what he had to say. They had hardly spoken after he told her he was meeting Anna for dinner. He had collected his bag from her apartment, telling her that he was going to a hotel because he needed to be alone that night to sort things out, and although she had tried not to let her feelings show, she had answered him in monosyllables.

He had considered not telling her anything at all. He knew he could just avoid her at work, and she would get the message in no time. The last thing he felt like this morning was having an ugly scene with her. But it was too cowardly a way out.

He walked down the carpeted hallway to her door and rang the bell. After a few moments the door opened, and she was standing before him, dressed up for work. He met her eyes briefly and then looked down.

Gail looked him over quickly and gave a slight laugh. "Moving in?" she asked.

Thomas did not smile. "I'm going to Boston today," he said.

"I know," she said, stepping aside to let him in.

He did not look at her as he passed into the living room. He could feel her eyes on him, appraising him, anticipating what he was about to say.

"I'm sorry about last night," he said. "I should have called you when I got back to the hotel."

"I didn't really expect to hear from you," she said. She walked over to where he stood gazing out her windows at the skyline. He glanced over at her and saw in the harsh daylight that there were dark circles under her eyes which she had mostly concealed with makeup.

"How was your meeting with Anna?" she asked. He thought about trying to explain it to her, but he did not know where to begin. How, he wondered, do you explain something, when you don't even understand it yourself? He turned to face her. "I've made a mess of things, Gail. I just didn't use my head. Now I'm afraid I'm going to hurt you, and I never intended to."

Gail nodded, but there was a remote look in her eyes, as if she were answering him from miles away. "No," she said softly. "I don't imagine you did."

* * *

Edward hung up the phone and returned to his chair in the dining room. What a piece of luck, he thought. What an incredible piece of luck.

Anna had called to ask him if he had seen or heard any sign of a prowler the night before. At first he had felt panicky, hearing her describe the open window, but he was able to assure her, as the police had, that there was absolutely nothing to worry about, that all had been quiet.

And then she had told him about the airport. She was taking the boy with her to the airport. What better place to abduct the boy than the sprawling, anonymous airport? He could easily think of some story to lure the boy off without being seen by either of his parents. Once he had the kid in his possession, it was just a matter of hiding the boy in the house and waiting until darkness fell to get rid of the body. Perfect. So simple. He only wished he had known about this last night, so that he could have gotten some sleep. Edward brushed the crumbs from his croissant off his fingers onto his plate.

Now, however, it was time to move. He checked his watch. They would be leaving soon. He decided to get ready quickly because he wanted to leave right behind them, keeping his distance of course. Tonight, he thought, this all will be over. He felt a huge sense of relief at the thought. He would have dinner at the club in peace, knowing that his potential accuser was safely dead and buried, somewhere far enough away, and all his worries buried with him.

CHAPTER 19

Anna pulled the car up into the line of cars beside the traffic island outside the Boston Shuttle terminal. She glanced over at Paul, who seemed mesmerized by the rush of airport activity.

"It's a good thing you were with me," she said. "I don't know how a person is supposed to drive and read all those signs at the same time. I could have ended up on the runway, for heaven's sake."

Paul shrugged. He had sulked on the way down at her insistence that he accompany her and not stay in the house, or go with Tracy. "You could have found it," he said.

"Well, maybe so. But it helps to have a copilot." She didn't want him to feel smothered and overprotected. But the thought of that open window in the basement plagued her. She kept thinking of Rambo's threatening predictions, although she would not have admitted it to anyone. He's safe, she thought, chiding herself. He's perfectly safe. But the sight of that window last night had reminded her that you could never be sure.

Anna realized guiltily that Thomas would never approve of this precaution. But today she needed the assurance of the boy beside her. Once Thomas was home again . . .

She reached into her purse and extracted a tube of lipstick. She carefully applied it, checking it in the rearview mirror. Then she snapped the tube shut and turned to her son. "Will you come in with me?" she asked.

The boy shook his head. Anna looked over at the busy entrance to the terminal. There were police and skycaps swarming all around the entrance to the building. "I guess you'll be pretty safe here," she said. "Just keep the doors locked. I'll tell that cop over there to keep an eye on the car while I run in."

"What for?" Paul asked.

"This is New York, darling. There is a lot of crime around here. You have to be careful around here. You sure you don't want to get out and have a look in the terminal? It might be boring sitting in the car."

"No," said the boy dispiritedly.

Anna frowned at him. "Do you feel all right?"

"Yes," he said, his voice rising in annoyance.

"All right," she said briskly. "I'll be back shortly." She slid out her side and locked the car door behind her. Then, giving him a wave, she looked both ways and hurried across the road to the doors of the terminal.

Paul leaned over and turned on the car radio. The announcer was talking loudly about back-to-school specials, and Paul's spirits sank as he listened. He was not looking forward to starting school. He had a feeling that everyone would be staring at him. He had no friends here, and while that wasn't so bad in classes, it was going to be creepy during lunch and free periods and stuff like that. He had a sneaking, newfound hope that Tracy might take him around a little. She had wanted him to go sailing with her today after all. It wasn't the best to be led around by your little sister, but it would be better than nothing.

A sudden rap on the window made him start, and he looked up, expecting at once to see Anna or some sinister-looking character with a gun trained on him. "New York," she had said. "Crime." Paul jerked his head around and saw the worried face of Edward Stewart peering in the window.

Paul gave him a bewildered look as Edward motioned for him to lower the window. Paul turned off the radio and pressed the button to lower the window.

"Paul," Edward began abruptly, "where's your mother?"

Paul nodded toward the airline terminal. "She went in," he said, "to see my father's plane off. What are you doing here?"

"Oh, no," Edward groaned, straightening up and grimacing at the terminal.

"What's the matter?" asked the boy.

"Oh, dear," said Edward. "Paul, your father's not in there. There was . . . Well, he had an accident this morning in the city. He was stabbed by a mugger. He's in the hospital."

"Uh-oh," the boy breathed.

"When they couldn't reach anyone at your house, they called ours. Oh, she's going to be frantic, looking all over for him."

"I can probably find her," Paul offered.

Edward seemed to consider the idea and then brushed it away. "Never mind. I'll find her. I've come to take you both to the hospital. My car is in that parking garage way over there." He indicated a building quite a distance down the road across from the main terminal. "It's in space H-thirteen. Can you find that?"

"Sure," said Paul.

"You go wait for me there. I'll find your mother inside."

"What about our car?" Paul asked, getting out of the Volvo and shutting the door.

"Leave it," Edward said. "I'll explain it to the policeman. You just get in my car and wait for us. The door's open."

"H-thirteen?"

"That's right."

Paul loped across the street and walked along the road until he finally reached the parking garage. It was dark inside, despite the brightness of the day, and very quiet. A couple of people were exiting as he came in, but mostly it was empty and looked like a graveyard for automobiles.

He noted that the letters marking the lot were low on the first floor, meaning he had to go up. He climbed the ramp into the second crowded level, but the letters only went up to F. With a sigh he walked up to the third level, where the cars had thinned out and it was as silent as a tomb. He thought about Thomas as he walked, bleeding on some sidewalk while a guy ran off with his wallet. The thought made him feel sick and a little apprehensive. The gloom of the garage suddenly felt very unfriendly, and he hurried to find the car and get into it. He would lock the door and just wait for Mr. Stewart. He began to scan the letters and numbers, making his way down the row of cars. He passed the parking lot elevator. The light above it indicated that the elevator was on its way up.

The space next to the elevator was H-7. Almost there. He counted the spaces as he walked and noted that he was coming up to a black car. As he approached it, he saw that it was a Cadillac, long and gleaming. He walked up to it and put his hand on the door handle. Then he stopped short and stared. The long hood of the car sloped down like a shining black mirror to the grillwork on the end. Perched on top of the grille was a hood ornament the likes of which he had never seen before. It was golden and in the shape of an eagle, its wings expanded, talons extended, its golden beak open, its eyes narrowed into angry slits.

Paul felt a pain shoot through his head, and he started to wince. His hand rested on the door handle; but all the muscles in his body felt limp, and nausea began to overwhelm him. His eyes riveted to the eagle, he began to back away from the car.

Suddenly he felt a thud on his back, and an arm reached around him and jerked the car door open. Paul toppled forward, through the open door, and fell into the front seat, his chin smacking hard against the dash. He was momentarily stunned, and then he scrambled backward with a cry as he faced his assailant.

Edward Stewart's cold eyes floated above him in the gloom of the black car in the empty lot. Paul raised a fist, but Edward grabbed it and pushed it down, pinning him with his weight under one bent knee. Paul had started to cry out when a damp rag descended on his face and a suffocating smell assaulted him.

In the few seconds before he passed out, he was a child again, lying limp on a grassy edge of the exit ramp, unable to move, as those cold eyes inspected him. He was pleading for help, but as those huge hands reached for him, he knew now, as he had known then, that they would only carry him deeper into danger.

* * *

Anna scanned the line of passengers waiting to have their bags inspected before boarding the plane. Her eye was caught by the dejected slope of his shoulders — a posture, she realized, that she recognized from Paul, who had stood just that way in the kitchen door this morning. Father and son, alike even in their stance. Thomas moved forward in the line, unaware of her scrutiny.

For a moment she wondered if she had the courage to proceed with her plan. The resolve which had propelled her from home to the airport now wavered as she looked at him moving toward the guards and the conveyor belt. Maybe she had misunderstood his intentions. Perhaps he intended to stay with the other woman after all. Anna felt her voice sticking in her throat.

It's Thomas, she reminded herself. Not some stranger. Even though she did not understand what he had done, she did know him. She could not be that wrong about his feelings. You're afraid, she told herself. That's all. Fight for him. You have to.

Forcing herself to move forward, Anna called out his name. Thomas turned and looked around with a puzzled glance. Then he saw her, and his troubled face was transformed by a smile. “Anna!” he exclaimed.

He broke from the line and rushed toward her. It’s going to be all right, she thought.

“What are you doing here?”

Suddenly she felt shy under the warmth of his smile. “I . . . I wanted to see you off,” she said.

He gazed at her, his tired eyes cautious but hopeful. He set his bags down on the ground and then rubbed his hands on his trouser legs.

Anna realized that he did not know how to reply. She had always smoothed the way for him. He needed her to do it now. “I hardly slept at all last night,” she said. “I was thinking about what you said. It hit me pretty hard at first.”

“I know,” he said quickly. “I was an idiot.”

“But I didn’t want you to go off today with this misunderstanding between us.”

Thomas nodded miserably.

“I know we can’t talk about this whole thing now,” she said. “But the more I thought about it, the more I realized that there was blame on both sides. I was so busy thinking about Paul that I guess I didn’t give much thought to what you were going through. Anyway, you asked me to forgive you, and I want you to know that I will. I do.”

They stood awkwardly, facing each other. Anna’s hands hung at her side. Thomas reached down and picked up her right hand. He placed it between his own hands, his eyes filling as he stroked it and then, hesitantly, squeezed it in his palm. She watched his face as he clutched her hand, the determined set of his mouth an indication that he was forcing back some insistent tears.

Anna felt herself swallowing her own. She was suffused by the peaceful sense that she had done the right thing by coming. Whatever needed to be unraveled could be done in time. They were joined again, she thought, looking down at their intertwined hands.

An amplified voice cut through the corridor. "All passengers for the 10 a.m. shuttle flight to Boston must have their baggage checked and be ready for boarding."

Thomas sighed. "That's me," he said.

"You'd better go." She smiled.

"I'll call you tonight," he said, but it was a question.

Anna nodded. "Where are you staying?"

"The Copley Plaza."

"Yes. Do call. I want to talk to you."

He picked up his suitcase and his briefcase. "How is everything at home?" he asked. "All right?"

Anna hesitated, thinking of the opened window in the basement. But he was poised to go, looking for reassurance. Besides, it would be all right soon, when he came home for good. She smiled at him. "Fine."

"Where are the kids?"

"Tracy went sailing with Mary Ellen. Paul's out in the car."

Anna saw a shadow pass over his face and knew that he felt hurt that the boy had not come in to see him. "He wanted to come in," she said, "but I asked him to stay with the car. I'm parked right out front."

Thomas glanced over at the dwindling line of check-in passengers. "Give them my love, will you?"

Anna nodded and smiled.

Impulsively he dropped his bags on the ground again and leaned toward her. She met his embrace, and they held each other tightly, his face buried in her hair. She could feel him shaking. Her own knees felt weak.

"You feel so good," he said softly.

She smiled and gave him a pat on the rear end. "You'd better get going."

He kissed her hard on the mouth and reluctantly released her. Then he was gone, turning to wave at her as he passed through the electric eye doorframe and sprinting toward the gate.

Anna waved back vigorously, forlorn and happy at once. He would be gone only overnight, she reminded herself. Tomorrow he would be back. Back in their home, to start over again. She waited until he had disappeared from sight and then she turned and started back. Men in suits streamed by, heading for the shuttles.

At the ticket counters, people in a variety of costumes waited and looked around. One young man wore dark glasses and running shoes and looked glamorous and insouciant. A woman in a neat, tailored summer suit rummaged in her purse, while a couple in leisure suits examined their tickets and tugged on the handles of their large wheeled suitcases.

People traveling, she thought. Going on vacations and trips and important business junkets. But she didn't envy them their travel plans. She was delighted to be going home, getting her house ready for her husband's return, and looking out for the children. She thought of the house on Hidden Woods Lane with a longing she could not muster for any strange city. Tomorrow they all would be home together, safe under that familiar roof. Again her thoughts flashed to the open window in the cellar, but she pushed them away. Thomas would be there, to make sure everything was all right.

Anna crossed through the modern vault of a lobby, past hustling employees dressed in blue and hurrying passengers. She opened the sliding doors with her step and left the air-conditioned hum of the terminal for the warm, racket-filled roads out in front. The car was parked beside the island where she had left it, and she was relieved that there was not a policeman standing beside it, issuing a parking violation.

Dodging the skycaps and the taxis that hovered in front of the terminal, Anna hurried across the street, craning her neck to see the top of Paul's head, which was not visible inside the car.

He's probably taking a nap, she thought. Teenagers. They eat and sleep with such a vengeance. She approached the door of the car, ready to tease him about his ability as a sentry, but she realized, when she arrived at the vehicle, that her son was no longer inside. For a moment she stood on the curb, staring into the car. Then she pulled the door open and got into the front seat.

There was no sign of him. She looked up through the windshield, half expecting him to come walking into her line of sight, but he was not there. He must have gone looking for me, she thought. Or gone inside to get some candy or something.

After locking the car doors, Anna hurried back across the street into the terminal. Coming through the doors, she looked in every direction, searching for the camouflage vest and black sneakers, but she didn't see him. The same people were in the terminal, but the sight of them no longer intrigued her, like guests at an overlong party after the novelty has worn off. She rushed over to the candy counter and was finally able to get the attention of the proprietor, who was busily collecting fees for paperbacks and newspapers.

"Excuse me," she interrupted him.

The man looked owlishly at her through thick glasses.

"Did you see a teenaged boy here, buying candy or anything? A kid in a camouflage vest, brown hair."

"Nope," said the man, and turned to another customer.

"He's kind of a thin kid, about this tall."

"No, lady," said the man, and turned his back on her.

Anna whirled around and studied the terminal. Maybe he had gone to see the plane off after all. She checked on the information board to remind herself of the gate and then began to walk swiftly down the carpeted corridors toward the waiting area. I'll probably meet him coming back, she thought.

The shuttle area was empty as she rushed up to it, except for a few employees who were joking and enjoying the letup between crowds. The woman who had checked Thomas's bags gave her a suspicious look. Anna repeated her question about Paul, but the woman, after consulting her disinterested colleagues, assured Anna that they hadn't seen him, or if they had, they didn't remember.

Damn kid, Anna thought as she walked away from the gate. Why did he have to wander off like that? I told him to watch the car. She tried to ignore the other feeling that was rising in her, like a long-dormant specter. She returned to the waiting room and looked around. The men's room was next to the phone booths on the far wall. She rushed over to the phone booths but could see at a glance that he wasn't there. Just then a man in a gray suit emerged from the men's lavatory.

Anna hesitated and then accosted him, trying to appear perfectly natural and matter-of-fact. "Excuse me," she said, "but I'm looking for my son. We . . . have a plane to catch. I wondered if he might be in there." She indicated the men's room door with a wave of her hand. "He's a teenager, about this height. He's wearing a camouflage vest."

Anna could see the man's face going through stages of surprise and an embarrassed uneasiness. He shook his head quickly in answer to her question. "I didn't see him," he said gruffly, and edged away from her.

Anna turned away from the man and walked slowly back across the terminal. She could feel herself starting to shake, even though she reminded herself that it was ridiculous. He's probably back in the car by now. He'd better be. Wait until I get hold of him.

She kept looking through the terminal as she walked, her eyes like two divining rods, trying to cover every inch of the place. She moved slowly, out the sliding doors, giving him time to return to the car. As she walked, she twisted the car keys in her hand.

The street was jammed with cars, and she picked her way through them, trying not to look at her own car as she crossed the road again. When at last she reached the door, she already knew what she would see. There was no sign of him anywhere. She stared down at the empty seat. Slowly she unlocked the door on the driver's side and got into the seat.

I'll just sit here and wait for him, she thought. He ought to be back in a minute.

She sat for a few minutes in the silent car, staring through the windshield, her mind as numb and blank as if it had been covered by a snowdrift.

A sharp rap on the window startled her, and she looked up to see a female security guard holding a pad and pencil and peering in at her.

"You're going to have to move this car, lady. This is a fifteen-minute-only parking area. Just move it out of here."

Anna looked up at the officer and opened her mouth.

The other woman's face softened and then wrinkled up in concern. "What's the matter?" asked the airport meter maid, suddenly abandoning her official stance at the sight of the face, white as death, which stared up at her. "Are you all right?"

"Help me," Anna whispered. "My son. He's gone. It's happened again. He's gone."

CHAPTER 20

Edward crawled on all fours across the surface of the loft, pushing piles of newspapers and half-empty brown cardboard cartons out of his way as he went. It was a small loft, but sturdily built. He had meant to house some of his finished work up there, but instead it was filled with broken pieces of ships and an assortment of garbage. Edward studied the post in the corner to which one side of the loft was anchored. That would suit his purposes. He sat back on his heels and folded his arms, lowering his head to avoid an overhead beam. There was no ceiling above him, for the windmill continued up with its narrowing sides. There was nothing to climb toward, just the dark, windowless tower above him. It looked satisfactory to him. He shifted awkwardly around to reach the ladder, and one of the cardboard boxes sailed off the edge of the loft and landed with a thud on the stone floor below.

Edward peered over the edge of the loft to the floor, where the box lay on its side, empty tubes of paint, brushes, and a coffee can of turpentine spilling from its open flaps onto the floor. The turpentine began to trail across the floor until it was stopped, and then absorbed, by the worn camouflage-patterned fabric of the vest worn by the boy sprawled on the stones.

Paul's inert body did not react to this disturbance. He lay with his mouth open, his eyelids only half-closed, the whites giving off a sickly gleam in the gloom of the stuffy windmill.

Edward sighed as he gazed down at the frail body. He did not relish the thought of carrying the boy up the ladder to the loft. Not at all. But the body would be safer there in case anyone should stumble in here by accident before the night fell. It was unlikely but not impossible. He thought again, glowering at the memory, of Iris's surprise of the night before. He continued to shove boxes aside, making a place for the boy among the trash. After it got dark, he could move the body to somewhere far from the house. A dump or possibly the landfill in Kingsburgh. It could be months before anyone found him.

A weak groan came from the figure lying on the windmill floor. Edward looked over the edge and saw the boy's eyelids flicker and his arm move slightly. Grabbing a few rags and a length of rope, Edward hurried down the ladder to the loft and approached the prone form.

"Help me," said the boy. Edward reached down and stuffed a rag in the boy's mouth as a reply. Paul's eyes opened wider in that expression of recognition and fear which Edward had seen in those same eyes, long ago. Edward lashed the boy's hands and feet together and rolled him over onto his back. The boy jerked his head from side to side, his eyes sick with fear.

Edward did not look at Paul. He staggered to his feet and picked his way through his equipment until he reached the odd-shaped windows that were cut into each of the six walls of the windmill. It was a hazy, uncomfortable afternoon now, and the Stewart estate was in perfect stillness, no sight of anyone to disturb the peace. Satisfied, Edward squeezed past his sewing machine and back to his prisoner, who was slumped on the floor. He looked up again at the loft. There was nothing to do but to take the boy up.

He took a deep breath and tried to ready himself for the unaccustomed exertion. It would all be over tonight, he reminded himself as he squatted down and reached under the sharp shoulder blades and bent knees. Edward lifted the boy and staggered to his feet. It took him a moment to regain his balance, and then he started toward the ladder, straining under the boy's weight.

As he did so, he remembered the last time he had carried the boy. Paul had been much lighter then. Just a toddler. He had been lying in the grass by the edge of the exit road, just after the car had struck him. Edward paused at the foot of the ladder, recalling the frightened, pleading expression in the child's eyes when Edward bent over him. He remembered the unpleasant shock he received when he recognized the injured, bleeding child as his neighbor's son.

Edward sighed, remembering the panic in his heart when he recognized Paul on that long-ago day. He felt a little sorry for himself, recalling the sudden choice he'd had to make. But he'd always been decisive. You didn't get to be rich and successful by backing away from a challenge. It had taken only a moment to make his decision. And then he had acted on it.

It had been such a bold action, and it would have worked, too, if Rambo had not seen it all and saved the child. Still, he reminded himself, for a long while he had been safe. Given the same choice, he would still have done the same thing.

Edward looked up the ladder and hoisted the boy up in his clumsy grip. Slowly he began to climb, resting with each step. The boy was stiff, but he did not struggle. His head lolled back, his mouth stuffed with the rag. Edward counted the stairs and made his ascent.

* * *

Anna closed her eyes and rested the base of her head against the back of the wooden chair. The area around her eyes stung, and she raised the heels of her hands to rub it, as if she could rub the pain away, but the piercing sensation lingered.

She blinked and looked around the Stanwich police station. There was a low level of activity that provided a constant hum, the blue-uniformed officers coming and going with papers in their hands, their holstered guns looking incongruous against their hips inside the station house.

Anna turned to the uniformed woman who was sitting at the desk beside her. "May I use your phone?" she asked. "It's long distance, but I can charge it to my home phone."

"Dial nine first," the policewoman instructed her.

Anna placed the call to Boston as she looked around the station house for the young officer who was supposed to be helping her. After two fruitless hours with Airport Security at LaGuardia, the officers there had suggested she go home and wait. A young officer had kindly driven her car back to Stanwich for her, advising her to take a nap and not to worry. Kids tended to roam. Anna had insisted on being taken to the Stanwich police station, where she had now been for half an hour.

"Copley Plaza." The operator's voice interrupted Anna's thoughts. She asked for Thomas but was not able to get an answer from his room.

"Do you wish to leave a message?" asked the operator.

"Yes," said Anna softly. She thought for a minute how to put it. "Please tell him that his wife called. Tell him, 'Please come home right away. Paul is missing.'"

The operator read back the message and promised to deliver it. The policewoman at the desk beside Anna pretended not to have overheard the conversation. Anna sat back and closed her eyes again.

She had debated whether or not to call him. Their reconciliation was so fragile. She was loath to put on it the strain of yet another crisis over Paul. But she needed Tom now. Something terrible had happened to Paul. She knew it in every fiber of her being, no matter what the police thought.

"Mrs. Lange?"

Anna opened her eyes and then rose to meet the young patrolman who had emerged from an office obscured by a clouded glass door. "Yes," she said anxiously.

"I think we have all the information we need now."

"What are you going to do?" she asked.

The young officer assumed a patient smile and put his notebook in his back pocket. "Well, there's not much we can do right now. We're just going to have to wait a little while and hope he turns up."

Anna stared at him incredulously. "What do you mean? Aren't you going to start looking for him?"

The young man shrugged apologetically. "We don't even know if he ran away or not. There was no note or anything. But that doesn't mean he didn't take off on a little jaunt. Kids do it all the time."

Anna could feel her anger rising, and she knew that her face was reddening; but she tried to control her voice. "This is not a case of a runaway. Officer Parker, I'm telling you that something happened to my boy. We can't just wait and see."

The young policeman folded his arms over his chest. "Mrs. Lange, technically I shouldn't have even made out the report. The boy is not officially missing yet."

"But he was right there in the car, and when I came back . . ." Anna heard her voice start to rise, and she made an effort to lower it. "What about the computers, the data bank on missing kids? I know you are connected to those systems. Believe me, I am familiar with everything about this process."

"We can access that information if we need it," the officer said. "But there's no evidence to indicate that your boy didn't just get out of the car and go off exploring."

Anna gazed at the young man intently. "Officer," she said, "I imagine you must know about some of the troubles I've had with regard to my son."

"Yes, ma'am, I do know," said the young cop respectfully.

"It's my belief," said Anna carefully, "that my boy's life may be in danger. It is just possible," she said, shivering involuntarily at her own words, "that someone has kidnapped him again."

The cop smiled at her sympathetically. "It's only natural that you would think the worst, ma'am. After all that's happened. But Paul is a teenager now. This kind of thing happens frequently. I'm sure he'll show up. He's probably back home already. Really."

Anna stared at the man's impenetrable smile for a few moments. Then she glanced over at the policewoman, who had ceased her paper work for a moment and was studying them. The policewoman quickly looked down at her desk.

Anna clenched her fists in frustration. "Oh God, if only Buddy were here. He'd understand. He'd do something."

The young officer did not take offense. "Try not to worry, Mrs. Lange. If Paul doesn't turn up by tomorrow, we will begin looking for him. By then, Lieutenant Ferraro should be back, and you can talk to him about it. Meanwhile, try to relax."

Without another word, Anna picked up her pocketbook and stalked out of the station. Officer Parker watched her go with a combination of pity and grudging admiration. For years, she had been something of a legend around the station, for her dogged pursuit of her kidnapped son. Every cop on the force had known of her obsession, although he had personally never come into contact with her before. Well, she had turned out to be right about the boy. He had to hand her that, but now it seemed the whole thing was too much for her.

Officer Parker had been taking some psychology courses at NYU at night, and he had his own theory about her. He'd heard that she'd called the station the night before about an open window in her house, and now this. It confirmed what he had been thinking: She was so obsessed with the boy's disappearance that she couldn't accept it when she got the boy back. She had to keep the ball rolling somehow. It was sad, really.

"I feel sorry for her," said the policewoman at the desk, interrupting his thoughts.

"Yeah, me, too," he said. "It's no wonder she's overreacting. After all she's been through, you can't really blame her. Well, Marian, I've got work to do."

The policewoman, Marian Hammerfeldt, leaned back in her chair and tapped her pencil on her desk, thinking about the conversation between the distraught woman and Parker. The young officer had scarcely been able to conceal the fact that he thought Mrs. Lange wasn't operating with a full deck. But Marian wasn't quite convinced. She had often talked with Buddy Ferraro about the Lange case over morning coffee. He had once told her that he had a lot of respect for a mother's instinct. It was something Marian believed in as well, being a mother herself.

She punched up the file on her computer with all the information about the on- and off-duty officers. The inn where Buddy was staying at his son's campus was listed there, along with a number where he could be reached in an emergency. She debated for a few minutes, and then she picked up the phone. It was his case, she thought. It always had been. And he'd want to know.

* * *

This is just the way it used to be, Anna thought as she sat limply in the wing chair, gazing around the living room. Everywhere she looked there were chores she could do. The plants needed watering, there was dusting to be done, and the refrigerator held nothing for dinner. But she could not move from the chair.

It had been that way for months after Paul had been taken and she had lost the baby. The house had been a prison to her; her household tasks, no matter how simple, had seemed more than she could do. It had taken every ounce of strength she had just to wait. Wait for the phone to ring, and when it did not, wait for the day to end. Wait in that numbed state of relentless dread that made inertia into a way of life. It was just as it had been then, but this time she doubted if she had the will to withstand it.

"The Lord doesn't give you more burdens than you can bear," her mother used to tell her. Anna turned her head and looked up at Paul's baby picture on the mantelpiece. She could not call her parents in Ohio and tell them this. Not yet. They were all excited, busily planning their visit to their long-lost grandson. They were old now. This news could precipitate another stroke in her father. You were wrong, Mother, she thought. It *is* more than I can bear.

But even as she sank deeper into her exhaustion, there was a sliver of will inside, nagging her to get up, to do something, anything, to try to recover her son.

There was that sheriff in West Virginia. She could call him up and try to find out if he knew anything. Or tell him to keep an eye out for the boy. If Paul *had* run away, he might be likely to go to a place he was familiar with, although even as she told herself that, she knew, with utter conviction, that the boy had not left of his own choice.

She recalled a psychic, a nice woman who was a New Jersey housewife, who had told her, some years back, that she saw Paul alive and in a warmer climate. She was right about that, Anna thought, remembering the prediction. Maybe she will know something.

The realization gave her the needed energy to get up from the chair. I have her number in the folders, Anna thought. She had kept voluminous folders in the years while Paul was gone, holding every scrap of information that had ever seemed useful. I'll dig them out and find the number. The thought of having to go back to the folders overwhelmed her with a sense of despair that almost sent her back to the chair, but she marshaled her strength and headed toward the den, where she kept all her papers in a desk drawer.

The sudden ringing of the phone sent a shock through her that made her jump. She raced to the telephone and grabbed it before the second ring. "Yes. Hello," she cried into the receiver.

There was a second's pause before Iris's anxious voice reached her ear. "Anna, it's me, Iris."

Anna closed her eyes and fell against the wall. "Oh, Iris. Hi."

Iris hesitated a little before she spoke again. "Am I interrupting you? Can you talk?"

Anna felt tears that she had held back all day rushing to her eyes at the sound of the familiar voice. "Oh, Iris. I'm sorry. I'm in kind of a bad way."

"What is it?" Iris asked. "What's the matter? Is it Tom?"

"No, it's not that," said Anna, unable to keep the tears out of her voice. "It's Paul. He's disappeared."

"Disappeared? What do you mean?"

"Oh, God, it's such a nightmare. I took him with me to the airport this morning to see Tom off on his trip to Boston, and when I came back to the car, he was gone. Gone. Just like that."

"Did you call the police?" Iris asked.

"Yes. I was there already. They weren't much help, I'm afraid. I thought this might be them now, on the phone with some news."

"I'm sorry," said Iris, feeling guilty for calling. "I won't keep you. I know how worried you must be."

"That's all right," said Anna wearily. "It's good to hear your voice. They probably won't call me anyway. They think I'm just an alarmist. I had them here last night because I thought someone broke into the house. And now this. I just don't think it's a coincidence."

"Someone broke in?" Iris exclaimed.

"I'm not sure. I thought so."

"How about that?" Iris said, half to herself. "Edward was right."

"Right about what?" Anna asked half-heartedly.

"About last night," Iris said. "He thought he heard a prowler; but he went out to check, and there was nobody there."

"He did?" Anna asked, gripping the phone tightly.

"He told me he heard someone outside, but then he decided it was nothing."

"But I called him this morning and asked him, and he said he didn't know anything about it."

Iris's voice took on a doubtful tone. "Maybe he didn't want to worry you, Anna."

Anna raised her voice. "I asked him specifically about it. He couldn't have misunderstood that."

"I'm sorry, Anna," Iris said in a small voice. "I can't think what else could have happened."

"No, you're right. It's not your fault. I . . . I'll just have to call him again, that's all."

"Do you want me to come over and stay with you?" Iris asked.

"No, that's all right. I'll be all right." Her mind was already racing, trying to absorb this news about the prowler. If only Edward had been honest . . .

"I'm sure he just didn't want to upset you," Iris suggested.

Anna murmured, "Of course. That was probably it." But she felt goose bumps rising on her flesh at the certainty she now felt. Someone had broken in. And Edward could confirm her story to the police.

"Are you sure you don't want me to come over?" Iris asked.

"No," said Anna. Then another thought intruded. "Where are you, Iris? I thought you were at the spa."

Iris's courage failed her. This was no time to get into her own situation. "I am," she said. "I just felt like talking to you."

"Oh." Anna was lost in thought again. The fact was, she realized with a flash of anger, that if someone had been lurking outside the house, then they could all have been in danger. How dare Edward keep that information from her, even if he was just being his usual overbearing self?

"Well," said Iris, "I won't tie up your phone. I'll call again tomorrow to see if there's any news. Try not to worry, Anna. He'll be all right. You'll see."

Before she had even hung up the receiver, Anna knew what she would do. She would go over to the Stewarts' and see if Edward was there. If he was, she intended to confront him with what Iris had said. If he would be willing to tell the police about the prowler, it might convince them to start their investigation right away. It could give them something to go on, more substantial, she thought, than a psychic's prediction. At least it was something she could do. It was better than just sitting here, waiting and wondering if she would ever see her son again.

CHAPTER 21

At the end of the driveway, which was almost as long as a private road, the Stewart mansion loomed dark against the afternoon sky. Anna walked slowly up the drive toward it, staring at the house. She had always felt that she could never enjoy living in a house like that, no matter how magnificent it might be. She often wondered if Iris, with her simple humdrum ways, felt out of place in that palatial house. It always struck her that the house must have been Edward's choice.

For a moment she stood, gazing up at the house. The windows throughout the mansion were dark, and the house was quiet. She wondered if she would find Edward at home. She knew that he only rarely spent a working day out of the city. Still, he had come home early the day before. Perhaps he had done the same today. She almost wished that Iris were here, to run interference for her. Anna never felt at ease with Edward and his stiff ways. She knew that he was only a few years older than she, but something about him made her feel many years his junior.

She decided to walk up and have a look in the garage windows to see if his car was there. The gravel crunched under her feet as she picked her way up to the expansive doors of the garage, which was in the same style as the house.

Anna pressed her face to the windows and looked in. It took her eyes a few moments to adjust to the darkness. She knew that Edward's car was black, so she was unlikely to see it until her eyes were accustomed to the dark interior. In a few seconds she was able to make out the long lines of the black Cadillac. He always drove the same kind of car, year after year, although he often traded it for new models.

As she recognized the car, she also picked out the golden eagle which he affected as a hood ornament and which was always transferred from one vehicle to the next. Privately she and Thomas had sometimes chuckled at this conceit since Edward's pompous nature bore so little resemblance to the majestic bird. As she looked at it now, though, something about the eagle bothered her. She stared at it through the window for a few moments, puzzled by her own feelings, and then turned away. It was a problem for another day, she decided. He was home. That was what counted.

Anna marched resolutely up the walk to the front door and rang the bell. She could hear the chimes echo through the halls of the house, but no one came in answer to her summons. For a few minutes she stood there impatiently, trying to peer through the lead-paned windows which surrounded the door. But the heavy silk-lined drapes were almost shut, and she would have had to pick her way through the rhododendron bushes to get a look inside. He might be taking a nap, she thought. She stepped down off the step and started back toward the driveway. Then she had another thought. He might be in the windmill. According to Iris, that was where he spent most of his free time. Anna glanced up at the huge Tudor structure. Maybe he didn't like the house either, Anna thought. You never know.

She walked over to the stone path that encircled the Stewart mansion and walked around to the back of the house. She came upon the terrace, the black, wrought-iron furniture facing the empty aqua pool. The top of the windmill was barely visible in the distance. He was probably out there. For a moment she hesitated, thinking that Edward might resent the intrusion. Then she continued on. She had something important on her mind, and she could ignore Edward's annoyance. Anything, if it would help to find Paul.

Behind her, the patio doors opened. Anna heard the sound and jumped, bumping her shin on the table legs as she whirled around.

Edward Stewart pushed out the French doors and came toward her, his cold eyes fixed on her startled face. "Where are you going?" he demanded.

"Edward," said Anna, "I didn't think you were in the house. I rang and rang."

"There are no servants here," he said, as if that explained why the door had gone unanswered. Anna let the explanation go. Maybe he just hadn't felt like company.

"I hope I didn't take you away from something."

"No," he said. "Do come in." He indicated the doors, and Anna passed by them and then waited for him while he closed them tight and led the way into the library.

"I was just about to look for you in the windmill." She noticed that his shoulders stiffened at the mention of his work room. He certainly is possessive of that space, she thought.

"Sit down," he said. He gestured toward a brown leather chair in the library.

Anna sat down on the edge of it, and Edward seated himself across from her

"I can't stay. I know you're probably working," said Anna. "I only came over to ask you something."

"Oh? What's that?"

Anna took a deep breath. "Iris called me just a little while ago."

Edward sat up. "Iris?"

"Yes."

"Whatever for? I was under the impression that they didn't have telephones at the spa she's staying at."

"I don't know about that," said Anna, realizing as she said it that she didn't really know why Iris had called. She had been so involved in her own concerns that she hadn't bothered to ask. For a moment it troubled her, but then she dismissed it. She couldn't worry about that now. She'd find out sooner or later. She looked back at Edward, interpreting the indignant expression on his face to mean that he was affronted that Iris had gone out of her way to call Anna, not him.

"What did Iris want?" he asked, his eyes narrowed slightly.

"I'm afraid I didn't give her a chance to say," Anna said apologetically.

Edward thought he knew. It was the same thing as last night, this kick she was on about not making him happy. Naturally she would be indiscreet and pour her heart out to Anna. They could compare notes about their marital problems. It was disgusting, Edward thought. Unseemly.

"I told her about Paul. Well, I guess you don't know what happened."

Edward felt a little shock. He shook his head and assumed an innocent, wondering look.

"I took him to the airport this morning, as I told you on the phone. I went to see Tom off, and when I got back to the car, Paul was gone. I haven't seen or heard from him since."

"Vanished?" Edward said.

"He didn't vanish." Anna corrected him sharply. "Something has happened to him."

Edward was silent for a moment. Then he cleared his throat. "Well," he said, "how can I help?"

"That's why I'm here," said Anna. "Remember this morning on the phone I told you about someone trying to break into my house last night?"

Edward looked at her blankly. Then he pretended to remember. "Oh, yes. The window. In the basement, wasn't it?" Immediately he knew that what Iris had told her had sent her running over here. He kept his expression puzzled as he searched his mind for a lie.

"Yes," said Anna. "Edward, why didn't you tell me you heard a prowler last night?"

"What?" he asked in apparent confusion, stalling for time.

"Today, when I mentioned to you about calling the police and the open window, you never said boo about it. But Iris told me that you thought you heard a prowler last night."

Edward rubbed his hands together and looked at her apologetically. "I didn't think it was important. I mean, I didn't want you to be needlessly alarmed. After all, I didn't see anyone."

"For heaven's sake, Edward, I'm not a child that needs to be protected. Why didn't you just tell me when I asked? It would have been a big help to me in dealing with the police to have known what really happened."

"There's no reason to shout," Edward said, and Anna was brought up short by the chill in his voice. "I did what I thought best."

Anna took a deep breath and nodded. "I know. I'm sorry. That's just what Iris said."

"What?" Edward asked suspiciously.

"That you probably kept it to yourself so I wouldn't worry."

Edward tried to stifle a smile. Iris. Was it any wonder that his life with her had been so simple? She had never been able to keep up with him. He always had his own way.

"I need to know," said Anna. "What did you see or hear last night?"

Edward picked up the Dunhill lighter which rested in one of Iris's little clay ashtrays and fiddled with it. "I was in my workroom, and I thought I heard something outside. So I went out to look. But there was no one there. Everything was perfectly quiet."

"Could you tell that to the police?" Anna asked.

"What for?" Edward exclaimed, dropping the lighter back into the ashtray. "I don't see what possible difference it could make."

"I think it could make a crucial difference," Anna insisted. "Right now the police aren't taking me seriously.

They are treating me as if I'm half insane with these complaints. If they were to hear it from you, they might start doing something to help."

Edward gave Anna a tight, chilly smile as he rapidly reviewed the options in his mind. If he refused her request, she might become suspicious of him, and he did not want to appear uncooperative. He loathed the idea of becoming involved with the police in any way on the subject of the boy; but if he didn't volunteer the information, Anna would simply take it to them herself, and he would be forced to answer their questions anyway. They might even want to come out here. He had to prevent that at all costs.

"I'd be happy to call them," he said smoothly, "if you think it would help."

"Oh, Edward, thank you," said Anna, exhaling and falling back into the leather seat.

"I'll call them right now," he said. He got up slowly from his chair, trying not to reveal the agitation he was feeling and headed for the phone. As he picked up the receiver and dialed, he mentally rehearsed the offhanded way in which he would present the information. As he listened to the phone ringing, it occurred to him that this call might ultimately work in his favor. A little neighborly concern, prompted by the mother's distress, was appropriate in this case. And Anna would be pleased with him for trying to help.

Anna closed her eyes briefly and then listened with one ear as Edward called the station. His manner of reporting the incident was infinitely casual and in no way reflected the kind of urgency she felt. Ah, but that was Edward, she reminded herself. At least he was calling. She gazed around the library as she waited, thinking what a handsome, if somewhat forbidding, room it was. The leather furniture was all in perfect condition, as if no one had ever sat in it. The antique furniture glowed from being polished and untouched. Several of the models that Edward had built adorned various tables and the bookcases. She had to admit to herself that he had a gift for it. They were elegant vessels, perfect in their details.

Across from her, hanging on the paneled wall, was a series of engraved etchings of various birds of prey. There were owls, eagles, hawks, falcons, and others she could not identify. It struck Anna that it was an odd choice for decoration. Most people of the Stewarts' ilk had pictures of mallard ducks on ponds or sleek Thoroughbreds. She could not help noticing that the eyes on some of the birds reminded her a little of Edward's. Perhaps, she thought, that's why he likes them.

Then, as a strange sensation flooded through her in a warm rush, her eyes focused again on the center etching in the group. It was a golden eagle, much like the one that adorned Edward's car, and Anna suddenly remembered where she had recently heard of a golden eagle.

"There," said Edward, coming back around in front of her. "I've alerted the police."

"Thank you," Anna mumbled, tearing her eyes from the picture to look at him.

"Now," he said, "why don't you go on home and try not to worry? The boy will probably turn up before you know it. This is all probably some youthful prank."

Anna got up carefully from the chair, avoiding his eyes. "I hope you're right," she said. "I know that's what the police think."

"Well," said Edward, "we have to trust our men in blue."

"Yes," she said, and then she forced herself to smile apologetically. "I just can't help worrying."

"I'm sure they would, too, if they were you," Edward said, thinking, with a great sense of relief that the policeman he spoke to had not offered to come out and look around again.

Anna drew in a breath and started toward the door. She turned to her neighbor. "I really appreciate your calling them," she said. "I'm sorry if I disturbed you."

"No trouble," he said expansively, relaxing at the sight of her leaving the house. "I was happy to do it."

He accompanied her to the door and watched as she started to walk toward the driveway. Before she disappeared from sight, she waved to him. He smiled, and waved back, and then closed the door to the house.

As she walked down the path to the driveway, she pondered the revelation she'd had in the library. The eagle coming toward him on a black mass was the image Paul remembered from his nightmare. The connection had stunned her for a moment when she made it. There were other eagles in the world, of course. It didn't have to have anything to do with the one on Edward's car.

She reached the driveway and stopped short. She knew she should start walking home, but she felt as if she were frozen where she was, her eyes fixed on the garage. She was staring so hard that she felt as if she could see through the doors to the car inside. She had the reckless, unreasonable sensation that if she could stand in front of that eagle and put her hand on it, she might almost be able to reach Paul, to remember something vital that could help her search. She felt suddenly compelled to get closer to that eagle, to stare at it and try to think. As if in a trance, she walked to the garage door, opened it, and slipped inside.

She knew that she should probably have asked Edward if she could look at the car and explained about the dream. But as soon as she had made the connection in the library, she knew instantly that she would not mention it to him. It was an instinct, almost animal in nature, and she trusted it. For a moment she berated herself for it, but then she reminded herself that she had been right before. She was Paul's mother, and there were things she felt that she knew. If that was madness, so be it.

The interior of the garage was dark and empty, except for the Cadillac. It was a beautiful car, in perfect condition. Anna placed a hand on its cold, shiny side, as if to steady herself, and walked around to the front of the car. The eagle was poised in flight, wings outstretched, its angry eyes focused on the pavement below, just as Paul had described it in his dream.

Maybe he had seen the car, and the hood ornament had made an impression on him, she reasoned. But that would not explain why it frightened him so or why the dream recurred. She felt her breath growing short as she stared at the bird. She wanted to get out of the garage before Edward realized she was there. She was loath to deal with him again. She needed to get home and think about the impressions which seemed to be colliding in her mind. She started back around the car, admiring, in spite of herself, its glossy finish. Just as she passed the windshield, she noticed a piece of paper stuck under one windshield wiper. The letters *LaG* jumped off the paper in the gloom and caught her eye. Carefully she reached over the hood and extracted the slip from under the wiper blade.

The paper in her fingers was a receipt for parking, with the number of a space on it, for a parking garage at LaGuardia Airport. It was timed and dated that morning.

Anna's knees started to buckle as she stared at it. She willed herself to stand up, to recover from the fainting feeling that came over her as she crushed the paper in her hand.

In a few moments she thought she could walk. She hurried toward the side door of the garage, which she had pulled shut behind her as she came in. There was light coming through the windowpanes on the door, and she kept her eyes on the light as she stumbled toward the door.

She turned the knob and pushed it open. A force from the other side jerked the door back, and Anna fell forward. She looked up into the unblinking eyes of Edward Stewart.

For a moment she stared at the white, fine-boned face that was contorted with anger. Then she began to stammer. "I was just looking for something . . ."

"What have you got there?" he said, reaching for the paper clenched in her hand.

"Nothing," she protested, trying to lift it away from him. But he was too quick. He grasped her hand, and unclenched her fingers. His light complexion grew even paler as he recognized the parking ticket.

"Careless," he said in a gloomy tone.

Recognizing the danger, Anna tried to get past him, to reach the door. His hand shot out and grabbed her by the jaw. She felt her teeth crack together, and there was a clicking sound as if the bone were separating from her skull. The force of his grip lifted her off the cement floor, and then he tossed her back inside the garage. She landed on her hands and knees, on the concrete, and cracked into the side of the Cadillac. She felt the skin tear from her palms and her kneecaps. A foot came down on her back from behind. Anna lifted her head and cried out.

She heard Edward growl like an animal above her; then something sharp and hard caught her in the temple, and she passed out.

CHAPTER 22

Buddy Ferraro took a sip from his plastic glass filled with pink punch topped by a disintegrating grapefruit section and gently nudged his wife with his elbow. "Look at Mr. Popularity," he said, nodding toward his son, who was huddled with a group of boys across the reception room crowded with freshmen and their parents in the student union.

Sandy gazed wistfully at her eldest son and sighed. "He seems to like it here," she said.

"He'd better like it here if he knows what's good for him," Buddy said gruffly. "At these prices."

Sandy smiled and slipped her arm through her husband's. "I'm going to miss having him around the house."

"Yeah, me, too," said Buddy. "I'll miss him swiping my razor, and leaving his dirty socks all over the bathroom floor, and his girlfriends calling and waking me up at midnight."

Sandy pressed her lips together in a shaky smile. "Seems like a long time until Thanksgiving," she said.

Buddy quickly looked in all directions and gave her a peck on the forehead. She squeezed her husband's hand.

"Come on," he said. "Let's go back to the hotel and take a nap before this dinner tonight. He doesn't need us."

Sandy raised an eyebrow at him, but she did not resist as her husband edged her toward the cluster of students where their son was standing.

"Hey, son," said Buddy, "your mother and I are going to take off for a while."

Mark tore his gaze away from a pretty blonde girl who had joined the group and was tossing her hair. "Oh, okay, Dad."

"We'll meet you at the dorm tonight at six thirty for the dinner."

"Okay," said Mark. "See you then." He and his new schoolmates returned to their conversation as Buddy steered Sandy toward the door, smiling at the various relaxed-looking faculty members and the pairs of nervous, correctly dressed parents.

"That kid can't wait to get rid of us," said Buddy, as they left the student union and began to stroll across the campus toward the hotel on the other side of the street.

"I know," said Sandy sadly. Then, after a pause, she smiled. "I guess that's good, huh?"

Buddy nodded. They walked in silence toward the cobbled walkway to the hotel lobby.

"Mr. Ferraro," the desk clerk called out as they passed through the lobby.

Buddy looked over at him in surprise. The clerk held up a slip of paper. "There's a message here for you."

Buddy excused himself from his wife and walked over to the desk. Sandy thumbed through a blue folder that she found on one of the tables in the lobby. On the cover of the folder was a picture of the campus in fall, with students scuffling through the leaves and laughing as they passed a handsome old classroom building.

She looked up to see Buddy standing by the desk with a grim look on his face. "What's the matter?" she asked, walking over to him.

Buddy shook his head. "That was from Marian at the station. She called to tell me that Paul Lange has been reported missing. She figured I would want to know."

"Oh, no," Sandy said. "How is that possible?"

"Listen, honey," he said, "I'm going to have to go back right away. I'm sorry."

"But what happened?" she said.

"I don't know," said Buddy. "But I knew something wasn't right." He crushed the message slip in his hands. "I'm afraid for that boy, Sandy."

* * *

Anna came to in the darkness, her head throbbing, her limbs stiff and painful. She tried to move her arms to rub her eyes and realized, through a groggy haze, that her hands were tied behind her and her feet were bound at the ankles. Her aching head rested on a cold stone floor. Her tongue felt like a lead weight in her mouth as she tried to maneuver it over her dry lips. For a moment she was tempted to slip back into the relative painlessness of an unconscious state. Scattered thoughts flickered and disappeared in her mind, and she was aware only of the pain and a desire to sleep.

Forcing herself to keep her eyes open, she gazed dully around her prison. The cold floor and the darkness led her to think she was still in the garage, and she was further disoriented when she saw that she was not. The piles of wood and pieces of boats confused her at first. It required all her concentration to tally her surroundings and finally understand that she must be in the windmill.

The recognition of Edward's workroom brought back, with full force, her confrontation with him in the garage. Panic gripped her by the throat as she remembered. She gritted her teeth and waited for it to pass. Edward had done this to her. Everything familiar had suddenly been turned upside down. For one second she wondered if this was some kind of misguided practical joke. Then she remembered the parking ticket on his windshield and knew for a certainty that it was not.

A low moan from the loft above her startled her clouded senses into total alertness. In an instant she remembered why she was here.

"Paul," she cried. Her voice came out in a whispered croak. She did not dare yell, even if she could, for fear that their captor might be just outside. "Paul, is that you?"

"I'm up here," he said in a weak voice. She heard him make a thrashing motion, and a cardboard box and two pieces of plywood sailed off the edge of the loft and crashed to the floor.

Anna grimaced at the crash. "Don't, don't," she called out. "Stay quiet. Don't get near the edge of that thing. You'll fall over."

The thrashing sounds subsided, and then Anna heard a groan that caused her more pain than all her bonds. "Are you all right?" she cried. "Did he hurt you?"

He groaned again, and his voice was weak but steady. "I guess I'm all right," he said.

"Thank God," she said.

"He put a gag in my mouth, but I worked it off against my shoulder," Paul said. "He tied me up. I can't move too well. Let's start screaming. Maybe someone will come."

"I'm afraid the only one who'll come is . . . is him. Paul," she said, "how did he get you here?"

"He tricked me into getting into his car at the airport. He told me . . . he said my . . . father was in the hospital. Then he brought me here."

A sickening thought made Anna tremble. "He didn't do anything . . . you know . . . molest you . . ." she whispered.

"No, not that," said the boy emphatically.

Anna felt relief at this denial. There was no reasonable explanation. "He's gone mad," she said.

"No," said the boy calmly. "He was afraid I'd remember him. And finally I did." He tried to laugh, but a sob caught him short. "A little late, I guess."

Anna shifted her aching body and stared at the floorboards of the loft above her. "Remember him?" She felt the confusion overtaking her again, like spots before her eyes.

"Yeah, from that day. Back then."

"What, darling? I don't know what you mean."

"I finally remembered today, when I saw the car, just before he knocked me out. I've been dreaming of it ever since I came back here. But today it came back to me. I got hit by a car. I must have been playing by the road. I got hit by a black car with an eagle on it."

"The eagle," she said, knowing now that she had been right about it. "Edward's car."

"And then he was there, bending over me."

"You can remember that?" said Anna.

"Yeah. I was only little. I guess it hurt. I don't remember. I guess it did. I was lying in the grass by the road, and I couldn't move. And he was there. I was scared. That I do know. And I was reaching up to him. I knew him, and I thought he came to help me. I reached up, and I think I was crying. And then he picked me up, and he started to carry me."

"Paul, are you sure this really happened? You were never hit by a car, that I know of. Never. I would have known. Are you saying that Edward hit you in his car? It's impossible."

"Yes. He hit me, and then he got out and picked me up."

"But I would have known that. If you had been injured, I would have known. And you never played alone near the road. You were only a small child."

"He picked me up, and he carried me a little ways, and then he put me down again." Paul's voice was dull and matter-of-fact. "In the highway. He put me down in the highway. And then he left me there. I remembered it today,"

Anna lay rigid on the floor, visualizing the scene her son described. For a moment she could not speak. Then her voice came out in a whisper. "He left you . . . in the highway."

"Someone came and picked me up. Someone I didn't know. I think it was my . . . you know . . . Rambo, my father. Only he was a stranger then. He picked me up and carried me off the highway."

For a few moments the windmill was silent, save for the sounds of their breathing. The boy was quiet, relieved of his story.

It took Anna a few minutes to absorb what she had heard and to understand its truth. Suddenly her body began to shake with a violence so fierce it seemed that the ground must be trembling beneath her.

"He did that to you," she said. It made sense to her now. This man, her neighbor, had hit her son by accident and then left the child in the road to die. Moved him, so that his death would not be left to chance. For a few intense moments Anna knew what it was to want to kill. With electrifying clarity she realized that she could plunge a knife into Edward Stewart's heart without remorse. Without pity. She closed her eyes as the murderous rage engulfed her helpless body, and then she began to breathe again as slowly it subsided. When the anger passed over her, like the angel of death, she was left with only an intense pity that brought tears to her eyes as she pictured her child, helpless in that open roadway. For a moment she blessed Albert Rambo with her entire being for rescuing her son from a certain death.

Anna began to inhale deeply, trying to will herself to be calm. She had to think of a way out of here. She and Paul had to survive this torture. That was what was important now. She did not have energy to spare on hatred. She needed her wits to get them free. And then, then she would see Edward Stewart punished for what he had done.

She counted backward to herself, slowly, trying to focus on something other than the vision of her child in the road, left to die by a "friend." Her mind refused to release the image. Then she heard Paul moan again from the loft above. She reminded herself of how scared he must be. Finally she found her voice. "Don't worry, darling. We'll get out of this. I won't ever let him hurt you again."

Paul was quiet for a moment. "Okay," he said. "What'll we do?"

In his voice was the innocent trust of a child, turning to his mother for the answer. And although she did not know the answer, his trust made her feel strong, made her sure that she could find it. "We'll get out of here," she said.

But as her defiant promise hung in the air, the door to the windmill opened, and Edward Stewart appeared. He was carrying a large suitcase. Anna stared at him, her loathing for him oozing from her body like sweat. Edward did not speak but turned on one small wall lamp and set down his valise. He began to search through the built-in cabinets. On one of the shelves he located an electric hot plate with one burner. He removed it and closed the cabinet door, then placed the hot plate on the workbench.

The sight of Edward's face made Anna's stomach churn with revulsion, but she understood the helplessness of her position. She kept her voice calm and steady as she spoke.

"Edward, untie these bonds and let us out of here. This has gone on long enough."

"Please don't speak to me, Anna."

"Be reasonable," she said coldly, "and stop this before it goes any further. Before you know it, people are going to be looking for us. This property is the first place they'll look."

Without answering her, Edward began pulling out drawers and emptying them on the floor, scattering papers and parts of boats around the room. Then he collected a bunch of rags that were in a bag on a workbench. They were stiff and stained with varnishes and turpentine. He examined them for a moment and then put them together in a pile. "By the time they find you," he said, "it won't matter."

"As soon as Thomas or Tracy gets home, they're going to come right over here and look for us. What are you planning to do? Take us away somewhere?" Anna asked.

"No," he said, "you're not going anywhere." He opened the suitcase he had been carrying and laid it on the trash-covered floor. He began to select the models which were finished, or partially finished, and load them into the valise. He was only able to fit about three boats into the bag. With a sigh he snapped it shut.

Anna watched him in fascination as he tested the weight of the suitcase. She thought she understood and felt a momentary relief. He only wanted a head start on getting away. She could not resist tormenting him. "What's the point of running?" she said. "You'll get caught in the end."

For the first time Edward looked at her incredulously. Then he started to laugh. It was a hollow laugh, over as soon as it began. "Oh, heavens," he said, "I'm not going anywhere. I'm just going to the club for dinner. No, no. I simply wanted to rescue some of these from the fire."

Anna's and Edward's eyes locked for a moment. At first she could not comprehend what he was saying. And then she recognized, in his steely gaze, the calm determination of one who had made an irrevocable decision. "The fire," Anna repeated.

Edward nodded and began to pile together some papers that crinkled. "I had planned to dispose of the boy somewhere else. But then you got involved, and it all became too complicated. So I thought it over and decided that the best solution was for a tragic accident to occur right here, while I was away from the house, of course."

"You wouldn't," Anna said.

"There's no one in the vicinity to alert the fire department. At least not before it's too late. I suspect you're right, that your husband or your daughter will eventually come looking for you and will find . . . what's left of you. Forgive me, that was crude."

Edward stepped over to the workbench and lifted the hot plate. He turned and looked at her, holding the hot plate awkwardly under one arm. "You shouldn't have interfered with my plan, Anna." He placed the hot plate on a low bench and plugged it into a socket on the wall. Then he picked up the pile of rags which he had collected. He carefully distributed them and the newspapers around the hot plate, with one corner of a rag overlapping the ring of the burner. "There," he said. "That will heat up and start to catch."

Anna's heart was hammering from fear, but suddenly the rage which she had held in check, hoping to reason with him, surged up from inside her, displacing every other feeling. "You loathsome, vile excuse for a man," she said through clenched teeth. "You disgusting pig . . ."

“Don’t talk to me like that, Anna,” he said tonelessly.

“Wasn’t it enough that you left my son in the road to die?” she cried. “You weak coward. You scum . . .”

Edward wheeled around, his eyes blazing wildly. He took a step toward her and kicked her hard in the side. Anna gasped and cried out.

“Yell all you want,” he said. “No one will hear you.” Edward turned around and picked up the valise. Then he looked up into the loft at the boy imprisoned there. “Good-bye,” he said evenly. Paul spit at him, and the spittle landed on Edward’s sleeve. He wiped his sleeve off gingerly with a paper towel and tossed the roll down next to the hot plate. Without another word he left the windmill and closed the door behind him.

Anna lay on her side, staring across the floor at the hot plate. The burner was starting to glow now. The edge of the rag rested on the brightening burner. Anna saw a faint brown border begin to appear on the cloth.

Paul’s small voice drifted down from above. “Did he hurt you?” he asked softly.

Gathering her breath to reply caused a sharp pain in her chest. But her voice was steady when she spoke. “I’m all right,” she said.

Slowly, painfully, she began to inch her way across the floor toward the menacing burner. The edge of the rag was black now, and a tiny lick of flame began to flicker across at its rim.

“Don’t be afraid,” she called out to him. “Don’t be afraid.”

CHAPTER 23

Thomas pulled his suitcase and his briefcase from the back seat of the cab and leaned over to pay the taxi driver his fare.

"Thanks, Mac," said the driver. "Have a good night."

Thomas nodded and watched as the driver backed slowly down the Langes' driveway. He turned and looked up at the house. He had somehow expected that Anna would rush out to the porch to meet him; but all the lights in the house were dark, and there was no sign of her, except for her Volvo parked in the driveway. He checked the garage window and saw his car parked inside. He walked up the pathway and let himself into the house.

He stood for a moment in the silent foyer and looked around. It was not the homecoming he had hoped for, but, he thought, it was probably the one he deserved. "Anna," he called out, but there was no reply.

He went into the living room and turned on a light. It was getting late in the day, that hour which is neither dark nor light. He set his bags down on a chair and walked through the house.

It was just lucky that he had decided to go back to his hotel room after lunch to pick up some papers. That was when he had gotten the message from Anna about Paul.

With a few phone calls he had canceled all his meetings and prepared for the trip back.

He walked into the kitchen and went straight to the counter where she always left her notes for him. There was nothing, no indication of where she had gone.

Thomas sighed and punched a fist lightly into the counter top. "Tracy," he called out, but he knew there would be no answer. For a moment he felt as if he were in every child's nightmare, when you come home from school and find that your family has moved. He shook the feeling off. He remembered that Tracy had gone sailing with Mary Ellen. Walking over to the phone, he dialed Mary Ellen's house and waited. The girl's mother answered and told him that the boat was still out. He told her to have Tracy call the moment she got in and he would come to pick her up. Mary Ellen's mother agreed, and Thomas hung up.

Anna was probably with the police, he decided. If Paul were missing, she would go straight to Buddy for help. She and Buddy must be out looking for him. Thomas could not help wondering, as he had on the shuttle back to New York, if the boy had decided to run away. And with that speculation came the guilty feeling that his own selfish behavior might be the cause. He gave a quick and silent prayer that his wife and son would walk in the door, but even as he prayed, he was dialing the phone number of the Stanwich police station.

The phone rang five times before anybody answered; it seemed to Thomas an unconscionably long time. When the receptionist finally answered, Thomas barked out his request to speak to Buddy Ferraro.

The woman on the other end explained that Buddy was not there.

"Well, this is Thomas Lange," he said. "My son is missing, and I was wondering if my wife might be out looking for him with Detective Ferraro. I just got in from Boston."

The woman at the other end was silent for a moment. "Oh, hello, Mr. Lange," she said finally. "I'm sorry about your son."

"Can you possibly tell me what is going on?" he said.

"I'm Officer Hammerfeldt. I was here when your wife came in this morning. Your boy disappeared at the airport this morning."

"I don't understand. Does Buddy Ferraro know about this?"

"Detective Ferraro was out of town when it happened. He just came back himself on account of it. He called me from home a few minutes ago, and he's on his way to the station. But your wife is not with him. We haven't seen her since this morning."

Thomas stared at the phone as if the instrument were deliberately confounding him.

"Detective Ferraro ought to be here in about twenty minutes," said the woman. "You want me to have him call you when he gets in? Or shall I tell him just to go on up to your house?"

Thomas thought for a moment, trying to decide what to do. "No," he said. "I may have to go pick up my daughter. I don't want him to waste a trip if I'm not home. Just have him call me. That'll be fine."

Thomas hung up the phone. His clothes felt wrinkled and uncomfortable. He decided to go upstairs and change them while he waited. Going back through the living room, he picked up his bags and climbed the stairs. He pushed the door open to his and Anna's room and looked inside. The room was orderly and welcoming as always, the wedding ring quilt spread neatly across the bed, a bedside vase filled with flowers.

It was unlike Anna not to leave him a message. Perhaps she thought that he wouldn't come home, wouldn't answer her call for help. It occurred to him again that he had done a lot of damage to their marriage, and along with the guilt he felt a powerful urge to make it up to her. He wanted to start right away, and the emptiness of the house filled him with a sense of impotence and frustration.

He put on his jeans, and pulled a sweatshirt over his head. As he was tying on his running shoes, he suddenly realized where she must be. She would not bother to leave a note if she were only going over to see Iris. It might mean that she would be back at any time. That was it. A feeling of relief flooded him. She had probably walked over there, needing someone to talk to. He leaned across the bed and picked up the bedside extension. The Stewarts' number was taped across the front, along with the police and the fire station, to call in case of emergency. He dialed the number eagerly, impatient to hear Iris's voice, so he could tell Anna that he was back. The phone began to ring and then continued ringing, as he realized, with a sinking heart, that there was nobody home. He slammed down the receiver and sat dejectedly on the edge of the bed.

He could not think of where else she might have gone. Maybe she had gone out somewhere with Iris, he thought. That was possible. Maybe they had gone out to search for the boy. He rubbed his eyes and stared at the phone. Or they might be out on the grounds somewhere. That could be. He thought of going over to check. They could be sitting out by the pool. Then he shook his head. Anna wouldn't be out reclining by the pool with Paul lost to her. He considered taking a walk over. If Iris were there, she might know something. Then he thought of Edward. He did not much like the idea of running into him. Edward always made him feel as welcome as a case of hepatitis.

Thomas sat down on the bed. Tracy might call at any minute, and he had promised to pick her up. And then there was Buddy. He would be calling, too. There's nothing to do but wait.

* * *

Using her bound feet and hands to make tiny, jerky pushes, Anna rolled her body across the cold stone floor toward the hot plate. The path was strewn with the flammable debris which Edward had collected. She forced herself to roll on it, crushing a half-finished hull into splinters that stabbed through her clothes, and tangling her limbs in the rags. Paper crinkled under her, and she bruised her side on the cold head of a hammer which lay on the floor. Her rotating feet caught the leg of a chair, which tipped over, and the cardboard box on top of it, which was filled with tiny silken sails, overturned. Triangles of bright fabric floated down and landed on the glowing ring of the hot plate. It flared up and flamed brightly for a few moments, casting a small but eerie glow in that corner before it turned to ash on the ring.

The edge of the rag left by Edward was flaming now, little licks of flame dancing on its blackened edges, eating in toward the center of the cloth. Anna hesitated, tempted to try to extinguish the rag, but she was nearer the cord of the hot plate. She looked up at the outlet where it was plugged. If she could lift her head up enough to grab the cord between her teeth, she thought, she could pull it from the wall. The thought of putting that cord in her teeth was daunting; but the rag was burning vigorously now, and she had to cut off the threatening burner.

"What are you doing?" Paul called out from above.

"Hang on, honey," she said. "I'm going to stop this burner."

"Be careful," he cried.

Anna stared resolutely at the cord. Dragging herself up on one raw elbow, she caught the cord in her mouth, carefully covering the sheath of the cord with her tongue as well as she could. Cocking her head to one side, she wedged a loop of the cord between her chin and her shoulder blade. Here goes, she thought. Don't bite down.

Anna squeezed her eyes shut and jerked her body away from the wall. The plug resisted and then came free from the wall. The violent motion pulled the hot plate off its perch on a low bench, and it overturned, a foot away against the treadle of the sewing machine.

Anna quickly dropped the cord from her mouth. "It worked," she cried. "I unplugged it."

"Good work, Mom," he cried. Anna felt a moment's giddy pleasure at the fact that he had called her Mom, but she was instantly sober again. "Now I'm going to put these ropes on my hands against the coils as they cool down and try to burn through them. First though, I have to put that rag out."

"Be careful," he said.

The tails of the rag were aflame, and Anna dreaded what she had to do next; but she felt there was no choice. It might take a while to free herself, and they would not be safe unless the rag was out. Once it was extinguished, she could concentrate on her bonds. The hot plate would not cool off that quickly. Now, however, she knew she had to smother the flames, and there was only one conceivable way to do it. She began to work her way toward the burning cloth, determined to crush it like a steamroller and flatten the flames before they could spread.

Anna tensed her body, prepared to roll. She hoped she could land squarely on it, so that it would be over in one try. She whispered a prayer and then drew back for momentum. The little flames working in toward the center of the rag suddenly reached a brown, stained patch. In that instant the rag exploded with a burst that shot licks of fire out across the room.

Anna checked her forward motion with a cry, her face seared by the intense and sudden heat. She shot backward as Paul let out a yelp. "What happened?"

"The rag," she gasped. "It exploded." Shards of the flaming rag landed in different spots in the small space. A few hissed on the cold floor and died. Others landed on hospitable boxes and other piles of rags and papers. One fell on a broom, propped up against the wall. The flames ate their way hungrily down the bristles as Anna watched helplessly. There were small fires all around her now as smoke began to rise in the windmill.

* * *

Edward's fingers trembled as he knotted his tie, but otherwise he felt relatively calm. The ringing of the phone a while before had unnerved him, but he had ignored it. Whoever was calling would be able to testify that he had not even been at home when they tried to reach him. He pulled on his jacket and checked himself in the mirror to be sure he was properly dressed. He always enjoyed dining at the club without Iris. When she was with him, no matter how well he looked, she always looked just dowdy enough to embarrass him as they walked through the dining room. Tonight, though, it would be perfect. It was a spot where he would be highly visible. He would eat, drink, and socialize, and by the time he returned from the evening all his problems would have turned to ashes. The windmill would be an inferno or a smoking shell. Inside, the searchers would find the remains of mother and son, the victims of a tragic mishap, their bonds incinerated in the blaze.

It was a bold plan, staging the accident right here on his own property, but he had finally decided it was the right move. It had infuriated him that Anna had stumbled into the middle of his perfect setup, and he had considered trying to dispose of two corpses instead of one, as he had originally planned. But the more he thought about it, the better it seemed to have them killed right here. Aside from the fact that he had no motive that anyone knew of, he felt sure that no one would ever believe that he would start such a fire on his own property. Anyone who knew him at all knew how attached he was to that windmill. In fact, it was his one regret that he had to sacrifice it in order to get rid of the boy and his snooping mother.

The Langes, he further reassured himself, were just the kind of people to come trespassing on his property, letting themselves into the windmill. It was one of their lowbrow habits to turn up, uninvited. Iris could certainly attest to that. He would tell the police that he had urged the boy to make use of the windmill anytime he pleased. He would be as blameless as could be. A victim, in fact, of their carelessness.

But now, he thought, it was time to get on the road. Edward picked up the keys to the Cadillac on the dresser and then opened the dresser drawer. Inside were his gold money clip and a leather billfold full of cash. He stuffed some bills into the clip and slipped it into his pocket. Then he snapped off the lamp and started out the door and down the hall to the stairs. He was halfway down the staircase when he heard the knock at the front door.

Edward froze, staring down at the door. For one moment he considered not answering it, thinking that perhaps whoever it was would go away. But then he realized that the person might go around to the back of the house instead, and he could not take that chance. He doubted whether there would be any sign of the fire yet, but he couldn't risk it. He would simply have to open the door and get rid of whoever was there. He reminded himself that he was a busy man on the way to his club.

Edward quickly took the remaining stairs. He peered out through one of the front windows but did not see a car in the drive. Tiptoeing to the front door, he pulled back one of the curtains surrounding the lead windows a fraction of an inch and looked out.

Thomas Lange stood on the doorstep. Edward's heart constricted in his chest. What is he doing here? He was supposed to be in Boston. Be calm, he commanded himself. Anna must have summoned him home. Behave normally. He is looking for Anna, and you have not seen her since this afternoon. Edward straightened up and brushed a piece of lint off the front of his suit. Then he opened the door.

"Thomas," he said pleasantly, "what can I do for you? I'm just on my way out."

"Can I come in for a minute?" said Tom. "I'm so glad to find you home."

Edward looked pointedly at his watch, but Thomas seemed too agitated to notice. "Well," he said hesitantly, "for a minute, certainly."

Tom passed by him and into the living room.

"Tom," said Edward, following him into the room, "I thought you were on a trip. When Anna called this morning, she said she was seeing you off at the airport."

Thomas shook his head wearily. "I went up to Boston, but then I got a message from Anna at my hotel that Paul was missing again. So I came home. And now Anna's nowhere to be found either."

"Oh, I'm sure she's not far," said Edward soberly.

"I was trying to wait for her call, but it was driving me out of my mind. I had to come over and see if you or Iris knew anything about what happened or where Anna is."

"Well, Iris is away for a few days. I saw Anna earlier this afternoon, but not since then, I'm afraid."

"What did she want?" Thomas asked.

"She was looking for the boy," Edward said. "My goodness, what a terrible time you've all had."

Thomas frowned slightly.

"What's the problem?" Edward asked.

Thomas looked at him closely. "I called before. No one answered."

"I've been in and out," Edward explained, looking at his watch.

"I guess I'm keeping you," said Thomas. "I ought to be getting home."

"No, no, you don't," said Edward, aware that Thomas would be much too close for comfort if he went home, even though the house was a good distance away. He still might smell the smoke from there. "I'll tell you what," said Edward. "I have an idea. Why don't I take you out and we'll drive around town and look for Anna? I'm sure you're in no mood to drive yourself right now."

Tom was surprised by the offer. "We wouldn't even know where to look, and I have to pick up Tracy in a while."

"We can get her on our way. Then, we'll swing by the police station and see if they have any news."

Thomas hesitated, suddenly looking extremely weary. "You're right," he said. "I can't just sit home by the telephone, doing nothing about this situation. It's driving me nuts."

"That's right," said Edward, gripping Thomas by the elbow. "You come along with me."

Thomas allowed Edward to steer him to the front door, and the two men walked out toward the garage.

"I hate to drag you away from what you were doing," Thomas said.

"I was only going to the club for dinner," Edward said. He glanced back behind the house in the direction of the windmill. There was nothing to give him away. The smoke was not yet rising. "Believe me, I can do that anytime. It's not every day you can help out a friend." The two men entered the garage, and Edward unlocked the door to the Cadillac on the passenger side. Thomas looked at him in surprise for a moment, and then he shrugged and got in the passenger side. He's as cold a fish as ever, Tom thought, but at least he's making an effort.

A sense of elation and smugness filled Edward as he opened his own side and slid back behind the wheel. He tried to compose his face to appear properly serious as he turned on the engine and looked sympathetically at his neighbor. These people are so simple, he thought. They're like sheep.

The car, which was facing forward, purred as it backed out of the garage and down the driveway.

* * *

The combined heat of the various fires was intensifying, causing the inside of the windmill to feel like a warming oven. With a recklessness born of desperation, Anna rolled back toward the hot plate, smothering the flames in her path.

Squirming up against the leg of the sewing machine, she groped behind her for the hot plate. At first she burned her fingers, noting with indifference that she felt the pain, but it no longer mattered. She held her bonds against the ring and tugged at them.

"Please," she whispered as a flaming rag torched the cane seat of a chair by the workbench. "Please."

She wriggled her hands against the burner, pulling and tugging at the ropes that held her. It was becoming more difficult to breathe. Her eyes were smarting, and she squeezed them shut.

"Mom," Paul cried from the loft. "Help." She heard him begin to cough.

The burning broom fell over, igniting a pile of notebooks. Anna tried to jerk her hands apart, but the hot plate was cooling now, its mission accomplished.

"Mom," the boy cried again. Don't give up, she ordered herself. He needs you. Don't give up. But the scene before her streaming eyes was like a vision of hell. She mustered all her breath. "Try to cover your nose and mouth," she cried, straining to be heard above the crackle in the room. "Try not to breathe the smoke." Her eyes were watering uncontrollably now, but whether from smoke or from tears, she was unable to tell.

"Do you hear me?" she cried. "Paul!" But there was no answer from the loft above.

CHAPTER 24

"I'm sure there's some perfectly simple explanation," said Edward, cranking up the air-conditioning in the car, "although it's a shame you have to go through all this."

Thomas, who was slumped in the seat beside him, did not appear to be listening.

"If I know Anna," Edward went on, "she probably couldn't sit still either. She's probably out looking—"

Thomas pressed the button beside him and rolled down his window. "Can't stand air-conditioning," he explained. "It's my wife's influence. It always feels too cold for me."

Edward glared at his passenger. "I prefer that you keep the windows up."

But Thomas was cocking his head at the open window. "The telephone's ringing in your house," he said.

"Let it ring," said Edward. "The machine will get it. It's probably just the Meechams, calling about dinner," said Edward. "I'll see them at the club later."

"It could be Anna," said Thomas. "She might have tried our house first and couldn't get me. Stop the car. Let's go back and get it."

"They've probably hung up by now," said Edward irritably.

"If it's Anna, she'll leave a message." Before Edward could prevent it, Thomas had jumped from the car and was sprinting back toward the house. Edward pulled up the emergency brake and slid out of the car to follow him.

He reached the front door of the house some seconds after Thomas and leaned against it, panting from lack of breath. Thomas stood with his ear pressed to the door.

"You see," said Edward. "It's stopped ringing."

"I'm sure it was Anna. Open the door," said Tom.

Edward glared at Thomas as he struggled to catch his breath. He glanced out toward the windmill and saw a faint plume of smoke rising in the air. "Don't be ridiculous," said Edward.

"She might need me. Maybe she had an accident. I don't know. Open the door."

"I think you're overreacting a little," Edward said coolly, "don't you?"

Thomas turned to his neighbor with eyes that were wholly determined. "You said you wanted to help me," said Thomas in a voice colder than Edward's. "If you want to help me, then open this fucking door, or I'll break a window and let myself in."

The two men stared at each other for a moment. Edward struggled to check his fury and not to bash in Thomas's insolent face. If Thomas broke the window, it would set off the alarms in the police station, and there would be squad cars here all too soon. Whoever was on the phone, Edward knew it wasn't Anna. If he could satisfy Thomas, he might still get him out of here in time. "You're acting irrationally, Thomas," he said, putting the key in the lock and opening the door.

Tom followed Edward through the house to the library. The light on the machine was blinking. Edward sighed, and pushed the button. Tom heard his daughter's voice on the tape.

"Mr. Stewart," said Tracy, "I'm sorry to bother you, but I'm looking for my parents. There's nobody answering at my house. If you see my mom or dad, tell them to call me at this number."

Edward turned to Thomas, who was memorizing the number that Tracy recited. "Why don't you call her when we get back?" said Edward.

Thomas shook his head. "Spoken like a man who has no children." Thomas picked up the phone and punched in the number as Edward walked back out into the foyer.

There was no time to waste. No time at all. He had to get Thomas safely out of there before the fire began to blaze. Edward looked at his watch again.

"I suppose she needs her ride," said Edward, as Thomas came out into the foyer.

Thomas did not reply but preceded Edward out the door. He waited for Edward down by the driveway. Edward fished in his pocket for the keys and locked the front door again. Then he followed in Thomas's path.

"Look, Edward," said Tom, "thanks for the offer, but I think I'm going to look for Anna by myself. I'm going to take a ride down and pick up Tracy, and then she and I can drive around for a while."

Edward was about to protest, but then he thought better of it. Any which way that Thomas left the house was fine with him. Just as long as he got out of there. "Are you sure?" he asked stiffly. "I really don't mind."

Thomas shook his head. "Thanks anyway."

"Well, then, let me at least give you a ride home," said Edward, opening the door to the car.

"I'll walk home," said Thomas politely. "I don't want to trouble you any further."

"Don't be silly. Let me drive you. I'm on my way out."

Thomas raised a hand in protest. "I've already made you late. You go ahead without me. I can use the walk."

Edward could feel his face reddening, but he spoke calmly. "It's a long walk from here," he said. "Why don't you just get in the car?"

"It's not that far," said Tom. "I'll cut through the back."

Edward felt his heart pounding in his chest. He had to persuade him to get in the car. He could not let him walk through the back. Not now. He was sure to see the smoke. "No," Edward insisted. "I'll drive you."

Thomas sighed wearily. "Look, I'd rather walk. I think I've about exhausted your generosity as it is." He turned and started toward the back.

Edward clenched his jaw, and then he shouted, "How dare you?"

Thomas stopped short and stared at him.

"How dare you assume you can go trampling and trespassing over my property anytime you please? You and the members of your family treat this estate like a public park, and I've had enough of it."

Thomas could hardly believe his ears. A minute ago, this man had been offering to drive him all over town in an effort to help. You arrogant, pompous ass, he thought. So much for the neighborly gesture. Now I know how you really feel about us, and it's just what I suspected. The thoughts raced through his head, but Thomas didn't voice them. "Sorry, neighbor," Thomas said slowly. "I feel like taking the shortcut."

With a deliberate stride he started around the side of the house.

Edward raced after him. "Stop this minute," he cried. Thomas continued on a few more strides, and then he did stop. Slowly he turned and faced Edward, who was right behind him.

The two men stared at each other. Then Thomas spoke. "There is smoke," he said evenly, "coming from the direction of your windmill. It looks as if there's a fire out there."

Edward's eyes were suddenly anxious. "Oh, nonsense," he said. "Get off my property."

"Why didn't you want me to see it?" Thomas asked quietly. Edward tore his eyes away from Thomas's accusing gaze.

"Get out of here, before I call the police on you," Edward cried.

"You better call the firehouse," said Thomas. Desperately, Edward tried to block his path. With a powerful swing of his right arm Thomas caught Edward in the side of the head and knocked him to the ground. Before Edward could scramble to his feet again, Thomas had disappeared around the back of the house and emerged on the patio. He could see the gusts of smoke more clearly now, gray against the darkening sky. He began to run.

His shoes made dents in the manicured lawn as he flew up over the rolling landscape of the estate. He leaped over a stone wall, staggered for a few steps, and then ran again. A clear view of the windmill was obscured by a bank of trees, but as he approached, he could see the unnatural brightness of flames inside. Flames were licking the frames of the tiny windows, and smoke issued from them. The area around the door was already beginning to blacken. And from inside he could hear the crackling and the faint sound of a familiar cry, which made his blood turn icy. Tears sprang to his eyes, although he did not know it. His chest rose and fell in a rapid motion. "Anna," he said. Then he ran for the door.

He put his fingers on the doorknob but pulled them back again, burned by the heat it conducted. Tearing off his jacket, he wrapped it around the doorknob and jerked it open.

Heat and smoke billowed out, blackening his face and his shirt. Inside, he could see flames in clumps burning up piles of junk and climbing the walls. The heavy smoke made the air in the room opaque, except where it was punctured by flames.

"Anna!" he screamed. "Anna!" Through the growing roar of the fire, he heard an answering groan. He pushed into the windmill, knocking over piles of burning debris and brushing off the flaming scraps that tried to settle on him. "Anna!" he cried. "Where are you?"

As his eyes adjusted to the gathering inferno, he saw a dark mass huddled behind the sewing machine. He lurched toward it, covering his mouth with the tails of his shirt, and bent down to see his wife, bound by ropes, crumpled in the corner, with one sleeve already on fire. She lifted her gaze to his, and then her eyes rolled back. After beating her flaming garment out with his hands, Thomas crouched down and carefully put his arms under her to lift her up. As he pulled her toward him, a line of flames burst into view where her arm dangled behind her. He gathered her stiff arms in close to him and tried to beat out the fire around her. The sight of her, bound like that, revolted and enraged him. But there was no time to loosen her bonds. It would have to wait until he had her safely outside. The flames were spreading, and he was coughing from the smoke that filled his lungs.

Tom glanced up toward the door and saw that the path was alive with fingers of flame that he would have to skirt. Clutching Anna close to him, Thomas rose carefully to his feet, teetering under his burden. He murmured to her nonsensically as he tried to plan a path through the flames. They were all around him now, burning piles of rubbish raising the temperature in the windmill to an unbearable heat, raging and hungry for the fuel that was everywhere.

Like a man treading in a snake pit, Thomas picked his way through the fire, aiming for the door, his wife bundled in his arms like a child. A chunk of flaming wood fell from the loft above him, narrowly missing Anna's legs. Thomas jerked her clear of the blazing projectile and pushed his way through the fire to the door, disregarding the singeing on his flesh where licks of flame had whipped him like a lash and left their mark.

As they reached the doorway, a flaming hull from one of Edward's ships fell into his path. Tom jumped back, then over it, and they were through the door and out on the lawn. He staggered a few yards away from the windmill and then, gulping in air, dropped on his knees to the ground, carefully placing Anna down on the well-tended grass. Anna moaned, lying on her side, her arms and feet still bound behind her. Tom rested for a minute, and then he turned to her and put his head to her chest. She was coughing and breathing hard, but without grave difficulty. He reached over and began to untie her.

Anna started to stir as her bonds were removed, and then her eyes opened and she rolled over. She looked up at the soot-smudged face of her husband, smiling down at her.

"Are you all right?" he asked between coughs. She reached her hand up, and he grabbed it and held it to his cheek. Anna struggled to sit up, and then she looked around.

"Paul," she croaked in a voice hoarse from smoke. Thomas looked at her blankly.

The dazed expression in Anna's eyes turned to one of frantic alarm. "Tom, he's in the windmill," she whispered, an occasional normal tone breaking through the hoarse, frantic croak.

Thomas shook his head. "I didn't see him."

She grabbed his shirt. "In the loft," she cried.

Without another word Thomas sprang to his feet and ran back to the door of the windmill. Anna could see the flames shooting from the windows, framing the door as smoke poured forth.

She clutched her hands to her mouth, shaking her head slowly from side to side, as she watched her husband hesitate and then plunge back into the inferno. Tears began to trickle down her face, leaving tracks in the soot on her cheeks.

* * *

It took several seconds after Thomas had bolted away from him for Edward to realize that he was ruined. Thomas would discover that his wife and son had been imprisoned in the windmill. It wouldn't be possible to kill them all. Not now.

Wiping his face on his sleeve, Edward staggered back toward the house. He would lose everything now, he thought numbly. His mind could not absorb the possibility. His perfect plan was ruined, and there was no time to think of another. With that realization Edward was jolted again into an awareness of his predicament. Running was his only hope. He charged into the house, not knowing what to grab first. He thought of the money in the dresser drawer. He raced up the stairs, yanked out the drawer roughly, and stuffed the money into his pants pockets. His next thought was for his boats. He grabbed the suitcase full of boats, which he lugged down the stairs. In the foyer, at the foot of the stairs, he stopped, looking around at all the expensive things he owned. For a moment he thought that he could not leave them. Then, with an effort, he started to move.

Alternately running and walking, he reached the car where it was parked in the driveway. He was out of breath as he put his hand on the door handle and slipped inside. He placed the suitcase full of boats in the back seat. With trembling fingers he switched on the ignition and pressed his foot down on the gas. For one second he glanced behind him and saw the smoke rising from behind the house. He faced forward and gripped the wheel tightly. He did not have much time.

With all his weight he pressed down on the gas pedal. The car shot forward and began to careen down the long driveway. He whizzed past the manicured grounds which had been his refuge for so long. Edward kept his eye on the drive, thinking about which way to go. He decided to head for the Millgate Parkway and head north. He was unable to think about any more than that.

The car approached the end of the drive, and Edward turned the wheel, applying the brakes so that the tires squealed as he made the corner. He glanced left and saw no one coming, as he had expected. The car, which had been going at a considerable speed, took the turn in a wide arc. As the Cadillac swung out into the road, Edward looked to his right and saw the police car, a few hundred feet from him, coming at a clip.

He spun the wheel frantically, trying to get the Cadillac back into its lane, but the automobile was out of control now and spun out wide, starting to jackknife. The police car tried to swerve out of the way but was unable to avoid the Cadillac. The two cars collided, and both cars jerked to a halt.

For a moment Edward sat, stunned, in his seat. Then, he saw the doors to the squad car open. A uniformed officer climbed out of the driver's seat. Edward recognized the plainclothes officer getting out on the passenger side. It was Buddy Ferraro, the detective who was always hanging around the Langes'. Calm down, Edward thought. Remember your position in this town. Intimidate them into letting you go. By the time they realize they're mistake, you'll be long gone.

Edward remained seated in the driver's seat, composing his expression into one of icy rage.

Buddy Ferraro walked up to the window and indicated that Edward should lower it. Edward pressed the button and the window came down.

"Mr. Stewart," said Buddy. "You were in an awful hurry."

"And your officer was driving carelessly and recklessly. I will have your badge for this, Detective. You've put a big dent in my car. Now kindly get out of my way and let me pass. I will settle this matter with your superiors, I promise you."

Buddy grimaced, and shook his head. "No, I'm afraid we're not going to be able to do that. You see, we were on our way over here to talk to you just now."

"To talk to me?" Edward said. "What in the world would you have to say that might interest me?"

"We have some things to discuss. Please get out of the car, Mr. Stewart," said Buddy.

"How dare you?" Edward demanded. "You're going to be looking for another place to work."

Buddy looked at Edward with narrowed eyes and then glanced into the back seat where he saw the suitcases. "Are you going on a trip, Mr. Stewart?"

"That is none of your business."

"On the contrary. I think it's very much my business, Mr. Stewart. Now, get out."

Trembling with genuine indignation, Edward opened the door of the car. He could hardly believe that this policeman was continuing to defy him. As if Edward's wealth and position were of no importance. Edward knew all about people like this detective. People with humdrum lives who could only dream of the kind of life Edward had achieved. They enjoyed trying to prove that they were equals. The nobility of the common man and all that. What a sham, Edward thought. He struggled out of the car and peered at the damage to his Cadillac. Then he began to shake his head. "You know, Detective. I doubt very much if, on your salary, you're going to be able to afford to pay for the repair of my car. I don't know how familiar you are with automobiles of this caliber but . . ."

"I'm not worried, Mr. Stewart. And neither should you be. Not about that," said Buddy. "But there is something you might be worried about."

Instantly, Edward thought of the fire. He was worried about that, all right. He had to get away before they discovered it. He glanced over at the patrolman who was crouched down beside the police cruiser, examining the damage. The patrolman straightened up and looked around with a puzzled expression on his face. He sniffed the air. "Hey, Lieutenant," he said.

"Not right now," said Buddy. "Mr. Stewart. A Mr. deBlakey called the station today. He's been trying to get ahold of me for a couple of days. He wanted me to know that he had, in his possession, a Bible that was written in by Albert Rambo during his stay at Mr. deBlakey's motel."

Edward rolled his eyes, and looked bored. "And this would matter to me because . . . ?"

"Because Albert Rambo wrote your name and phone number in his Bible on the night before he died. Can you explain to me why he did that, Mr. Stewart?"

Edward felt the blood draining out of his face, and he swayed slightly. It's nothing, he told himself. Nothing. They can't hold you because a madman wrote your name in his Bible. But even as he was reassuring himself, he felt his confidence beginning to wobble. Could it be? Could it happen?

Buddy stared at Edward, and Edward stared straight ahead. "Mr. Stewart?"

"I don't have to discuss anything with you," Edward said stiffly.

The patrolman who was sniffing the air made a face. "Hey, Lieutenant," he said. "I'm sorry to interrupt, but I gotta tell ya. I smell smoke. I think that house is on fire."

* * *

I should never have let him go back in there, she thought. He'll never get out alive. I'll lose them both. I have to go after them.

Anna tried to stand but couldn't. She couldn't hoist herself up any higher than her hands and knees. Her head felt like a cannonball on her neck. She tried to crawl forward, toward the burning building, but collapsed almost immediately. Tom, she thought. Paul. She had to go after them.

Then she thought of Tracy. She still had a daughter, who needed her. Maybe God had left her alive for Tracy. "Please save them," she whispered.

Anna groaned. Her arms trembled under her weight, and her wrists felt as if they could snap. She struggled up and sat back on her heels, her bruised knees digging into the ground. He had been gone too long. Too long. There were no human sounds.

The urge to go in rose in her again. Part of her wanted to plunge in and throw herself on the flames like a grieving widow on the funeral pyre. The idea was almost tempting. It would be a way to relieve the horror. "Tom," she wailed. But she thought of Tracy again, and she knew she wouldn't do it.

Somewhere in the distance the sirens of fire engines began their plaintive wail. Anna heard them keening, but in her distraction she did not understand that they were coming to her. The sound grew louder as they came closer, and then she realized it.

Suddenly, in the doorway of the windmill, a dark, crouching figure burst forth, carrying another. Anna let out a cry of relief at the sight of her husband, grimy and gasping for breath.

"Tom," she cried, lurching to her feet. "Darling."

Then she looked at the burden in his arms. The boy was utterly still, except for his head, which bobbed lifelessly as Thomas carried him from the fire. On parts of his limp body the flesh appeared to be smoking through charred tissue. His eyes were closed, his mouth thrown open as if he had been crying out for the precious air that never came.

Anna looked from the boy to her husband, and then she raised her hands as if to ward off a blow. She began to scream.

Thomas placed the boy gently on the ground and looked up at her.

"No, Anna," he whispered, coughing hard into his hand. "He's alive. He is. Believe me."

Anna clapped her hands over her mouth and sank to her knees as Thomas bent over Paul's body and began to try to resuscitate him. She watched, transfixed, as Thomas placed his mouth over his son's and exhaled his own breath into him, turning his head to the side and listening for a response after each puff. On about the tenth breath the boy's chest moved, and Thomas looked up and met her eyes.

"See," he said. Anna nodded and closed her eyes. She placed one hand on the boy's arm and the other on her husband. Thomas bent over Paul's body again, holding his head back in preparation for breathing.

"Can you do that?" Anna demanded. "Do you have the strength?"

Thomas only nodded, not wanting to waste the oxygen. Once again he put his mouth on Paul's and continued to breathe into the boy's mouth, while Anna watched as the boy's chest began to rise and fall in a steady rhythm and a semblance of color returned to his face. There was a commotion in the distance now as the fire engines and ambulance which Buddy had summoned on the police radio converged in the Stewarts' driveway.

"Tom, look," said Anna as Paul's eyes opened and rolled around to her. Thomas straightened up beside her. They both looked worriedly down at the boy and smiled at him.

"You okay?" Anna asked softly. The boy nodded and then began to cough as if he would choke. "Tom," said Anna, grabbing his arm, "I think he's choking."

"No, he's got to get the smoke out." Thomas gripped Paul's hand as he coughed until the spasm ended. "He'll be all right. You're stubborn, right? You're a fighter."

Paul managed a feeble smile and wrapped his fingers around his father's. Tom smiled at Anna. "I think he gets that from you." Tom lowered his head to the boy's ear and spoke softly. "We'll get you to the hospital in no time, don't worry." Even as he spoke, the fire trucks and the ambulance came screeching up over the Stewarts' well-manicured grounds.

Paul nodded and closed his eyes, which were bloodshot and still tearing from the smoke. Tom gazed down, studying his son's haggard face. "I wonder what he gets from me," he said with a sad sigh.

Anna put her arm around him and watched her son's steady breathing. "Everything there is," she said gently. "Every good thing there is."

THE END

THE JOFFE BOOKS STORY

We began in 2014 when Jasper agreed to publish his mum's much-rejected romance novel and it became a bestseller.

Since then we've grown into the largest independent publisher in the UK. We're extremely proud to publish some of the very best writers in the world, including Joy Ellis, Faith Martin, Caro Ramsay, Helen Forrester, Simon Brett and Robert Goddard. Everyone at Joffe Books loves reading and we never forget that it all begins with the magic of an author telling a story.

We are proud to publish talented first-time authors, as well as established writers whose books we love introducing to a new generation of readers.

We have been shortlisted for Independent Publisher of the Year at the British Book Awards three times, in 2020, 2021 and 2022, and for the Diversity and Inclusivity Award at the Independent Publishing Awards in 2022.

We built this company with your help, and we love to hear from you, so please email us about absolutely anything bookish at feedback@joffebooks.com

If you want to receive free books every Friday and hear about all our new releases, join our mailing list: www.joffebooks.com/contact

And when you tell your friends about us, just remember: it's pronounced Joffe as in coffee or toffee!

ALSO BY PATRICIA MACDONALD

FROM CRADLE TO GRAVE
SISTERS
MISSING CHILD
I SEE YOU
CAST INTO DOUBT
DON'T BELIEVE A WORD
THE GIRL IN THE WOODS
SAFE HAVEN
MOTHER'S DAY
SECRET ADMIRER
LOST INNOCENTS
LITTLE SISTER
MARRIED TO A STRANGER
STOLEN IN THE NIGHT
NOT GUILTY
SUSPICIOUS ORIGIN
THE GIRL NEXT DOOR
NO WAY HOME
STRANGER IN THE HOUSE

Printed in Great Britain
by Amazon

23827552R00169